# GODS OF BLOOD AND BONE

AZALEA ELLIS

Seladore Publishing

*To Jared. Be not afraid.*

# Chapter 1

You may know *of* me, but you have no idea who I *am*.
— Eve Redding

THE ELECTRICAL IMMOBILIZERS clamped on my wrists and ankles caused the areas around them to burn with a strangely tingling sensation. It felt like touching my tongue to the tip of a nine-volt battery.

I tried to arch my back and kick out, and the sensation spread violently, causing my muscles to go rigid-limp against my will. I whimpered against the rubber-tasting patch covering my mouth, and tried to imbue some rage into the glare I leveled at my captors. The masked woman chuckled at me. The other one, a man, placed a large metal case on the ground and unlocked it with the hissing sound of hydraulics.

"Please, you said I'd get a Seed. Can I have it now?" the boy said, desperation lacing his voice.

I turned my glare on their sniveling accomplice. How could I have been so stupid? I should have ignored his fake distress, like everyone else. I'd almost done so, but then he met my eyes, his own pitiful and full of fear. He'd mouthed, "help" at me. So I'd walked into the alley.

And here I was now, bound and gagged by two masked people. A large transport vehicle had pulled up to oh-so-conveniently hide the mouth of the alley, and thus my current predicament, from the people on the street. They probably wouldn't have helped, anyway. Strangers would take one look at the girl being abducted by masked, vaguely military-looking people, and scurry on with their eyes firmly pointed to the gray pavement. Gotta get to work. Lucky to be among the steadily decreasing percentage with a job. No time to deal with other people's problems.

The boy looked away from me and snatched eagerly at something in the silent man's outstretched hand. "I'm sorry," he mumbled to me. "I wish I was stronger." Then he shuddered and unclenched his fist around a little glass ball, which dropped to the ground.

"What do you think you're doing? Pick that up!" the woman hissed. "You can't leave stuff like that just lying around. There can't be any evidence we were here. None."

The boy gulped and snatched it back up, then met my eyes again. "I had to. I didn't have a choice. You don't know what it's like." His voice dropped to a whisper, and his chin quivered a bit. "But you will."

"Shut up," the man spoke for the first time, drawing something from his metal case and stepping ominously over to me.

At that, I tried once more to move my useless body. My muscles locked themselves into a painful half-relaxation, and though the force of my scream burned my throat, it came out of my nose weak and muffled.

The man bent over me and jammed a pen-sized piece of metal into my leg. It pierced the skin, and a second later he withdrew it and handed it to the woman, who plugged the other end into the side of a clunky link pad.

My breath heaved out of my lungs, and my eyes opened

painfully wide, but every attempt at movement only forced me to lie more and more still.

The screen of the pad popped up with my face, under my name, Eve Redding, and a slew of other data.

What the hell? It was me in a white hospital gown—the same picture I'd had taken a few months before, when people had come to do a surprise, school-wide medical examination. We'd been told it was to ensure none of the students had communicable diseases. Why did they have that picture?

I swallowed. In a situation like this, there could be no good reason.

"It's her," the woman said. "Hurry. We don't have much time. We'll have to leave her here."

That didn't sound good, either. But if they were leaving me, at least I wasn't being kidnapped for human trafficking or something. I'd make a bad slave to some rich foreigner. Too rebellious, and not pretty enough to make up for it.

The man nodded and grabbed me by my arm, which was bound behind my back. He lifted my weight roughly. He turned me onto my stomach and lifted the hair off the nape of my neck. There was pressure, and then a sharp pain at the base of my skull.

I tried to jerk away, but I couldn't even move an inch. Frustration, terror, and rage boiled up in me, pushing out any forced humor, and a tear slipped down my nose onto the painfully rough concrete pressed against my cheek.

Tears—the only outlet my body had. I hated crying.

Another pain, slightly lower down.

Another tear of rage.

He flipped me back over and the woman came forward, another glass ball in her hand, but this one was filled with a creamy liquid. She knelt in front of me and pressed it to my neck. "I hope this one survives."

Wait, what?

There was one last quick, sharp pain.

She stripped off my electrical immobilizers and tapped the

back of her wrist port against the patch on my mouth, causing it to disintegrate. I drew breath to scream, and tried to jerk away from her, but my body didn't listen. The alley walls and the woman's back as she stepped into the transport vehicle all spun crazily. I realized it was because my eyes were rolling back into my head as I passed out.

---

CONSCIOUSNESS CAME LURCHING BACK to me with a wave of sickness. I rolled to my hands and knees and heaved up bitter-apple bile onto the concrete. My dark brown hair hung unrestrained around my face, and my hands got splashed a little, but I barely noticed.

"Oh, God," I moaned, heaving once again. I retched until nothing came out, then crawled to the alley wall and used it to pull myself up. My body shuddered uncontrollably. I looked up through the smoggy air to the sky above. The sun wasn't overhead yet, but even in the shade of the towering buildings, the early summer heat made me feel like I was baking inside the city-stench all around me.

But I didn't have time to stand there contemplating my own misery.

I needed to move *right then,* or I wouldn't be able to.

I stumbled out onto the sidewalk, causing a businesswoman to rear back and sidestep to avoid colliding with me. She curled her lip at me in disgust and clacked away in her towering heels. Scag.

I stumbled on my way, using the walls to support myself when my legs couldn't. The other people on the sidewalk veered out of my way, avoiding my eyes or throwing me the derisive glance reserved for homeless people and half-crazed addicts.

My brain was tingling.

What the hell had they done to me? Everything spun crazily, and every time I blinked random images and sounds flashed in my head. White walls, a frowning man in a lab coat, monitors blinking and beeping, shouting in a foreign language, a chest straining against restraints, a bright light…blindingly bright.

I opened my eyes and found myself leaning back against the side of a building, hot window glass against my back, and my head tilted toward the light of the rising sun. I jerked back and closed my lids against the white-hot heat starting to throb down from the orb. When I opened my eyes again, I saw a man looking suspiciously my way.

Fear gave me temporary mental clarity and the boost of adrenaline needed to straighten up. "Stupid," I hissed to myself. "What the heck are you doing, on the street in broad daylight?" I took a deep breath of the dirty air and propelled myself forward, off the sidewalk and into the street. I raised my hand for a taxi pod and anxiously looked at the people around me out of the corner of my eye.

My attackers had left, but what if they were coming back? What if there were others? I stood out, obvious in the stupid uniform all high school students were forced to wear. I was spaced out on the streets, looking delirious, smelling of vomit, and in serious danger. I thought of filing a report with the enforcers, the military troops that policed us civilians after the attempted air strikes seven years ago, but everyone knew they were useless when it came to actually helping the civilians, unless you had money. I didn't have money, but whoever my attackers were, they obviously did. The enforcers weren't an option.

A taxi stopped in front of me. I opened the door and threw myself inside, blurting out my address to the computer-operated vehicle. It pulled leisurely away from the sidewalk and hurled itself full-speed into the flow of traffic. My stomach lurched, and I heaved onto the plastine seat. The computerized voice said something about financial responsibility, but I wasn't paying attention.

My body started to vibrate, and when I looked down, I saw my pieces coming apart. Then I blinked, and I was normal again. "Must be hallucinating," I mumbled. When I finally looked up from the fascinating myriad lines and crags in the skin of my palms, the taxi pod was stopped outside my building.

The automated voice was loud, and I don't think I was imagining the irritation as it asked me once again, "Valued customer, we have arrived at the specified destination. The charge is three hundred twelve credits. Please swipe your identity link over the payment center and exit the vehicle promptly." I looked out the pod window to my building. Thanks to my single mother's workaholic nature, we lived in an area just far enough from the unemployment slums that it was safe enough to walk to school. Or should have been.

I swiped the sheath around my left forearm over the scanner in the center of the pod and climbed out. I couldn't feel my legs, and had to look down to ensure they were still attached to my torso, but somehow I made it inside, through the doors, into the elevator, and then into our house.

The dark interior of my house was comfortably familiar. Safe.

"I hope this one survives," rang through my head again. Perhaps not so safe after all.

"Please," I whispered to the air. What was wrong with me? I was sick. Much too sick.

Before I could contemplate it any longer, my body was swept with a wave of heat. As soon as that passed, a wave of bone-creaking cold spread through me. My brain seemed to be tingling again, along with my spine, and when I took a step toward my room, my vision went dark and blurry. Then the cold floor smashed hard into the side of my head.

---

VOICES SEEPED THROUGH MY EARS, as if from very far away.

"Got a call from the school saying she was absent…Can't believe her!"

Some mumbling, and then louder, "Well, I don't work to send

her to school so she can become some delinquent and put us on the enforcers' radar! Live quietly, I say…"

The door opened, and I tried to talk, to ask for help, but I couldn't muster the strength to push the air out of my lungs.

"Oh my god. Eve, are you okay?" My mother shook my shoulder.

"Something's wrong. Go get the medbot, Mom!" my brother said.

Someone rolled me over onto my back, and then the medbot's cold sensors were being pushed into my armpits and mouth.

They were saying something else, but speaking in a man's deep voice, and once again it wasn't English. What? I didn't remember them being bilingual. But in any case, the sound was quite soothing, and I found I didn't care where it came from.

"Evaluation complete. Diagnosis unknown. Treatment unknown. Patient has fever of 105.4 degrees Fahrenheit. Please contact a medical professional immediately." The robotic voice sounded next to my ear, loud enough to scramble my brains.

My mom's voice on the phone, rapid-fire and shaking, grating, loud.

Hands on my skin, picking me up and pressing so hard the pain made me black out again. I woke up for a few seconds, in my own bed and staring up at Zed's worried face.

He just barely squeezed my hand, and it felt like my bones would disintegrate, but I couldn't move, couldn't talk.

"You're gonna be fine. The doctor's on his way."

I closed my eyes and drifted off to the sound of the other man's voice, murmuring gently.

# Log Of Captivity 1

Mental Log of Captivity-Estimated Day: Two thousand, five hundred eighty-four.

I felt the initiation of a *blood-covenant* today. It was unlike the others, not another sordid violation. She is a Matrix, perhaps brought here in the exodus. I did not understand what was happening, at first, when I felt her. I fear that the stunted *two-leg-maggots* have captured her, and are using her for experimentation, like me. But if they are the cause of my *blood-covenant* being initiated, it shows only how ignorant they are. For the first time in many cycles, I feel hope.

## Chapter 2

He that dies pays all debts.
— William Shakespeare

I WAS DREAMING. In my dream, I was a thousand little sparks of light, of life, of energy. I was sinking into the flowing expanse. As I settled, I started to reach out and connect to the other pieces of myself. Vibrations traveled through us, and I felt as if I was on the cusp, about to fall over the edge into understanding. Then I woke up.

I sat straight up in bed, gasping. My mind was reeling, dizzy, as if it had snapped back with the force of a once-taut rubber band. I found myself listening for something that wasn't there.

I let some of the tension go and looked around. I was in my room, tucked under the covers of my bed, and wearing my favorite pajama set. My brother sat in a chair beside my bed, asleep. The room was still dark, just starting to gray with the approaching dawn.

I shivered and wrinkled my nose. My clothing was damp and my skin grungy from sweat. I really needed a shower. Badly. I peeled back the covers and sheets and crawled out of bed, careful not to wake Zed.

I noticed then that I was attached to an IV, the little needle piercing the flesh at the bend of my elbow. I've never been squeamish about needles, so I carefully pulled it back out of my skin and put pressure on the spot with my thumb for a while. My knees almost buckled when I tried to stand. By the time I'd made it to the bathroom, just around the corner from my room, I was panting, dizzy, and completely exhausted.

I turned on the sink and leaned against the counter for support while scooping water into my desert-dry mouth. I slurped too hard and started to cough, violently enough to hawk up a loogie. I spit the glob of mucus and dried blood into the sink, and the water carried it down the drain.

I looked at the bedraggled girl in the mirror. My dark, straight hair floated around my head in a tangled halo, my lips were dry and cracked in bloody lines, skin deathly pale, and the bags underneath my eyes looked bruised. Literally. My jaw was sharper, my cheekbones more defined, and I must have lost ten pounds. Just what I'd always wanted. Except not.

I met my pale blue eyes in the mirror. "You look like crap," I croaked out, and then started coughing again.

The exertion drained me, and I sat down on the toilet for a few minutes of rest.after I relieved myself—which was indeed a relief —I stayed on the toilet for a few minutes, resting. My body felt strange in a way that I'd never felt before, even after being sick. Something was...different. And my hands and feet ached around the faint scars that still remained from having my extra fingers and toes removed as a baby. I rubbed at the skin where my sixth finger had been absentmindedly.

I remembered strange, crazy things. Nightmares. People had grabbed me when I tried to help some random guy. They'd injected me with something.

I lifted my hand to the back of my neck and pressed around at the base of my skull, then the spot an inch below that, then ran my finger over the skin of my throat where the woman had held the marble-injector-thing. There was no pain, no nicks or cuts that I could feel. I'd miraculously made it home, after they'd left me passed out in the alley.

And then what? I remembered flashes of a sterile room, strange machines, doctors, and some deep and soothing sound. I frowned and shook my head with a sigh. I couldn't remember. I'd been way too out of it. Sick.

What had they done to me? Injected me with some sort of disease, perhaps. We were always hearing about terrorism on the news. That was one of the main reasons for the establishment of the enforcers a few years ago. Maybe I'd just been unlucky enough to meet some terrorists.

But, no, that didn't make sense. They knew who I was. They'd said, "It's her." If they'd injected me with something infectious, I wouldn't be here, in my room, with Zed not even wearing a mask. I would be quarantined. So maybe it had been some sort of poison?

I groaned. I couldn't think. Maybe Zed would be able to tell me what my diagnosis was. If the doctor had come, my brother would know the result, since he'd obviously been at my bedside since the day before.

I went back into my room, sat down on my bed, and gently shook Zed's shoulder.

He jerked awake, eyes wide and bleary, and looked around. "I'm up, I'm up! What's wrong?" His eyes focused on me, and then his lips parted in a relieved smile. "Oh, thank goodness. I'm so glad you finally woke up. I mean, the doctor did say we should expect you to sleep for a long time as your body fought off the virus, but when you didn't wake up for three days, I started to wonder—"

"Whoa, whoa," I said, holding out my hand to stop him. "*Three days?* I've been sleeping all this time?"

"Well, yeah. I mean, mostly. I think so." He looked uncomfortable, awkward, which was rare.

I frowned suspiciously. “What do you mean, ‘mostly?’ ”

He grimaced. “You were having nightmares. Or hallucinations, maybe. The doctor said…”

“Mom really did pay for a doctor?”

“Well, yeah. Of course. I mean, she wanted to take you to the hospital, but you know we don’t have that kind of money. What do you remember?”

I narrowed my eyes. “I got attacked on the street, and they injected me with something. People in masks. I was trying to get home, and I thought maybe they were watching, and there were doctors and machines in a small room. I was tied down…” I trailed off, frowning. “I guess I did get quarantined or something? I thought you said I didn’t go to the hospital.”

Zed bit his lip. “Umm, okay. So the doctor said this might be a side effect. All of that stuff didn’t happen. You were probably hallucinating, or maybe just dreaming. He said that in most cases, patients experience paranoid hallucinations during the fever, and possibly afterward, too, and that we should keep an eye on you, and he gave me some sedatives because he said sometimes they continue for a little while after the fever’s over and that if you get too worked up you should take one…” he rambled.

I let myself tune out his voice as he went on. Hallucinations. Is that what everything had been? Just my stressed out, overheated brain creating imaginary terrors? “But they seemed so real,” I murmured, cutting off his explanation of the sedatives. But maybe I was wrong. “What could cause something like that?”

“He said it’s a new strand of virus. Usually not deadly, but there’s no treatment for it yet, so he said to just give you lots of fluids and rest and to try to make sure you stayed grounded in reality.” His fingers tapped nervously on his knees, full of nervous energy and the need to help.

They were testing out some sort of bioterrorism, then? “Zed, I could have gotten you sick!”

“No. The doc said it’s not very contagious, and isn’t normally translated through anything except blood. Do you know what may have happened?"

"I don't remember anything like that. And I promise I haven't stuck myself with any used needles lately." I smirked, then met Zed's concerned eyes and changed it to a softer smile. "Do you think you could get me something to eat? I'm feeling a bit empty."

He grinned. "Not eating in three days will do that to you, I hear. I'll go get something. Be right back."

As soon as he was gone, I picked up my ID sheath link and looked up my most recent transaction. Three hundred twelve credits, transportation and sanitation fee.

I wasn't hallucinating everything. So how could I tell what had actually happened?

---

THE BACK of my neck tingled, and then pulsed out a little shock that felt like static electricity. *Unlike* static electricity, it caused me to go blind for a second, and then my vision sputtered back to life like an old car's engine.

Except now, a paper-thin, translucent screen hung in front of my face. I let out a stifled shriek and scrambled backward, shoving my covers into a pile in my haste to place myself as far away from it as possible. I stopped once my back was pressed firmly against the wall and I could go no further.

The screen floated unperturbed, the same distance from my face.

My eyes read the words on it without conscious thought.

WARNING: DO NOT DISCUSS THE GAME OR YOUR STATUS AS A PLAYER TO CIVILIANS.

I reached out and tentatively hovered my hands over and around the edges of the screen, careful not to touch it. There were no wires, no strings holding it in place. I slipped my hand behind it and watched my slightly blurred fingers wiggle back at me.

"This is not good." I hesitated, then reached out and poked it with a finger. It reacted to my touch, though I felt nothing, and it popped out of existence as if I'd burst a bubble. Another one replaced it a second later.

EVE REDDING, CONGRATULATIONS ON YOUR INITIATION TO THE GAME.

That one faded away on its own, and was replaced by another.

YOU HAVE REACHED LEVEL ONE!
YOU HAVE GAINED ONE SEED!
PLEASE EXTEND YOUR HAND PALM UP TO RECEIVE YOUR SEED.

"Oh, hell," I croaked. "This isn't real. It's not real." Even so, I couldn't help but hold my hand out, facing upward in shaky supplication. I was screaming inside, wondering what the hell was wrong with me. Resisting insanity was a much better idea, but my curiosity got the best of me. It seemed too real.

Over my hand the air rippled strangely, like a heat wave rushing out from my palm, distorting my vision. It was similar to the mirage of distant water on the ground that you can see on a really hot day.

Then it was gone, and where the air had once been, one of those glass balls my captors and the boy had used sat in my palm.

I closed my eyes and took a deep breath, so freaked out I felt I might start sputtering gibberish and banging my head against the wall. My heart beat like a subwoofer inside my chest as I opened my eyes and brought the ball closer to my face for inspection.

The early morning sunlight angled through my window and glinted off the marble-like sphere. A branching, maze-like pattern was etched into the clear glass in spidery, metallic lines. Inside the glass shell some sort of shimmering liquid swirled slowly around. Across the face of the marble, a string of letters rose to the surface and flowed past my eyes. The words read "MAKE A WISH."

That was too much for me. "Zed!" I screamed.

He came rushing into the room, still holding a piece of bread in his hand and looking around frantically. "What's wrong?"

"Do you see this?" I held up the ball, my hand shuddering. "Tell me!"

"Yes, I see it. Calm down, what's wrong?" He held his hands in up a calming motion and pushed my arm down. "What's the matter?"

I pulled my hand free and shook the marble. "Look closer. What do you see?"

He frowned and peered at it. "It's a marble, Eve. Probably from a street vendor. Are you feeling all right?" He placed his hand on my forehead to test my temperature, and I brushed it away in irritation.

"What about that?" I pointed to the screen hanging in front of my face. "Do you see that?"

His eyebrows scrunched together further and his voice grew tight. "See what, Eve? What am I supposed to be seeing?"

I shook my head and pressed the palms of my hands hard to my eyes. "You'd know what I was talking about if you could see it. It's hanging in the air, dammit!"

"I'm going to get you one of those sedative pills. You stay right there, Eve. Don't move, and try to calm down. Just stay there, okay?"

Where would I go to get away from my own head? Besides, I barely had the strength to get to the bathroom. Did he think I'd run away? Jump out the window?

I took my hands away from my face and nodded, and he bolted away, the piece of bread now squished in his fist, forgotten.

The bread was so ludicrous, so removed from everything my crazy brain was trying to smash me with that I couldn't help but laugh.

I was still giggling when another window popped up, different than the others.

—Eve, you're perilously close to breaking the rule about disclosing Game information to non-Players. You really don't want to do that.—
-Bunny-

My laughter died in my chest, and I froze.

—When he comes back, you better realize that you're feeling sick and feverish, and had another hallucination, if you care for his or your own safety. Oh, and by the way...nice to meet you. :P—
-Bunny-

"Who are you?"

—I'm Bunny, your Game Moderator.—
-Bunny-

# Chapter 3

I desire the things that will destroy me in the end.
— Sylvia Plath

ZED SAT WATCHING ME EAT, concern etched all over his face.

I stuffed the fresh sausage, eggs, biscuits, and gravy into my mouth ravenously, both to satiate my hunger and to excuse me from discussing my "hallucination" with him.

My heart was beating fast, too fast, as if I'd had too much caffeine and couldn't calm down. It was a sour feeling.

When I'd finished, I licked the plate and plopped backward onto my pillows with a big sigh.

He pushed a glass of cloudy yellow liquid toward me. "Drink this. It's vitamix and lemon water. You need to get some nutrients to help rebuild your strength."

I sighed and shot my little brother a look.

He grinned back at me and rolled his eyes. "It's good for you. Just drink it. Doctor's orders."

"Oh, really?"

"Yeah, just think of this as practice for when I join the Peace Corps. You're my dummy patient."

I snorted and complied, gulping down the mixture made only slightly better by the taste of lemon. "Okay, I feel better now. I think I just needed something in my stomach." I let out a loud yawn, not fake at all. "I'm really tired now. I don't think I'll need that pill. I'm just gonna go back to sleep." I studied his worn face and bloodshot eyes. "You should probably go to sleep, too. I know you don't have anything important to do. And I'm fine, so you don't need to keep 'mother hen-ing' me."

He studied me for a moment while I did my best to look sane, calm, and not as if I were trying to make him leave for some ulterior motive. Even though I was hallucinating invisible screens who called themselves Bunny, freaking out, and trying to shoo Zed away so I could talk to them. In short, I was lying.

"Okay. If you need anything, just shout."

"Roger."

Zed was a genuinely good person, and the opposite of me in almost every way. Brave, popular, handsome, and he had an unselfish nature.

That's why I sent him away, and didn't say anything about the reason my heart was beating so frighteningly hard. Because if I *wasn't* crazy, whatever was going on wasn't good, and he didn't deserve to be involved in it. And if I was crazy, it would pass along with my lingering sickness, and no harm would come of it.

Alone, I took a deep breath and whispered, "Umm … Bunny? Are you there?"

—YES. NOW THAT HE'S GONE, LET ME EXPLAIN WHAT'S GOING ON.—
-BUNNY-

"First things first. Am I crazy? Is this a paranoid delusion?"

—NO. THE DOCTOR WAS ONE OF OURS. HE TOLD YOUR

FAMILY THAT SO THEY WOULD IGNORE ANY STRANGE ACTIONS OR ACCUSATIONS YOU MIGHT MAKE ABOUT BEING ATTACKED, OR THE GAME.—
-BUNNY-

"That's just what a paranoid delusion would say. How do I know you're really there? Is this really happening? And why do you want to keep it a secret?"

—THERE WILL BE PLENTY OF PROOF, IN TIME. THE FIRST PIECE BEING THAT YOUR BROTHER ACKNOWLEDGED THE "MARBLE'S" EXISTENCE. IT'S NOT A MARBLE, BUT IT *IS* OBVIOUSLY REAL.—
-BUNNY-

I slid the ball from under my pillow where I'd hidden it, and rolled it around my palm. "But he couldn't see these…hologram screens."

—THAT'S BECAUSE THEY'RE ONLY IN YOUR OWN MIND. AND DON'T MAKE THAT FACE. JUST BECAUSE THE SCREENS AREN'T REALLY THERE DOESN'T MEAN YOU'RE IMAGINING THEM. SOMETHING ELSE *IS* REAL. THE VR CHIP EMBEDDED IN THE BASE OF YOUR BRAIN.—
-BUNNY-

"VR…Virtual Reality? Embedded in my brain? Is that what they were doing to the back of my neck?" I paused. "Wait, you can see me?"

—I'VE GOT ACCESS TO YOUR LINK CAMERA, AND OUR DOCTOR PUT A COUPLE DIFFERENT MONITORING DEVICES IN YOUR HOUSE UNDER THE GUISE OF CHECKING OF DANGEROUS MOLD SPORES THAT COULD EXACERBATE YOUR CONDITION, SO WE CAN KEEP AN EYE ON YOUR INITIATION. SIGH. IF

YOU'D JUST LET ME EXPLAIN WITHOUT INTERRUPTING, ALL OF THIS WOULD BE A LOT EASIER. JUS BE QUIET FOR FIVE MINUTES.—
-BUNNY-

I raised an eyebrow, but said nothing.

—YOU ARE NOW A PLAYER OF THE GAME. AND AS FAR AS I KNOW, YOU'RE NOT CRAZY. WE TEST FOR THAT BEFOREHAND. THE GAME ISN'T THE CONSOLE OR COMPUTER TYPE YOU MAY BE USED TO. IT'S COMPLETELY INTERACTIVE, COMPLETELY REAL. THE OUTCOME IS ONLY DEPENDENT ON YOU, AND BY LEVELING UP, YOU CAN GAIN THE ABILITY TO CHANGE EVERYTHING ABOUT YOURSELF, IN REAL LIFE. YOU LEVEL UP BY COMPLETING QUESTS GIVEN TO YOU BY ME, YOUR MODERATOR, AND BY ACHIEVEMENTS IN THE TRIALS, WHICH ARE GAME-LIKE TESTS OF YOUR ABILITY. YOU'VE BEEN GIVEN I FREE SED, TO USE AS YOU SE FIT. YOU MAY NOT TALK ABOUT OR DISTRIBUTE INFORMATION ON THE GAME TO NON-PLAYERS.
AND EVE...THERE ARE NO DO-OVERS. YOU ONLY HAVE I LIFE.
—
-BUNNY-

---

BUNNY HAD GIVEN me an introductory quest to familiarize myself with the Game's "user interface," and then left me in visual silence, writing that he had something more important to tend to.

I didn't proceed with the quest, but instead thought about what he'd said till the lingering fatigue of my sickness overpowered everything, and I slept. I woke and raided the fridge, my body ravenous for the nutrients to rebuild itself, then slept again.

The next morning, I was ready to deal with the situation once more.

"Bunny?" I called into the empty air of my room, hoping nothing reacted, and I could write it all off as a crazy dream.

—Yes—
-Bunny-

Tch. No such luck. "I've got some more questions."

—I have answers. Some of them, anyway.—
-Bunny-

"How are you talking to me like this?"

—We both have VR implants, and they send signals to each other. Your brain knows when you're trying to communicate with me and activates the chip.—
-Bunny-

"You can read my *thoughts*?"

—Haha, they may want us to tell you we're all-knowing, but we can't receive messages you don't want us to. Your private thoughts are your own.—
-Bunny-

"Did they do the same thing to you they did to me, or did you accept it willingly?"

—This is my job.—
-Bunny-

"Working for who?"

—Hah! Nice try.—
-Bunny-

"You warned me to keep this Game a secret. What happens if I talk about it with other people?"

—Trust me. You don't want to do that.—
-Bunny-

"But what if I did?"

—Let's just say that the information you revealed would never make it anywhere further.—
-Bunny-

I wondered exactly what that might entail, but the gist was pretty obvious. If I told someone, they'd never be able to tell anyone else. The easiest way I could think to ensure silence was death. "Okay. Next question. What if I refuse to play?"

—Haha. You can't refuse. You're a Player, and there's no going back. Refusing to play would really only be deciding to play *badly*. Well...perhaps you could kill yourself, but rather than 'not playing,' I tend to think of death more on the terms 'losing.'—
-Bunny-

I swallowed. "Well, what happens if I play well?"

—If you play well, you get more Seeds. And the Seeds are really the point of it all. They allow you to change everything about yourself, except personality. The 13 Attributes. They make your wished come true, literally.—
-Bunny-

"Thirteen Attributes?"

—Part of the Quest I gave you, which you obviously haven't done.—
-Bunny-

I bit the inside of my lip. "I had a lot of things to think about. This is overwhelming."

—You're going to have to become a lot more adaptable. Sigh. Let's run through it now, then.—
-Bunny-

I frowned, and hesitated. "Umm, what do I…?"

—Double sigh. You're a bit useless, aren't you? Say "Display Quests.—
-Bunny-

I bit the inside of my lip again, this time for a different reason, but held my irritation back as I always did. I wanted to set Bunny straight, but there was nothing I could say. There was nothing special about me at all. I wasn't a great student, I wasn't pretty, and I was especially nonathletic. I was the type of person who was mostly ignored, except for the occasional bullying. An invisible girl. But that didn't mean my jaw didn't clench and my tongue didn't burn with the desire to spit something cutting at the screen.

Instead, I said, "Display Quests."

INTRODUCTION TO USER INTERFACE–STATUS WINDOW
USE VOICE COMMAND "DISPLAY STATUS WINDOW."
COMPLETION REWARD: 5 EXP
NON-COMPLETION PENALTY: NONE

I followed its instructions, and a larger window popped up.

PLAYER NAME: EVE REDDING
TITLE: NONE
CHARACTERISTIC SKILL: N/A
LEVEL: 1 UNPLANTED SEEDS: 1
SKILLS: NONE

STRENGTH: 7
LIFE: 12
AGILITY: 4
GRACE: 4
INTELLIGENCE: 10
FOCUS: 8
BEAUTY: 4
PHYSIQUE: 5
MANUAL DEXTERITY: 7
MENTAL ACUITY: 10
RESILIENCE: 5
STAMINA: 6
PERCEPTION: 7

A SMALL, quickly fading window slid into my peripheral vision, telling me I'd gained five experience points, and giving me instructions for the next part of the "chain" quest.

"These are measures of…me?"

—YES.—
-BUNNY-

I poked at the word "Strength" on the screen.

STRENGTH: ABILITY TO EXERT PHYSICAL FORCE.

"I'm level seven strength? Seven out of what?"

—7 out of infinity. Though if you don't level up any of the balancing Attributes, you will reach a point where your body is so strong it'll destroy itself. Use the Attribute Window to display all of them at once.

—

-Bunny-

"Display Attributes," I said. Another EXP gain notification popped up, along with a larger window.

STRENGTH (7): ABILITY TO EXERT PHYSICAL FORCE.

AGILITY (4): PHYSICAL ABILITY TO INITIATE QUICK-TWITCH MUSCLE MOVEMENTS.

MANUAL DEXTERITY (7): ABILITY TO UTILIZE FINE MOTOR CONTROL.

INTELLIGENCE (10): ABILITY TO REMEMBER DATA AND EMPLOY REASONING.

MENTAL ACUITY (10): ABILITY TO THINK AND DRAW CONCLUSIONS QUICKLY.

FOCUS (8): ABILITY TO CONCENTRATE ATTENTION ON A SPECIFIC ISSUE.

PHYSIQUE (5): PHYSICAL APPEARANCE OF THE BODY'S FORM, CONFORMING TO THE WISHES OF THE PLAYER.

BEAUTY (4): ATTRACTIVENESS OF THE OUTWARD APPEARANCE, SPECIFICALLY THE FACE, CONFORMING TO THE WISHES OF THE PLAYER.

GRACE (4): ABILITY TO CONTROL THE FLOW AND CONSEQUENCE OF BODY MOVEMENTS.

RESILIENCE (5): ABILITY TO RECOVER FROM DAMAGE AND MENTAL AND PHYSICAL EXHAUSTION.

STAMINA (6): MEASURE OF HOW MUCH PHYSICAL OR MENTAL FORCE CAN BE EXERTED BEFORE BECOMING EXHAUSTED.

PERCEPTION (7): ABILITY TO SENSE BOTH THE PHYSICAL AND THE IMPLIED.

LIFE (12): MEASURE OF HOW MUCH DAMAGE CAN BE ABSORBED BEFORE DYING.

UNPLANTED SEEDS: 1

—Now pick an Attribute, hold your Seed to your wrist or your neck, and make a wish for whichever one you want to increase levels.—
-Bunny-

I pulled out the little marble-like ball from under my pillow again and held it in my hand, studying it. The sun shone through my window and fell onto the Seed. It was beautiful, that liquid swirling around inside, glimmering in the light. Once again, the words rose to the surface, prompting me to make a wish.

"Is it addictive, like, a drug? That guy who got me into all this, he seemed pretty desperate to get his hands on another one."

—You've already had 1. Do you feel addicted?—
-Bunny-

I raised an eyebrow and snorted. "Quite the opposite. That thing almost killed me."

—Well, that won't happen again. Your body's already adjusted to it.—
-Bunny-

"How do you know?"

—Because you're alive.—
-Bunny-

I stilled and let out a slow breath.

—And no, there are no physically addictive properties to the Seeds.—
-Bunny-

"Physically, huh? What about mentally, or psychologically?" I wasn't stupid enough to be comforted by his not-quite-a-lie words.

—...Some people do become obsessed. For obvious reasons. We're giving you the ability to make yourself *better*.—
-Bunny-

Ah. That was the question. "Why are you doing this? All this?" I gestured vaguely to myself and the screens hanging invisibly in the air. "*Giving* us this?"

—That one, I'll leave to your imagination. Perhaps you'll discover the answer in time.—
-Bunny-

I shook my head, frustrated at the general lack of answers. A wish? What could I wish for that would make my life better if it actually worked? This was the modern day, and I wasn't an athlete or a man, so things like strength would be largely useless. Intelligence would be good, but hard to measure. Would I *feel* smarter? My eyes caught on Beauty. That would be easy to compare, before and after. And all that crap about the inside being what mattered and people who professed not to be affected by appearances…it was all bull. People cared about appearances. Attractiveness, *beauty*, made a big difference. And as someone who didn't have it, I felt its lack.

I grabbed the Seed, went to the bathroom, and locked the door, then stripped down to my underwear. I started the video recording function on both the body length wall mirror and the half-size one above the sink, and said, "Okay. What exactly do I have to say?"

—Just say something like, "I wish I were more agile," and the Seed will inject itself into you. It's called "planting" the Seed.—
-Bunny-

I swallowed painfully and stared at myself in the mirror. Body too tall, and chubby. Slightly crooked nose, pale, thin lips, pimples. "There's no way this is going to work." I pressed the Seed into my wrist, above the veins. "I wish I were more beautiful."

There was a sharp pain, and the Seed injected its contents into me.

As soon as it was empty, I felt it detach from my skin, and peered at the place it had cut. The small piercing was almost gone already, and as I watched, it healed itself.

I put the Seed down on the tiled counter as a horrible realization swept through me. "What have I done?" This was dangerous. Reckless. And I just went ahead with this strange entity in my head and injected an unknown substance into myself?

I waited to feel sick or dizzy, like I had the last time. I waited to die, to feel high, anything. But nothing happened.

It seemed like an eternity, but after no more than a minute had passed, it started. My skin began to warm and tingle strangely, especially the skin of my face. It itched painfully, and when I put my hand to my cheek, I could feel the heat radiating outward.

I sat down on the toilet seat and tried to control my panicked breathing. I put my hands underneath my butt to resist the urge to claw at my skin. Just when I was about to rush out of the bathroom and do something stupid, though I didn't know what that might be just yet, the tingling-burning-itching calmed down, and continued to dissipate with each passing second. My skin cooled, and I stood up and shakily walked over to the bathroom counter, leaning on it for support.

I leaned toward the mirror above the sink, looking at my face for any sign of change, good or bad. "It's my imagination."

—It's not.—
-Bunny-

I lifted a hand and ran my fingers lightly over my skin. Soft, fewer blemishes. My nose was still crooked, but perhaps not as much. My eyes, my best feature, stood out, and I brushed my fingers over the thickened eyelashes framing them, and then over my lips. Still thin and pale, but … better? I took a deep breath and closed my eyes against the view in the mirror. This could be a placebo effect—me wanting it to be true so badly I imagined an improvement.

"Calm down." I took another deep breath and said it again. "Calm down." It wasn't time to get excited yet. I stopped the mirrors' recording and downloaded the videos to my ID sheath. Then I snapped the sheath straight and replayed the two video viewpoints side by side on its clear surface. Once over my whole body, and again zoomed in to my face. Then I watched in fast forward, again, and again.

I couldn't stay still; I pushed back from the counter to pace back and forth across the room. My hands were shaking, and I wrapped my arms around my torso as if to keep myself from exploding and flying apart. I muttered calming words to myself, trying to slow my ragged breathing.

There was a light tapping on the bathroom door. "Eve? Are you okay?" Zed's voice filtered through. "You've been in there a while."

I cleared my throat and steadied my voice. "I'll be right out. I'm fine." I slipped my clothes back on.

Zed's voice was soft, hesitant. "Are you sure?"

I flushed the toilet to give some rationale to my long stay in the bathroom, and spritzed the "fresh air scent" dispenser. I needed to pull myself together. "Yeah, I'm fine. Thanks, though."

In the mirror above the sink, I looked at myself. Pale, pale blue eyes, wide and shocked, stared back at me. The lids slid down over those eyes, and I turned on the sink to splash cold water over my face and rinse my mouth out.

I lifted the hem of my T-shirt and used it to dry my face, pushed back my shoulders, and opened the door. "Promise, I'm feeling much better."

My brother stood right outside with, jaw clenched hard and a worried frown across his handsome face. When he saw me, it slipped a little. "You do look…recovered, but you were just really sick. Do you want to go lay down? I'll bring you some lemon water with a straw, if you want."

I rolled my eyes, patted him on the shoulder, and shook my head. "No, I'm really fine. Don't worry. I had to poop. Thanks for making such a huge deal of it."

He looked chagrined, and I slipped past him, back to my room, and closed the door behind me.

"Thinking about it abstractly is one thing. Seeing is another thing entirely," I murmured, looking at my new, slightly more beautiful face in the mirror on my wall.

I PACED the carpeted floor of my room, back and forth, back and forth. "Bunny!" I hissed into the empty air. "I need to talk to you!" It was the umpteenth time I'd called, and at this point I wasn't even expecting a response anymore.

But as if to prove me wrong, a window popped up in front of my face.

—WILL YOU STOP CALLING ME FOR TWO SECONDS? EVERY TIME YOU SAY MY NAME I'M FORCED TO DIVERT MY ATTENTION FROM MORE IMPORTANT THINGS. JUST BE QUIET, WILL YOU?—
-BUNNY-

"What more important things? I'm freaking out here. I need answers! How do these things work? What just happened should be impossible." I'd searched the net for any reference to what I'd just experienced, but couldn't find anything. Not surprising, as that would be a violation of the Game rules.

—I HAVE OTHER PLAYERS TO DEAL WITH. ONES WITH REAL PROBLEMS. AND QUITE FRANKLY, YOUR CURIOSITY IS NOT OF GREAT INTEREST TO ME.—
-BUNNY-

I paused. "Other Players? How many? Are there other Moderators, too?"

—EVE. STOP. IF YOU'LL LEAVE ME ALONE FOR NOW, WE'LL TALK LATER. HERE'S SOMETHING TO OCCUPY ME. DON'T CALL ME AGAIN UNTIL YOU'VE FINISHED THE QUEST.—
-BUNNY-

EXERCISE
RUN 2 MILES

COMPLETION REWARD: 15 EXP
NON-COMPLETION PENALTY: BUNNY WILL NOT ANSWER QUESTIONS.

I waved my hand across the screen as if waving away a fly, and it disintegrated. But I didn't call for Bunny again. I was impatient, but I would wait to do as Bunny said. It…he…*she*? was the source of all my information and my Seeds, and its good will was valuable. Plus, fifteen more experience points would put me over the halfway mark toward my next Seed.

"Breakfast!" My mother's voice rang out from the kitchen, and I realized that I was once again starving.

I went into the kitchen and piled my plate high with food.

She sat down across from Zed and me, tapping a message or report for work on her forearm sheath. I shot Zed a look, and he rolled his eyes at her bowed head with an amused smile. She always insisted that we have at least one meal per week together as a family, but still managed to be half-distracted, every time. We acknowledged the irony, but that was a sort of tradition in its own right.

My mother's eyes caught on me as she looked up. Her lips tightened imperceptibly as her gaze roamed over me and then to my plate. "Eve, do you really think you should be eating…all that? If you want to be healthy, you really need to monitor yourself a bit more." Her voice paused noticeably before "healthy," and I knew what she really meant was, "skinny." She herself was a beauty, but the only thing we had in common was thick, straight, almost-black hair.

"You've just lost some weight. Wouldn't you feel better if you could keep it off?" She smiled at me gently, but there was something else hiding in her voice. Disappointment, and maybe some sadness, too. I was less than the beautiful, popular, perfect counterpart to Zed.

Her words stung, but I knew she didn't say them to be cruel. She was just lacking in tact. At least that's what I told myself.

"Your brother is an athlete, and a man besides that, and you're eating more than he is," she finally added.

I swallowed, and felt the food sitting heavy in my stomach. I'd lost my appetite, and anyway, running two miles on a full stomach was just begging to throw it all back up. Especially in the shape I was in.

I stood up and shoveled the food on my plate down the disposal chute, then went to my room to slip on a pair of runners and a sports bra. "I'm going for a jog," I called out as I left the house, and I saw Zed throw a hard glance at my mother over my shoulder.

I started out at a nice slow run. Almost instantly I was down to a jog, and not long after that I was doing some floundery, bouncing motion that had people on the street passing me at a brisk walk. I took the same path I normally walked on my way to school and stopped when I saw the alley.

It was empty. Innocent-looking.

I stopped jogging and walked toward it, my chest heaving, air and smog burning in and out of my lungs.

They'd known where I was going to be that morning. They'd known who I was. And Bunny could see me, I knew, though he hadn't affirmed my suspicion. Which meant… I looked around suspiciously. Was I being monitored, watched? That guy across the street just shot me a look. Was he following me? I looked behind myself, and a woman briefly met my eyes and then looked away.

"I'm probably just being paranoid," I gasped to myself. But even so, I started pushing my body harder. I took an abrupt turn at the next alley, and then ran through it, turning once again when it opened up on the parallel street. I kept going till a Window slid up, telling me I'd completed my quest. I found myself in an old dilapidated parking lot, gasping for breath and unable to keep moving.

—GOOD JOB. THOUGH…YOU LOOK KIND OF LIKE A SEAL GIVING BIRTH, SO SWEATY AND GASPING LIKE THAT.—

-Bunny-

"You were…watching me?"

—Hmm. More or less. I didn't have anything more pressing to do at the moment, since I dealt with my other situation.—
-Bunny-

I hobbled over to a light pole and leaned against it. That was why I didn't like to exercise. It freaking hurt! "Do you have people…following me?" A few more deep breaths of disgusting air. "Keeping tabs on me?"

—Why would we waste resources like that? Your location is tracked electronically, and at any second, I can find a camera to monitor you.—
-Bunny-

"You've got GPS on me?"

—Yes. Duh. You're an asset; do you think we'd just let you run around without knowing where you are and being able to find out what you're doing?—
-Bunny-

So, GPS, and obviously he could see and hear me, which meant the people behind all this probably had access to the government's internal surveillance network. And probably satellites, too.

Around the time they'd created the enforcers, the government planted listening devices and cameras throughout every city, to monitor and search for potential threats to the nation's safety.

"Plus you put cameras in my house?"

—Yes. But don't bother trying to find them. You won't.—
-Bunny-

"Do other people watch me, or is it just you? Is Bunny even your name? What kind of name is that? You could be a hundred different people for all I know, all pretending to be 'Bunny.' "

—Rude much? I don't insult *your* name. >:(
My superiors have access to the files of individual Players, but they never use them. It's just me watching you, almost exclusively, and I'm not a hundred guys. Just one. It's my job to keep tabs on you and write reports that no one ever reads about your progress and achievements.—
-Bunny-

I closed my eyes. These people were powerful, had extensive resources, could access my high school medical tests, and had forcefully implanted a wish-fulfilling substance into me. "Who *are* you?"

—That's a secret.—
-Bunny-

# Chapter 4

Everyone is a moon and has a dark side which he never shows to anybody.

— Mark Twain

I RAN-WALKED AS QUIETLY and inconspicuously as I could through my school's halls. I'd left the last class of the day early, saying I had a stomachache. Honestly, I had very little idea what I was doing. While I was ignoring the on-screen lectures in class, a quest window had popped up almost directly in front of my face, as if Bunny were trying especially hard to attract my attention.

OPEN LOCKER 113 IN C HALL AND REMOVE THE KNIFE WITHIN, WITHOUT GETTING CAUGHT.
LOCKER COMBINATION: 13-49-01.
COMPLETION REWARD: 3 SEEDS
NON-COMPLETION PENALTY: POSSIBLE PUNISHMENT FROM SCHOOL FACULTY AND/OR ENFORCERS.

Along with it, another, smaller screen popped up, displaying only a two-minute countdown. No matter how I looked at that, it screamed "dangerous!" and I didn't know if I'd be able to pull it off within the time limit. C Hall wasn't close. Then I thought of getting three Seeds, and started running as fast as I could, in the opposite direction of the infirmary. As if I could refuse! My legs screamed in pain with every step, sore from the previous day's run, but I ignored them.

I skidded to a stop in front of locker #113 and used a voice command to pull up the quest information again. "Thirteen... forty-nine...one," I whispered, twisting the combination into the lock. It popped open, and I quickly rifled through the locker, finding the butterfly knife easily. It belonged to a guy named Adam Coyle, according to the label on the back of his school link. I stuffed it into my pocket and was about to close the locker door and leave with plenty of time to spare when a strange, niggling thought popped into my mind. I hurried to tear out a piece of paper from the back of one of the notebooks inside, and scribbled, "I saved your scalp. You owe me one." I rolled the note up small, and slipped it inside the cap lying on top of the locker's jumbled contents.

I had just closed the locker door when an enforcer turned the corner. Our eyes met for a split second before I turned and started walking away as nonchalantly as I could. I felt like a puppet on strings, walking stiffly and comically, until I turned the corner at the end of the corridor.

At that moment, the bell rang, and students poured into the hallway, rushing out of their classrooms and creating a wonderful, sprawling sea of chaos. I slipped between the rushing, inconsiderate bodies, and felt a smile of glee come to my face when the quest completion screen slid up in my peripheral vision.

---

"SO, Bunny, what was that all about?" I asked, walking safely home.

—WHAT?—
-BUNNY-

I dodged a mother with two screaming toddlers taking up most of the sidewalk. "That quest. Why did you need me to do that? Who does that locker belong to?"

There was no immediate response, and I wondered if Bunny was trying to figure out what to say. "Just tell me. That locker belonged to another Player, right?" I couldn't help the excited grin growing on my face. "And you were trying to protect them from that locker search?"

—YEAH, SOMETHING LIKE THAT. BUT MORE IMPORTANTLY, WHAT ARE YOU GOING TO DO WITH YOUR 3 SEEDS?—
-BUNNY-

I raised an eyebrow and smirked. Was he trying to divert my attention? Way too obvious. "That's another thing. Three Seeds? Quite a reward. You were pretty desperate to make sure they didn't get caught. Why?"

—BECAUSE THAT PERSON WAS ON THEIR LAST CHANCE. IF THEY'D GOTTEN CAUGHT, THEY'D HAVE BEEN SENT TO A JUVENILE DETENTION CENTER. BECAUSE IF THEY WERE UNDER SURVEILLANCE, IT'D BE KIND OF HARD FOR HIM TO DO THE TRIALS. AND PLAYERS HAVE TO DO THE TRIALS.—
-BUNNY-

"What happens if they can't?" I didn't comment on Bunny's slip, but smiled. Now I knew Player was a boy.

—UNLESS THEY'RE DEAD, A PLAYER WILL DO THE TRIALS.—

-BUNNY-

"And this made you panic because...?" I trailed off, thinking out loud. "If they have to do the Trials, but you don't want people to know about what you're doing..." I stopped walking and looked up at the sky, visible only in patches between the towering buildings. "If he got caught, you were going to kill him. Maybe not you, specifically, but one of your people, like the ones that grabbed me."

There was a pause before the response came back, and that told me the answer, as clear as anything.

—I'M SURE WE COULD HAVE FOUND ANOTHER WAY. WE HAVE A LOT OF INFLUENCE, RESOURCES. BUT IT'S NOT SOMETHING TO WORRY ABOUT, BECAUSE THANKS TO YOU, HE DIDN'T GET CAUGHT.—

-BUNNY-

I didn't know what to say to that, so I kept my silence for a while, until another thought popped into my mind. "What happens in the Trials that you don't want people to see?"

—I'M NOT AN EXAMINER. I DON'T REALLY DEAL WITH THE TRIALS. ALL I WILL SAY IS THAT YOU SHOULD PREPARE, EVE. —

-BUNNY-

I entered my building and rode the elevator to our empty house, then went inside to my room. "Let me get those Seeds, Bunny."

—HOLD OUT YOUR HAND.—

-BUNNY-

I did so, and three creamy spheres appeared after the mini wave distortion. I went into the bathroom again after stashing the knife in my closet, and recorded as I put another of the Seeds into Beauty. I was expecting the side effects, and much better able to handle them. This time I watched in the mirror as my slightly crooked nose, which I'd focused on specifically while planting the Seed, straightened slowly, almost imperceptibly.

Once the crazy burning and itching wore off, I looked at my nose in the mirror and thought that perhaps one more Seed would make it straight. But I hesitated to plant the other two into Beauty, because of what I sensed was behind Bunny's unwritten words. I needed to prepare for something. And if it didn't matter which Attribute I planted the Seeds into, why would he have brought it up? Maybe it was meant as more than a distraction. A subtle hint that perhaps it shouldn't be Beauty, over and over again.

I pulled up the Attribute screen and looked them over. Intelligence or Mental Acuity seemed like a smart choice, but perhaps I would be better off putting a Seed into one of my weaker areas. I sighed. Without knowing what I might need, it was hard to choose.

In the end, I chose Resilience and Stamina, because they seemed like areas that could be useful in many different situations, and dealt with the mind *and* the body.

I injected the Seed for Stamina and waited tensely for painful side effects like those of Beauty. But instead, my whole body tingled with pleasant warmth, even my brain. It felt good, and when it was over, I felt strangely like my veins had been injected with a very mild, slow-burning coffee. If I were a pod, I would have said my gas mileage just got better.

Resilience didn't hurt, either. Warmth and tingling spread through me, but after it was over, I didn't feel much of anything different. In fact, it was a tad bit disappointing.

But I'd gained three valuable things that day. One, I now held a debt over another Player. Two, the knowledge that Bunny did, reluctantly, care for the wellbeing of his Players. That meant that with the right stimulation, he could be coerced, manipulated. Third, the foreboding reminder that behind all this seeming magic, there was bound to be a catch.

I wish I'd listened to that bad feeling. But even if I had, there's no way I would have been prepared for what came next.

# Chapter 5

If death has no cost, life has no worth.
— Ilium Troia

BUNNY WOULDN'T GIVE me any more information on the Game, but instead gave me exercise quest upon exercise quest. I did them all because I wanted the Seeds he offered. I'd put a few into different areas, but mostly Beauty. My nose was now straight, my skin clear, and my body was sore from head to toe. My mother and brother had both commented on how lovely I was looking lately, but of course didn't realize the reason. It was strange and wonderful, to look in the mirror and think I was pretty. I worked out hard at Bunny's urging, pushing myself to meet the requirements of his quest. If I didn't, I would fail it, and there would be no experience points. Already, it was harder and harder to reach the next level, as more points were needed.

Zed had offered his company in my new workouts, and did a great job at being a secondary motivator. He was extremely fit, always a member of the school's sports team, and the baffling type that actually liked to work out, even if he didn't strictly have to. I think he thought I was working out to lose weight so I could be prettier and live up to my mother's expectations, and while in general he wasn't wrong, he'd taken to giving my mother silently accusing looks whenever he thought I wasn't looking. He'd never liked the way she seemed to be perpetually disappointed in me, while conversely praising him. I guess he thought I'd finally broken under the pressure, and it was like he couldn't decide whether to he happy I was finally taking care of myself or angry at her. He settled on doing both at once.

I'd continued to search the net for clues to my situation, but found nothing. I felt a strange mixture of trepidation and glee at the amazing things I was doing, and the cost I knew deep in my bones had to come along with the ability.

After a night run, I stood with Zed in my building's backyard, a small park area with a few tall trees and some benches, and looked up at the night sky.

"You're getting better quickly," he said, breathing hard but not nearly panting. "Just be careful not to push yourself too hard. Your joints and tendons might not strengthen as quickly as your muscles, and you don't want to injure yourself while you're still just getting started."

I grinned and gave him a light shove, catching him off guard and making him stumble. "Hah! Just watch, Mr. I'm-going-to-be-a-doctor. In a few months, I'm going to be the one telling you to, 'take it easy and make sure you don't hurt yourself, okay kiddo?' And then you'll look back on this moment and realize this is the point where it all started going downhill for you."

He gaped at me in mock shock for a moment, then drew himself up to his full height, which wasn't actually taller than my own Amazonian frame. "Just because I'm your little brother, doesn't mean you can push me around. Someday I'll be bigger than you, and you'll regret it!" He lunged for me then, wrapping an arm around my neck and pulling my torso down, where he proceeded to rub his knuckles over my head, completely mussing up my ponytail.

"Miscalculation!" I shouted, wrapping one of my own arms around his waist to keep him from escaping, and using the other to tickle him. "You played right into my evil plan."

He shrieked in a way that wasn't quite manly, and immediately let go of my neck, trying to escape my fingers. He finally struggled free and ran a few steps away from me, then turned to see if I would give chase. This time it was him gasping for breath, as he recovered from his laughter.

I waved an arm limply at him. "Oh, no…" I whined fakely. "He's run away and I can't catch up. Drat."

We both burst out laughing at ourselves then, and he left to go into the house and finish up some homework, while I stayed outside, relishing the way my body ached in a way that meant I was growing stronger, and was one more step closer to getting another Seed out of Bunny.

My Agility and Stamina Attributes had each spontaneously leveled up from the workouts Bunny had been giving me, with no Seed input needed. I let the warm evening breeze blow over my skin and through my hair. I was a bit euphoric, and a bit exhausted, from my earlier exertions. As I watched, more and more stars appeared, and seeing them spread out infinitely before me, I felt a tingle in my chest at my own tininess, and how very *not* tiny the universe was.

I smiled into the darkness, listening to faint strains of music. As I listened, they grew louder. It was a bit creepy—a child's voice singing softly in what could have been English, but…wasn't, wind chimes and reed instruments adding a level of strangeness. A shiver ran up my spine despite the warmth of the evening, and I wrapped my arms around myself.

It grew louder and louder, seeming to be coming from the air around me, from every direction at once. The child's voice sang nonsense words, and they echoed off the inside of my skull as if it was a small sound-enhancing room.

I couldn't move, couldn't think. The song was in my chest, in my bones, and then in a wave that rolled out from the center of me, it was gone.

I was on my hands and knees, eyes clenched tight. My head spun dizzily, and I choked down bile, suddenly nauseous.

Deep, slow breaths helped to settle my vertigo.

But then I opened my eyes.

The manicured grass was gone. My hands rested on dead leaves, twigs, and damp soil. My eyes traveled upward, and my first inane thought was that the trees had grown, or maybe I had shrunk. But I quickly realized that these were not the trees of my communal backyard.

They towered above me, reaching high into the sky, so tall I wasn't sure where they ended and the night sky began. Moonlight filtered through the branches as if through mud, just bright enough to see by.

I stood and turned in a slow circle. My body seemed to have weights attached to it, like the feeling of heaviness you get after crawling out of a swimming pool you've been floating in for a long time. My building was gone, the park was gone, and the noise was gone. In the city where I lived, there was a constant hum of life and energy. Distant noise and the undercurrent of electricity ran through everything, vibrating inaudible beneath the surface.

Here, the lack of that hum was like a dark blanket that, instead of muting my senses, brought them to life. It was terrifying.

A twig snapped beneath my foot, the sound so sharp and cutting, I jumped and barely held back a scream. Somehow the thought of adding noise to the darkness seemed horrible.

The wind blew across my body, suddenly chilly, and I realized it smelled of cut grass and peaches. My legs shook, and I wrapped my arms around my torso, trying to hold myself together.

A Window popped up in front of my face, causing me to jump and almost let out another scream of surprise. I half-choked on keeping it inside, and didn't make a sound.

The Window was a two-dimensional mini-map, with an arrow

labeled "Eve," and a blinking "X" positioned almost all the way across the map.

Attached to it were a quest window and a timer, counting down the time from fifteen minutes.

GATHER
USE THE MINI MAP TO MAKE YOUR WAY TO THE PLAYING FIELD.
COMPLETION REWARD: ENTER THE TRIAL
NON-COMPLETION PENALTY: DEATH

"Bunny? What the hell is going on?" I asked, putting as much force into my quiet voice as possible. There was no response, and I called again. "Bunny, answer me!"

Then I realized. Bunny had said he didn't deal with the Trials, which were some mysterious tests that I should prepare for. And the "Gather" quest's reward was to enter the Trial. "Hello? Is there a Moderator listening? Or, what was it again, an Examiner?"

There was no response, and the time limit was still ticking away. I was down to fourteen minutes. I raised my left arm to try and make a call from my ID link, but it was missing, and I remembered that I'd left it in my room for its weekly charge. "Stupid, stupid, stupid." I started walking. The X on the mini map was a long way away from the little Eve-arrow, and I didn't know how long it would take me to get there. "Hopefully not more than fourteen minutes," I muttered. As I continued, my eyes grew more accustomed to the inky darkness, and I moved faster. Every rustle of the forest made my heartbeat quicken. The hair on the back of my neck stood up straight, sensing something wrong.

Something rustled to my right and I froze, listening, watching, my eyes open wide to let in as much light as possible. Whatever it was moved again, low to the ground, a shadow amongst shadows.

Then a terrified scream pierced through the air, high-pitched and drawn out.

I bolted, sprinting as fast as I could, jumping over fallen trees at the last second, whacking into low-hanging branches with my bare face and arms. Something was following behind me, and catching up fast.

My instinct was to turn and look, but I kept my head straight and continued moving. I wouldn't be one of those stupid girls in the horror films who looks back to see her pursuer gaining on her, and then trips and falls. My breathing was loud, but even so I heard another one, following along to my right. They were pinning me in.

Then something tackled me, slamming into my right side. I tumbled to a stop with it on top of me, its small hand clamped over my mouth to prevent me from screaming. A voice hissed in my ear, "Be quiet! Do you want to lure more of them? We've only got a few seconds till it comes back. We've got to fight."

I nodded, and the girl, by the sound of her voice, helped me to my feet.

"Do you have a weapon?"

"No, I don't. I'm sorry, I don't know what the hell is going on. What was that thing chasing me?"

"There's no time for that." There was a loud cracking sound, and then something hard pressed across my chest. "Here, take this."

I closed my fingers around it, and realized she'd broken off an old branch to form a sort of staff.

"Is this your first Trial? Never mind. Of course it is. Damn," she muttered. "It's here!"

There was a shuffling sound. She stumbled against me, and grunted with effort. At the same time a meaty *thunk* came from in front of me. Something snarled, and then the shadows shifted again as the two struggled. Then a wet *snuk,* a low whine, and one of the shadows slunk off into the darkness, whimpering.

We waited a few moments in silence, and then she grabbed my hand. "Come on. We've got to get to the starting point. I'm Chanelle, by the way."

"Eve," I replied.

We moved quickly, but she pointed out things that might cause me to stumble, seemingly able to see in the darkness.

"I'm—what—" I stopped and gathered my thoughts. "What was that thing? Where are we?"

"That was a monster. They don't have a name, or if they do, I don't know it. And where we are is the big mystery. One of them, anyway." She paused. "I think it's not Earth. Or maybe it's all in our heads. Super-vivid, shared hallucinations caused by whatever they put in us."

"The Virtual Reality chips? So all this is just a game?" I felt air easing out of my lungs, along with tension.

"It's not a game!" she snapped. "Believe me, this is as real as anything you'll ever experience. You get hurt here, you're hurt in real life. You die here…"

I didn't ask her to complete her sentence. It was obvious. "What happens in the Trials?"

"The Trials are always different. They test different things, play to different strengths. Most of them have some physical aspect, though." She paused to jump over the eight-foot-high trunk of a fallen tree. "If you're breathing that heavy already, you're in trouble."

I felt a bit self-conscious, but there was nothing I could do to disguise my panting. "Exercise. Got it. How do you know what the Trial will be testing?"

"You know when you're told how to get through it—what the objective is. Or if there's no Examiner, then it's usually a mental-type, and you have to work out how to survive all on your own."

Another scream carried clearly through the strange-scented night air, changing from piercing and clear to gurgling, and then strangling out into silence.

"Monster?" I said.

"Yes. Let's be quiet now. Sound draws them."

A few minutes later, the gargantuan trees opened up to a small clearing, and the unobscured moonlight seemed bright enough to read by. Other people were standing about, obviously waiting.

"Other Players," I murmured. There must have been fifteen of them. "So many!"

"This is only a few of us. There are other Trials going on simultaneously right now."

I looked down and saw the source of my helper's voice was a small blonde girl. She scanned the group of Players with a frown and bit her lip, hard.

"What's wrong?"

She shook her head. "My sister's not here."

Even as we entered the clearing, others came from the trees and joined together in the middle. I walked slowly forward, watching. "Maybe she just hasn't arrived yet."

"Maybe." But she didn't sound reassured.

Some of the Players seemed confused, disoriented, and frightened like me. Others' moods seemed to vary from watchful preparation to absolute terror. I wondered what they knew that I didn't. One extraordinarily gorgeous latte-colored girl seemed to be warming up. She must have spent a lot of Seeds on Beauty, because I'd never seen a more alluring face.

In the center of the clearing, a black cube hung in mid-air. A message was written, the same on every side.

HERE YOU WILL BE TRIED, YOUR MEASURE TAKEN.
THE WORTHY WILL BE GRANTED THE POWER OF
THE GODS.

"What does it mean?" I asked Chanelle.

She shook her head, looking distracted. "I don't know. It's part of the Game. You get Seeds after the Trial's over if you 'perform' well."

"How—" I started to ask, but a screaming voice cut me off.

"People, it's a trap! It's a lie!" A boy stood at the edge of the forest, waving urgently at us. "If you stay there and enter the Trial, you're all going to die. Please, believe me. I've done this before. It's a death trap—" his voice cracked out, either from the stress of screaming, or the force of his memories.

People inside the clearing murmured to each other, some unsure, some shaking their heads at him.

Chanelle gripped my arm. "Don't even think about it. Remember the penalty for not completing the quest? At least we have a chance of living if we can win the Trial. If we leave, we're dead for sure."

The beautiful girl heard her words and cracked her neck back and forth. "He's obviously a newbie." She had an accent. Spanish? "Watch what happens to him."

"Please, believe me. At least out here we have chance. We can help each other survive," he called.

Across the clearing, a girl let out a whimper and raced toward him.

He took her hand and squeezed it, then yelled to the rest of us again. "Run away before it's too late. We can—"

His voice cut off again as the fifteen-minute timer reached zero and winked out of existence in front of all our eyes.

I drew a deep breath to calm myself. All this terror was really getting to me.

Clutching the girl's hand, he took a step backward toward the blackness of the forest.

But then the tree above him moved, its whole form writhing. Something sprinkled down onto the two of them. At first I thought it was just fallen leaves, but the two started frantically brushing at their bare skin.

Their movements grew more and more frenzied, and then the girl started to scream, and ran back toward us. He followed, stumbling. "No, no, no, please, no," the words scratched out of him.

As they got closer, I saw that whatever the tree had dropped onto them was sticking. I frowned and pushed forward through to the edge of the group of Players.

The boy stumbled first, and then the girl. "I take it back. I'll do the Trial! Please, *forgive* me!" she wailed, clawing her way forward.

"Oh, damn," I said aloud as I saw what was happening to them.

The things that had fallen onto exposed areas were burying themselves within the skin, growing, pulling at the flesh. As I watched, a tendril sprouted from the boy's cheek, and a leaf grew from it, so rapidly it was like watching one of those time-lapse videos of the life of a plant over weeks. From seed to thriving adult, they only took a few minutes.

These were using the boy and girl as fuel. As the plants grew from them, unfolding beautifully, they sucked up the flesh beneath through their roots. The pair screamed, and kept screaming, wordless.

The girl looked like a corpse, skin thin enough that her bones were almost visible through it. Her voice trickled away into silence. An eyeball burst as a tendril forced its way outward, then shriveled as it was sucked up. But she didn't move, and her expression of terror didn't change, because she was dead.

I took an involuntary step backward, only able to watch as the two of them were consumed. The plants grew thicker and higher. The only sounds now were that of branches creaking and snapping, their leaves rustling as they reached for the sky, and the Players' flesh and bones squelching and crumbling.

Finally, two trees stood in the place where the pair had fallen. The bases of the trunks were a vague memory of the shapes of their tortured bodies, like surrealist sculptures. The trees were miniature versions of all the others in the forest, and still growing upward.

I choked on nothing, my throat spasming involuntarily. I thought I might throw up. "They failed the quest," I murmured under my breath, but the sound was loud enough to carry in the absolute silence of the clearing.

"Oh, we've got a smart one here!" a mocking voice rang out from behind me. A man in a three-piece suit walked out of the trees. He was dressed immaculately, from his white, starched collar to his shiny black dress shoes. The only incongruous thing was the huge costume wolf head that he wore, which completely covered his own head.

The cube hanging in mid-air rose higher and grew bright, causing those standing next to it to jump. It lit up most of the clearing, a spotlight shining down and forming a distinct circle of brightness. The newly grown additions to the forest stood just outside the light.

He stopped and took out a gold pocket watch from his vest. "Seems like time's up." He looked us over. "And a few are missing?" He shook his huge wolf's head back and forth. "Tch. Too bad. So sad."

I moved back to Chanelle, who'd been my savior. She shook her head at me before I had a chance to open my mouth. "It's over. The Trial's started now. Focus on that," she said.

I had a sudden realization. "Your sister…?" I murmured, clenching my trembling hands and trying hard not to think about what I'd just witnessed.

She shook her head. "China's not here. Maybe she entered a different Trial," she said, but looked grim.

I knew we were both thinking of those anonymous screams we'd heard from the forest. The image of a new tree growing in the darkness flashed in my mind, and I shuddered from deep in the pit of my stomach.

The suited man moved farther into the circle of light. He bounced on his toes, and I could swear the wolf's head smiled just a bit, its felt tongue falling out of the side of its mouth. "There are consequences. You were all warned. This isn't just some child's game…" he trailed off with a giggle to himself. "Well, except it is, tonight."

He clasped his hands formally behind his back, stood up even straighter, and announced, "This Trial will be a game of 'What's the Time, Mr. Wolf?' Has anyone played it before?" It seemed almost as if the costume head had moved a bit, the tongue adjusting itself to lie properly inside the mouth, instead of hanging lasciviously over the side.

No one said anything.

"Well, that's fine. You'll all get the hang of it quickly, I'm sure. I am Mr. Wolf, obviously." He gestured to his head, and paused as if for laughter.

There was none.

He sighed, but continued. "I stand in the center of the playing field with my eyes closed. You all start around the edges, wherever you want. You will all ask me 'What's the time, Mr. Wolf?' " He called out the last part in a high-pitched, singsong voice. "And I will respond with, say…'Three o'clock.' You must all take three steps at that point, and then you ask me again. You may not take any more, or any less than the amount given. Repeat ad nauseam, until it's 'Dinner Time.' "

The lips of his wolf head stretched back from the teeth in a strange parody of a smile.

I swallowed. Rather than being ludicrous, it was terrifying. The teeth looked sharper and harder than stuffing-filled cloth possibly could, the eyes brighter, and the gums pinker. He snapped his fingers in the air.

From the forest, dark shadows moved forward, slinking up to Mr. Wolf's heels. They looked a bit like feral dogs, except that their eyes and ears were bigger than any dog I'd ever seen, and they had teeth that curved out of their mouths like saber-tooth tigers.

"What the hell are those?" I whispered, afraid to draw attention to myself with noise.

"The same monsters that attacked us in the forest," Chanelle whispered back.

"When 'Dinner Time' is called, my wolves will eat you," he waved a pointed finger, encompassing our group, "who are dinner. *If* they can catch you before you get back past the safe line again, that is. If you can make it out of the light, you'll be safe. So run fast, little bunnies."

The gorgeous girl with the Spanish accent cracked her knuckles. "How do we win this game?"

He focused on her intently for a few, incredibly long seconds.

She didn't seem fazed by the psychological pressure at all, as I knew I would have been. Instead, she took the time to crack her neck again and roll her shoulders backward in a circular motion.

"The game is won either by surviving for twenty rounds, or if one of the prey is able to touch me before I call 'Dinner Time.' Everyone who makes it to the end will be rewarded with Seeds, according to their performance, as always."

"Got it." She nodded. "But…I'm not the prey here. I'm the predator." She licked her chops exaggeratedly and grinned.

Mr. Wolf threw back his head and laughed. His eyes shone wetly when he looked at us again. "Let the Trial begin."

Chanelle gripped my hand and pulled me out of the circle.

I stumbled, my legs feeling weak. Outside of the light's edge, I couldn't help but look at the fresh twin trees.

She let out a sigh, gripped my face, and pulled, forcing me to bend over and look her straight in the eye. "Things are about to get dangerous, okay? You need to pull it together. Focus. From now on, concentrate on staying alive. Don't think about what happened to those other people. There's no room for that."

I stared into her big blue eyes and tried to stop trembling.

She gripped my face tighter. "Do you want to live, newbie?"

I swallowed and nodded. "Yes."

"Then stop thinking about those two. Forget them. The Trial and surviving it are the most important things in the world to you right now. Got it?"

"Why are you being so nice to me?"

She let go of my face and stepped back, turning to face the light. "Does there need to be a reason? That's not important."

Mr. Wolf placed himself in the center of the circle, his hands covering his eyes. "Let the Trial begin. Loudly, now, and all of you together."

"What's the time, Mr. Wolf?" we chorused.

"Twelve o'clock, little bunnies!"

We stepped forward twelve times, moving from the outside of the circle inward. This repeated with different "times," until a few Players drew dangerously close to Mr. Wolf and his saber tooth dogs.

It would be the next round, I knew. And it was.

"Dinner Time!" he sang, uncovering his eyes as he turned around to look at the majority of us, who'd walked toward him from behind.

His stuffed animal head was no longer stuffed. It was a grotesque, huge wolf's head, alive atop his human body. His too-large eyes moved, taking in our positions relative to him, and the dogs sprang forward. His nostrils flared, and saliva swung from his hanging tongue, falling toward the tip of his polished shoe.

Seeing it hit snapped me out of my trance, and I turned around to sprint back to the safe line. Someone screamed. I didn't turn my head to look back, didn't wonder about the safety of my fellow Players, and didn't think about my own already aching legs. I just ran.

Ahead of me, a guy stuck out his foot to trip another, and the second guy went down hard. I jumped over him, and kept running.

I passed the line by quite a bit because of my momentum, and turned around to make sure I was safe. Others stampeded toward and past me, obscuring my view of Mr. Wolf for a moment. When the small field had cleared of terrified people, I saw him standing still in the middle of it.

Two of the dog-things had caught someone, and one was the boy who'd been tripped. The monster's jaw was clenched around his upper arm, long curving teeth piercing into the flesh. Blood mixed with saliva ran down, soaking the boy's blue T-shirt. His face was white and contorted with pain and fear.

Someone laughed beside me. It was the one who tripped him. Our eyes met, and he gave me a small shrug and a smile. "Less survivors mean more Seeds for the rest of us."

The fallen boy reached out a pleading hand to all of us watching safely from behind the line, and then his eyes rolled back in his head, and he started to convulse. He looked like he was having a seizure, and foam dripped down his chin. The other downed Player started to flail, too. The dog-monsters retreated back to Mr. Wolf's side, and soon the bodies lay still.

Not saber-tooth tiger teeth, then. More like cobra fangs. Poisonous.

People screamed and cried on the edge of the light.

But then the boy in the blue T-shirt twitched. Silence crashed down as we watched him.

He moved bit by bit, jerky, like a battery-powered doll running on the last bit of its juice. He stood up, but his stance was strange, alien. Limp arms hung down past slightly bent knees, and his head lolled to the side. His eyes were vacant, and he turned his back on us to join Mr. Wolf in the center of the light.

Mr. Wolf giggled. "Oh. Bitten Players become wolves. I may have forgotten to mention that."

# Chapter 6

What reinforcement we may gain from Hope. If not, what resolution from despair.

— John Milton

THE NEXT ROUND, we all inched forward, moving our feet only enough to count as taking a step, and no more. When "Dinner Time" was called, the two bitten Players turned and chased after us, just like the monsters. The boy's mouth was stretched in a wide grin, and slobber ran down his chin and neck.

I turned after reaching safety and watched a thin guy run desperately from the strangely loping former Player. He…*it* reached out a hand and grazed the back of the guy's shirt. Terrified, the guy took a dangerous chance, trying to feint away. He stopped abruptly and turned to run at a different angle, but he wasn't counting on a dog-monster being there. The creature vaulted at him, and his neck was caught between its massive, wide-open jaws, his head disappearing inside the mouth.

Blood gushed out between the teeth.

My knees were shaking. I took deep breaths and looked away

from the gruesome scene. I wanted to deny that this was real, just pretend it was all a horrible dream that I would wake from soon. But I couldn't do that, because I knew the fear was the only thing keeping me going. Without the slight edge that it gave me, boosting my slow, ungainly movements with adrenaline, I would die here tonight.

I knew that, and so I didn't pretend that it wasn't real. I looked away, swallowed, and tried to steady my shaking legs.

Chanelle caught my eye, and gave me a silent nod of approval.

We started forward again. The speed was glacial, each of us doing our best to move forward less than the others.

I panted for breath, my muscles burning and trembling, and I felt so grateful to Bunny for enticing me to exercise. He must have known I would need the strength I was using now. He knew, I realized. He knew about this.

Chanelle crept beside me on one side, the beautiful Spanish girl on the other.

I felt incrementally safer between them, and found myself watching Chanelle's white runners dragging through a puddle of dark blood half-soaked into the ground where the last Player had fallen. Her pretty white shoes were ruined.

I realized my mind was trying to play tricks on me—to disconnect from the horror. I grabbed the pad of my left hand between my forefinger and thumb and pinched as hard as I could. Pain brought some clarity to my mind, and I focused on it, trying to get a grip.

When "Dinner Time" was called, we all turned to run. Out of the corner of my eye, I saw the Spanish girl slip in that same puddle of blood covering the ground. But I didn't stop. How could I stop?

When I reached the safe line and looked back, she was pinned to the ground by the blue T-shirt "wolf." He snarled down at her, drool dripping onto her cheek.

The fingers of her left hand were wrapped around his neck,

holding him off. She formed the other into a fist and slammed it into his ear. Once, twice, three times.

He fell sideways off her, eyes unfocused for a second. He shook his head and rallied, but she'd already scrambled to her feet.

She pulled back her right fist and slammed it down into the back of his head, propelling it with the force of her entire body.

His face smashed flat into the ground. He twitched, and she pulled back and punched once more. He didn't move that time, but she kicked him in the side before racing back to the safe line, weaving to avoid the remaining monsters and bitten Players.

I watched her in awe. What kind of strength was that?

By the start of the next round, we were down to almost half of our original numbers, while Mr. Wolf's had grown again.

Everyone's tension inched toward the breaking point as we got closer and closer to Mr. Wolf. A girl tried to bolt back to the safety line early, but vines burst from the earth, tripped her, and held her down. She screamed and struggled, but was trapped. When Mr. Wolf sang out "Dinner Time!" all the attackers ignored her, leaving the easy pickings for last.

Only a few seconds from the safety line, a turned Player lunged for a boy running close to Chanelle. The boy swerved and spun to avoid it, smashing his elbow hard into her temple.

She went down.

I stumbled the last few meters across the line and looked back, gasping.

She knelt on her hands and knees, blood dripping down the side of her head. Beside her, the boy who'd elbowed her was being bitten.

"Run!" I screamed at her.

She crept forward a few inches and tried to stand, but couldn't get her feet solidly under her, and fell forward again.

The turned Player released its catch and turned to her.

I took a step into the light, but she snarled at me, "Get back!" Her voice was slurred, groggy.

It grabbed her head between two hands and bit into the curve where her neck met her shoulder. It ripped its head back viciously, and a bite-sized chunk of flesh went with it.

She flopped awkwardly in its grip, like a fish stranded on the shore, and let out a choked scream.

"No!" I shouted.

"My sister…China. Find her. Thirteen hundred Brine Street. Tell her…to live!" She squeezed the words out, rapid-fire.

It bit into her neck again, this time digging its teeth in and shaking its head like a dog with a toy.

She ignored it, keeping her eyes locked on mine.

I nodded, and her eyes rolled back into her head, and she started to thrash around.

I pinched the inside of my thumb pad, hard. Once again, the pain allowed me to focus. But not enough, so I bit my bottom lip, until the iron taste of blood blossomed on the tip of my tongue and spread throughout my mouth.

---

MR. WOLF, drool running down the collar of his once immaculate suit, looked at the number of new "wolves," and laughed.

Our numbers were severely depleted, and the danger of each round grew exponentially greater.

I looked at his grotesque, laughing head, and I hated him. I hated him, and I was absolutely terrified. I shuffled forward as the next round started, and thought of the Seeds I'd wasted. What good was Beauty to me now, when my life was on the line?

Each round seemed to be taking longer and longer, as if Mr. Wolf was trying to get us as close to him as possible before calling Dinner Time, and because we were moving so slowly, it was a tedious affair of constant, mind-eroding tension. But Mr. Wolf never called for any time greater than ten o'clock.

When he finally turned and called "Dinner Time!" I pivoted toward the starting line as quickly as I could. As my head swung around, I met Chanelle's eyes for a second, as if in slow motion. Then I broke the connection, running away.

Behind me, I heard light footsteps and bubbling gasps, as if someone were breathing through a layer of water.

My heart beat so fast it felt like it might literally burst out of my chest. I'd never understood those words before, but now I could feel it, expanding large and squeezing hard with each hummingbird-fast pump. My legs felt like fat, heavy logs, and wouldn't move as I wanted. They were slow, too slow, much too slow compared to the light footsteps behind me, gaining on me.

As I approached the safe line, I started to let out great, gasping sobs. I was almost there when something grabbed the back of my knees. I went down hard, smashing into the ground and sliding just a bit.

I flipped over onto my back, scrambling to see who'd tackled me.

The-thing-that-had-once-been-Chanelle was on its knees, grabbing desperately onto my legs. Her jaw hung open halfway, and so much saliva bubbled up in her mouth that her breathing rattled with the fluid she'd inhaled. Her eyes locked on mine. There was no compassion, no recognition, only hunger.

I pulled back a knee without even thinking and slammed my foot into her face, hard enough that her small hands lost their grip on my legs. I scrambled backward like a crab, clumsily, as my arms slipped and collapsed.

She came for me, and I kicked her again and again, keeping her off until I somehow made it over the safe line.

We sat on either side of that division between light and darkness, and her eyes met mine again.

She seemed to strain forward, but was held back by some invisible force. Those blue eyes held nothing but hunger. No anger, no humanity.

Then they lost even the hunger and her interest in her escaped prey seemed to slip away. She limply rose to her feet and turned to walk back toward Mr. Wolf.

On the field, two other people were convulsing in their own blood.

My arms collapsed from the weight of my upper body, and I rolled into a ball with my eyes facing the ground and my torso bent over my knees.

It was too much. I couldn't stand up, couldn't do this again. That's what I thought, but somehow I was on my feet again when the next round started.

Mr. Wolf called out "twelve o'clock" for the first time since the beginning of his sick game. I took my twelve shuffling steps forward. How many rounds had it been? Not close enough to twenty. I didn't think I could make it till the end. But I would keep trying until I could move no more, or I got turned into a "wolf."

I saw quick movement to my right, and looked up. The tough Spanish girl jumped forward with a huge, half-leaping, half-running step. What was she doing? My weary brain struggled to compute.

But then I saw the shrinking distance between her and Mr. Wolf.

I gasped, and in an instant I was urging her on with every fiber of my being.

She grinned viciously, and I remembered what she'd said in the beginning about being a predator. Her jumps weren't the type I'd ever seen before from a human. Something was slightly off about them, as if despite the heaviness of this place, she was bending the rules of gravity just a bit, moving too high from the pull of the Earth, and traveling too far.

Jump, jump, jump, she went, drawing dangerously near Mr. Wolf.

How many steps did she have left? I hoped it was enough.

She jumped and landed one last time, stopping obviously too far away to reach Mr. Wolf without moving her legs. "Dammit!" she growled. The sound carried well in the taut silence.

I felt the pit in my stomach yawn open and suck the air out of me.

Mr. Wolf chuckled.

But before we asked the time again, she stiffened her body, stood up on the tips of her toes, and extended her hands toward the sky. Even her fingers were straining to move higher.

It looked like she was trying to fly away.

Then, with her body extended and stiffly clenched, she started to tilt forward. She tilted until she was falling, and didn't flinch even a bit as she slammed face-first into the ground.

A few moments of frozen silence passed, and then I saw that Mr. Wolf's ankle was caught in her outstretched hand. Her feet were still planted on the ground where she'd stopped, at exactly twelve steps.

"She's touching him!" I whispered. Then I shouted it desperately, as if making sure everyone heard it would make it irrefutably true.

The Spanish girl stood up stiffly. She'd probably knocked the air out of her lungs when she hit the ground. She rested her hands on her knees for a moment, taking a few deep breaths. Then she let out a low chuckle, spit, and straightened, wiping her mouth with the back of her hand. "Screw you," she said succinctly.

Mr. Wolf seemed to be frozen at first, but then turned around. His head was once again an innocent stuffed costume head, except for the saliva drenching the lower half of it and his entire torso. "It would've been a waste to eat you, anyway," he said to her. Then he lifted his arms wide, palms facing toward the sky. "The game is won, and the Trial completed. Congratulations, Players!" His voice was jovial, pleased.

The sound made me shudder, because I knew his true nature.

He took a step toward us, and I flinched, but he didn't move to bite the Spanish girl or chase after any of us. He walked through our pitiful group and away, into the darkness of the trees from where he'd come. On his whistle, the ones who'd been bitten followed him, shuffling strangely off into oblivion.

Was it over, now that she'd won the Trial? No, no, not yet. Don't trust, don't relax, I ordered myself.

In the middle of the field, where we'd first gathered, the floating cube sank down to head-level once again.

I waited to see that nothing happened to the ones who moved close to it, and then followed.

CONGRATULATIONS ON SURVIVING THE TRIAL.
THERE ARE NO BESTOWALS.

The beautiful girl scowled, pacing back and forth in front of the cube.

I watched her without realizing what I did. Every step made my wire-taut nerves stretch even more precariously tight, her agitation feeding my own. Every sense was on the alert for danger, and the hair on my sweat-slick skin stood up. I couldn't take any more.

Then the cube's message changed.

DO YOU WISH TO RETURN FROM THE TRIAL?
YES / NO

The girl's face lit with relief, and she lunged forward to press, "Yes" without hesitating. A mirage-like wave, like those formed when I received new Seeds, rolled out of her body, and then she disappeared.

Nothing remained where she had been standing. She was just gone.

After her, others pressed, "Yes," and the same thing happened to them.

I swallowed, reached out, and touched the cube before I could worry about it any longer. I thought I heard a snippet of the eerie children's song again, loud in my bones, and then it exploded out of me.

I was dizzy and nauseous, but my knees didn't buckle this time.

The breeze was warm on my skin, and the grass under my feet was the normal grass of my backyard, not the too-green, too-sharp stuff of the Trial.

The tree was a normal oak, large, but not towering, and the smell of the air was fresh, but with a bit of a smog-like tang. The darkness wasn't true-black pierced only by distant light from the expanse of sky. Rather, the grey-tinged, half-sick haze of an insomniac city.

I threw up from relief, all over my shoes.

# Chapter 7

Death is not the greatest loss in life.
The greatest loss is what dies inside us while we live.
— Norman Cousins

WHEN MY STOMACH WAS EMPTY, I noticed the window hanging in front of my face.

YOUR ACTIONS IN THE TRIAL HAVE AWARDED YOU 2 LEVELS.
YOU HAVE GAINED 2 SEEDS.

I wiped the back of my hand across my mouth and stared at the words for a long while.

It was easy to slip into the house without my family noticing me. I went into the bathroom, stripped off my dirty, torn clothing, and stepped slowly into the tub, using my hand on the wall to support myself. Every muscle in my legs seemed to be shivering in a violent threat of collapse, so I turned on the faucet and sat down in the tub.

A bath was better, anyway, because I wouldn't have to close my eyes under the stream of water.

My skin was scraped and sliced everywhere it'd made direct contact with the ground and grass of that place, but I hadn't even noticed. Now that the overwhelming tension was gone, the raw skin started to hurt.

I ran the water hot, as hot as I could stand it, and soaked in it till it turned tepid. Then I got out and went to my room. I shoved my clothes to the bottom of my trashcan so my mom wouldn't see them. My shoes went into a plastic bag in the closet until I could find time to wash them in secret.

I dressed in a long-sleeved shirt, pants, and socks, wanting to have as much of my skin covered as possible. I twisted my hair into a single braid and tied it off with a hair band, out of the way. Then, with my light on full brightness, I checked in every corner and possible hiding spot of my room, just in case. There was no one, nothing new.

As prepared as I was going to get, I turned off my light so that no one would think I was still awake and come checking in on me during the middle of the night. I couldn't handle that right now. I crawled into bed and tucked myself into the corner between two walls of my room, so I could see both the door and window, and any movement without turning.

"Bunny?"

—I'm here.—
-Bunny-

"What was that?"

—I think you know.—
-Bunny-

"No, I mean—It was a Trial. But what *was* it? What happened —it was…It's not freaking possible! It's not possible."

—Don't be obtuse. It happened, didn't it? Therefore it *is* possible. You just don't understand it.—
-Bunny-

"But…how?" I whispered.

—I can't tell you that.—
-Bunny-

"Why not?"

—I just can't. I'm not involved with the Trials, Eve. I'm just your normal Game Moderator.—
-Bunny-

He didn't *know*, I realized. I bit my split bottom lip again. That's why he couldn't tell me. "Please, can't you let me go? I don't want to be a Player. I'll give back all the Seeds. You can change back the things I leveled up. Just, *please*, let me go. I don't want to do this anymore."

—There's no way out but through. Once you're a Player, there's no going back.—
-Bunny-

"How do you get through?"

—I don't know.—
-Bunny-

"Has anyone ever done it before?"
There was a delay in the answer that time.

—Not yet. Not that I know of.—
-Bunny-

I swallowed the blood welling from my re-opened lip, but didn't say anything.

Bunny didn't prompt me for more words, and left me alone in the darkness, the almost-silence of my room.

Perhaps it was then that I began to change.

If any evidence of the true nature of humanity was needed, I only had to look at myself. I wasn't thinking about those Players' families or the tragedy of their deaths. I wasn't sad, or guilty about not being brave enough to stop and help them.

I was only scared for myself. My mind was focused not on regret, but rather on exactly how I could ensure I didn't lose to the Game, like them. I wanted to live.

I tucked my knees to my chest, wrapped my arms around my legs, and stared into the darkness. There was no way I would be able to sleep that night, despite my physical and mental exhaustion. Even if I could, I didn't want to. I was afraid I'd dream of the Trial, but never wake up.

I stayed curled up on the far corner of my bed till morning, watching my room, my door, and my window for any danger. The sunrise was a relief of epic proportions. For some reason, humans always feel safer in the light. They're not creatures of the dark.

---

I CRAWLED STIFFLY OUT of bed shortly after the first hint of sunrise and dressed in silence. Then I peeked in on my sleeping mother and brother to make sure they were okay. They had to be kept separate from all of this. Safe.

I went outside to examine the ground where I'd been the night before, when *it* happened. There was only grass, manicured and sedate, and completely unhelpful. I stood up and sighed. "Fine."

I angled my left arm across my body and used my right hand to type an address into my forearm sheath link. "China, right?" I muttered to myself, and started walking toward the street.

Two public transport pods and a short walk later, I was in front of the house from the address Chanelle had given me.

It was nice. Not mansion-rich, but it wasn't stacked next to or on top of any other houses, and there was a large fenced backyard, exclusive to their family. Even the pollution was lighter there, so far from the jobless slums.

I stood awkwardly, shifting from foot to foot. "What now, dumbass?" It didn't seem right to just knock on the front door. What would I say? 'Hi, I think one of your daughters is gone forever, possibly dead, because she got bit by a crazy, salivating Player in a secret Game your daughters and I are being forced to play? But no worries, because I'm here looking for the other daughter?' Probably not a good idea.

I slipped around the side and hauled myself painfully over the tall wooden fence enclosing their backyard. My decimated muscles gave out and dropped me on the other side with a painful *thunk.*

I held in a groan and stood up, then crouched and started to move through the huge bushes, flower plants, and trees of the backyard garden. I realized belatedly that sneaking around and peaking in the windows probably wasn't the best way to earn someone's trust. But I didn't want to interact with anyone but China. No non-Players.

Then something dropped out of the tree beside me onto my back, flattened me to the ground, and knocked the air from my lungs.

Panic flooded me and I struggled wildly to turn around, sucking desperately for air that just wouldn't come.

When I saw my attacker, my lungs finally accepted a surprised gasp of air. A small girl with blonde hair and big blue eyes scowled down at me. "Who are you? Why are you here?" she whispered.

"Chanelle?" I croaked. "What are you doing here? I thought—"

She pressed her hand over my mouth and leaned over to hiss in my ear. "Where is she? What did you do to my sister?" Her hand pressed harder, and I could only let out a muffled, "mmph."

"Be quiet. If you alert the others, I'll kill you." She took her hand away. "Now, tell me. What did you do with Chanelle, and where is she?" China looked exactly like her sister.

I shook my head. "I didn't do anything to her, I swear. After the Trial, she went with the Examiner. She told me to come find you." I paused as a horrible thought filled my head. "You *are* China, right?"

She nodded, scowling.

"And you're a…Player?"

Hesitation, but another nod.

I hadn't broken the silence rule, then. "I know this looks suspicious, me sneaking around and all, but I promise I'm not here to do anything bad. I was just trying to find you."

"What do you mean, Chanelle went with the Examiner? Is she all right? And what are those people doing in her room?"

When I didn't answer immediately she leaned down with narrowed eyes and said, "Talk! Just because you're a Player doesn't mean anything. For all I know, this could be a quest, and you're here to trick me. If I don't start getting answers right away, you're going to start hurting."

I nodded. "China, I'll tell you everything I know. I promise I'm only here because of Chanelle." I tried to imbue my voice with calm trustworthiness and confidence. "You can trust me. But you just said someone's in her room. What are they doing?" I said the last slowly, emphasizing the importance.

She pulled back and frowned. "I don't know. Going through her stuff. I snuck out here to hide, but then you came. I wouldn't even have noticed them if I hadn't been waiting up all night for her." Her eyes were wide, half wild and unstable from fear.

I nodded again and swallowed. If I was going to gain her as an ally, now was the time to act, to be confident. "Let me up, China. We should find out what they're doing. It could be important—about what happened to Chanelle."

She stared down at me for a few seconds, and then the tension in her face loosened, and she scrambled up and offered a hand to help me stand.

I took it, and the two of us hurried to the back of a huge, leafy bush. China pushed aside one of its branches, and I saw there was enough space in the center for the two of us to crouch uncomfortably. I crawled in, and she came after me.

"What a great spot. It's perfect." From within, we could see out through the leaves, but anyone who looked in our direction would see nothing but a bush.

"My sister and I used to play in here all the time when we were kids. It was our secret place. And it's got a perfect view through her bedroom window." She pointed.

Through the window, I saw three masked people moving around inside the bedroom. One was on Chanelle's computer, one was rifling through her drawers, and the other was waving a scanning wand of some kind over every inch of her room. Visible through the breathing holes in the masks, their mouths moved silently behind the window glass. I scooted forward in a futile attempt to hear. "We're too far away."

China shook her head and closed her eyes. "I think I can hear them. I've got a lot of Seeds in Perception. Give me a second to focus."

She took a few deep breaths and seemed to be concentrating so hard I found myself holding my own breath for fear of disturbing her. Then she started to speak. "Hurry up! The sun's almost all the way up; we need to be out of here soon."

"I'm going as fast as I can. It's not our fault that Davis girl had a party going on at her house. Took us forever to get in and out without being seen."

The other laughed. "Yeah, but with a girl like that, no one would have any trouble believing she ran away."

I let out a slow, silent breath. She was relaying their conversation to me, somehow hearing their voices clearly through a window and ten meters of air. Amazing.

She continued repeating, "Wonder what NIX is going to do with all of them."

"Research, idiot. They're going to study them three ways from Tuesday. I betcha we'll be doing the Mendell drop with samples from them within days."

"Would you two *shut up*? There are other people in this house, you know. What if they heard your voices and decided to come check up on the little sleeping girly, and found us instead? Keep it quiet."

China waited for a while longer and then opened her eyes again. "Seems like they listened to him. I can't hear anything."

I nodded. The masked figures inside weren't moving their mouths anymore. They took some of Chanelle's things and put them in a bag. A couple minutes later, they climbed deftly out of the window and left over the fence on the other side, much the same way I had, only more graceful. The gentle rumble of an engine cut the silence, and a plain multi-member pod slipped off down the brightening street.

I relaxed in their absence. "That was amazing, China. Good job."

She bit her lip. "Not amazing enough. All we got was some cryptic conversation. I should have been listening from the beginning, but I was too focused on hiding."

I smiled. "It was more than just some cryptic conversation, China. We got plenty."

China closed her eyes and took a deep, deep breath, then released it along with some of her tension. "Yeah. Chanelle's still alive." She opened her eyes, and they locked on mine. "At least for now. Tell me everything that happened last night."

I did, starting from the time Chanelle tackled and protected me to the point where she followed Mr. Wolf into the darkness, conveniently glossing over my weaker moments and general uselessness.

"So…NIX has her. Who, or what, is NIX?"

"It's probably the ones who created this Game. Not a person. An organization. They're too powerful for anything else," I said.

"And as long as they've got tests or whatever to run on her, they'll keep her alive, right? What's the Mendell drop?"

I shook my head. "I don't know. But perhaps it's some sort of testing facility. They said they'd be taking samples. And when I was made a Player, they matched my blood to confirm my identity." I bit my much abused bottom lip and held a finger to my lips. "Bunny might be listening," I mouthed silently.

She nodded understanding and took off her link, tossing it away. She motioned for me to do the same. "There aren't any mics out here," she said. "Chanelle and I searched."

"How?"

"If you concentrate really hard, and your Perception is really high, you can hear them."

What a useful skill. I made sure to consciously keep my thoughts shielded from any intention to communicate with Bunny, and said, "Did you have a medical test at your school a few months ago?"

Her pale eyebrows drew down. "Yes. Blood and tissue tests, physical exam, and they took our pictures…" she trailed off. "You think that was them? NIX?"

"Maybe. They had access to that test, even if it wasn't them implementing it. It makes sense though, doesn't it? I've got a theory. They're using us like test subjects. Human rats. That's what the examination was for. To make sure we were healthy, because they didn't want to waste their money on a faulty product." I leaned forward, talking faster. "I mean, can you imagine how expensive we must be? The technology they're displaying, I can't imagine what kind of funding they must have…"

"Why are they doing this to us?" She looked like a small, wounded animal, a look fairly designed to inspire protective feelings.

But I was reminded of my goal, instead. "I don't know. But remember the message Chanelle gave me for you?"

"She said for me to live?" China frowned. "What does that mean?"

I shrugged. "I think it means exactly that. She wanted you to be safe, to stay alive. And she sent me to you so we could help each other. As long as we're alive, there's hope that we can escape. For us, and for Chanelle. I want to help you, if you'll do the same for me. I want us both to live." I imbued my voice with sincerity.

The truth of it all was *I* wanted to live, and I thought she might be able to help me with that. "In the Trial, I saw people trip each other so they could get more Seeds. Killing people who are stuck in the same hell right next to them, just to get ahead a step or two. That's not right." It wasn't *smart.* "Let's have each other's backs. I'll look out for you if you do the same for me." I held out my hand to her. "Allies?"

She stared into my eyes searchingly, then nodded and gripped my hand with her smaller one. "Allies."

We talked for a bit longer, exchanging contact information and speculation, and then I left for my home, and she for her room. If Bunny were to check in on me, I didn't want my GPS to reveal my knowledge of the cleanup crew. I looked back at the house, standing deceptively sturdy against the backdrop of the sunrise-stained sky. "I'm sorry, China." I whispered, so low even I could barely hear my own voice, safe from even her superhuman hearing. "But I need your strength, because I'm not going to die yet."

# Chapter 8

We stopped checking for monsters under our beds when we realized they were inside us.

— The Joker

TWO DAYS LATER, the song played again, and I entered my second Trial.

I'd been walking down a crowded street, thinking about the things my most recent net searches had uncovered. With more information, I knew better what clues to search for. There were online conspiracy groups who questioned the increased number of child runaways and mysterious disappearances. It had started five years ago, and they had theories from serial-killer cover ups, to human trafficking, to government experiments. The enforcers of course found nothing, and these were dismissed as the crazy ravings of distraught parents. And because I knew what to look for, I noticed the connection to parenting groups, where they worried about their children being victims of a bullying ring, or part of some sort of secret fight club. Of course, their children were fighting for their lives in the Trials, but they had to keep it a secret from their families, so other explanations for the wounds were created.

As the first faint strains of music entered my head, I'd panicked a little. I scrambled for the nearest side street, and the nearest alley from there, all the while muttering under my breath, "Bunny? Bunny, I need to talk to you. Now!"

—What is it?—
-Bunny-

"I'm hearing the song again, that one that filled me up, and then I was in the other place, in the Trial, and it's too soon. I'm not ready, I haven't prepared yet, and I thought I'd have more time..." I took a deep breath and swallowed hard to cut off my babbling.

—It's probably a special Trial, separate from the normal ones. I think this is your Characteristic Trial. It's going to test your reactions, and then you'll get a Skill based on your performance.—
-Bunny-

"It's too soon, Bunny! I'm not even recovered from the last time yet! I thought we were supposed to have ten days! That's what China said, and I'm—" once again I cut myself off. I was scared. But I didn't want to say it aloud, because if I didn't, I could pretend the fear wasn't real. And then maybe it wouldn't be.

—Suck it up. You don't have time to whine. The Boneshaker doesn't last for long, and you're almost out of time. Pull it together, kick some ass, and we'll talk about it when you get back.—
-Bunny-

I wanted to throw a few choice cuss words back at Bunny, but the song was in my bones. I closed my eyes to keep them from rattling out of my head, and it stopped.

I was prepared for the nausea and dizziness, so I stood up and observed my surroundings despite the sickness, knowing it would pass.

I stood in the midst of a field with tall green grass up to my chest. The sun shone down so brightly I had to squint until my eyes didn't burn from the light. The colors were somehow *deeper* than any I'd seen before. The sky was a clear, piercing blue, a bit too dark a color. The grass was a green that made me think of strength, life, and the insatiable desire to *grow*. The air smelled…*off*, fruity and earthy and green. I breathed it in, and shuddered. Normally it would be a pleasant smell, but I couldn't help but associate it with blood and death.

I saw that other Players were there, too, poking out of the gently waving green sea. Furrows were cut through the grass in straight lines, paths leading to a few scattered buildings a couple hundred meters away. The buildings weren't like any I'd seen before. They seemed to have been built for beauty rather than economy of space, and twisted and lounged in strange, sometimes organic and sometimes geometric shapes.

On the other side, the field stopped abruptly at the edge of a line of thick trees. These weren't the giant trees of my last Trial, but thick and so closely spaced they blocked out the light beneath their leaves.

Players were moving to where the cube hung, over a place where the paths in the field converged. I started toward it as well, slowly, because being heavier made me clumsy. I stumbled from the grass onto a narrow road. It was lined with thin strips of metal running along the stone path in straight lines.

I leaned down to touch them, and the sight of my trembling arm widened my eyes. "My ID link!" It was basically a computer, mobile phone, and official identification all rolled into one. I tried to call my mother, but the screen was blank, and the link lay unresponsive on my forearm. "Am I out of range? The only places out of range are caves and lead boxes! Don't screw with me! I can see the sky; I should have service." I smacked the forearm sheath in sudden desperation, but it continued to ignore me.

A young boy giggled at me, and shook his head. "They don't work here. I tried last time. You shouldn't bring electric things with you. They get scrambled and broke by the Boneshaker."

Bunny had used that word before, too. The Boneshaker must be the creepy song that brought me to the Trials. "But the VR chip in my neck still works, even though it goes through the Boneshaker."

The kid shrugged. "It's inside your body."

"Oh." I stood up. "How many times have you been here?"

"Once before," he said, and a different emotion wiped the smile off his face.

I knew that feeling like a close friend. It was fear. "Me, too."

A guy my age laughed softly. "Oh, that's too bad. Usually you've got time to strengthen a bit more before the Characteristic Trial."

I focused on his handsome face. "You know about this, about what's going on?"

He smirked, and looked me up and down. "I do. This is our chance to gain the weapons to become gods."

"What does that mean?" I took a step forward, wanting to drag an explanation for all this out of him.

"That's the point of all this, you know. They're seeing who can become a god." He gestured to the floating cube. "What did you think it meant?"

It read slightly different than the last time.

HERE YOU WILL BE TRIED, YOUR MEASURE TAKEN.
THE LIVING WILL BE GRANTED A POWER TO MATCH.

I wanted to scream, but restrained myself to a flurry of questions. "What does that mean? Who's 'seeing?' What is this place, this game? What weapons do you mean? Illegal things, like guns or knives?"

He smiled again, and looked up at the sky. A flapping sound filled the air, and I followed his gaze. Hundreds of crows flew towards us from every direction.

I threw myself backward into the grass and crouched down.

The guy gave me a surprised look and laughed. "It's only the Examiner. Relax."

The small boy smiled at me, an innocent expression that made me wonder just how old he was. Definitely too young to be playing in this Game. Just what kind of monster would do that to a child?

The crows settled around the group of Players in the small stone clearing like a shimmering black shroud over the earth. When nothing happened, I crept back out again.

One crow, larger than the others, landed on top of the cube and looked down at all of us with a cocked head and beady little bird eye. It opened its mouth, and a half-mechanic, half-cute voice came from it. "Hello, Players. I am this Trial's Examiner." Its beak stayed constantly open while the words came out, as if a speaker in the back of its throat did all the "talking."

"Those are my eyes and ears." It gestured to the other crows with its beak.

Their little eyes glittered, a sea of sparkles. It was unnatural, revolting, and the hair of my arms and the back of my neck prickled stiff.

The crow's voice came out again. "This Trial is a special type of test. All the choices and actions you make, your every move, is measured. If you survive until the end, you will be given a Skill that matches your assessment. Please reach into the cube and retrieve your token."

The handsome guy sunk his hand eagerly into the wall of the

cube, which melted over his disappearing skin until he drew something out.

Nothing happened to him, so I thrust my own hand forward. I clenched my teeth when the cube didn't stop me, instead seeming to suck and pull at my flesh. I felt something small and hard, clenched my fist around it, and yanked backward. In my hand was a small black ball.

I examined it for markings while the other Players took their own tokens, but it was perfectly smooth, and surprisingly heavy. I tucked it into my shirt pocket.

The crow started to speak again. "There are only two rules to win. Do not give up possession of your token. You will not be able to return without it. And do not die. You may take each other's tokens through battle or trickery, but greater potential rewards create a harder challenge. If you are not prepared for an increased difficulty level, do not take additional tokens." It cocked its head as if listening to something in the distance. "Let the Trial begin." And with that, all the crows flapped into chaos, rising into the sky like a cloud of darkness.

---

I COVERED my face with my hands to protect it from the crows' beating wings and claws, and when I lifted them, I saw everyone had burst into motion. I saw some running through the field for the trees in the distance, some fighting over each other's tokens already, and some going for the strange buildings. The small boy and the guy who'd known what was happening were both gone already.

I hesitated for a moment, and then ran down the lined stone path toward the buildings. Protective walls around me and a small place to hide sounded perfect.

The path split in three directions, and I turned to the right. The path split again, and I took the right again, which led to an oval building that looked like a gargantuan, half-sunken egg. Vines sprung from the ground and curled up its surface as if anchoring it to the earth.

A shriek, like that from a bird of prey, cut through the air behind me like a high-pitched razor. Someone shouted, and then the shouting changed to screaming. I could tell the difference, because the screams were desperate and filled with fear.

I shuddered and didn't look back as I entered a small doorway cut through the side of the vine-covered building. That was stupid, because the floor dropped away beneath my feet as soon as I touched it, and I fell, screaming.

My scream cut off abruptly as my landing knocked the air out of my lungs. I rolled to my hands and knees and sucked desperately for the dust-filled air. Something *snicked* above me, and every last drop of light cut out. When I could once again breathe, I patted at the ground, sweeping my arms around to get my bearings. Heavy dust and…sticks. I followed the sticks to other, attached sticks, and came to a horrible realization. "Not sticks…" I snatched my hands back, coughed, and gagged.

I fumbled with my link, but though its display wouldn't come on, my eyes adjusted to the low light in the small compartment I sat in. A large skeleton lay beside me, and I scuttled back only to rattle another stack of old bones. I turned in a circle, and saw that I was in a seamless square box, about three meters in every direction. Three large skeletons and one normal-sized one kept me company.

I saw a small black ball amongst the half-inch layer of dust made of their decayed bodies. I brushed it off, and realized it was a token, just like the one I had. I dropped it immediately. The crow had said having more than one made the Trial even harder, and I didn't want the walls to suddenly start pouring water down on me and filling up the room, or some other equally deadly twist. I only needed my own token to get out alive.

I stood up and put my hand on one of the walls, hoping to feel some seam or crack I could get at, but it slid away at the touch of my hand, meshing into the adjacent wall. A corridor stretched out in front of me, lit with warm light. Beautiful pale blue flowers with large, droopy petals stretched out over the floor and walls.

I stared out, and then back to the four skeletons lying inside the room. "Unless they were moved here after dying, there's a reason why they didn't escape," I muttered.

I turned back to the bones and noticed something on the normal-sized skeleton's arm. I slid it off and held it up. "Damn." It was an old ID link, completely out of power. My heart beat even faster, and the hair on the back of my neck stood up in warning.

I turned in a circle, searching for danger, but nothing had changed. I tried to fold the link to tuck it into my waistband and take it home, but it was as brittle as if it had been lying there for decades, and crumbled in my hands. I clenched my jaw and went to examine the other three, larger skeletons.

All wore armor of some sort; one had a larger hammer, and the other a short, wide sword. I couldn't lift either of them. But there were two bands crossing the empty chest cavity of one, and I dragged them off, shifting the heavy chest, arm, and skull until I had pulled them free.

The bands seemed to be made from hundreds of pieces of metal, stuck together into straps. I examined them quickly as the feeling of danger grew, and the sweet scent of the flowers from the hall floated toward me. I looked around again, and knew that I couldn't wait any longer. I slipped the bands over my head and positioned them across my chest in an X, like the corpse had.

I stepped cautiously into the corridor, droopy petals crushing beneath my feet and releasing their perfume. Adrenaline flowed into my veins with a burn. Danger. Death was coming, I knew.

I breathed heavier and started to run. The faster and farther I went, the more the sweet scent filled my lungs, and the more I shuddered with irrational fear. I bit the inside of my cheek while running, since my bottom lip was still healing. The blossom of pain and taste of blood distracted me from the danger for a moment, and I realized something was wrong. The panic was raging out of control, for no apparent reason. The farther I went, the worse it got. I knew something bad was ahead. I could feel myself getting closer to it as the instinctual sense of danger increased.

I stumbled over a branching vine and fell to my hands and knees. The blue flowers puffed up their cloying scent, right into my face, and my heart squeezed so fast and hard I became quite literally lightheaded from fear.

"The flowers." I took another breath, and thought back to the safety of that small room with the skeletons. I knew I should go back. I'd be safe there. "Damn." I stood up, grabbed my shirt's sleeve, and ripped it off, then rapped it twice around my head, covering my mouth and nose like a mask.

The flowers were messing with my head. Something in their scent made my brain think of death and torment. And as I went further, they grew thicker and thicker, and the fear grew worse.

I started running again, gasping for air through the thick filter. It helped somewhat, and I was able to continue until the corridor grew so thick with flowers I had trouble moving. Finally, the hallway ended abruptly, and I stumbled into a large room with steps leading down from the outside to the center, like a coliseum, or a small version of a football stadium.

I looked around and shuddered. The room was filled with new monsters, and they were all looking my direction. For a few awkward seconds, we all just stared.

The corpses of strange animals littered the floor, some newer, and some old enough that the bones had been picked clean already. There were a few human skeletons.

The monsters were short, close to the ground. The bigger ones had six stubby legs, three on either side of their grub-like bodies. Their heads resembled a retarded pug dog's. Their eyes bulged out on either side of their skull, and their mouths dripped thick green slime.

They had been slurping up the liquefied flesh of the bodies. Smaller monsters with no legs, the babies, wormed around like maggots, blindly sucking up the fleshy slush beneath them. I realized then that some of the carcasses were their own species, being cannibalized.

One of them sniffled loudly, lifting its head as if to scent the air. Then it ran toward me, moving surprisingly fast on its six stubbly little legs. The other adults followed, mouths hanging open like happy dogs. Most of them were on the lower levels of the room, and seemed to struggle moving up the large steps.

I didn't wait for them to reach me and see what they would do. That much was obvious by the contents of the room. I turned and ran, heading sideways around the outside of the stadium, close to the wall and on the highest level.

I heard the snuffling behind me from a grub-pug that must have already been on the top level, and ran faster, barely keeping ahead of it. I looked frantically around for an escape, and saw a door at the other end of the room.

I felt something warm on the back of my calf and snapped from fear, just a bit. I took a huge leap out over the abnormally large steps leading down to the middle. Things seemed to slow down for a moment as I hung in the air, falling forward onto the steps far below. Then I was plummeting at full speed.

I landed on my feet, but my legs couldn't handle the pressure or the forward momentum, and I tumbled over. I came down on my back and flung out my arms to keep from rolling any more. I had probably hurt myself quite a bit with that little stunt, but there was so much adrenaline pumping through my veins that I didn't notice.

I'd put some distance between myself and the one on the top level, but conversely put myself closer to the ones still struggling to climb up from the bottom. I stood and ran forward, careful to maintain my footing on the vines and small plants that grew everywhere at this lower level.

When I reached the far end of the room near the second doorway, I started up the stairs again, my thighs burning from the exertion of moving my weight upward at such a fast pace.

When I reached the top, I used some of my precious air on a chuckle.

The grub-pug on top had followed me down and across, but was now struggling along with the others to move up the steps below me. Its short legs scrabbled desperately before finally heaving it over the edge of a step.

I pointed at it and spit. "Screw you! I'm not that easy to kill."

Of course, fate took that moment to show me the consequence of hubris. A sniffling sound came from the doorway behind me, and I jumped out of the way just in time to avoid the huge grub-pug lunging for me. It sniffed and came for me at full speed.

I turned and ran all the way back to the blue-flower doorway, then down and back up again, avoiding decaying bodies along the way.

Some of the grub-pugs were thrown off, but more came through the doorway, and others seemed to catch on to my trick and ignore my descent, waiting for me at the top level. Soon, I found myself trapped on three sides, with my back to the outside wall. I was caught, too far away from either of the doorways to escape into them. Helpless rage took hold of me at the unfairness of my situation. I hadn't asked for any of this, had done nothing to deserve it. My whole life I'd gone about silently, invisibly, never standing out or voicing the anger, irritation, and derision that filled my head.

Now, I screamed at the monsters, a wordless shriek of challenge. Let them try and fight me, eat me, if they could. I wouldn't hold back my rage at Death's attempt to take me any longer.

So I put my back to the curve of the wall and braced myself for the first one to come close. I was ready when it did. I kicked it in its drooling face as hard as I could.

Its pug-nose squished in a little bit, and it fell back, dazed. Another came, and I did the same to it. But they were big creatures, and my kicks weren't having much effect other than to keep them off.

So I kicked harder. I slid my back farther down the wall, so that my legs could push outward rather than just down.

The drooling, maggot-like monsters gathered around me, watching warily, and looking for a chance to rush me. Thick, slimy fluid from their mouths coated the stone floor, making it slippery.

When I kicked them from my lowered position, they slid away. I was hoping to knock them over the edge, but then others that'd been on the lower steps heaved themselves up to the top level, and joined the others in pinning me to the wall.

I let out a choked sob. There were too many of them, and I wasn't strong enough.

Then, one of them made a horrible snorting sound, like it was gathering up a stubborn loogie from the back of its throat. It spit at me, a wad of green slime flying forward and hitting me in the middle of my left shin.

I shook my leg and most of its spit glob dripped reluctantly to the floor. But my pants were wet where it had hit, and they clung to my leg.

Then another snorted, and another.

I didn't know what the heck the green stuff was, but the fact that they were standing at a distance and spitting it on me meant it couldn't be good. I only had to look around to see it had to be a poison or acid of some sort. I highly doubted they were going for the gross-out factor.

They aimed for my legs again, and I use my left shin to shield my still loogie-free right leg.

The heavy fluid soaked through my pant leg and pooled in my shoe.

I prepared for the pain of acid eating through my skin or at least *something* horrible. But nothing happened. Then I realized my lower left leg and foot didn't hurt at all. I'd had blisters all over my foot and my calf had been absolutely screaming in ignored pain, just like my right leg. I tried to wiggle my left toes, but couldn't feel them to tell if they'd moved or not.

Blood rushed in my ears as I comprehended my situation.

They would keep me pinned, and spit on me from afar until I was paralyzed, and then they would eat me, feeding their young on my dissolving, putrid body.

"Screw that." I spit back at the monster that'd spit on me first. Then I screamed, and pushed forward from the wall. I balanced on my good leg and used the numb one to kick out viciously. I pushed two down a few steps, letting them slip in their own green slime, and then limped after the ones still on the top level. I kicked one in the head hard enough that it seemed to grow woozy for a second, and I used the opportunity to shove it over the edge.

The last one on the top level made the snorting, gathering sound again, but I kicked it before it could spit. Its head snapped sharply to the side and it stopped. It opened its mouth wide and rushed me, but I threw myself at it, stomping with all weight down on its head. My foot was so numb I couldn't even feel the impact, but I saw it sink down in the blubbery creature's head.

I did it again and again, as hard as I could. My breath shuddered in and out of my lungs, and I sobbed desperately, a sound of fear and mindless rage.

It had stopped moving, its skull thoroughly smashed in, its eyes bulging out even more. I stepped back from it and placed my back against the wall again.

"I killed it," I said to myself. And then again, "I killed it! It's dead!" It was a giddy feeling. And when the monsters I'd kicked down a few steps reached the top, I killed them, too. I screamed defiance at them, a grin stretching my mouth painfully wide.

More came from below, and still more from the far door, but their skulls weren't designed for stability against hard impacts. I stayed in my circle of slippery, smashed carcasses, and killed my attackers with vicious kicks when they came close.

I didn't know how much time passed, but they stopped coming, and I realized that all the adults were dead, too stupid to realize my superiority and run away.

I stood panting in the circle of squished-headed monsters for a bit, then limped away and sat down with my back against the wall.

I leaned my head toward the low-hanging ceiling and laughed, and then started to cry. "I'm alive," I whispered. I hadn't thought I would be.

Lethargy started to crawl over me, and I struggled to my feet. If I didn't keep moving, I might fall into the sleep of exhaustion and never wake again.

# Chapter 9

I knew nothing but shadows and I thought them to be real.
— Oscar Wilde

I WALKED through the far doorway and dragged myself up the huge steps of a dark stairwell. The remnants of light evaporated as I climbed, until I moved in absolute darkness. It frightened me at first, but as I went on, I lost even the strength for fear, and thought longingly of rest. My dragging left leg felt like a heavy log.

I sucked on my much-abused bottom lip, and the quick spike of pain pushed through my foggy head like a fresh breeze. "Works like a charm," I whispered into the blackness. I continued on, pinching or biting myself when I started to grow lethargic.

By the end I was panting, my legs so worn that even the good one felt numb, and I couldn't tell if my dizziness was imagined, or a result of over-exertion. The stairwell ended abruptly, and my face smashed into something solid. The pain made me jerk away, and brought me tingling back to a level of awareness I didn't remember losing.

I felt along the wall I'd run into. It was actually more like the ceiling. It slanted toward me, and warmth radiated from the stone in waves that felt soothing, despite the heat of my body. I pushed, and the stone slid away. Hot air wafted down on me, and I peeked my head up through the floor and looked around.

The room was a compact cylinder with a low ceiling and images of different kinds of strange animals carved into the walls at regular intervals.

No monsters appeared, and nothing happened. I spat as far as I could into the room and ducked down, waiting for a reaction. Nothing. So I climbed up the rest of the way into the room. As soon as I was in, the opening *snicked* closed behind me, as seamless as if it had never been there.

Then the air around me let out a pulsing boom. It hit me from every side at once, and suddenly I was burning. Heat tightened my skin, and my dust dry eyes stung with tears that evaporated before they even wet my eyeballs.

I screamed, but couldn't hear myself, and ran mindlessly, trying to get *away*. I slammed into a section of the wall with a gazelle-like creature on it. The stone once again slid open, this time onto a room full of deer-like monsters, separated from the room I was in by what looked like a seamless sheet of water.

A thin and muscular monster turned to look at me. It reminded me of a cross between a Chihuahua and a deer. Rather than hooves, two claws tipped each of its four legs. Its snout was long and pointed, and its teeth sharp. Two triangular ears swiveled around warily, and it ran towards me and stopped at what it seemed to judge as a safe distance.

I pushed my fingers through the layer of water. They cooled immediately, and I had to resist the urge to plunge my body through, too.

The creature let out a high-pitched chattering sound. "Tikitik-tiktik!" Its eyes were locked on my own, and something about it, small bony frame and all, settled worry into my heart. It might be cute, if I didn't know it wanted to kill me. Drawn by its call, others slipped into my line of sight, one after the other, until a crowd waited on the other side of the barrier.

The taut skin of my lips cracked from the heat, and a drop of blood fell to the bands across my chest, then dried up and fell away like dust.

I could fight the monsters. I couldn't fight the heat. I stepped forward, and the absence of the burning felt so pleasurable I wanted to weep in relief. But I didn't have time.

I knew from their body language they were going to rush me all at once, so I made the first move. I stepped forward and crushed one of them under my left foot with one giant stomp.

Its legs snapped out from underneath its body at a bad angle, and it died with a pitiful, high-pitched scream.

I almost felt bad for it, until its friends jumped at me from all sides. Their little legs propelled them through the air as if they were made to run and jump. But unlike the delicate creatures they resembled, they were the hunters, not the hunted. Their legs clawed at my clothes, my face, and my arms, and their teeth ripped at my skin.

They came at me from so many different directions I could only flail around and try to protect my head. But there were too many of them, and I was already weakening. I bled from a myriad of tiny slashes, and each time they sank their teeth into me, they tore loose small chunks of flesh.

So I clenched my jaw and stopped trying to blindly protect my head. It was instinct to react defensively to something I couldn't fight head on, but it was going to get me killed.

A tik-tik was on my leg, biting into my thigh with its Chihuahua-sized jaw. I grabbed it by the nape of its neck and twisted with both my hands as if wringing out a washcloth. Its bones crunched and broke, and I used the body to bat away another that jumped at me. It slammed into the ground, hard, and didn't get up again. Some were attached to my back, so I stumbled against the nearest wall and crushed my body against the stone once, then again, and again.

Blood ran from me, and some splashed against the metal bands I'd taken, right in the middle where they crossed each other. Metallic scales rippled out from the center point in waves, rising like the back hair of a frightened cat. Then it tightened over me and the bands started to spread, the little scales filling in the gaps between the bands. In less than a second, my torso up to the neck and down to my waist was covered. I gave it a sharp rap of my knuckles, and it silently spread the force of the impact with a ripple of scales. "Freaking body armor," I croaked. "Hell, yeah."

The creatures sank back for a second, wary, and a few of them let out that high-pitched "Tik tik!" sound again.

I knew I needed to finish them quickly, before they overwhelmed me again. I was already exhausted, and losing blood to boot. So I lunged forward in attack, picking them off one by one.

They wouldn't run away, and instead encircled me, trying to keep me contained. I had the feeling they were stalling for time until reinforcements were drawn by their cute calls.

I used the bodies of their dead against them. If a little deer got knocked over, I was on it, and it was dead before it had the chance to stand back up. I killed them, and kept killing them. They were so weak, compared to the grub-pugs.

But more came, and more. They were determined, smart, and vicious. One would dart in and make a feint at me, while two more attacked when my attention was diverted. My torso was protected, but they ripped at my legs, arms, and head. Rather than latching on like in the beginning, they'd dart in to give small wounds, and then dart right back out to rejoin the encircling pack. They were like a pack of relentless arctic wolves, hell-bent on bringing down their prey.

But fear of death is a powerful motivator, and I refused to fall. I killed them until finally one let out a sharp "Tik!" and they all backed up a few steps and repeated the sound.

I made a feinting lunge toward them as if to attack, screaming with all the intimidation I could muster. My dry throat cracked, and my voice broke under the pressure, turning my scream into a growling shriek of bloodlust.

They jumped in surprise, and dashed away almost quicker than I would have thought possible, going "Tik! Tik!" in alarm.

After that, I took a long minute to just lean against the wall and rest. I knew I needed to keep moving. I knew that. But at the moment, I couldn't. That scream had been a desperate attempt to scare them. And luckily it had worked, because no matter how much I wanted it to, my body couldn't keep going without a break.

As I sat among the small carcasses, I felt elation roll over me. I'd won, with my own strength. I'd fought and won.

---

I SAT near the entrance barrier and looked around the room. I'd been too busy with the more immediate danger to examine it before.

It was a section of the top of the building, cut somewhat like a piece of Bundt cake, the center being the heat-room I'd come from, and the other slices undoubtedly being filled with other types of monsters. There were three doorways in the far wall, each leading into darkness. But the small crisscrossing grooves lining the walls and the holes in the ceiling that let in beams of sunlight were of more interest to me.

I looked to the three doors, and then to the skylights, and then to the grooved walls. "Damn. I wish I'd exercised more." With one last deep breath, I swallowed to moisten my still-dry throat, crawled to my feet, and hobbled toward the doors.

When I reached the outward facing wall I carefully avoided the doorways and the danger I knew would lurk somewhere on the other side. Instead, I wedged my fingers and toes into the slanted grooves in the wall, and started to shuffle diagonally upward. When I'd gone to the far wall, I carefully moved to a higher set of grooves and started in the other direction, inching my way toward the ceiling.

As I neared one of the glass-less windows, I realized it was eerily silent outside, and the faint smell of something else mixed with the light perfume of the air. When I'd entered the building, already there had been horrible screams, but they were absent now. When I reached the window and hauled my upper body through the opening, I discovered why.

"Oh. God," I murmured.

It was a scene of carnage. Countless bodies were strewn across the ground in every direction, lying on the stone paths and amongst the trampled grass of the fields. Many of them were monsters, but I saw a human head with brown hair lying below my vantage point, face down.

It was just the head, the body nowhere to be seen.

I reared back from the opening, gasping for air as my stomach heaved. But even so, the taste of the air, filled with the scent of blood and feces and the meaty, food-smell of raw meat and internal organs…the smell filled my mouth, and I could taste it on my tongue and the back of my throat.

My stomach convulsed, and I spewed down onto the floor below. I wiped my mouth with the back of my hand, and looked out again.

Under a nearby tree, whose trunk had broken like a snapped toothpick, a pack of the tik-tiks piled on top of something on the ground, ripping and biting. A small arm flailed out, helpless, and I gasped. It was the boy, the small boy from earlier. They were killing him.

I shouted and waved my hands, but none of the monsters so much as twitched. I crawled out of the opening, angled my feet down, and pushed off down the outside of the curved building. I slid quickly, and then shot off the side almost straight down.

I hit hard, and despite crumpling to the ground and rolling, sharp pain shot up through my un-numbed ankle, my knees, and my hips. The scaly vest I wore absorbed some of the impact, and protected my spine. I groaned and stumbled to my feet, then hobbled to the pack, shouting in rage.

They saw me coming, and lifted red-stained muzzles, teeth bared in warning.

When I reached them, I snapped one's neck with my two hands while I cracked the spine and brittle legs of another under my foot, screaming all the while. That took care of that. They ran off, chattering at me resentfully.

I knelt in front of the small Player. It looked like maybe he had been hiding in the branches of the tree, which had been knocked over by some huge force. The boy that I'd thought earlier looked too young to be here lay bleeding—way, way too much blood.

My hands shook as they hovered above him, trying to figure out the best spot to apply pressure. "Oh, god. Please. Are you okay?" I knew the answer. There were too many wounds, he was too small, and he'd already bled so much. It was everywhere, the blood.

He gasped up at me, chest heaving for breath, eyes wide and terrified.

I smiled at him, hoping it looked honest. "You're going to be fine, okay? They're gone, and I'm here now. I'll keep you safe, and as soon as this is over we're going to get you out of here, to a hospital, so don't you worry." I looked around for someplace to hide. "Everything's okay," I chattered, not sure if I was trying to soothe the boy or myself with my words.

The sleeve I'd wound around my face earlier had fallen down around my neck. I took it off, tore it down the middle, and used it to tie off both of the boy's arms as close to his body as possible. Then I tore off my other sleeve and did the same to his upper thighs. "Need to keep the blood near your core," I explained.

His torso was still leaking blood everywhere, but I didn't have anything to bind it with.

I heard a shriek, and a huge shadow passed overhead, blocking out the heat and glaring harshness of the sun for a fraction of a second. I looked up at the tail end of a huge flying bird creature. "Crap. We need to move."

I looked around for somewhere small, somewhere defensible. Definitely not another mysterious, *surprise-it's-a-trap*! building. Somewhere I could keep the boy safe. A crow sat in a nearby tree, watching us with its beady little eyes. I ignored it and looked past to a bullet-shaped glass container, big enough to fit a couple humans inside. It lay overturned nearby, on one of the grooved stone paths.

I slid my arms under the boy's light body and lifted him, trying not to jostle him despite my limpy leg, and carried him to the human-sized bullet. It had metal tracks on one side, and as I stared at the aerodynamic shape, I suddenly understood. "It's a pod! A transport pod."

I set the boy down on the ground and wedged my shoulder against the side of the pod, giving it a hard shove. It lifted slightly, but settled back down again. I shoved harder, and kept shoving, and it lifted, then rolled over and settled with its tracks along the grooves in the stone path. I pulled at the handle I'd uncovered and opened the glass door, then lifted the boy and slid him inside.

He groaned and tossed his head back and forth, pale with pain and blood-loss.

I went behind the pod and tried to push it along the tracks, but it ground against the stone roughly and I ran out of energy in less than a minute. I had to stop. I peeked my head inside the door to check on the boy, but instead noticed a cartridge in the front of the pod, attached to the end of the metal tracks. On the floor of the pod lay another, covered in rust.

I picked it up and buffed it thoughtfully against my pants, blew hard into its end, and took the other cartridge out of the slot. They were the same. I slipped the old one into my waistband, and then put the one from the floor into the slot. It took a good hard shove to push it into place, but when I finally got it, the pod hummed to life.

After only a few seconds, the glass tinted over to protect the interior from the sun. I laughed aloud. "Hell yeah!"

The boy giggled, despite his injuries. "This is awesome."

"How do you drive this thing?" I said, before noticing movement on the other side of the pod.

I stilled in fear as a large creature stalked around the corner of a nearby building, straight toward us. It looked like a humongous wildcat, except for the third eye in its head. I had half a moment to hope that it had already eaten someone or something else and wasn't hungry any more. Then its nose twitched, and it shot forward, slamming into the side of the pod and almost rocking it off the path again, clawing at the glass as if trying to get inside.

The boy screamed shrilly.

The three-eyed wildcat growled and scored lines into the tinted glass with its claws.

I took an involuntary step back, and it pushed away from the pod, padding purposefully around to my side. I stepped backward, and then remembered something I'd heard once about dealing with wildcats. I spread my arms and legs wide to try and look large, and resisted the urge to turn my back and run.

It merely threw me a warning snarl and turned to the boy, exposed by the open door of the pod.

"Damn it," I groaned. I lunged forward and slammed the pod door closed, leaving the boy protected inside.

The creature seemed to assess me anew in surprise, and bared its teeth in warning, letting out a rumbling growl, like the sound of far-away thunder rolling across the earth.

"I can't let you. He's just a little kid." I said aloud, though I knew it wouldn't make a difference to the creature.

It lunged for me, and I pushed sideways just soon enough to avoid its long claws. I fell onto my numb leg, now unfeeling all the way up to the hip, and scrambled backward. My hand landed on a rock, and I threw it at the cat, but it struck nothing more than a glancing blow.

All three of its eyes focused on me unwaveringly, a hunter's glare.

I continued to scuttle away as it stalked forward, until I came up against the trunk of the split tree from earlier.

The cat let out a series of raspy coughs, almost as if it was laughing.

I used the trunk to haul myself to my feet and snatched one of the snapped branches, pointing the sharp end toward the cat and shouting in wordless, empty threat.

It swiped one large paw and ripped the awkward weapon from my grasp. Another step and another swipe, and it knocked me into a tumbling roll across the ground.

I crawled to my hands and knees, holding the bleeding scratch marks on my arm, and wondering if the bone might be broken. My ID link definitely was, cracked and split like the ground of a desert land.

The cat pounced on me again, batting at me like a toy and sending me flying.

I dragged my limp left leg toward the pod, and used its smooth side to haul myself to my feet. My eyes met the boy's through the tinted glass, and I saw a fear in them that mirrored my own. I also saw the reflection of the cat behind me, and I knew that it would play with me until it killed me, and then it would eat me, and the boy would die.

There was no escape.

So I turned around, balled my hands into tight, bloodless fists, and screamed defiance at the monster. "Come!"

It smashed me against the side of the pod and pinned me with its front paws, towering over me on its hind legs.

I punched and flailed and even tried to bite at it, but it held still, looking at me with those three beautiful golden eyes. It opened its mouth to bite off my head.

I refused to close my eyes against death. But when it lowered its head, instead of teeth biting at me, a sandpaper tongue rasped against my forehead. I blinked twice as my mind stuttered in confusion. A lick?

The creature pushed back and landed on all fours, looked at my astonished face once more, and let out another coughing laugh. Then it ambled away, disappearing around a bend of the stone path between the tall grasses.

I shakily opened the door of the slim pod and sat down inside. "Are you okay?"

The boy nodded faintly. "I'm glad…you're okay," he whispered, taking rapid, shallow breaths.

I chuckled. "Me, too." There was a small lever in the center of the pod. I pushed it forward, and with a rusty groan, the pod started to slide forward.

The boy started shivering, and when I placed my hand on his forehead, it was cold and clammy. I pushed the lever down harder, and the pod shuddered with the effort to add more speed.

With some difficulty and a lot of worrying, we finally made it back to the starting point and the cube, the pod dying as the clearing came into view.

I got out, lifted the boy into my arms, and hobbled toward the still black cube. I laid the boy at the edge of the clearing, went to poke and prod at the cube, but got no reaction. I smashed my palm against it in frustration and then went back to the boy. "It'll be over soon, and then we'll be able to go back. I'll get you help."

He smiled sweetly at me and whispered, "No, you won't. But that's okay. Take it." He gestured to the front pocket of his jeans.

"What?"

"Take it."

He fumbled with the stiff fabric, so I reached into the small denim pouch to help him and drew out his black token.

"No." I shook my head, moving to put it back.

He smiled again, and blood ran out of the corner of his mouth as he whispered, "It's okay. Thank you." And then he was gone. I didn't want to believe it, but there's a horrible sense humans have for the souls of others. His was gone.

I blinked and let out a hitching, sobbing breath, though my eyes stayed dry.

Then the crow flapped down from the deep blue sky, landing atop the cube once more.

A screen flashed in front of my face.

THE TRIAL IS OVER. PLEASE RETURN TO THE STARTING POINT.

I waited numbly until others started to drag themselves back to the cube, weary and half-beaten. Then I stood up, clenching the second token in my fist. Words appeared on the cube.

YOU HAVE PROVEN YOURSELVES WORTHY.

I watched as the survivors filtered back. A man and woman came back okay, or so I thought. He dragged her, her arm thrown around his shoulder. Her eyes were wide and staring, and her throat had been slashed open, deep.

He was chanting to the dead woman mindlessly, as I had done to the boy. "It's okay, Honey. I'm here with you, and everything's going to be okay. It'll all be back to normal once we get back to the real world. It's okay, Honey…" This time, I knew for sure that the words were to comfort him, not her.

The cocky guy who'd claimed to know what was going on at the beginning of the Trial popped out of the tall grass and stumbled over the body of the boy. He grimaced in distaste, and then knelt down to pat the boy over and search his pockets.

"He doesn't have a token," I said without thinking.

He looked up and smiled at me. "You made it, huh? Though a bit worse for wear, I see," he said, looking at my bleeding, bedraggled and bruised body. "How do you know he doesn't have one?"

I stared at him emotionlessly, and his lips twisted into a knowing smile. "You took it, that's how. Well, well. I must say I'm impressed. Going for the weaker targets doesn't pay in strong

Skills, but you decrease risk that way, too. Personally I prefer the ones with fight in them. That way you know you'll get something good." He nodded at me approvingly. "And you got some armor. You've got more guts than I thought. You might do well in this Game."

I turned my head away without responding, and watched the others. There had been many at the start, but we were fewer now. "More than fifty percent casualty rate," I muttered.

"How else to cull the weak from the strong?" he said.

The crow moderator opened its mouth. "Everyone has arrived. Congratulations on surviving. Now, for the special awards! Please take out your tokens."

I slipped my finger between my strange vest and my shirt and pulled out my original token from the pocket where I'd stashed it. As the cube hummed, both mine and the boy's token started to vibrate sympathetically, and then melted and reformed into strange shapes that reminded me vaguely of old Chinese characters, or maybe Egyptian hieroglyphs.

Words rolled out across the screen from left to right.

WISHER'S PENNY: JENNY SHEEN
GREEN WHISPERER: JACK URBAN
SECOND WIND: VAUGHN RIDLEY
AURA OF LIGHT: VAUGHN RIDLEY
FLICKER: VAUGHN RIDLEY
MADRIGAL'S SHELL: VAUGHN RIDLEY
NOSE_

I watched the guy next to me. As Vaughn Ridley's name rolled out, over and over, his smile grew wider and wider. He held a handful of transformed tokens in his hand, watching the screen.

I grew cold inside, but was soon distracted as my own name rolled across the screen.

TUMBLING FEATHER: EVE REDDING
SPIRIT OF THE HUNTRESS: EVE REDDING

"Wow," Vaughn said. "You got a spirit-type Skill? Impressive."

I frowned at him. "What does that mean? What are 'Skills?' "

He shook his head at my ignorance. "They're just like the 'skills' in a video game. They let you do special things once you plant them, things you couldn't do normally. They're quite useful."

I stared at the two tokens, sitting so innocently in my palm. "They'll help me survive?" For a second, I was elated at my good fortune. I could hardly wait to plant them.

"They help you do more than survive. They allow you to become god!" He announced, looking at me with narrowed eyes. "I am the strongest Player to ever enter the Game, and I'm aiming for the ultimate power. I'm looking for allies to help me on my way. Strong people who will do whatever it takes, and don't mind getting their hands dirty. How about it?"

It took a minute for my overwhelmed brain to understand what the braggart was asking. "You want me to join you?"

"Yes. You're the only one here with more than one token, besides me. Even if you did only kill a little kid to get it, at least you're ruthless. And I know you're a bit strong, because you've got a spirit-type Skill. I'm going to dominate this Game and all the other useless Players, and I'll take you with me to the top."

I almost said yes. But then I saw the happy, charming smile on his face, and over his shoulder, the empty little body lying on the ground. Putrid disgust for myself washed over me. I hated myself, truly, at that moment.

"No. I'm not the one you want." I turned and dragged my left leg slowly toward the cube, which now displayed the "Do you want to leave?" message, and pushed "Yes."

# Chapter 10

I carry death in my left pocket.
— Charles Bukowski

THE FEEL of my suddenly lighter body and the sight of concrete walls rising up into smoggy air on either side allowed me to let out a sigh of relief. A window popped up, telling me I'd earned a few levels and Seeds. As the tension left my body, the pain and exhaustion washed over me like the waves of a rising tide. My head spun, and I fell against the wall and started to shiver. Blobs of light and dark swam across my vision, and a distant voice shocked me to alertness again.

With a gasp, I looked around. I didn't know how long I'd been sitting on the ground, but numbness had overtaken my whole left leg and butt, and was spreading through my torso. I was shivering and clammy from blood loss, and my heart beat fast trying to keep my body oxygenated. "Damn it. No, no." I shook my head helplessly. Soon, the numbness and paralysis would spread to my lungs.

I jabbed at my ID sheath, but the shattered surface didn't

respond. No phone call possible. I called out weakly toward the sidewalk, but the alley took a sharp turn, so no one could see me, and I was too weak to shout.

One last resort. "Bunny?"

He responded immediately.

—You're back.
Shit. You look like crap.—
-Bunny-

I swallowed. "I need help. If I don't get to the hospital, I'm going to die."

—What's wrong? What exactly happened?—
-Bunny-

My tongue felt furry and thick. "Got spit on by some monsters and my whole body's getting paralyzed. Bit up pretty bad, blood loss..." I struggled for another breath. "Maybe a couple broken bones. Please, call an ambulance."

—I can't do that. What are you going to say happened to you? There'll be questions.—
-Bunny-

A surge of rage and desperation gave me a few morsels of energy. "If you don't help me, I'm going to die right here on the ground! You will remember my death forever. How I begged you for help, and how you murdered me."

No response, and then,

—I can't call an ambulance. But maybe I can get help...—
-Bunny-

The rage slipped away, and with it went my strength. My eyes closed, and when I opened them, I was somehow lying on the ground.

A bright orange screen pulsed inches from my face.

—Stay awake! Help is on the way.
Talk to me.—
-Bunny-

I heard a deep voice speaking, panting and hoarse, but I couldn't make out the words. I roused a bit, and tried to tell it I couldn't understand, but all that came out was a ragged wheeze. I thought my eyes were open, but black crept in from the edges of my vision, wiping out the alley.

Running feet appeared in my last pinprick of sight, and then I knew only the black nothingness.

---

I WOKE with a gasp to a blonde boy giving me CPR.

He drew back with a relieved sigh and slumped against the opposite wall of the alley as I sucked for the air every cell in my body screamed for.

When I was re-oxygenated I sat up and stretched carefully. My legs both moved, and though the left one was considerably stiff, and still numb, I could now feel the ankle swelling painfully.

What had he done to save me? I narrowed my eyes and looked him over. Sandy blond hair, blue eyes, white teeth, and clothes that were worth more than everything in my closet put together. But the interesting things were the look in his eyes, and his exhausted shivering.

"Did Bunny send you?" My voice scratched against my throat and sent me into a fit of coughing.

He slipped off a light backpack and tossed me a half-empty water bottle from within.

I downed the contents in a few gulps, water overflowing and running over my cheeks and down my throat. “Thanks.” I handed the empty bottle back. "So? Did he?"

The boy took a deep breath and nodded.

"Did you heal me?"

He nodded again.

"How?"

He raised the corners of his mouth in an unhappy smile. "It's my Skill."

"Your Skill? You mean from the Characteristic Trial?" I didn't wait for his response. "Show me."

He frowned at me and didn’t move, so I smiled back as innocently as possible. "I'm Eve. What's your name?"

"Sam. Samuel, but I go by Sam." He smiled back at me, wide and open, and I decided that I liked him.

"How long have you been a Player, Sam?"

"A few months."

"Wow. I'm a new Player. I don't have any Skills yet, and I'd love to see your Skill in action. Would you show me?" I tried again, this time with a smile.

He'd stopped shivering, and gave me a half-shrug. "I guess something small couldn't hurt." He moved toward me and took my hand, which had long scratches along the palm, outlined in blood.

He held out his other hand. His skin separated and started to bleed, the same pattern as the cuts on my hand. Then it closed up again, gone as if it had never been.

He wiped the blood off on his jeans and showed me the unmarred skin. Then he rubbed at my cuts with his thumb, and the dried blood flaked off, showing skin just as smooth as if I'd never been cut.

My mouth hung open and I flexed my hand. It didn’t hurt. "It's gone. You took the injury from me?"

He nodded. "That's my Skill. I take the injury on myself and heal it." He looked down for a moment and in the blue depths of his eyes, I saw a shadow move, but it passed.

"That's completely amazing!"

He gave me a small smile. "Not really. I can't heal everything as easily as that cut. For instance, your poison. I only took a bit of that. I can't do anything about your previous blood loss, and I'll have to do a few more passes before you can be safely left alone. But I took care of the lung paralysis, so we've got time."

I shook my head. "No. It really is amazing. And you've been a Player for months. That in itself is amazing, too. Do you have others to help you?"

He shook his head. "No. I play alone."

Good. That meant I might be able to use him without the hindrance of other Players.

"And you'll want to burn or bury these pants. Don't wash them. The saliva might be reactivated if you do, and you don't want that spreading through the city's water system." He placed his hand on my hip, and some of the numbness from that area receded. He took a few minutes of rest while his body fought off the effects of the poison, and then did it again, and again, moving down my left leg toward the original point of contact.

Then he placed his hand on my rib and some of the pain of each breath flowed away. My armored vest had returned to its original state of two black bands crossing my chest sometime while I'd been too out of it to notice the change.

"You've got a few fractures there. I'm not healing them completely, but I've given you a jumpstart on the process."

"Why did you come?"

He shrugged. "I came because I heard you needed me. What else could I do?"

I laughed. "You could have ignored me. Or you could have used my weakness against me."

"Well, I guess I could have. But for what?"

"I can think of a few things. Like Seeds. But you wouldn't do that, would you? Because you're a genuinely good person."

His eyes rose to mine in surprise. "I'm not, really. I use good behavior to mask the truth."

"The truth?" I parroted.

"I'm not an angel. I'm the harbinger of death," he murmured, and stood up, obviously exhausted from his efforts. "I've got to get home. My parents might be wondering where I'm at."

I nodded and rose carefully to my feet. If he didn't want to discuss his secret with me, that was fine. I could understand that. But it didn't change the judgment I'd made of him. "Thank you, Sam. Really. You saved my life." I met his eyes, making sure my own held that judgment of him clear to see.

He looked at me for a moment, then smiled happily, gave me a nod of acknowledgment, and started to walk away.

"Wait!"

He turned.

"Give me your contact information."

He hesitated, so I stepped forward, limping from the pain of my sprained ankle. "Please. I just want to be able to contact you in case something happens. You can trust me."

He held out his wrist with an ID bracelet on it, but my link was too broken to accept the flashed information.

"Just tell me. I'll remember your number," I said.

I stood in silence for a while after he'd gone, and then spoke into the empty air. "Bunny. Thank you."

—You're welcome, Eve.—
-Bunny-

---

I ENTERED my house carefully in case my mother and brother were there. My clothes were once again ruined, and despite what Sam had done for me, injuries riddled my body. How would I explain that? 'I got mugged by a meat processor?' I placed my hand on the doorknob to my bedroom and turned the handle slowly so as not to make too much noise.

"Where were y— What happened?" Zed's urgent voice came from his bedroom doorway, which he had just opened.

I opened my mouth and closed it again, like a fish.

He looked me up and down, then rushed toward me and grabbed my shoulders as if I might collapse at any moment. "Oh my god. Are you okay? What the hell happened?"

I shook my head sharply. "Shh! Be quiet."

He frowned down at me as if I was crazy. "What do you mean, be quiet? You're hurt bad, Eve! I'm going to call Mom."

I clapped my hand over his mouth and shook my head vehemently, then dragged him into my room. I closed and locked the door behind us and turned back to him. "You can't tell anyone about this. Please."

"Tell anyone about *what*? Were you bullied? Did someone hurt you? Just tell me who it was, Eve. I'll make sure they never touch you again."

I smiled and shook my head, looking at his clenched fists. He wanted to be the savior, but there was nothing he could do about this. He couldn't know. I didn't want him to be the subject of one of NIX's cleanup operations. Would they make it look like another run away? Or maybe an accidental death? "Trust me, Zed. You don't understand. I'm doing this for your own good. Please, just listen to me. Trust me. Have I ever led you wrong before?"

He sputtered and shook his head. "I can't just *ignore* this. I—"

I cut him off. "I'm not asking you to ignore it. I'm asking you to keep it a secret. I'm asking you to not ask questions. Please. I need you to do this for me." I looked into his eyes and imbued my voice with as much sincerity as possible.

He clenched his jaw and frowned at me as if in pain. After a long, tense moment, he said, "Can't you let me help you?"

I smiled widely, knowing I'd won. "I can. Help me put on some ointment and wrap up all these little cuts," I said, though I knew that wasn't what he meant. I went into the bathroom and pulled out the small energy cartridge digging into my stomach. It was strange to see it in my ordinary bathroom, something from *that place* infiltrating the mundane life. I wrapped it and the armored vest bands in my ruined clothes to hide it and took a quick shower.

I returned to my room in baggy pajamas to find Zed waiting with the medbot. I tossed the bundle of clothes into my closet.

He helped me to rub the disinfectant cream over most of my cuts. "What did this to you? Never mind." He snorted. "I suppose you won't tell me."

I smiled. "That's right. Thank you."

The sound of the front door opening filtered through the house, and we looked at each other in panic.

Zed quickly shooed me into my bed and pulled the cover over me, then slipped the first aid kit and medbot next to my feet as my mother called out to us.

"Go," I said.

"I'll keep her away." He opened my door and called, "Welcome home," to her. He turned and threw me a glance over his shoulder. A look that said I owed him one.

I raised an eyebrow and smiled. I did owe him one. But I couldn't repay him with the answers I knew he craved.

When he was gone, I rose and locked the door again. Then I returned to my bed and extended my palm. Seeds appeared in a ripple of the air and dropped into my hand. I chose two and held them to my neck, planting them into Resilience.

By the morning, I had healed more than I thought possible. "Note to self. Resilience is useful."

# Log Of Captivity 2

Mental Log of Captivity-Estimated Day: Two thousand, five hundred ninety-seven.

My link to my master has been growing stronger, but only today did I realize how weak she is. She must be still young, still new. I am needed as a protector, and yet I am confined by these *two-leg-maggots* while she is in danger. I could do nothing but send my words to her again, but I received nothing back. I suspect this is because the *blood-covenant* is still incomplete, only one-sided. I despise my own uselessness. If my *mother-lord* saw me, she would spit at my feet.

# Chapter 11

The caged bird sings of freedom.
— Maya Angelou

I OPENED my window to let warm summer air flow through my room and placed the two black tokens on the windowsill. My own token, sharp and bold, with hidden edges that just might cut if touched the wrong way. The boy's, looping and delicate. It matched him, too fragile to protect himself.

An exploding heat inside of me forced its way out. Hatred, helplessness and self-loathing raged in me, and I swallowed them down, slumping boneless to the floor. Small sounds like those of a wounded animal came from my throat as I cried—great, heaving sobs.

I'd thought I deserved better than the horror NIX put me through, thought I was just another victim, thought I was good. But it turned out I was just a hypocrite.

Zed would have made a better Player than me. He wouldn't have used his first Seeds so selfishly, so stupidly, and he would never have seen a small child gather for a Trial, and then leave to protect himself without a second thought for the boy.

I cried until snot and tears soaked into the rough carpet under my face. When I finally stopped, I felt better. Zed would have handled the situation better, definitely, but thank God the universe didn't see fit to punish him that way and make him a Player. However, I *was* a Player, and that wasn't going to change.

"Who I am isn't going to change, either." I wiped my wet face against my sleeve. I couldn't change, and I didn't want to. I cared about my own survival. I wanted to live, and I would do anything to make that happen. But if I could do it all again, I'd protect the kid from the beginning. Now it was too late for him, but there would be other chances. Other chances to make sure I didn't regret my actions.

I went to the bathroom, washed my face with cold water, and looked at myself hard in the mirror. Blotches covered my face and my eyes were puffy and red from crying, but my gaze didn't waver.

I wouldn't feel guilty again, I vowed. I returned to my Skill tokens and picked them up. I would need power to back that promise.

---

I ASKED Bunny a question I'd been wondering about for a while. "Do Players ever commit suicide?"

He took his time answering.

—YES. YOU'RE NOT THINKING OF...—
-BUNNY-

"No, no, I'm not. I'm more the type to cling to life with my fingernails. I don't have the constitution to kill myself. I was just curious."

—Well, I've only heard rumors from other Moderators. It hasn't happened to me.—
-Bunny-

"What happens to them—the Players that kill themselves?"

—Well, they'd dead. But other than that, we send out the cleaners for the body, make sure there's no suicide not with incriminating evidence, etc. No one will find out what happened to them.—
-Bunny-

"What do the cleaners do with the bodies?"

—I don't know. That's not part of my job, and I'm not privy to that information.—
-Bunny-

"Well, I've never seen someone start out as a dead body at the beginning of the Trial. That's happens later," I joked bitterly. "So at least they escaped that."

—Dead Players are taken off the lists of active Players, so I think so. What would be the point to send a dead person to the Trial?—
-Bunny-

"Yeah," I said, and dropped the issue. But I filed that tidbit away in the back of my mind. All information was important when it came to NIX and the Game. I never knew what might someday save my life.

That didn't end up being the information that saved my life. In fact, it very nearly got me killed.

I HELD the token the boy had given me to my neck and spoke aloud, experimenting. “I wish I had the Skill ‘Tumbling Feather.’ ”

I felt a familiar pain as it pricked my skin and injected its hidden contents into me.

A window popped up.

YOU HAVE GAINED A NEW SKILL: TUMBLING FEATHER

I waited for side effects, something strange or burning or a sense of strength or well-being, but nothing happened. So I held my own token to my neck and spoke again. “I wish I had the Skill 'Spirit of the Huntress.' "

Again, no response in my body.

I looked out over the communal park stretching out beneath my fourth-floor window. My backyard. A tree obscured some of the view, its branches almost close enough to touch. I leaned forward absentmindedly to see if I could reach.

A small bird fluttered toward me, chirping angrily, and then disappeared into the thick foliage.

My breathing slowed as I watched for it to appear again. A flutter, a flap of wings, and a flash of movement between the leaves. I crawled onto my windowsill and reached forward, then pulled myself onto the closest branch. It dipped a little under my weight, but held strong.

I crept forward, and found the bird again. It darted away, chittering what I could tell were insults from the tone. My head snapped around to follow its path, and I pressed myself closer to the branch. I wanted to chase it, to see if I could catch it. Then I realized what I was doing. The trance-like state snapped away.

I gasped and froze, but before I could move to safety, my vision went blurry, my head started to spin, and my whole body began to burn and tingle. I wrapped my arms around the tree branch and hung on, squeezing from the terror of not knowing if I was about to fall off or not, because my balance was shot. My stomach rolled and I heaved a little, bile spilling out of my mouth.

My fingers felt like burning hot knives were piercing through the tips of them, and suddenly something was cutting my skin where my hands overlapped the opposite forearm. It hurt, but I was too disoriented and terrified to loosen my grip. Was I dying? Was NIX finally killing me?

"No," I groaned, and heaved again, spewing sourness as my body started into mini convulsions. I bit my lip until the iron taste of blood spilled onto my tongue. I realized I was probably having an adverse reaction to the Skills I'd just gained. If so, I only had to wait a few minutes and it would subside.

So I held on even tighter as both stars and waves of darkness burst across my eyes, my arms bled, and my body burned and shook.

But the symptoms didn't subside. They grew worse, my grip on the trunk somehow slipped, and then my body twisted off, and I fell.

The wind brushed my skin like a caress as I plummeted, and I slammed into the branch below and bounced off. Then the next branch, and the next. I felt like a little metal ball in one of those old pinball machines. But somewhere on the way down, I started to understand the twisting of my body, the pushes and pulls that moved it. I caught a branch with my arms and almost ripped them out of the sockets trying to slow myself. The next branch I hit with both feet, but still slipped.

Then I slammed into the ground, but spread some impact through my ankles and knees before throwing myself sideways. A few bruising tumbles later and I came to a stop, four stories below where I'd started out, and still alive.

I crawled to my hands and knees, making a mental examination of my body. The wounds from the day before, though somewhat better, were all still there. Duh. The pain, shaking, and sensory disorientation were gone. A few cuts, definitely some bruises. But nothing serious compared to what I'd been through lately. Except that below my face, pressed into the weak grass, short bloody claws tipped my fingers.

I rose to my feet and held my hands in front of me, curling and uncurling my fingers. Everything was strangely clear and light, as if the sun had gotten brighter. I looked around to make sure I hadn't been transferred to a Trial without realizing it, but it was the same world I'd always known. The same backyard, unexceptional except for me, the girl who'd just fallen four stories out a window and landed on her feet.

My forearms bled from puncture wounds, no doubt caused by the claws, when I was clinging onto the branch for dear life. I spit red and tried to wipe the blood from my ravaged lip. I was shaking, tired and feeling half-drunk. I took a few deep breaths to steady myself and shut out the outside world. "Display Characteristic Skills," I choked out.

CHARACTERISTIC SKILLS

TUMBLING FEATHER (KINETIC CLASS): INCREASES GRACE AND AGILITY. IMPROVES SENSE OF BALANCE AND MOTION. SKILL EFFECTS WILL EXPAND AND STRENGTHEN WITH PLAYER GROWTH.

SPIRIT OF THE HUNTRESS (SPIRIT CLASS): INCREASES GRACE, AGILITY, PERCEPTION, FOCUS, PHYSIQUE, AND STAMINA. NAILS EXTEND AND SHARPEN ON COMMAND. INCREASES CHANCE TO LAND ON FEET AFTER A FALL. AGGRESSIVE TENDENCIES INCREASE. SKILL EFFECTS WILL EXPAND AND STRENGTHEN WITH PLAYER GROWTH.

I SWALLOWED. "OH. MY. GOD." This type of thing was something I hadn't even imagined. The bonuses were amazing. "Bunny!

What just happened? This Skill, it's—I've—" I searched for words, hitching.

—Hey. Looks like you've got a couple Characteristic Skills. And one is quite good. The percentage of Spirit Class Skills is very low, from what I understand.—
-Bunny-

A few moments passed while I took it all in, and then a slow smile spread across my face. "Lucky me."

I slunk back into my house and hid out in my room, and hid the empty Characteristic token shells in a side pocket of my pack. Somewhere along the way my nails returned to normal, which I was grateful for. I decided to skip school, and stayed in my room trying to make the claws come out again.

Zed helped to cover for me again with my mom, though not without some frustration when he saw the new cuts on my forearms. I felt guilty for causing him so much worry, but I couldn't tell him the truth. Even if I did, it would do nothing but cause him more stress.

I fell asleep at some point, with the sun shining on me through my open window, and woke when a shadow passed in front of the light, darkening my closed eyelids. Something poked my shoulder.

I jumped and shot straight up, attacking.

By the time I registered that little China was the one standing in front of me, I had both of her thin arms squeezed in my hands, the claws were bared, and my lips pulled back from my teeth in silent menace.

Her eyes and mouth gaped open, surprised and speechless.

I relaxed my grip on her and sat back onto the bed. "Sorry, China. You surprised me."

"Yeah, apparently." She rubbed her arms where I'd grabbed them. "You weren't at school today, what happened?" Her eyes caught on the cuts and bruises that covered my exposed skin. "Are you okay?"

I frowned and nodded. "Yeah. But why are you here?" I pushed my hair back from my face as if scraping the cobwebs from my mind. "How did you know I wasn't at school?"

"I go to Jefferson High, Eve. Didn't you know?"

I looked her up and down. She didn't look old enough to be a high school student.

She must have seen the doubt on my face, because she said, "I do!" and punctuated her words with emphatic stomp of her small foot. "Why does everybody think I look like a little kid?" She crossed her arms.

I chuckled. "Well, maybe you would be more convincing as a high school student if you didn't stomp your foot like a little girl."

She opened her mouth, closed it, looked down at the offending foot, and uncrossed her arms. "Well, I'm a freshman."

I resisted the urge to continue teasing her and said, "I didn't know you went to Jefferson."

"Well, I do. But that's not the point. What happened to you? You look like you just had a Trial, or got hit by a train, but there shouldn't be any Trials for another six days or so, except for people with a Characteristic..." She trailed off. "Did you just have your Characteristic Trial?"

I paused, then nodded. "Yeah."

"Oh. I thought those normally happened somewhere in the first few weeks. I assumed you'd already had yours."

That's because I wanted her to think I was more experienced, so she'd trust me more and accept my usefulness. But not too experienced, so she wouldn't think it was weird when I pumped her for information. I shrugged and grinned. "Well, I'm relatively new. But I got some good Skills, apparently. Just haven't quite figured out how to use them yet."

She sat down in my chair, the only other seating in the room beside my bed, and grinned. "What did you get? I might be able to help."

"Something called Tumbling Feather, and Spirit of the Huntress. Spirit of the Huntress is the one I'm more focused on. It gives me these claws." I held up my hands to show her, but my fingertips had already gone back to normal. "Well, I don't know how to make them come out. Seems to just happen involuntarily."

"Like when you're scared or angry?"

"Yeah. How'd you know?"

"Because they came out when I startled you just now. Good thing you just grabbed me and didn't slice. Why don't you try and bring out that same emotion again?"

I took a deep breath and searched for the feeling again. Something like anger, but more confident. My fingertips itched, and I looked down to see the short claws poking out once again. I flexed my fingers and felt the longing to assert my superiority over something, over someone.

China stared at me in awe, and I felt a heady sense of pleasure at her open acknowledgment of my power.

I willed my fast-pumping heart to calm down, and the exhilarating feeling slipped away, along with the claws. "Damn. That was crazy." I let out a shuddering breath. "Aggression is one of the side effects. Maybe not the best idea for me to do that with you around right now."

After a moment of incomprehension, her eyes widened and she leaned backward. "Oh. Yeah. Good thinking. Umm…so how was the Trial?"

I bit my poor lip. "I'd rather not talk about it."

She frowned and shook her head at her lap. "Of course. That was stupid. Sorry."

I shrugged. "No big deal. But what about you? Your Skill, I mean? Will you show me?"

She hesitated for a second, but went to my still-open window. "I can speak to animals."

I almost snorted, thinking she was joking, until I saw the bird from earlier fly to the edge of the sill, and then hop onto her finger, cheeping curiously.

"He says you jumped out of the tree earlier." She lifted wide eyes to me.

I coughed behind a fist and looked away. "Uh…well, that's impressive, I'll admit. But you said there'd be another Trial in six days?" I changed the subject.

"Yeah." The bird flew away. "The normal ones happen every ten days or so. I heard that it used to be longer, before, but then it just suddenly changed. Who knows? It might change again someday, but for now you can pretty much count on ten days in between."

"So if we know we've got six days, we should start to prepare. There are some things I think would be useful for the Trials. I'd also like to spend some time with you practicing our Skills and working out strategies for different scenarios."

"If we're lucky enough to get the same Trial," she muttered.

"What?"

She looked up, startled. "Oh. It's just that the Trial you enter is somewhat randomized. Unless you form a recognized team, from what I understand it's just luck if you get put with the same people. Being close together when the Boneshaker starts helps, but it's no guarantee."

"Well, how do you form a recognized team? Bunny?"

When he acknowledged me with a pop-up screen, I repeated my question.

—You have to have more than two people.—
-Bunny-

"How many?"

—Four or more. One leader, three or more followers for a team, which is the first level of command.—
-Bunny-

My mind was racing. "And once I've got them, what then? Just tell you we're a team?"

—YES, BASICALLY. AT THAT POINT YOU'LL BE GROUPED TOGETHER FOR TRIALS. TEAMWORK IS A RECOGNIZED, IMPORTANT PART OF THE GAME, AND BEING PART OF A GROUP GIVES CERTAIN EXTRA REWARDS.—
-BUNNY-

"Four." I grinned. "That's not so hard."

# Chapter 12

I must not fear. Fear is the mind-killer. Fear is the little-death that brings total obliteration. I will face my fear. I will permit it to pass over me and through me. And when it has gone past I will turn the inner eye to see its path. Where the fear has gone there will be nothing. Only I will remain.

— Frank Herbert

I SPENT the next six days planning and preparing for a Trial. I met in person with China to discuss her previous Trial experience. My link was broken, and my mom refused to get me a new one. From China, I gained knowledge of the different types of Trials, and some insight into Skills and the effects of the various Attributes.

I continued to level up and train my body, and put Seeds into Intelligence and Mental Acuity. Being able to think quickly in a tight spot might allow me to avoid situations where I *needed* brute strength or speed. Plus, the brain was much harder for me to spontaneously level up with training than my physical Attributes were.

I sheathed and unsheathed my claws until they obeyed more reliably.

Zed continued to keep my secret. Although he reluctantly stopped asking me to confide in him, he still watched me suspiciously.

When I heard the Boneshaker, I woke from a dead sleep with a choking gasp, as if I'd been drowning and had just broken the surface of the water. I clenched my thin summer blanket so hard I felt the bones in my hands creak like the hinges of a rusty door.

After a few seconds of panic, I scrambled out of bed, dressed in cargo pants, a long sleeve shirt, and a jacket, the closest I could come to military-type gear. Underneath it all I had the two-banded, transforming vest armor that I'd taken off the skeleton my last time around. I started recording with a small mirror I'd brought to my room. Then I grabbed the small backpack I'd prepared and slung it on.

I stood there in the dark, trembling in my bedroom as I waited to be taken into the Trial by that dizzying wave. The song filled me and burst outward.

I stood in a city. The buildings were taller, twisting and flowing and more beautiful than any I'd seen before, and overgrown with tenacious greenery. Only the occasionally boring rectangle was there, unlike the city where I'd come from.

The little map popped up, and I followed its directions to a big, squat building. Light peeked out through its windows, making it stand out. The only other light was that of the stars and the…*two* moons? I stood for a few seconds, just staring up at the sky and trying to figure out what the heck I was seeing.

It's funny how the brain tries to reject things it doesn't want to believe. I actually rubbed my eyes to make sure I wasn't seeing double, despite the fact that the two orbs were different sizes, and had different markings on their surfaces.

Then the side of the building opened as a piece of the wall slid upward. I jumped in surprise, but then saw other Players and the floating cube waiting inside, and entered.

Players milled about, but I didn't have much time to observe them, because one of the pieces of wall slid upwards, and a large mouse walked into the room. Large meaning gigantic. It was four feet tall walking with all paws on the ground, and probably seven or eight feet tall standing on its hind legs. A spiked ball that looked like it could do serious damage tipped the end of its tail. The creature wore a military hat and jacket with colorful stripes and medals decorating the collar and chest.

The mouse—Or maybe it was a rat. How do you tell?—walked silently across the room, sniffing the air and inspecting us Players, who'd all gone silent. Someone whimpered.

It sat up on its haunches to address us. "Time is up. Those who are not here will be summarily executed." The lights seemed harsh and bright under the weight of its presence. It twitched its whiskers, and another door slid up in the side of the wall, releasing an orderly row of long-limbed…soldiers? Well, they were dressed in uniform. Their arms and legs seemed abnormally elongated, but still corded with wiry muscle. Black goggles hid their eyes, and their noses were long and wide-nostriled. Something about their pale skin and twitching noses reminded me of rodents.

"I am the General." The rat's voice was loud, and traveled throughout the room. "For every two of you, there is one soldier. Once you leave this building, you are effectively fugitives, and they will be hunting you. You will escape to one of the extraction points."

A mini map popped up in front of me, and everyone else, too, I assumed. It showed a 3-D model of the organically designed city. Yellow dots blinked—the extraction points. An arrow showed where I was, on the center of the map. I played with the model, using hand movements to turn the view and zoom in and out as the giant mouse continued to speak.

"If you are able to escape from enemy territory to the extraction point without being captured, you survive, and you win. If you are caught, you lose. Along the way, there are a few 'concerned citizens' of this wonderful city." He grimaced. "They will give away your location to your pursuers if they notice you, so beware. You will be given a small window of opportunity to leave the starting point. Exactly three minutes will pass before my soldiers are deployed." He gestured with his tail to the creatures standing tall and silent behind it. "Are there any questions?"

I bit the inside of my cheek until blood flowed, slipped a finger inside my cheek to pick up some of the blood, then moved the hand under my shirt to rub the drop onto the center spot of the armor bands hidden beneath. Right over my sternum, they fit together with a small opening for their fuel. They picked up the blood and spread in secrecy to protect me. I was as ready as I could get.

A familiar voice called out lazily. "What happens if the soldiers catch us…but we kill them?"

My head snapped around. It was the girl from my first Trial. The gorgeous one who'd caught Mr. Wolf and ended the game of terror.

The General responded. "My soldiers are authorized to use deadly force to ensure fugitives do not escape. You are free to do the same to ensure the opposite." He seemed impatient. "There will be no more questions. When the doors go up, you all have thirty seconds to leave this safe point. Then the countdown will start." And at that, pieces of the walls all around us opened to the darkness.

I watched as the crowd disbursed through the various exits. The Spanish girl passed me on her way out but didn't spare me a glance. I would have called out or followed her, but I needed to stay and make sure no kids had been put into the Trial again. I saw a few confused and scared people, but they weren't children, and I knew I didn't have the power to expend protecting them. So I left, alone.

Outside, many dispersed through the unlit streets, sprinting frantically to gain distance from their pursuers, while others huddled in groups, discussing plans in murmurs.

Behind me, the wall slid shut and a three-minute timer

popped up. The seconds ticked away at a seemingly impossible speed, pushing a sense of urgency on me.

I looked at the city map again, trying to figure out the smartest move. My brain spun, but could only come up with best guesses, because I didn't have enough to go on. The seconds flashed away. I took a deep breath and ignored the timer. If I didn't have enough information, that meant I needed to gather more.

Instead of running away, I went to a nearby building with windows overlooking the starting point. It didn't have any doors, and I supposed whatever pieces of the wall would have slid open for me were powered off. But it did have a broken window.

I leaned my back against the wall and jabbed my elbow at the remaining chunks of glass, then crawled through the cleared opening.

My eyes adjusted to the lack of moonlight quickly, and I saw something had caused part of the ceiling, otherwise known as the second floor, to collapse. I peeked up under the hole all the way through to the roof, and into the night sky. A huge chain with links I could fit my arm through hung down from somewhere above. I had the urge to tug on it, but resisted. The ground below the opening was cracked and crushed in a circular crater. Whatever caused that, I wanted to stay far away from.

I climbed up the staircase and crouched in front of an intact window. The remaining Players below ran off as the last few seconds ticked away, and the doors of the starting building slid up, spilling out light and rat-men soldiers.

Their silhouettes moved into the darkness silently, and stood with their heads tilted, noses twitching as they scented the air. A few bent to the ground and sniffed, then pointed in the same direction many of the Players had run. With a few whistling sounds among themselves, they scattered, following scent trails.

I kept my eyes on the streets below and pulled up my map again, mentally marking the directions the rat-men had taken. "Hope they don't smell me in here," I breathed into the dark.

A different silhouette against one of the silver moons drew my attention. Someone stood atop the building adjacent to mine. I squinted and focused, able to distinguish the features of the Spanish girl. I didn't know her name yet, but I wanted her for my team.

She crouched and sprang off the edge of the roof, toward my building. As she moved through the air, a sick feeling built in my chest. I pushed, much too slowly, away from the wall, toward the hole piercing the building.

Sure enough, a muffled shout of surprise came through the hole, and then a few frantic scrabbles, like she had tried to grab onto something. She was falling, and I couldn't move fast enough to catch her.

My hand was outstretched, too far away from the tunnel of air piercing the building. As if I'd have been strong enough to catch her anyway. She plummeted through the air in front of me, her hand outstretched as well, as if reaching for me.

Our eyes met for a second, the image of her splattered on the broken stone of the ground floor already in my head. It would happen because I was too weak to save her.

Then she grabbed the huge metal chain with her outstretched hand.

I reached the edge of the hole just in time to see her body slam hard into the crater below. But not hard enough to kill her, as she'd slowed her descent with the chain.

Above, I heard a cracking sound, and a few pebbles fell past my head. I looked upward just in time to see the huge ball at the end of that chain roll through the hole in the roof, a perfect fit. It started to hurtle down through the opening that it had obviously created in the first place, blocking out the light from the sky. As it fell, the chain below piled up on top of itself like a messy soft-serve ice cream cone.

"Move!" I screamed.

She was just starting to look up at her impending doom, too

late to save herself, when something smashed into her from the side like a kamikaze fighter jet.

I jerked my head out of the tunnel, less than a second before the huge ball smashed down, loud and hard enough I felt it vibrate through the building. "Crap. Someone definitely heard that," I said.

I listened for movement below, wondering whether I should go down or not. Whatever had knocked the girl out of the way might be dangerous. And the rat-men would be coming back soon, too. Then I realized what I was doing and clenched my fists. Not again.

I rushed back down the stairs, and saw that she and someone else were lying in a tangle of limbs a few feet away from the metal ball. I dropped hard to my knees on the dusty stone beside them. "Are you okay?"

The other one, a boy, was panting hard.

She was still, and I smelled blood.

I patted her cheek. "Are you okay?"

She groaned and her long, thick eyelashes fluttered open. Dark eyes stared at me blankly, and then she stiffened. She looked at the boy next to her and jerked back, flailing frantically in the effort to disentangle their limbs and get away.

He groaned in pain as she pushed at his body, and I wrapped my arms around her shoulders and dragged her away to protect him from her panicked blows.

She clung to me in a vice-like grip, burying her face in my stomach.

I hesitated for a moment, and then patted her head. "It's okay. You're fine."

She started to shake and let out strange noises, and I realized with discomfort that she might be crying. She'd seemed a much stronger type than that. Then she drew her head back, and I realized she was laughing. It wasn't a beautiful laugh to match her looks, but it made me smile and want to laugh with her.

"Nucking futts, I thought I was gonna die," she said.

"But you didn't." I looked to the boy lying on the ground and clutching his arm, dark curly hair that was slightly too long hanging into his face. "But we need to move. The rat-men are already on their way back. Both of you, come on."

She grew serious and stood up, but weaved dizzily on her feet, and I had to grab her arm to keep her from falling. She pursed her lips apologetically. "Hit my head. Ground keeps tilting under me."

The guy ground out between clenched teeth, "My arm's broken, and my leg's not feeling great, either. I'm bleeding pretty bad. You guys better move soon, cause they're going to smell the blood."

The scent was everywhere, and I knew if I smelled it, the rat-men would too. "Crap. Okay, we can't travel, but at the least we need to move a bit. Somewhere less visible." I scanned the room and pointed to a corner blocked off by a half-wall only a few feet high. "There."

I threw the girl's arm over my shoulder and walked her to the corner.

As soon as she sat down, she struggled to rise again. "I don't hide. I'll fight 'em if they come."

"Okay." I didn't want to waste time arguing. Plus, even with a possible concussion, she would likely prove herself more useful than me in a fight. "For now, just wait. They're not here yet."

I went back for the boy, and knelt beside him. "Can you move? I'll help. If we can just get you to the corner…" I trailed off, because I didn't know if assurances that "things would be fine" might turn out empty.

His left arm was badly broken. The bone punctured jaggedly through the skin of his forearm, and the wound had already pumped a puddle of blood onto the floor. He was squeezing just below the elbow with his other hand to strangle off the blood flow, but not doing a great job.

"Shit." The breath left my lungs in a whoosh.

He was gritting his teeth and panting in pain, but still found the will to roll his eyes at me, as if to say, "No shit, Sherlock. I'm screwed." What he said aloud was, "Just leave."

"No thanks, I'd rather stay." I reached into one of the pockets of my pants, and pulled out a roll of medical gauze and unwound a long strip. I looped it around his bicep as tight as I could and rolled it into a tube that clung even tighter, helping to cut off the blood flow. Then I leaned over him and wrapped my arms around his torso. Being careful to avoid his arm, I helped him to his feet, and we hobbled to the corner with the girl.

I went to the nearest window and peeked out. Two rat-men were already slinking up to the building, their noses twitching as they whistled softly at each other.

I felt warmth at my back, and then the girl whispered in my ear. "They coming?"

I nodded. "If they come in, I'll take the first, and you get the partner before it can call for help." My whisper sounded barely louder than the rush of blood in my veins, but I knew she heard me.

A rat-man's ears twitched, and I prayed that it hadn't heard me, too. But perhaps it hadn't, because the two moved to the window I'd crawled through, their noses twitching furiously, and then one crawled through, headfirst and weasel-like.

Or maybe they were just confident in their ability to take us in a fight.

My claws slid out and my vision sharpened even more, and I held in a sigh of relief that my Skill hadn't failed me.

The girl's eyes met mine for a moment as the rat-man stood up and its partner moved to follow it. We attacked at the same moment.

I punched at the first soldier's neck, hoping to stop him from calling out. My fist caught, but not firmly enough to cause real damage, and he jerked back and automatically swung a fist at me. He smiled, and I realized that perhaps they *had* known where we were.

I moved back, but not fast enough, and he struck me on the shoulder. The pain made anger flow through me, instead of the fear I'd been expecting, and I moved back in to teach him a lesson. I jumped and kicked at his knees, and we went down.

He was definitely a better fighter, and stronger than me, too.

But I was big for a girl, and he didn't have a Skill that gave him claws and made him want to rip me open for daring to oppose him. I did. I clawed and hit at his face and throat, and when he moved to protect his head, I went for the belly and groin.

He let down his guard at the wrong moment, and I grabbed the front of his throat. The claws let my fingers get a better grip, and I sank them into the flesh, braced my other hand on his face for leverage, and ripped away. His throat opened up, and blood guzzled out onto the stone below as he jerked spasmodically.

When the last bit of life was gone from his body, I stood up and looked for the girl.

She was leaning against the wall, grinning at me. Her opponent laid motionless with his hind end hanging out the window and blood dripping from his forehead where she'd smashed his face into the windowsill. "Took you long enough."

I was panting, and the rush of triumph making my head tingle made it hard to concentrate. My claws slipped away with a tingle, and I looked back down to the body in front of me, and stumbled back. "Oh, god." Unlike the monsters before, it was distinctly humanoid, long arms and legs splayed awkwardly in the puddle of dark, metallic-smelling blood.

She shook her head and pushed off the wall. "So you're one of the crazies, yeah? Pretty gruesome."

I shook my head, but what could I say to negate the thing I'd just done? The evidence was the mutilated carcass at my feet. "Not crazy. I just need practice controlling myself," I muttered.

She opened her mouth to reply, but I saw movement out of the corner of my eye and cut her off with a sharp hand motion.

Down the street, another rat-man stood still, looking suspiciously in our direction. The girl's opponent still lay with his hind end hanging out the window. If it noticed… It was much too far away for us to keep it from sounding an alarm and calling more of them down on us.

Then someone far away screamed. It turned its body toward the sound, and with one last backward glance toward us, it slunk off, long limbs sliding around the darkness of the street corner.

We both let out silent sighs of relief, I jerked my head toward the boy, and we went back to him.

She held out a fingerless-gloved hand to me over his body. "I'm Jacqueline Santiago. Call me Jacky."

I gripped it firmly. "Eve Redding." The blood still on my hand clung to her as I pulled away. I looked down at the guy. "And you?"

"Me what?"

"Your name," I urged.

He scowled at me. "Adam."

I stared back at him, undeterred. "What were you doing? Why were you here, I mean?"

"I was watching them. NIX. Gathering information."

"What kind of information?"

"Any information," he said, and stared at me mulishly, obviously unwilling to continue talking.

I understood his lack of trust. I also understood the import of his information gathering. "Knowledge is power," I agreed. And I was in the process of accumulating power. Plus, I'd seen him tackle Jacky out of the way. Humans couldn't move that fast, not without what I calculated must be a large number of Seeds. Meaning he had experience surviving the Game.

I dug around in my pack and pulled out the makeshift emergency kit I'd brought. I ripped the top off a foil kit and sprinkled the blood-clotting powder within over the guy's wound. Then I took my can of numbing spray and applied it generously over his entire forearm. "I'm not sure how well this will work on your arm, but any relief is probably good in your situation."

He relaxed by a few degrees, so I knew it must have been helping.

I took an old skirt from the pack and ripped a strip from it. My claws came out with a second of concentration, and I used them to slice holes in the larger piece of fabric to wind the strip through. I held up the product of my efforts. "A sling. Hope it works okay." I'd packed the skirt for just such a need, along with many other things I wished I'd had in my last Trial.

He reached for it, and I brushed his hand out of the way. "I've got two hands free. I'll do it." As I leaned over and carefully slid the cloth around his broken arm, I noticed a stylistic, Celtic knot-like design snaking up and down his arms. I sat back on my heels and studied it. It was intricate and beautiful, delicate even. It ran from above his wrist to his bicep, the knot losing intricacy and finally disappearing as it rose. The inked skin was torn and scraped off around his wound.

"Your tattoo. Is that going to be alright?"

"I'll just redo it when everything's healed. It'll be good as new."

I stopped studying it and looked up at him. "You do that yourself?"

He was frowning at me. "Yes," snapped. "Why are you doing this?"

I didn't pretend to misunderstand him. "Because I want to. You saved Jacky. Thank you for that."

"You know her?" He winced as he used his good arm to adjust the sling and stood up on one leg.

I shook my head. "No, not really. But I will. And I'll know you, too."

He raised a derisive eyebrow.

"I will. Don't think I'm doing this just to be nice. You'll owe me." I stared hard at his eyes, refusing to be the first to look away. He needed to know I was serious in that.

He looked down at his body. "Why did I do something so stupid? Basically guaranteed I'd lose the Trial." He grumbled, and then looked back to me. "I'll accept my debt to you, only after you get me out alive. If you can."

"I will." I held out my hand.

After a pause, he shook it with his uninjured one.

"Do you have a weapon? Something to defend yourself with?"

He pulled something small from his pocket, and a familiar butterfly knife glinted in the darkness, bright to my sensitive eyes. "I've got a few skills besides fighting, too. If the situation demands, I'll show you something impressive."

I couldn't help a wolf-like grin stretching across my face.

# Chapter 13

I am your worst nightmare. And your wildest dream.
— Sonya Chloe

"SHARE MAP DISPLAY," I said. The three-dimensional model of our Trial arena popped up in front of me, and Adam and Jacky's eyes focused on it as well. Sharing my displays was a little trick China had taught me.

"Okay, this is us." I pointed to the blue arrow in the center, in the center of a rectangular building. "We'll be going here." I pointed to a blinking yellow dot on the top of a building only a few streets removed from our location.

"Why?" Adam frowned. "That's not the closest one, and it's all the way on the roof."

"We need to stay down-wind of the rat-men as much as possible. Most of them went this way." I pointed in the direction I thought was east. "We want to keep them between us and the wind. As for the ones that went the other way, we'll just have to deal with them."

Jacky licked her finger and raised it to the air to catch the direction of the breeze that filtered through the broken windows of the building. "Why don't we just roof-jump? It'll be faster than goin' through the streets."

I mentally mapped the route we'd take for both options, and nodded slowly. "Yes. That's a good idea. We'd leave no scent trail on the ground, so finding us might be a bit more difficult. And the faster we can get out of here, the better our chance of survival." I looked to Adam. "Could you make a jump like that with your arm?"

He took a beanie from his pocket and shoved it onto his head with his good hand, flattening his hair in the process. "I'll have to, won't I?"

I hoped he could keep to that statement when the time to act came. "Okay. Let's go."

We moved up the stairs, Jacky taking the lead, seemingly to avoid Adam, and me staying beside him to make sure he could keep up despite his injuries. Halfway up the third floor staircase, she raised her hand and we froze. I snuck up to her and saw what had caused her to stop us.

A small plant-like creature with slowly wriggling limbs spread out across the steps above our head. One long stalk rose from its base, on top of which sat an eyeball like a snail's. "Concerned citizen?" I whispered.

She stepped forward like flowing water in the darkness. Her feet made no sound on the ground, and her movement seemed to stir no air. I thought it was a Skill.

The creature didn't have time to let out more than a gasping squeak once it noticed her presence.

Her hands shot out and wrapped around its neck, squeezing and twisting, while she ground her boot into its body. The eyestalk snapped off, and the stump squirted some sort of fluid that smelled sweetly of antifreeze. The limbs at the base stopped wriggling, and the whole body seemed to deflate onto the ground like a popped balloon.

She looked at me, and I nodded.

We continued on, her taking the place of our scout again, until we reached the fifth floor.

Adam panted and leaned on the wall for every step, the pain of his injured leg wearing on him.

I couldn't help but think that if he hadn't saved Jacky, he'd probably be well enough to survive all on his own. But I was glad for his recklessness, because otherwise she would have died, and I would never be able to gain her alliance.

In the middle of the fifth floor, the staircase abruptly disappeared, having collapsed for about six steps. Big steps, as always.

My heart sank in my chest, but I clenched my jaw and tried to think of a solution. Going back down wasn't an option. I remembered the way Jacky had ended the first Trial.

I judged the distance of the gap. "Jacky. Could you jump that?"

She pursed her lips. "Yeah...probably. Maybe."

I nodded. "Okay. Give me a second." I rummaged in my bag and pulled out a coil of plastine rope.

They watched me as I tied the rope into a noose-like harness on both ends, pulling on my knots to test them. Thank God for the Internet, and my foresight in studying some survival channels during the last week. "Jacky, you're strong. I've seen your power. Could you lift one of us?"

She looked from me to the two-sided harness, and nodded. "Yeah, I'm strong. And I can be lightweight, too. I dunno if I can make it, but I'll try."

"Brace yourself around the corner at the top of the stairs so our weight doesn't pull you off the edge, too," Adam said. "It doesn't matter how strong you are if you can't keep your body from sliding because you're too light."

She grinned and wrapped one slipknot around her stomach, throwing the other over her arm. She stepped back down the stairs, and with a mutter that sounded like "fingers crossed," she lunged up the steps, and then sprang up off the edge of the last step. She slammed into the edge of the upper step, knocking her air out with an audible *oomph*, but she easily scrabbled the rest of the way up and sat gasping for breath. She adjusted the rope around her waist and stood, giving the victory sign, two fingers spread into a V.

Adam stepped to the edge and reached out his good hand. "Lower down the other end." He wrapped it gingerly around his waist and she stepped backward to brace herself on the edge of the stairwell.

A piercing screech split through the air, like a siren made of knives.

We all flinched, and Jacky turned around and ripped off the eyestalk of the "concerned citizen" that had sounded the alarm. "Sorry. I didn't see it," she said.

Adam shook his head. "Just hurry and pull us up." He swung off the edge gently, and she slid for only a few inches before getting a good grip and pulling him up.

He sat panting afterward with eyes closed against the pain, while she took the tightened harness from around him like he was made of maggots.

I went next, my weight causing the vines to tighten around my torso with bruising strength. I moved upward and rolled over the edge coughing as Jacky pulled unstoppably on the rope. Her body didn't look strong or heavy enough to stand firm and lift one man-sized person, let alone *two*, but it was impossible to deny the facts. I crawled to my feet, pulled my slipknot over my head and handed it back to her. "Impressive. Let's go. I'm sure they're on their way. Hopefully that little gap slows them down a bit extra." Unfortunately, I had a feeling it wouldn't.

We were all gasping for breath when we burst through the door to the rooftop. I shot a glance to my map to get our bearings, and pointed to the roof of a nearby building. While we had been climbing, storm clouds had oozed across the sky. The wind whipped at me, threatening to push me off my feet.

I took a few breaths of the electrically charged air to regain some strength, stepped back, and ran to the edge of the roof. I leapt out into the empty space between buildings, feeling the extra weight of that place pulling me down.

I landed barely inches away from the deadly drop and rolled over before coming to my hands and knees. My claws were out, digging into the cold material of the building's roof. I stood and moved to the edge. I could see the shadowy forms of rat-men passing by at a run, through a window halfway up the building we'd just ascended.

"They're coming!" I warned, hoping that fear would lighten our steps and bolster our recklessness.

Jacky came next, landing smoothly, and then tossed the harness back to Adam. He wrapped it around himself, took a few limping lunges, and jumped off. He didn't quite make it, but Jacky was already moving forward, taking up the slack in the line.

He smashed into the side of the building with a thump and muffled a scream.

I crawled to the edge and grabbed the back of his hoodie and his good arm and helped to pull him up.

He rolled to his back, half across my lap, and lay there shuddering visibly. He'd bitten through his lip, and blood trickled down the side of his face. "Can I get some more numbing spray?"

I nodded and pulled off my backpack, fumbling around in it until I felt the can. I sprayed inside the makeshift sling, close to the skin. "Do you want some for your leg, too?"

"No. Wouldn't do any good." He stood up and weaved on his feet for a second, then started toward the far side of the roof. "This way next, right?"

This time the jump was easier, and he made it on his own, without help from Jacky.

But the next roof was slightly higher than our own, and I worried that even Jacky might not be able to make it.

I had her wait to jump until I'd positioned myself with bent knees and cupped hands at the edge of the roof.

She moved to the far edge and came running at a full sprint, stepping right into my cupped hands and jumping as I pushed upward to give her a bit more lift.

She sprang away like she was flying, and tossed the harness back to me once she reached the roof above.

I jumped, slammed into the wall on the end of the rope, and was dragged up the building's rough side to the top.

I turned back to throw the harness to Adam, and saw the rat-men burst onto the roof as lightning shattered the sky in a burst of blinding light, followed by a rumble of thunder that I felt pass through the air like a physical force. The wind was screaming now, whistling in my ears so I had to shout to make myself heard. "They're on the roof! Hurry!"

Once again Jacky was already moving forward as Adam swung through the air, but the impact still jostled his whole body. His eyes rolled back in his head as his broken arm hit the wall, and he hung limp and still for a second until consciousness returned to him.

"Brace yourself with your feet and just walk up," I shouted.

He did, moving upward as Jacky moved forward.

I grabbed his good hand and gave him a boost over the edge.

The rat-men were standing on the edge of the roof of the first building, and as I looked, the first of them jumped across to the second building, landing easily. It turned to urge its fellows on. They would be on us soon.

I turned around and looked to the far side of our rooftop, where a long, oval shaped pod stood on its end. I pulled up my mini map and zoomed in as we hurried over to it. Sure enough, it was the extraction point. The front had an indentation like a shrunken handle, so I grabbed it and pulled. It popped open with the sound of hissing hydraulics.

I waited for a moment, but nothing happened.

"We have to get in," Adam said. "This type of teleportation pod will take us one by one. I've seen them before."

Jacky looked to the rat-men and then to Adam. "You go first."

He frowned, but she pursed her lips. "You're useless in a fight, *chico*. I don't wanna have to protect you *and* me, so you better get safe. Plus, I owe you one."

He stepped in with a single frustrated nod and sealed the door, stood there for a few moments, and then looked around in confusion and opened it again. "It's not working. It's not powering up."

"What?" Jacky ground out.

"It's broken." He snapped. "Like I said."

I turned to the rat-men. They would arrive in less than a minute at the rate they were going. "Shit." I pulled up my map to search for another extraction pod. There was one a few streets away, but on the ground, and the roof we stood on had no door, no way to move down through the building. Except for the one we'd just come from, all the buildings around were un-jumpable, either too high or in a weird shape that we'd just slide right off of. There was no way we were going to jump all the way to the ground, and climbing down it wasn't possible, either. "Shit," I said again.

We had only one option. "Okay. We're going to fight. There are more of them, but being on the high ground gives us an advantage. We'll kill them all, and then go find a working extraction point." Despite my words, I doubted we'd be leaving the Trial alive.

I turned back to them and saw Adam kneeling awkwardly at the back of the pod. He peeked around it. "One of the power sources has corroded. The other one's a bit rusted, but I think it still works. I might be able to fix the pod, if I could get a charge in it."

I looked to the rat-men. Less than thirty seconds. I slung off my pack and tossed it to Adam. "There's another power cartridge in the side pocket. I don't know if it'll work, but I got it from a transport pod the last time I was in-Trial. I don't think it has any power."

He grabbed the pack and looked at me with surprise and a kind of consideration that bordered on respect. "I'll show you what I can do besides fighting, if you can keep them off me." He grinned with a sort of cockiness that made me smile back.

"It better be impressive," I said, and turned back to the rat-men below.

I watched the pack run across the roof below and felt a strange exultation melt through me. I would not die here today. I would destroy them. My claws tingled out and my senses sharpened and focused on them. I could hear their panting breaths and almost smell their eagerness. I smiled and looked to Jacky beside me on the edge of the roof. "Are you ready?"

She cracked her knuckles with more pops than should have been possible with ten fingers and smirked. "Are you?"

I turned back to the enemies below without answering. The first rat-man reached the edge of the roof and sprang at me. I lifted one knee to my chest and kicked outward and down, catching it at the base of the throat and knocking it down into the chasm of darkness between the buildings.

I watched it disappear, its hands reaching to the heavens as it plummeted. I raised my head and sucked in a breath of energy charged air as the next three came. I spun and clawed across the face of one as it reached me, and Jacky pummeled two with flurries of heavy blows and kicks that obviously stemmed from extensive training.

I aimed a kick to the knee of my opponent. He dodged and I thought for a minute that I would fall, off balance, but something instinctual kicked in and I slid to my hands and knees and swung a leg to take him off his feet. Then I thrust my hand at his throat, fingers straight, and cut into it, still crouching. I curled my fingers before ripping them out, and then drug him by his ears and dropped him off the edge.

More of them had already jumped across the gap, and I turned to fight without thinking.

As I fought, I caught a glimpse of Jacky, far outnumbered and overwhelmed. Two grabbed her from behind while another three attacked her from the front. She snapped her head back and aimed a kick at their knees, but they were undeterred. They moved to the edge and swung her much smaller body out over the edge.

I moved before I realized what I was doing, springing like an animal onto the back of the rat-man with the main grip on her. I clawed into the front of its throat and sliced my hands backward, opening up its jugular veins to the world. "She's mine," I said. Jacky had the type of fighting power that would significantly increase my chances at living through this Trial, and the following ones. "I won't let you take her."

It dropped to its knees and loosened its grip on Jacky, dropping her over the edge.

I pulled myself atop its shoulders and lunged for her. My hand barely caught her wrist, and my claws dug into her. But I'd caught her. I drug her up as the rat-men punched and kicked at my unprotected, kneeling body, while the rat-man under me jerked and bled out like a slaughtered animal.

My armored vest spread some of the impact of their blows, but could only do so much. A blow to the back of my skull rattled my balance and made the darkness seep in around the edges of my vision.

But Jacky had already regained her footing. With a scream, she attacked with a new savageness born from the fear of her near-death. She held them off while I regained my feet, both of us now in the disadvantageous position of being surrounded on the edge of the roof and cut off from Adam.

Before I could join her in the fight, light exploded on the other side of the roof and knocked us all off our feet. My ears rang and I crawled to my hands and knees, my blinded eyes streaming tears from the sudden brightness.

I heard faint shouting, and then Adam's voice filtered through the ringing. "Working! Hurry…not much…"

I stood on shaking legs and blinked till I could see the pod, lit up and powered on, and Adam leaning on it with a charred rat-man at his feet. He waved to me urgently, still shouting, then bent over at the waist and hung onto the pod as if to keep himself from collapsing.

I looked to the ground and saw Jacky lying on her back with her eyes closed. I fumbled over to her, stepping on the still-disoriented bodies of our enemies.

She didn't move when I smacked her face and yelled at her to get up, and then I saw the blood seeping from the side of her head. She must have smashed it into the ground for the second time that evening when the blast hit.

"Crap," I muttered, unable to hear myself over the ringing still echoing through my skull. I grabbed her by the collar of her shirt and stepped forward, pulling until her smaller body started to slide. I dragged her slowly across the roof, right over the rat-men when necessary, until we reached the pod. The ringing and disorientation had already decreased, and I could hear the rat-men rising to their feet behind me.

I shoved Jacky's unconscious body into the pod and shut the door on her. The pod started to vibrate and hum, and then it let out a familiar shock wave, and she was gone.

I turned back to the group of rat-men, already stumbling toward us. "Hurry and get in, Adam."

He was as tense as a tightly strung guitar wire as he watched them, but he shook his head. "I have to be here to charge it again. Get in. I'll be right behind you."

I hesitated, and he turned on me. "Go! You're wasting our time," he snapped.

I stepped in and closed the door.

He reached upward with his good hand, the other resting on the power cartridges, and another explosion of light connected the ground and sky, as he called down the lighting.

I had a last glimpse of him before the wave of energy filled my bones and took me away. A half-blind image of his back, his silhouette standing against the low-hanging moons.

I FOUND myself back at the starting building along with a few others and the General, the standard dizziness and nausea making the room spin, along with the effects of being less than five feet away from a lightning strike only moments before. My claws had slipped away sometime without me realizing it, but my hands were still covered in layers of dried and drying blood, sticky and uncomfortable. I lay on the ground for a few moments, and then crawled over to Jacky's body to check her head wound. She lay motionless, except for the slight rise and fall of her chest as she breathed.

"At least she's alive," I sighed. I waited for Adam, my heart sinking in my chest with every passing moment. It had been too long. If he were going to return, he would have done so already. The rat-men must have gotten to him. With his arm like that, there was no way he could have fought all of them off.

But in the space between one moment and the next, Adam appeared in a shockwave. His beanie was gone, and his hair floated around his head with static electricity. Little sparks jumped around him, and I could literally smell the charge suffusing his skin.

Our eyes caught, and he smirked again. "Told you I'd do something impressive." Despite his words, his muscles were rebelling in mini spasmodic tremors, and he smelled burnt.

I nodded, nothing clever coming to my weary brain. "Glad you made it." I looked him over. "You left my pack?"

He opened his mouth and then closed it again. "Uh, yeah. Sorry. I hope there wasn't anything important in there."

"It's fine." I'd gladly pay the contents of my pack in exchange for his life.

He slipped it into his pocket with a weary nod, then we sat next to Jacky's body and waited.

No other Players returned, and after a few minutes General Zarack boomed out, "Eleven survivors. That is everyone. Quite a surprising number this time."

"Surprisingly high, or surprisingly low?" I murmured.

The floating cube buzzed, and rolled out the same words I'd seen before.

CONGRATULATIONS ON SURVIVING THE TRIAL.
THERE ARE NO BESTOWALS.

"No bestowals? That's nucking futts," Jacky said weakly. She sat up and grinned at my surprise. "I'm pretty damn tough. A little knock on the head isn't gonna put me down."

DO YOU WISH TO RETURN FROM THE TRIAL?
YES / NO

She turned to Adam. "Consider my debt to you paid. You saved me, and I helped get you through."

He snorted. "We saved you again after you passed out. How do you think you got back?"

She scowled. "You're the one who knocked me out in the first place, no? Twice, I believe. I don't owe you nothing."

"Knocked you out? If I hadn't been there—"

I put my hand up to stop their bickering. "Guys. Each of us saved the others out there. None of us would have survived if we hadn't all been there. We made a great team." I smiled at them both.

Jacky grinned back. "We kicked their asses, crazy Eve."

But Adam noticed a deeper intention beneath my words, and narrowed his eyes in silence.

"Will you two meet me in the real world? Tomorrow?" I asked.

"Why?" He asked.

"I've got something I want to talk about, a proposition I think you'll want to hear. Just come and listen. I'm not going to force you to do anything, but if we're talking about who owes who... maybe you'll remember a little note in your locker?" I knew it was him from the combination of name and the twin to his butterfly knife, which I had hidden in my closet.

His eyes widened. "That was *you*? You thief! You stole my—"

"I *saved* your ass," I snapped. "They were about to do a locker check on you."

That gave him pause. "Well, do you still have it?"

I nodded. "I do. If you come tomorrow, I'll bring it for you."

"How do I know I can trust you?"

"Well, it's obvious, isn't it? You *don't* know that. But come anyway. You won't regret it."

He thought for a while, and then said, "Where?"

"I'll message you the information. Give me your contact info."

He did, reluctantly, and then I turned to Jacky. She grinned like the Cheshire cat and said, "Give me *your* contact info. I'll call you in the morning, and you can tell me the meeting place then."

I laughed, letting some of my tension out. It was unavoidable, and when Jacky's infectious snorting joined me, even Adam couldn't hold back. I stood up and walked to the cube. "I'll see you guys tomorrow."

My bones vibrated as the cube returned me to my room, back in the dark, and alone.

---

MY LEGS TREMBLED as my body realized that the danger was gone, for the moment. A window popped up, telling me I'd gained three levels. The Seeds appeared from the ether, and I tucked them into the back of my bedside drawer. I'd decide what to do with them later.

"More importantly…" I murmured, and picked up the small mirror I'd set to recording. I hit 'stop,' and then 'replay' in fast forward, to see what had gone on in my room for the hour or two I'd been absent.

I saw my nervous self from before the Trial disappear like the product of special effects, and then a few minutes of empty, silent room, and then I was back again, stumbling, dirty, torn, and tired, and full of relief. "What? That can't be right," I muttered.

I rewound it to the beginning and played through again. Only fourteen minutes had passed in the recording, but I knew the Trial had lasted for at least an hour. "Maybe it's broken."

I checked the time on my clock. Less than one hour had passed since I left for the Trial, and I'd already been back for half of that time.

I showered and laid down to try and sleep, my mind spinning with the possible implications of my discovery.

# Chapter 14

Our torments also may in length of time
Become our Elements.
— John Milton

"YOU WANT US TO DO WHAT?" Adam snorted incredulously.

"Join me." I said again, looking at the four others I'd called together to China's backyard after school. Adam, Jacky, Sam, and of course China herself. Her parents had gone to her grandparents' house, so no one would be able to observe us.

"I want to create a team that works together to survive the Trials and the Game. People that we enter every Trial with, who can have each other's backs in the Trial, and in the real world, with the ones behind it. We'll be organized. Prepared. It would increase our chances of survival," I said.

"How do we know we can trust any of these people?" Adam looked at the others. "I don't know them. Why should I trust them to have my back, with my life? How do I know I can trust you? This could be a trap."

I resisted the urge to grind my teeth. I'd known he'd be difficult, but I'd still asked him to meet, and more than ever I wanted him for my team.

Before I could say anything, China spoke up. "We're not tricking you. What would we gain from that anyway? We want to team up, not make enemies."

"Even if that's true, what would I gain from allying with you? I've been playing for months, and I've gotten by just fine on my own. It just creates more risk for me if I've got to look after someone else along with keeping myself alive."

I settled back in my seat at one of the benches in China's backyard garden. "That may have been true in the past, Adam. But you're vulnerable right now." I looked pointedly at his arm. "You wouldn't have made it out of that last Trial if not for Jacky and me."

He opened his mouth to respond bitingly, but I held up a hand and continued. "And we wouldn't have made it without you, either. That's exactly my point. We all gain if everyone in the group looks out for the best interest of everyone else. You can trust us because you know that by looking out for you, we're really just looking out for ourselves. A symbiotic relationship." I stared into his eyes, knowing that my honesty would be more compelling to him than any reassurance of my good nature and morality.

Any such reassurance would be a lie, anyway. My own survival was my top priority. I didn't feel guilty for that; it was just biology. I smiled after I judged our silence had gone on long enough. "Plus, I know you understand the importance of gathering more information about our…situation. I have some things I'd like to share with you, that I think you'd find valuable."

He stayed silent, but scrutinized me with narrowed eyes.

I turned to the others to allow him time to decide. I didn't know how to persuade him further. "China, I know you're in. What about you, Jacky?"

She leaned back on her perch atop the back of a bench and shrugged. "That all sounds good to me. I know already you make a good teammate. I'll go with you, for now. But," she leaned forward, suddenly serious, "I won't be confined. I will not be trapped in this. I will leave when I want. I will follow what orders I want. I will not be forced."

I nodded. "That is as it should be. If you will listen to my reasoning and consider it, that is all I ask. The Game is quite enough enslavement for all of us, I think."

She grinned and spat on the ground. "Screw the Game."

China repeated it, the vehemence extra shocking coming from her child-like frame and angelic face.

Adam laughed, the barrier he'd been holding around himself seeming to fall away. "Screw the Game," he said with relish. "I guess I'm in."

I turned to Sam, who'd stayed noticeably silent until then. "Sam, what about you?"

He smiled, but shook his head. "I don't think being part of a team is for me, sorry. I'll be going." He turned to leave.

"Wait, Sam," I called out. "Why don't you want to work with a team?"

He looked at the ground for a second, and then back to me, but I'd caught the white-knuckled fist he made and then quickly released. It wasn't anger. He had the type of skin tone that blushed at a moment's notice, and would have flushed with anger. Instead he was pale beneath his tan. "I don't work well with others. Honestly. I'm better off alone."

What secret was he hiding? "I don't expect you to be best friends with any of us. Just to work together so that we can all live."

He frowned. "That's the problem. I'm not the one you want to have at your back in a life and death situation."

Ah, maybe that was it. I could understand fear. "Sam, I know what you can do. I don't want you fighting at my back during a life and death situation. I want you safe right beside me so that when I need you, you'll be ready and able to help. We've got fighters. I didn't ask you here to be one of them."

He shuffled his feet. "But still, I don't think—"

"I have no doubt that you'll save all our lives at least once. If you walk away now, you'll be leaving us to die without you if something happens. We need you, Sam. Please join us."

"You're kinda manipulative," he said wonderingly.

I smiled widely. "I am. But I'm also being honest. I want you on my team. I want each of you, specifically. That's why I called you here."

He still hesitated, and I rolled my eyes. "You know you want to, Sam. Just say yes."

He took a deep breath. "Okay, yes. I just hope you don't regret it."

I settled back in my seat again, legs and arms spread wide to show my confidence. "I won't. I made a promise to myself to never regret anything again."

"Bunny, you heard all that, right? I've got a consenting team. Register us."

—Already? You move fast.—
-Bunny-

"I'm single-minded." Singly focused on my own survival, to be exact. But I didn't say that last bit aloud.

A window misted into existence like a mirage in front of my face.

YOU HAVE BECOME THE LEADER OF A TEAM.
SPECIAL CONDITION ACTIVATED
YOU HAVE GAINED THE SKILL "COMMAND."

A new Skill? My eyes widened and I sat forward. "Display Skill Window," I murmured under my breath.

COMMAND (MUNDANE CLASS): ALLOWS LEADER ACCESS TO THE TEAM MANAGEMENT WINDOW. LEADER CAN COMMUNICATE WITH TEAM MEMBERS

THROUGH GAME WINDOWS, SEE LOCATION OF TEAM MEMBERS ON TEAM MANAGEMENT MAP, AND IS ABLE TO ACCESS BASIC GAME INFORMATION OF TEAM MEMBERS.

My tongue twitched with the desire to display the team management Window, but I held myself back. "Did you guys get a Skill?"

China tilted her head to the side. "It says we can communicate with our leader via Game Windows."

Adam frowned at the invisible screen in front of his face, and then at me. "And I suppose that would be you," he said resignedly.

"Yes. It is me." I hadn't known the leader would be appointed like that, but I wouldn't apologize that it was me. The situation and my seeming power play made me a bit uncomfortable, but I kept it hidden and tried to begin as I meant to go on, with outward confidence and control.

Sam shuffled his feet and looked between Adam and me nervously.

Jacky chuckled. "Did you expect different? It's not like anything changed. There's just a pretty label on it now."

We stared each other down for a moment, and then Adam relented. "So I'm your subordinate now. What information do you have that you thought I'd be interested in?"

"You're my ally," I corrected. I very deliberately took off my link, and handed it to China, who put it in her bag.

Adam's eyes widened, and he did the same.

When everyone in our group had removed their links with varying levels of understanding why we were doing so, China carried her backpack away, out of the links' audio receptors' range.

"Everyone, be careful to shield your thoughts from Bunny. Just consciously acknowledge that you don't want him to overhear this." When China returned, I looked to her. "What I have is a name, I believe."

She knew immediately to what I referred. "Mendell."

"Mendell? One name? Is that first or last? What context is the name in? How, exactly, is something like that going to be useful?" He was rolling a coin over and between his knuckles with angry energy, tiny sparks of static electricity jumping off it.

China replied before I could. "My sister was taken by them, by NIX. We think that's the name of the people who run the Game." Her voice wavered in the beginning, but strengthened as she continued. "Eve was there when it happened. And then people in masks came to my house to make it look like my sister ran away. They were talking about what they would do with the ones they'd taken, and we listened. They said they'd be taking samples from them to Mendell. That's the context."

The irritated look slipped off his face, replaced with intense focus. "A research lab, maybe? A place, or maybe a person…" he muttered. He'd already begun tapping on the ID arm sheath link clamped onto the cast around his arm, entering in information.

"That's what I want you to find out," I said.

He took a deep breath and held his hand up in the air, and as he let the breath out, his hand started to spark visibly, and his curls started to float upward from the electricity coursing through his body.

Sam and China watched him with avid curiosity, while Jacky stepped back in alarm, probably remembering her last incident with his abilities.

Adam laid his hand onto his arm sheath, and though his body was still, his eyes twitched back and forth with bug-like, skittering speed, focused on nothing in the real world.

I pulled up the team control Window under my breath while the others were all focused on him.

PLAYER NAME: ADAM COYLE
TITLE: NONE
CHARACTERISTIC SKILL: ELECTRIC SOVEREIGN
LEVEL: 58
SKILLS: HYPER FOCUS

STRENGTH: 13
LIFE: 11
AGILITY: 28
GRACE: 13
INTELLIGENCE: 19
FOCUS: 22
BEAUTY: 8
PHYSIQUE: 13
MANUAL DEXTERITY: 15
MENTAL ACUITY: 29
RESILIENCE: 14
STAMINA: 10
PERCEPTION: 8

He obviously focused his points in the mental Attributes and Speed, and Electric Sovereign would be the Skill that allowed him to manipulate electricity. Hyper Focus was also self-explanatory. But the irritating thing was the average level of his Attributes was far above mine. He must have started out with high points, and only added from there, because even fifty-eight level-ups didn't explain those numbers. If he hadn't broken his arm, he would never have needed protection from Jacky and me. He was definitely the highest leveled Player in the group

Adam fairly vibrated with the intensity of his concentration for a while. Then, he took his hand away from the ID sheath and its connection to the Internet and let out a shuddering breath. He rubbed now bloodshot eyes and then looked at me. "I've found something."

We all leaned forward in anticipation, holding our breath after the display he'd just given us.

He continued, "A person. An engineer, slash physicist, slash biologist, former genius that's been out of the scientific community and the public eye for a while now. It's not much, but he's suspicious. I hacked into the city property databases, and I found a place under the name of his deceased sister that's paying extraordinarily high electricity bills. Which doesn't mean much, but when I tried to figure out where the money was coming from to pay those bills, I couldn't."

I nodded, understanding the direction his thoughts had gone.

Jacky pursed her lips. "So? That doesn't tell us nothing."

He smirked. "I'm able to understand the electrical impulses that run through a computer, and manipulate them. There should be no hiding the money trail from me, but it was in the form of a large credit deposit from a company I'd never heard of, and beyond that I couldn't track its path." He paused for emphasis. "It was purposefully hidden. Now, who would want their mysterious payments to a genius hermit researcher to be untraceable?"

China bounced on her toes and grabbed my arm in excitement as if to stop herself from flying away. "Oh my god. Yes! He's connected to NIX. He has to know something about Chanelle, and maybe she's even there right now, being held in some sort of research lab..." She tugged on my arm. "Eve, we have to go get her, before it's too late."

I refused to bring the team that very instant to look for China's sister. She would have rushed to Mendell's secret lair alone, but I was able to dissuade China with a compromise that we would go after the team had some time to prepare and gain information.

"But I'm not going to keep waiting indefinitely, Eve. If my sister's in there, I'm going to save her." She frowned at me with that face identical to Chanelle's.

I nodded and laid a hand on her shoulder. "I know. But if she is there, it's better that we wait until we're actually able to save her, rather than making an attempt and failing, and her being trapped forever."

Adam snorted. "I'll go there with the team, but no way am I risking my life for some random girl I don't even know."

I smirked, but said nothing. What was it exactly that got him that broken arm? Saving some random girl he didn't even know, if I remembered correctly. If the situation arose, I'd bet credits that

Adam would save Chanelle and a hundred others, grumbling about it all the while.

But Sam knew him even less well than I did, and frowned. "If there are people there that need our help, we have to help them. We have the responsibility to do what we can."

"Right. While you're being a martyr, I'll be keeping myself alive," Adam said.

I raised a hand. "Guys. We don't even know what we're going to find there yet. We'll deal with that when we come to it. Right now, let's get to know each other better, so I know exactly what we're working with and how best to allocate our limited manpower."

Jacky tilted her head back and forth to crack her neck. "So basically you want us to tell about our Skills, right?"

"More or less. Skills, Attribute point delegation, any other special skill or ability you might have…basically anything that might be useful for me to know."

Jacky gave a mischievous smirk and grabbed a short branch from a nearby decorative tree, ripping it off.

I pulled up her statistics in the leadership Window, to compare her real stats with what she told us. Her Characteristic Skill was "Gravitational Autonomy." When I touched the Skill, the words "Kinetic Class" appeared, but that was it.

She squeezed hard enough that her arm trembled with the effort, and her fingers sank into the wood, sap leaking from between her fingers and dripping onto the ground in milky spatters. With another smirk, she opened her hand and showed the pulverized wood pulp within. "I'm strong. Really strong, and sturdy enough to support my own strength, so I don't rip my own muscles and bones apart. My points are almost all in the physical Attributes. My Skill lets me change the force of gravity on my own body, just a little bit. I can't fly or nothing, but it's good for fighting." She wiped her sap-covered hand on the ground, and then moved to me and placed her hands on my shoulders. First, she bounced up and hovered just an instant longer than she should have, and the weight of her on my shoulders was surprisingly light. Then she pressed down on me, and I had to strain to keep my posture straight under the pressure her significantly smaller frame exerted on mine.

I could imagine the surprising strength behind a punch aided by the force of gravity.

"I've never put even one point into Beauty." She looked each of us, as if to challenge us to argue. "I didn't need to, since I was born beautiful, yeah?"

I couldn't help but laugh at her aggressive confidence, though inside my emotions were tinged with more than a hint of jealousy. To be born that beautiful, it was like a blessing from a fairy godmother, or a cheat code from the game of life. That beauty must have made things easier. No doubt it had much to do with her almost arrogant confidence. "I've seen you fight, too," I prompted.

"Yes, I'm also a fighter. Even before the Game. Since I was a child."

"Do you think you could train us to fight more effectively?" I asked.

"I've never taught, but I remember what my teachers did. Maybe I can teach. I'll try, but I'll need to watch you all fight, yes?" Jacky returned to her perch atop the bench.

China stood next. "My Skill…I can understand some animals, more or less."

Sam's eyebrows rose. "Like a Disney princess?"

She scowled at him, but her peach and cream complexion, big blue eyes, and thick blond hair showed a definite resemblance to a small Disney princess from the films. Except if this were a film, it would be a horror film, not all fun, acapella songs, and happily-ever-afters.

Jacky started laughing, hard. Not a beautiful laugh to match her appearance, but a snorting, rough sound that shook her whole body and irresistibly drew a laugh from me, as well. She laughed so hard she fell off her perch, and then we were all laughing.

China continued, after the mirth subsided, "I can't understand animals completely, but I get better at it as my Perception increases. And I can kinda talk back to the easiest ones, though they don't always understand me. It's a Skill of limited use. I'm not good at close combat, but I use throwing knives and that kind of thing."

Adam stood next, once again rolling a quarter between his fingers, perhaps unconsciously. "You've already seen both of my Skills. I can manipulate electrical currents, and increase my brain's processing speed for short periods of time. High Intelligence, Mental Acuity, and Focus. Indirectly, I use all of those things to allow myself direct access to a computer's processes, and through that, even to the Internet."

"And you can call down lightning," Jacky added.

"Yeah." He smirked. "I focus mainly on Agility when fighting. In and out, critical hits with the least possibility of damage to myself."

I nodded, pleased that he'd been honest.

Sam shook his head wonderingly. "Wow. This group's powers are strange enough, even I feel relatively normal."

"What do you do?" Jacky asked.

I had already pulled up his Window, and was looking at his Characteristic Skill in confusion.

He hesitated for a moment, and something about the strained look on his face made me step in to save him. "Sam's a healer. He saved my life after my Characteristic Trial. It was pretty amazing."

He looked at me with an indecipherable expression that might have contained relief or gratitude, but with something else locked away behind the surface. "Yeah. I can heal wounds, and poisoning, and stuff like that, as long as it's not too serious. I can't bring anyone back from the dead or anything, but..." he pointed to Adam's arm. "I could probably do something about your bone."

While Sam used Adam's broken forearm to do a demonstration, I examined his status window.

PLAYER NAME: SAMUEL HAWES
TITLE: NONE
CHARACTERISTIC SKILL: HARBINGER OF DEATH
LEVEL: 33
SKILLS: N/A

STRENGTH: 11
LIFE: 19
AGILITY: 12
GRACE: 12
INTELLIGENCE: 13
FOCUS: 9
BEAUTY: 13
PHYSIQUE: 12
MANUAL DEXTERITY: 10
MENTAL ACUITY: 9
RESILIENCE: 30
STAMINA: 18
PERCEPTION: 7

I tried to bring up more information on the Harbinger of Death Skill, but I could only see basic player information with the Command Skill. Even so, the words "Ruination Class" popped up. What did that mean? I remembered his words the first time we'd met. He'd said his good exterior hid something else beneath, and he'd been reluctant to join us. He wasn't the type I wanted at my back?

I watched him kneeling next to Adam, controlling a grimace as the broken bone he'd taken from the other boy started to heal, and then grinning hugely at Adam's look of amazement at his own half-healed hand and wrist.

No. I wasn't wrong to call on Sam. The type of person I didn't want on my team were those like Vaughn, who may have gained power and Skills through his actions in the Characteristic Trial, but who was rotten on the inside. That type of person would corrupt my soul, only feeding my own desire for control and cowardly power. I'd take Sam any day.

I stood up. "My turn, then. I don't have any exceptionally high Attributes. More or less an all-rounder for now. I'm a close-combat fighter. I'm the leader of this team, so I've got a Command skill that lets me know where you guys are in relation to me, send you windows like Bunny does, and I can also see your basic statistics."

Sam's gaze snapped to mine, but I didn't let my face acknowledge anything out of the ordinary, and continued on. "I have two Characteristic Skills. One is a spirit-type." Whatever that meant. I willed my body to perform its now-practiced transformation. My claws slid out and my senses sharpened with a rush of excitement that made me want to run and jump. "The other Skill basically just makes me more graceful, acrobatics and stuff."

“To be explicit, since I knew we're not being listened to at the moment, my goal is really to survive the Game, but I don't want to do that just by doing better in the Trials. The real threat to us are the ones who control the Game, and the disparity of power and knowledge between us. I want to level the playing field. So, why don't we go check out this Mendell person's house?" I grinned at them.

# Chapter 15

I am terrified by this dark thing that sleeps in me.
— Sylvia Plath

A COUPLE NIGHTS LATER, I put pillows and an extra blanket under my sheets to fake a sleeping body, like I'd seen in teen movies, and hoped no one would notice my absence. Then I grabbed my backpack and climbed out my window, tentatively reaching for the tree limb just outside.

—EVE, DO YOU REALLY THINK THIS IS A GOOD IDEA?—
-BUNNY-

When the monitoring devices in my room had picked up my suspicious actions, Bunny had happened to noticed and ask me what I was doing. I took a risk and decided to tell him. I wanted his aid someday, and despite the danger, I had a feeling he'd stay silent for us.

My heart pounded crazily and I had to force myself to move toward the trunk, but my body reacted to the danger, my claws slipped out to grip the wood better, and my balanced sharpened noticeably. "Yes. I do."

Since learning our plan, Bunny had spent the rest of the evening trying to change my mind. But he was appalled by the fact we even knew NIX's name, and the more he tried to stop me, the more I thought we were doing exactly the right thing. Otherwise he wouldn't have cared so much.

—YOU DON'T KNOW WHAT YOU'RE GETTING INTO. AS SOON AS YOU BREAK IN, YOU'VE COMMITTED A CRIME. AND WHAT IF IT REALLY IS ONE OF NIX'S RESEARCH LABS? DO YOU THINK THEY'LL JUST LET YOU TAKE THE PLAYERS AND LEAVE?—
-BUNNY-

I moved from the base of the limb to the one below, and then the one below that, again and again until I reached the wonderfully stable ground. It had been much easier than I expected, and I reveled a bit in my body's new power as I headed on foot to the meeting point. "We've done our research. We've watched the place and accessed the recorded satellite feeds. If NIX had a base with a lot of people, there'd be more traffic in and out of the property. Even if this Mendell person does have guards or assistants, it can't be very many."

—YOU'VE DONE YOUR RESEARCH? PLEASE. IT'S ONLY BEEN A COUPLE DAYS. WE HAVE NO IDEA WHAT YOU'RE GOING TO FIND INSIDE. DO YOU EVEN KNOW HOW YOU'RE GOING TO GET IN? THIS ISN'T SAFE, EVE. YOU'RE ENDANGERING YOURSELF, AND YOUR TEAM.—
-BUNNY-

He was worried. And he'd used "we" instead of "you," a slip that gave me confidence in my earlier assessment of him. He felt sorry for us, though he tried to hide it, and I might use that weakness against him if I could cultivate the compassion in him.

I knew he was right about the danger. Even the GPS chip in our necks might give us away, when we got too close. But from the observation we'd been able to do, we hadn't noticed a lot of people at the house. In fact, the only people in and out seemed to be fast food and delivery pods. I didn't know what to do except take a risk, and hope it paid off. And for whatever it was worth, it wasn't technically against Game rules to search for info on NIX, as long as we didn't talk about it to civilians.

I let out a panting laugh as I ran. "*This* isn't safe? Come on, Bunny. Think about that. I'm a Player. Every day I have to wonder whether or not I'm going to survive my next Trial. We all do. If we can learn something here that will help us to live, the danger is an acceptable risk. And the sooner, the better." I softened my voice. "You know we have to do this. We want to live, so please don't try to stop us. And don't get us caught."

There was a long pause before his next window appeared.

—DON'T GET YOURSELF KILLED.—
-BUNNY-

"I'll do my best," I said sarcastically, noting his silent acquiescence for what it was, and ran in silence till I reached the meeting point. Sam was already waiting for me, and the others would all arrive separately, in case we needed to leave in a hurry. I slipped into the passenger seat of his pod. No doubt an expensive gift from his parents when he'd reached driving age.

"You know…that my Skill isn't just healing, don't you?" Sam said into the silence.

"Well, you don't waste any time, do you?" I laughed. "I wasn't sure, but you've just confirmed it."

He opened his mouth, and closed it again silently, like a fish. "Oh. Umm…" He clenched and unclenched his fingers around the steering wheel.

"It's okay, Sam. We don't have to talk about this now. I don't need to know all your secrets. I just need to know that you're loyal to the team." I would find out his secrets eventually, anyway.

"Okay." He let out a big breath.

We drove to a deserted side road far from the edge of town and parked the pod between a couple trees, then got out and jogged.

"Psst! Over here." A hand waved to us from the darkness, and we headed for it.

China, Jacky, and Adam were crouched in a semicircle on the ground, and I sank down beside them, trying to quiet my breathing. "Any new developments?"

China rubbed her arms, apparently cold even though the temperature was perfect. That's what came of being so thin and waif-like. "Nothing, really." She'd been observing for most of the last twenty-four hours, watching for movement and determining what security measures were in effect.

Jacky chuckled and pulled a twig she was chewing out of her perfectly shaped mouth. "Except this guy's loaded. I mean…really, really, *rich*."

Adam nodded. "Which is going to make breaking in much more difficult. From my best guess, there's an automatic alarm system set up all around the property. No dogs, but there are cameras and motion detectors."

Jacky smiled cruelly, her teeth white in the darkness. "Good thing he's a long way away from the nearest police station. We'll have plenty of time to get away if things go bad."

Sam bit his lip. "But what if the alarm doesn't go to the police station? What if…?"

"It's connected to NIX?" I finished for him. "Well, there's a simple solution. Let's just not get caught."

Jacky sighed and shook her head. "No way we're gonna break in under an alarm. Not all of us, anyway. If it's cops, they'll be here in twenty, and we'll have time to get in and out. If it's not the cops…we'll be screwed."

I shook my head. "There's got to be a way."

Jacky shrugged. "I say we just move in fast and get out fast.

They'll never tell who we are from the cameras since we brought the masks like you said."

Just then, the sound of another vehicle driving up the winding road behind us filtered through the trees. "China," I hissed, "go see what it is."

She gave me a sharp nod and murmured, "Got it," then sprinted off into the darkness.

We all waited in apprehension for almost a minute before she came back, breathing hard. "It's a pizza delivery pod. Must be going up to the house."

I grinned and took off my backpack. "Great." I pulled out a mask and a pair of gloves, and slipped them on.

Jacky watched me with an excited grin on her face. "We gonna do what I think we're gonna do?"

"Yep." I turned to the others. "We're hijacking that pod. Pizza delivery pods get free access onto the property, all the way to the front door. No one suspects them."

By the time the old pod came rumbling up, we were prepared. China stood in the middle of the road with her hoodie pulled up to hide her features. The delivery boy would see just her small, fragile looking form standing in the middle in the road.

He stopped the pod and rolled down the window. "You okay?" He stuck his head out and called to her.

China shook, sobbing loudly.

He opened the door, but only had one foot on the road before Jacky rushed out from the trees and gave him a quick chop to the back of the neck.

He crumpled to the ground, and she dragged him off the side of the road.

"Neat trick," I said.

"Dangerous if you dunno what you're doing." She nodded sagely. "Lucky it worked, since I dunno what I'm doing." She grinned at Sam's shocked expression.

China pulled a small knife with a blue sticker from a sheath wrapped around her waist and pricked the boy's arm. "Coated with sleeping poison. Chanelle had the idea to collect it in one of our Trials. He won't wake up for a while."

"He'll be fine to stay here until we're finished." I said, nudging his still form with my foot. "If something happens, he'll be safer here anyway." I turned to the car. "Sam, you're going to be our pizza delivery guy. Strip him and take his clothes."

He looked back and forth from the unconscious boy to me. "Really?"

"You're the most trustworthy-looking out of all of us. Except China. But she looks like she's twelve. No one would believe she's old enough to drive."

I laughed under my breath at her protestations against my teasing jibe, and in a few minutes we were pulling up to the mansion's gate. The rest of us crouched down, out of sight of any cameras that might cause suspicion over a pizza delivery car full of people, while Sam drove.

"Pizza delivery?" Sam said.

A man's voice crackled back through the speaker. "Please wait. I will be down shortly."

---

SAM STOOD at the front door wearing the stolen outfit and a nervous smile on his face. He had a pizza in his hands, but a hat pulled low over his head for the benefit of the cameras. There was a beeping sound as someone on the other side entered a code, and then the door opened. Without giving the man time to react, Sam dropped the pizza, stepped forward, and pushed him backward, clamping his gloved hand over the man's mouth.

We rushed in behind Sam and helped him hold down, tie up, and gag the man.

Jacky brought in the pizza box and closed the front door behind us, while Adam made sure the alarm system was disabled, and turned off the home security system, along with NIX's possible view of the break-in. China helped him, checking for hidden cameras like the ones in Players' houses.

I looked around curiously. "Wow." The inside was a modern, open-air design, everything spacious and bright. The air smelled clean–evidence of a carbon filter air purifying system. A small fountain burbled in the middle of the lounge area beneath the stairs to the upper floors, and everything seemed to be made of marble and genuine wood. The place had been professionally decorated, was beautiful, and must have cost a fortune. It was also messy, with empty takeout containers and trash strewn around.

Jacky, Adam, and China did a quick recon of the mansion to make sure no one else was there, while Sam and I stayed with the man. I grabbed his ID link, in the shape of a bracelet, and pulled up his information.

Dr. Blaine Mendell. He was in his early thirties, wore thick glasses, and had floppy brown hair and a smile that made him look like he sponsored a child in Africa, volunteered at the nearest orphanage, and saved sick puppies in his spare time. If I hadn't been almost positive he worked for the most evil people in the world, I would have thought he looked like a nice person.

I maneuvered him into a chair and took the gag out of his mouth. "Don't scream. If you do, I'll take you over to that fountain and hold your head underwater until you learn to conserve your air for breathing."

He nodded.

"Doctor Blaine Mendell, tell me, who do you work for?"

His eyes darted back and forth between me, who wore a black mask, gloves, and sturdy clothing, and Sam, still in the pizza delivery outfit, which was somehow more disturbing.

I sighed, steeled myself, and backhanded the doctor across the face, making Sam jump in surprise. "Focus! I'm speaking to you," I said. I wasn't as strong as Jacky, but he'd have a bruise. "Let's try again. Who do you work for?"

He swallowed. "I—I don't work for anyone. I am unemployed; I just live off my savings and investments. I—I'm truly unsure what is going on here. Who are you people, and what do you want with me?"

Jacky came back into the room, having found no one in her section of the mansion. She opened the pizza box and took a slice, and then came to stand beside us, looking down at him with malice as she took a huge bite.

Blaine was looking at the three of us with a lot of confusion, but with much too much curiosity and not nearly enough naked terror.

His eyes met mine again, and I smiled calmly. "There are other ways to make you talk, if asking nicely doesn't work." I wasn't bluffing. I would do anything necessary to get the information from him, but I hoped that he saw my resolve and would spare me from having to do anything messy.

"I think you should see this!" Adam called from the doorway.

China stood behind him, eyes open wide and breathing shallowly, her body almost vibrating.

"What is it?"

Adam smiled. "I'm not sure yet. It's best if you see for yourself, I think. It's downstairs."

Blaine's eyes widened, and I saw the first hint of true fear come into his eyes.

"Well, Blaine, let's see what you've got down there, shall we?" I said.

He looked between Adam and me. "Who are you? Why are you doing this?"

I nodded to Jacky. "Bring him, please."

She drug him by his bound legs, bouncing him painfully behind us down the stairs to the cement and metal basement door, where Adam proceeded to override the electronic locking system.

China was as tense as a coiled spring, ready to shoot toward whatever was on the other side.

The door opened into a large lab. It had stone chemist tables and drains in the floor, research equipment and electronics everywhere, half-built gadgets, a wall lined with computers, and vials of strange liquids all laid out haphazardly. There were several other closed cement doors leading through to other basement rooms.

I started to walk through the room, examining the pieces of scattered machinery and the samples he'd been working on, while Adam and China started opening the other doors.

Jacky bumped Dr. Mendell down the last few stairs, ignoring his loud protests. "You've been quite naughty, have you not, Doctor?" she said, her Spanish accent growing strong.

Sam grabbed him by the arms and helped him to sit on one of the stools. "Why don't you tell us all what you've been doing here? We're not here to hurt you, if you'd just talk to us…"

He swallowed, but croaked, "I'm doing medical research. Attempting to find a cure for cancer."

My heart beat faster as adrenaline surged through my veins. He was lying. I knew, because on the table in front of me lay something that definitely didn't look like cancer research. Pinched between two slides, under one of the microscope lenses, was a fluid that sparkled like a Seed.

I looked through the lens and saw wiggling, teeny tiny microscopic organisms, so thickly packed I could barely tell where one ended and the other began. Little bug-like creatures. I snapped my head back, away from the microscope's eye piece. I unclipped the slide and gently took it out, holding it up to the harsh light above.

It shimmered and swirled over and under itself, moving constantly.

My breath came hard, and my hands shook. I cradled the slide in my hand and walked back to Blaine, showing it to him.

His loud protests, declarations of innocence, and wriggling ceased.

I touched him under the chin with the forefinger of my free hand and forced him to look at me, barely holding back my sharp nails from sliding forth. "Do you know what this is?"

He didn't shake his head this time. He didn't say anything. He just swallowed and looked into my eyes, desperation growing in his own.

"*I* know what it is," I said. "And I know you do, too. I also know who you work for. You absolutely *are* going to tell us what you know. Because we're patient, you haven't been trained to withstand torture, and no one is coming to save you."

I turned to Jacky. "Please pulverize the pinky finger of his left hand from the last knuckle to the tip." I turned to him. "Oh, and do it slowly, please."

Sam's voice came out, almost silent. "Is this really necessary?"

"If he's going to talk without it, then no." I raised an eyebrow. "Well, are you? Tell us everything you know and we won't hurt you, how about it?"

Blaine had stilled, but he said nothing.

"So be it. This is my question. What are you working on, down here in your secret lab?"

Jacky had grabbed his left hand already, a vicious, white grin stretching behind her mask. She pressed on the tip of his pinky, pinching it harder and harder until his face grew white with shock.

He turned red, and then white again, and started to pant and buck against his restraints.

Sam stepped forward. "This isn't right. Torturing him makes it like we're the bad guys."

Jacky looked to me, still pressing, obviously reluctant to quit.

I nodded to her and motioned with my hand, and she dropped his bound hands with a disappointed sigh.

Sam sighed as well, and smiled at me.

"Move on to the next finger," I said.

Sam's eyes widened, and he moved to stand in front of Blaine. "Come on, guys. Just stop!"

I stepped forward and placed a hand on his arm, and murmured so that the scientist couldn't hear. "I know this is difficult. But you have to understand we're not the ones in the wrong. He knows about what NIX does. He helps them. Think about the people whose lives he's had a hand in destroying, how many people he's helped them kill. He's part of the people that did this to you, to *us*. He doesn't deserve your protection." I pulled gently, and as if the strength to oppose me had left him, Sam stepped away. "If it's too much for you to watch, why don't you go explore the other rooms with those two?" I pointed to Adam and China.

He swallowed. "No; I'll stay."

Blaine held his trembling hands in front of his face, and I saw that his left pinky was flattened unnaturally, a white color that was quickly turning purplish red as it filled with blood. Jacky had pulverized it, similar to what she'd demonstrated with the tree limb in China's backyard.

She shook her head ruefully. "That's gonna be hard to use from now on. You shoulda cooperated from the beginning. There's no mercy to be found here."

Sam swallowed again, staring at the crushed finger intently. He looked away after a second and took a deep breath, but his own hands were clenched at his sides, and he didn't try to stop us.

"She's right," I said. "Now, once again. What exactly are you working on?"

Blaine sputtered and panted. "I'm working on a cure for cancer," he repeated.

Before Jacky could start to press again, China stomped past her, grabbed Blaine by the hair on the back of his head, and held a knife to his throat. She was panting and red-faced. "Where is she?" Her voice cracked.

I looked over my shoulder to Adam, who shook his head. All the doors were open, but apparently none of the rooms contained human subjects.

When the scientist didn't respond, her voice morphed into a scream. "Where is she! Where? Tell me, right now!" She pressed the knife forward, and a generous line of blood started to run down his neck.

He held himself still to avoid cutting his own neck. "What? I don't know who you are talking about."

She screamed again, spit flying into his face. "Don't. *Lie!* I *know* you took her. NIX took her to do research on. I know you have her. My sister! Where is she?"

His shoulders slumped, whatever had been keeping him strong slipping away. “They took your sister?”

“Why the hell do you think I’m here? They were supposed to bring her here. You’re doing research on her! I’m going to save her, and if you don’t tell me where she is, I’ll slit your throat, right now.”

He closed his eyes for a second, pain radiating from him. “I’m sorry. She’s not here. I don’t have her.” He looked at me, over her shoulder. “I’m sorry. I was told if I revealed information about them, they would…” he swallowed against the blade. “They took my niece and nephew, too. As hostages.”

---

“WHAT? You have to have her. If she isn’t here…” China stared at him for a few moments, and then slipped away like she’d been deboned. “Where is she?” She looked to me.

I shook my head. “I don’t know. But it’s not the end yet. There’s still hope.”

She leaned forward until her head rested against my torso, and wrapped her arms loosely around my waist. “Promise me we’ll find her, Eve. I can’t stand it, imagining what she’s going through. If they haven’t killed her…” Her small body shuddered, and she squeezed tighter.

Despite myself, my heart clenched in response. I petted her blonde head and said, “She’s strong. She’s a fighter. You know that better than anyone. We’ll find her. I promise.” The last part felt like it might be a lie, but even I couldn’t tell for sure. I looked up at the doctor. “You’d better start talking, right now.”

He nodded quickly as Jacky reached for his bound hands again. “I was a researcher. Before all this. A physicist, an engineer, and I loved it, the work, the respect, the money,” he blurted. “Then, my sister got diagnosed with cancer, and when she died, I quit all that because I promised I’d take care of her kids. NIX contacted me, requested I work for them, but I refused. So they took my remaining family to use as blackmail against me. I had no choice but to work for them. They furnished this place with equipment and deposit money into my bank account every month. In return, whenever I'm able to produce something valuable—research, or an invention—for them, they give me proof of life."

Adam's eyes narrowed. "How do you turn over your results to them?"

"I send them a message," he jerked his head toward the computers lined up against the wall, "and they respond with a time to meet, and GPS coordinates."

"How far away and how far in advance is the average meeting they give you?"

"It's usually quite immediate. A couple hours of warning, and most of the time is used up driving to wherever they want to meet." He looked at China, who had calmed down, but was still letting herself be petted by me, and then to me. "I'm sorry. I had no options. I didn't know what to do. I had to keep my sister's kids safe, and it's not like I could go to the police. Even now, if they learn that you were here, I don't know what they will do. But if they are doing this to other people, too…you're the same as me. I don't know what, but if there is anything I can do to help, I will do it."

I nodded immediately. "I'll take you up on that offer."

Adam's head snapped toward me with a deep frown, but I ignored him and continued talking. "But you must be willing to accept the risk involved."

Blaine smiled for the first time, despite the fact he was still tied up by four masked people who'd tortured him, and his crushed finger must have been screaming with pain. "I've been in danger since they decided they wanted my help in the first place. I don't want things to continue on as they have been, so something must change. It is insanity to keep doing the same fruitless thing in the hope that it will suddenly become profitable. They're never going to give my niece and nephew back on their own."

China pulled back from me, and gave him a weak smile. "Sorry for threatening to kill you."

"I would have done the same," he murmured, "if I thought the kiddos were being held here."

I untied Blaine's bonds, and nodded to Sam, who I knew had been itching with the desire to heal him. "Go ahead."

Blaine's eyes grew wide as he watched Sam's Skill go to work. When it was done, he gently touched the healed finger, his mouth hanging open. "Spontaneous regeneration. That's amazing. This is decades ahead of the research in the field right now. What did you use to do that? Could I see it? I'd like to examine how it works." His eyes searched Sam's empty hands for the cause of his healing, and then went back to his finger.

"Do you know what NIX does?" I asked.

He drug his eyes to mine for a second. "From the things I've been asked to research, I've gathered that they're an arms manufacturer. Advanced weapons technology, biological warfare, that sort of thing. Maybe selling on the black market to the highest bidding country, or maybe they're a military operation."

"Do you know what this is?" I held up the slide of shimmering Seed material.

His face brightened. "It's the most amazing thing—completely autonomous organisms that seem to share a common consciousness, I've never seen anything like them before. I received that sample just a few days ago. Honestly, I think, I think they might be a cure to cancer." He blinked, "Isn't that ironic? But of course that's not what they want me to do with them. Even so, my research could be beneficial, if I could release it to the world."

—Do it and you'll die, dumbass. NIX would never allow that to happen.—

-Bunny-

"Have you heard of the Game, Blaine?" I ignored Bunny's

warning to Blaine, who'd couldn't receive our Moderator's message anyway.

—Don't *you* do something stupid, Eve. Don't you remember the first rule? You can't divulge information to non-Players.—
-Bunny-

"Are you going to kill him if I do? He's already unable to tell anyone else. And he's already involved in all of this. Hell, he's studying the Seeds! Just because he doesn't use them like we do doesn't mean he's not the same as us. He's trapped, too, already dealing with everything. He just doesn't know what that is. I'm not going to *reveal* it to him, just *explain* it."

Bunny didn't respond, and I knew it was because he couldn't technically argue with my logic.

Blaine was staring at me strangely. "Umm, who are you talking to? Are you wearing an earpiece?"

I laughed. "No. It's the voice in my head." I ignored his look of bewilderment, and explained the Game and Trials, our status as Players, and the little we knew about NIX. While Blaine's head still seemed to be spinning from that, I had him show us around his laboratory and explain what he was working on.

Projects in various states of completion were strewn all about the room. "I prefer to work on defensive capability things, rather than weapons, though I do both types of projects. I've got a few going on right now, as you can see." He gestured all around us. "But most recently I've been examining the samples they sent to me…the Seeds, you called them, and something else, which I'm assuming are the samples from…the ones they took, like your sister. I'm trying to figure out how exactly they work, and from there how I can make them do other things. Other than that, I'm working on a lightweight synthetic armor—better than Kevlar, a serum that temporarily stops the pain receptors in your brain from working, and a substance that can stay strong while being thin enough to slice apart molecules. I just finished a mecha suit, an electrically powered framework for soldiers to wear, but the energy requirements make it unfeasible for extended use in combat. Of course, I'm particularly excited about the Seed material, and the things you've just described to me. I'd gotten some things from NIX to research before. Things that made me wonder why they even needed my help, if they had technology like that. I even considered that they might have excavated some ancient alien city." He laughed.

That gave me pause, and I didn't know how to respond, but Adam spoke up. "Why *does* NIX need you? I find it hard to believe an organization like theirs is lacking in scientists of their own. And even so, why do they allow you to do your research here? Why not just keep you wherever their actual base is and have you work there?" he challenged.

Blaine shrugged. "They need me because I'm very, very good at what I do. And I've always preferred to work in solitude no assistants, no distractions. I'm kinda known for not wanting a research team; idiots only hinder me. Maybe they want to preserve my working environment. Or maybe they don't want me anywhere near my niece and nephew, or they don't want me within their base for some other reason. Honestly, I don't know."

I walked around to investigate the connecting basement rooms. One was a quarantine room, with an air-sealed large glass box within, and I wondered just what he worked on that might require such precautions. Another was a storage room for supplies and equipment, another a small closet with a cot in it, but the last was pay dirt.

"Hell yes," I said aloud. Windows cut into the concrete walls near the high ceiling right at ground level would have let light into the large room, if there were any outside. But it didn't matter, because my eyes automatically compensated.

It was dusty and cobwebby enough to be on the set of a horror movie. Random, rusty bits of metal, tools, and various boxes laid all around and stacked against the walls. Two staircases on either side of the room led up to a second-story loft that ran a third of the width and the whole length of the room. I stepped forward. "This place is awesome."

I waved away a spider web and stepped onto the bottom step of the nearest staircase. A probing push with my foot proved it to be stable. "Except for the dirt." I turned to Blaine. "You said you wanted to help, right?"

He nodded, tilting his head to the side in an unspoken question.

"Guys," I spread my arms wide. "Behold our new base."

## Chapter 16

For evil to triumph it is enough only that good men do nothing.
— Edmund Burke

I CREPT BACK into my house late that night and curled up in bed. Adam had of course protested my decision, not trusting Blaine Mendell or his house-slash-secret-laboratory. We'd compromised by locking Blaine in the quarantine room and changing all the passwords to his security system. The scientist hadn't enjoyed that, but I'd told him to suck it up, because as punishments go, the things he'd participated in deserved much worse. That shut him up, and I told him I'd be back for him soon. I'd even left him the rest of the pizza and some water.

I'd told Adam to work on making our base safe from NIX, cutting off their access to the security cameras and microphones without them realizing. China would then thoroughly comb the house, making sure there weren't any other monitoring devices. My house was next on the list, but I figured the base took first priority.

A weariness like the weight of an ink ocean crushed me, suffocating me in dark silence. I'd crossed one more line tonight, created another barrier against my naivety, my normalcy, and my original invisible self. I felt like all the soft parts were being squished out of me, both mentally and physically. When the Game was done with me, all that would be left was a hard, jagged knife of a girl, able to cut through anything and everything. It would shave everything that wasn't survival away. If I didn't shatter in the process, that is.

I hugged my legs and rested my head on my knees, speaking into the darkness. "Don't you ever get tired of it, Bunny?

—Of what?—
-Bunny-

I'd known he would be there. "Of what you do. Kidnapping, human experimentation, murder…knowing how your Players live in fear?" When I paused, silence reigned. "How do you do it? Do you just not care? I know that's not true. So how do you do it?" Maybe if he explained it, I could do it, too.

More silence, and then a bright window appeared against the darkness of my room.

—I do this because it's my job. And they wouldn't do it if there weren't a good reason. I know it must seem like NIX is evil, but this is all necessary. They're working toward something.—
-Bunny-

"What could possibly be important enough to make this okay?"

—I don't know. That's above my security level until I pass muster as a Moderator. But I'm just here to monitor and guide you. I may not like what happens,

BUT I DO WHAT I CAN TO HELP. HAVEN'T I DONE THAT FOR YOU?—

-BUNNY-

"You don't know why this is supposedly necessary, and you just blindly believe? You're saying you're not *directly* involved, just a bystander, so that makes it easy? That's how you deal, how you cope? That makes it okay in your head?" I laughed. I took it back. I couldn't take any lessons from him. If I was dirty, I at least wanted to see the truth of it clearly in the mirror.

"Listen to yourself, Bunny. 'They' and 'you' are the same. You work with them! Those people kidnap children, inject them with microchips, force them into a game of death and abomination while experimenting on their bodies and having them monitored by cameras and microphones and...*you*!" I ran out of breath. "Do you realize what they did to China's sister? They turned her into a literal flesh-eating monster, and then took her and others like her somewhere to experiment on them. But it did double duty, since they let us watch, to give the survivors extra incentive to use the Seeds and play their Game even better, because we're afraid to end up like the losers. Chanelle wasn't even human anymore..." my scrambling voice petered off.

—IT'S HORRIBLE, YES. DO YOU THINK I DON'T REALIZE THAT? BUT WE HAVE TO PAY THE PRICE FOR URGENT ADVANCEMENT. WHAT DO YOU WANT ME TO DO?—

-BUNNY-

I took a shuddering breath and let it out, the weight of everything too tiring for me to continue. It was late, and I was tired. "I just want you to face the fact that maybe you *should* be doing something about it, even if you don't know what it is yet." The anger had left me, and left behind only crushing loneliness. "You've been decent to me, Bunny. But you can't keep hiding behind your intentions. Inaction is an action, too."

I LET myself into Blaine's house the next morning, breathing hard and dripping sweat after running from the closest bus stop. I wanted to come early to get a full day of cleaning and then training in with the weekend still in full swing. Soon, class would be out for seniors, and I'd be graduating. It's funny how the relative importance of graduating from high school had plummeted so abruptly.

The others were already cleaning our new base, and Blaine was still fidgeting in the quarantine box.

I helped clean, using a rag and bucket of already cloudy water to wipe things down. None of us had noticed anything unusual or worrying from NIX, which reassured me that Bunny had kept our actions to himself. Or if he'd written a report, no one had read it, like he grumbled about.

Sam, up above cleaning the spider webs from the loft area, leaned down to call a greeting. "Did you run here?"

"Yeah. Part of the way, anyway. I don't have a car." I shrugged. "Good exercise, and God knows I need every extra bit I can get."

Adam frowned. "It's best to have a vehicle. What if there's an emergency and you need to get somewhere fast, or get *away* fast? Except for China, who's too young, you're the only one of us who doesn't have a ride."

"Both you and Jacky own motorcycles, right?" Sam called down.

"I have one," Adam said. "Not sure what you'd call what Jacky does."

Sam cocked his head to the side. "What do you mean?"

Jacky pursed her lips. "I may have...*borrowed* that bike."

Really, now? I considered for a second if that bothered me, but I didn't find anything inside except a bit of curiosity about what skills that might entail, and if they could be useful. Things like the law were another thing that mattered so little now.

Sam smiled, innocent. "Oh. That's nice of your friend, to lend their motorcycle to you."

China, who'd been silently cleaning beside him in the loft, stopped and stared at him incredulously along with the rest of us.

"What?" He looked back and forth at our faces.

"When she says borrowed, she doesn't mean *borrowed*," Adam said.

"Borrowed?" His mental dialogue showed clearly on his face, changing from "I'm totally lost," to "Oh!," to "Oh-my-god-I-can't-believe-it," to "I'm worried," over the course of a few seconds. "But what if you get caught? Won't you get in trouble with the law? And your parents?" he said aloud.

Jacky smirked at him. "I'm an orphan, *chico*. And I've already been in trouble with the law enough it doesn't really matter. I'm living in a detention center already. What more are they gonna do to me? I'm a minor." Her voice was hard and challenging.

Sam froze, horror and then shame washing over his face, along with a dark blush. "I—I'm sorry. I didn't—I... God, that was so rude of me."

Jacky stood staring up at him expressionlessly for a few seconds, and then busted out laughing. She laughed loud and hard, a sound that reminded me of the braying of a donkey. After pounding at her knee and gasping for air, she finally calmed down enough to say, "Oh, Sam. You were just..." she slipped into mirth again. "I say that, and you just stand there looking at me so horrified. Like you just said... Like you just told me my baby was ugly. And then you look like you don't know how to apologize because I'm not even the mother. It's not my baby, I'm just fat!" She broke down again, wobbling over to the wall and leaning on it for balance.

Sam looked like he wasn't quite sure what she was saying, but was relieved all the same by the fact she wasn't angry. He cracked a smile, and a laugh of his own slipped out.

I thought about what Jacky had revealed. An orphan, and living in a detention center. "Jacky, how is it you're able to meet up with us at all hours of the night if you're in a detention center? Don't they have curfews and restrictions and things like that?"

She straightened, the residual mirth slipping from her mouth. "The warden has a soft spot for me. He lets me go out for some 'extracurricular classes', and beyond that, I just don't get caught." She grinned her cocky grin again.

But the look that had twisted her features for half a second when she spoke of the warden's soft spot was revulsion, maybe even hatred. It made me remember how she'd panicked when Adam had landed on top of her after saving her. I gave her a searching look that she resolutely ignored, and returned to my cleaning. We weren't close enough for me to probe further, and maybe I was just reading things between nonexistent lines.

After I judged the water in my pail dirty enough, I took it back to one of the sinks in Blaine's lab. Instead of returning to the others, I opened the door of the smaller quarantine room.

"Oh, God, thank goodness. I've been dying to get out of here," Blaine said.

"If you do anything stupid, I'll slice you up a bit, then I'll knock you out and lock you right back in here," I replied, sitting down at one of his lab tables. "Or I might kill you, if whatever you do is extra stupid."

He swallowed. "I want to help. But if I ally myself with you, and NIX discovers my duplicity, I may be putting the kiddos in danger."

"This is your chance to get them *out* of danger, for good, not just until the next time you can come up with something valuable to give to NIX. How long do you think your current situation can last? What if they decided that killing one of your 'kiddos' would be even better incentive for you to try and keep the other alive?"

He paled.

"And it's too late for you to go back now, you know. You're already our accomplice." I let my voice go gentle around the threat, but my gaze stayed hard and locked on his. "The only option is to get your family hidden, somewhere far away and safe."

"I am not going to do anything nefarious. Believe me, I fully understand the situation I'm in. And like I said, I want to help. But," he looked me up and down. "You may be tall, but you're still a girl, and I don't see any weapons. How would you kill me?" he referenced my earlier threat. "Are you crazy strong, like that—"

I knew what he was asking, and since that's what I wanted to talk about anyway, I decided to just show him. I held my hands up and let the claws slide out. They'd grown sharper and more menacing since the first time they'd appeared, and I saw his eyes dilate as he sucked in a choked breath.

Instead of scrambling back like I half expected, he stepped forward and grabbed my hand to examine my fingers, pushing and prodding at the tips and around the base of the claws. "A weaponized biological mutation, under active control..." he muttered aloud.

"Have you seen something like this before?"

"No, not in person. I mean, there's speculation, DNA splicing and all that, but no one's been able to figure out how to feasibly implement it." He drew a deep breath. "Would you mind if I...I'd like to study this. Study you." He waved his hand to encompass the whole team.

I grinned. "Glad you're on board. I want to know exactly what the Seeds are doing to us, and how NIX is causing all this to happen."

We sat down at one of his tables and chatted while he took samples of my blood, spit, hair, and skin, and shavings of both my claws and my normal nails, then prepared the samples for examination.

"You said they knew who you were, when they attacked and made you a Player?" he asked.

"Yeah. From what I've gathered it's more or less the same with everyone. They take you, inject you with a VR chip, tracking device, and a Seed. You get sick, and then you wake up a Player. Or you don't wake up. The ones who turned me said some things that make me think not everyone survives the process." I recounted the five minutes of helplessness that had concluded with me becoming a Player.

When I was finished, he frowned. "So the question that stands out to me is, 'Why you?' Other than the fact you're all young, I don't see an obvious pattern. I speculate there might be some genetic marker they are looking for. Something that increases your chances of adapting to the Seeds."

I nodded. "Exactly. Then the next question is 'What do they hope to accomplish?' It's got to be something big…" I thought about everything Bunny had told me, and what Vaughn had said. "Every Trial, we're trying to gain the power of the gods, the incentive being fear of death…" I mused. "Which means that's what NIX wants, too. They use fear to push us toward gaining it."

Adam walked through the open door and pulled out a stool to sit on. "Heard you talking and thought I'd join in. Next question, what would you do with the power of god if you were NIX?"

I frowned. "Before that, what exactly *is* the power of gods?"

Adam rubbed a hand through his floppy hair and came away with a few sparks jumping from hand to hand. "Miracles, right? Things we shouldn't be able to do, but we can because we gained something extra special as a Trial reward. Like this." He snapped his fingers and a spark jumped at me, stinging lightly where it landed. He grinned with childish smugness at my scowl.

"Which leads back around to two questions," Blaine held up a finger. "One, why do they want that power—what are they hoping to accomplish through their actions? Two, *how* are they doing this?" He bent over a microscope, peering at a slide of my blood. "Your blood has the Seed organisms floating around in it, but… something is off. Oh." He looked up at me, then back down to the slide, and started to mutter to himself. "Fascinating, never seen something like this before."

"What?" My voice sounded strained. "What do you see?"

He looked reluctantly away from the eyepiece. "The Seed organisms seem to have modified some of your blood cells. The majority are still normal, but a few seem to have been…enhanced. What I wouldn't give to know how they made those Seeds."

Know thine enemy. "Blaine, I have a present for you." I said. "Adam, do you still have that energy cartridge?"

"Of course."

"Lend it to the good doc." I turned back to Blaine. "I heard you had some issues with high energy requirements on one of your inventions. We've got something from the Trial world with enough capacity to power a single person's teleportation. It might help your research. Though it likely won't work, after coming back to Earth. The Boneshaker seems to have a deadly effect on electronics."

"Are you serious? An artifact from within the Game? Wait. So where exactly are they transporting you? What is the Game world?"

Adam and I exchanged a glance.

"That's a great question," I said. "Wherever it is, it's a real place. I mean, I'd considered it being a hallucination, or some sort of Virtual Reality simulation. But bringing back both injuries and objects…it wouldn't make sense."

Adam nodded, looking down. "I'm thinking…maybe an alternate dimension? Or maybe we're being beamed away to an alien planet. Or they're sending us way into the past or future. Some of the things we've seen would make sense, if the Trials are the future of Earth in a few thousand years. If NIX could gain advancements from the future, the technological and genetic advancements, they'd have a monopoly on…everything. They could take over the world."

"But what about the double moons?" The question popped out of my mouth as I thought it. "Earth has one moon."

"I don't know, maybe we got crazy and decided we'd build another one up there as a resort destination or something." He snorted. "But I was thinking, maybe something happens in the future. Some extinction-level event. That might explain an extra moon, and why there's no sentient life, despite evidence of humans."

"*Giant* humans?"

"Yeah. Which also makes me think it's thousands of years in the past. We have a few fossils of extremely oversized humans. Maybe before the dinosaurs, when the Earth could support life that large. Or maybe it's Atlantis." He snorted again.

I frowned, trying to understand the implication of any of his theories.

"Wait," Blaine said. "If it's the ancient past, that means bipedal, humanoid life evolved on Earth…Twice. The ramifications of that…"

Adam shrugged. "Maybe. Or maybe it's an alternate dimension. Or it's *not* Earth at all. It kinda feels like Hell, to me." He grimaced at his own quip. "This really isn't my area of expertise. I'm just speculating."

Blaine's eyes had grown even brighter with fascination. "So where is this energy cartridge? Perhaps I can gain some clues through examination!"

Adam rolled his eyes. "Not here. I'll bring it for you, tomorrow."

I decided to interrupt Blaine's impatient eagerness. "I don't want you to give NIX complete projects any more. Withhold as much as you can from your best effort, keeping it at the point where they won't notice. And keep the real product for us. Can you do that?"

"Maybe…I don't think they'd know the difference, either way. If they were intelligent enough to figure that out, they wouldn't need me. But why?"

I ignored the question, knowing both men at the table were more than smart enough to work it out. "How soon do you think you can have something ready to hand over to NIX?"

"If it doesn't have to be perfect? Maybe…two weeks?"

"Okay. Make it happen." Two weeks. I hoped it was enough time for the team to prepare, and me to turn a plan into reality.

It would have to be.

---

I CALLED Adam and China to my house the next day when I was alone, to stop all the monitoring equipment in my house from giving NIX accurate information. They hopefully wouldn't know the difference, but I would be able to speak and act a little more freely. My mind was still consumed by our lack of information, and Adam sent me a video from the Net to the new ID sheath my mom had reluctantly bought me. "Take a look at this. I think he might be one of us," he said.

I sat on the chair next to my bed and flicked up the video.

A young man stood in the midst of a kneeling group, brushing his fingers against their outstretched hands. His body was surrounded by a faint glow, and when his skin touched theirs, a ring of light pulsed from the joining, and for a second they joined him in glowing. He walked through them toward a large stone chair sitting on a pedestal, and sat looking out at his supplicants with a grim smile. His eyes flicked to the camera. "I am your god. Let those who recognize my power join me." The video clip cut out.

"What do you think? That thing about being god, and the light…it might just be fancy tricks, but maybe not," Adam said.

I shook my head. "No, it's not a trick. I know him. Vaughn Ridley. See what you can find on him, and let me know. ASAP."

"Got it. Give me a couple minutes."

I dressed quickly and opened my door to find my brother standing outside it.

We both jumped, and he smiled ruefully. "Hey, sorry. I was just going to ask, do you want some food? I made enough for both of us…"

"Um, I'm going out. But I am starving. I'll grab some to go, thanks."

"Where are you going?"

"To see a…friend." Vaughn was the farthest thing from a friend, but I couldn't say 'Oh, I'm going to see someone who I hate, even after only knowing him for ten minutes total, because I need information he might have about how to stay alive. After all, he may be a sociopath, but I'm dealing with a whole organization of sociopaths, and the enemy of my enemy is my friend…' now, could I?

"You've got a lot of new friends, lately," Zed said.

I frowned. "Yeah. I do." His suspicion was understandable, but it was just one more burden, one more thing to deal with, and I didn't have the strength to carry it.

"I'd like to meet them, if that's okay with you," he said, relenting in the face of my stare.

"Yeah, maybe sometime." I slipped past him, grabbed some food to sate my now constantly ravenous appetite, and left the house.

Adam sent me the location where the video had been taken, and I headed straight there at a loping run I never could have sustained when I was normal. Before the Game.

I arrived a half-hour later at an out-of-the-way, rundown building. It was in the jobless slum section, and despite knowing I could handle myself better than any normal girl, I couldn't help the wariness that prickled as I felt hungry, despairing eyes follow my running form. Before the attempted terrorist air strikes seven years ago, the area had been normal, if slightly lower income. Now even the air was bitter and faintly slimy. My breathing was heavy, and I was covered in sweat, so I stopped to compose myself before going further, and got bowled over by a large golden blur.

My first instinct was panic, followed instantaneously by the urge to attack, but the feel of a wet tongue on my face and the stink of an unbrushed mouth calmed me. It was only a dog.

But the dog was followed close on its heels by a laughing Vaughn. When he saw me, his eyes widened in surprise, and he hesitated a second, then reached out one hand to pull the dog back, and the other to help me up. "Well, if it isn't Little Miss

Spirit-Type. Come to join me? If it's for you, I've got space in my ranks anytime."

I ignored his hand and rose unaided to my feet. "Vaughn. You know my name. Please use it."

He chuckled. "Eve. What brings you here? And how did you find me?"

"I found you through that video you posted online. Are you trying to get yourself killed?"

"Hardly. I'm not revealing anything that I shouldn't. I'm simply…drawing attention. I'm surprised to have a response so quickly, though I somehow doubt you're here to answer my summons. That video only went up hours ago. How did you find me?"

"I've got resources. Not unlike yourself, I think?" I tilted my head to the side and forced a smile. "Though why you would want to draw attention to yourself, I still don't understand."

"Ooh. Charm and flattery will get you…" he trailed off suggestively.

"Your attention?" I supplied.

"But you already have that. Why are you here, Eve?"

I nibbled on the inside of my lip. "When we first met, you told me that you were aiming to become God. That the Trial was weeding out the weak from the strong. What did you mean by that?"

"Ah, you're here because you want information. I meant exactly what I said. Though I didn't mean God with a capital 'G.' " He winked at me. "You'll have to ask more specific questions if you want more specific answers, Eve."

The subtle smirk twisting one corner of his mouth made me want to claw his face. He hadn't really done anything to cause my current ire, but perhaps it was the fact I saw myself in his eyes, and didn't like the reflection. "Tell me about NIX. And how do the Seeds work?"

"You go right for the jugular. You've toughened up a bit since that Trial, burned off some softness. I like it." He looked me up and down, obviously giving his statement double meaning.

"Please, just answer the question."

"Now why would I do that? You obviously understand that information is valuable. What would I get in return, of sufficient value to match the knowledge I'd be sharing with you?"

Dammit. "What do you want?" What could I offer him that he didn't already have? And more important, what was I willing to give?

"Information would be good, but if you're coming to me, I assume you don't have anything I don't already know." He quirked an eyebrow, silently asking if he was right.

I wasn't so sure he *was* right, but I didn't want to test that by comparing notes. Any information I had that he didn't was likely specific to my team, and would only make us vulnerable to him. So I kept my voice silent and my face impassive.

"If you agreed to join me, I'd tell you everything I know, but I don't think that's going to happen," he continued. "So, I think I'll have to settle for one favor, the specifics of which are to be determined at a later date."

"One *small* favor."

"Those questions you asked weren't small. One large favor."

"You're only giving me words, which I have to take at face value. It's not big enough to qualify for a large favor. I'll do small-to-medium, and that's it. And whatever you tell me better be good and thorough."

He laughed. "Okay, I'll take it. NIX, though I don't know how you found out that name, is an organization searching for strength, for excellence. A type of power you can't find on Earth in this day and age. The Seeds allow them to search it out. A catalyst, you know? Those things separate you from all the other mere humans on the planet. They're like limit disablers. When you wish on them, they change your current self irreversibly from what you were before, but they also augment the bounds of what you can become. Eventually, if we prove ourselves worthy, we'll pass certain limits. The ones that separate humans from gods. The way—"

He stopped talking abruptly and looked over my shoulder. "You brought backup, I see."

I tensed and turned around slowly, following the direction of his gaze. I took three steps forward and looked around the corner of the building.

My brother stood there, eyes wide and mouth open, but no sound escaping.

"What the hell are you doing here, Zed?" I said, my voice low and grating.

He looked back and forth between Vaughn and me, still wordless.

"How long have you been standing there?" I said.

Vaughn stepped forward and touched the back of my elbow. "Please tell me he's a Player."

My heart paused for a minute as I took in the meaning of his words, and then crashed against my chest in a painful thump. My eyes snapped to his in wordless fear.

Reading my expression, Vaughn's face twisted in a way that almost ruined his handsomeness. "You set me up. Trying to get NIX to take me out for revealing information? Screw you."

I shook my head. "What? No. No, they can't know. I've got to get him out of here." I strode forward, grabbed Zed's arm, and yanked him away. "This never happened, Vaughn." I called desperately over my shoulder.

"What—what was going on back there, Eve?" Zed said. "What did he mean, 'take him out'? Are you in trouble? I mean, is something going on?"

I yanked harder on his arm, looking around in paranoia. Had they been monitoring our conversation? Did they know what Zed had heard? How soon could NIX's cleaners track him down? "How long were you there?" I snapped.

He looked around in confusion, following my darting eyes. "I'm sorry I followed you. I was just worried. You've been different lately, Eve. You don't talk to me anymore, and every time you think no one's looking, you've got this look on your face like…I can't even explain it." He pried my fingers off his arm and tugged to slow me down. "Scared, angry, exhausted, I don't know. But you're not happy, Eve. Please talk to me."

I grabbed him by the arm again and kept dragging. "Zed, what the hell?! What did you think you were doing? Following me, sneaking around, spying on me?" My voice got louder as I went, and I took a deep breath to calm myself.

I dragged him the rest of the way home, ignoring his worried pestering at me to talk to him. When we arrived, I slammed the door behind us, did a frantic search through the house to make sure no one had broken in, and then turned on him. "You've got to mind your own business. It's not cool to…do what you did!" I sighed, stepped forward and placed my hands on his shoulders, level with my own. "Please. I'm absolutely fine. You don't need to worry about me. I'm doing great. I've been working out as part of a group, sort of an exclusive club of friends. You just snooped on a private meeting."

He looked at me as if he didn't recognize me and shook his head. "Just talk to me. Let me help you."

"I don't need your help, Zed. Because nothing's *wrong*! Well, *one* thing's wrong, and it's you, acting like this. Why can't you just accept that for once I might have some friends? For once, I'm not the invisible girl. Just. Back. Off, okay?" I wished I was still the invisible girl, the one nothing extraordinary ever happened to. I'd been bitter, not even knowing how wonderfully good I had it.

He stared at me a while longer, and then stepped forward and wrapped his arms around me. "I'm sorry. I didn't even realize that's what I was doing. Of course you should have friends. I'm just not used to not being a part of every aspect of your life. I'll give you some space." His voice was contrite and sincere, but I couldn't see his face, and didn't catch the look in his eyes.

"Wait, Zed," I called out. I sighed deeply, letting some of the tension and anger go. "Sorry I got so upset," I mumbled reluctantly. I hated apologizing. "Do you want to…help me make pudding?"

He paused for a second, and then nodded.

In the kitchen, we got the ingredients for homemade pudding out quickly, working in easy harmony.

"Do you remember the first time we made pudding?" he asked. I did, but I let him keep talking. "I remember it was my first day of school, and I saw those kids teasing you in the hallway because you were so tall. I got mad and started yelling at them, but you just grabbed my hand and told me they were stupid and *short!* Then you laughed and we made up all those short-people jokes. 'You shouldn't listen to short people 'cause their body is too worried trying to make them grow to work on their brain. The air is different all the way down there were short people breath, so if they say stupid stuff just take a good breath and feel sorry for them… A blonde and a short person walk into a bar, and then a chair, and a table. Short people never clean the tops of their refrigerators, filthy animals!" He laughed. "We were so silly, but you distracted me from being upset. I remember when we got home Mom was still at work, and I was hungry, so you said you knew how to make pudding. You totally didn't!"

I elbowed him lightly. "But at least I was smart enough to look up a recipe!"

"Which I promptly screwed up. Hey, I didn't know how to read yet! How was I supposed to know the difference between flour and starch? And you're the one who added the yum-powder."

"It's supposed to make everything taste better! That's what the commercial says!"

He affected a high-pitched little girl's voice. "Oh, it's okay you added the flour, we'll just put the pudding in the oven and make pudding-cake! It'll be delicious! I'm sure the huge warning on the yum-powder not to cook it isn't important!"

I flicked some starch into his face, making him sputter and shutting up his mimicry. "I did not sound like that."

His eyes narrowed, and his own hand darted out for a fistful of starch. "That's the part you're going to focus on?" He eyed me up threateningly. "Not the fact that you almost blew up the stove and turned the kitchen purple?"

I backed up slowly, eyeing him warily. "*Me*? I seem to remember—" I was cut off by a fistful of starch flying at my face in a cloudy explosion, and then our argument descended into a food fight.

I was kneeling on Zed's back and rubbing an egg into his hair with one hand as I incapacitated him with tickling from the other when our mother walked into the room, just home from work. I froze, and Zed choked on his laughter.

My mother's eyes tracked over the food-strewn kitchen, and the back to the two of us on the floor. "Pudding is cursed in this house," she said succinctly, and then walked away.

Zed started guffawing first, and then I followed, laughing so hard I rolled off him and couldn't pick myself up off the floor for a long while.

Pudding had always been the thing for us to make together, when we were feeling down about something. It never failed to lift our moods, no matter how many years passed. That hadn't changed, and for a while, I forgot everything else that wanted my attention, and just had fun with the only person in the world who I could count on to have my back. Which was also the reason he was the only person in the world I wanted to protect from myself.

Later, I went back to find Vaughn again, but he was gone, with no trace that he or any of his fanatic followers had ever been there.

## Chapter 17

Corruption, do not take it gently. You must rip it out and burn it. Then spit on the ashes.
— Kaiser Fell

I JERKED from sleep to the sound of my alarm before the sun rose all the way over the horizon. Seniors didn't have school that week as we'd already taken our exit tests, and I needed every spare second to prepare. I stood and dressed, thinking wistfully of my soft, comfortable bed. Then I thought of the Trial in a few days and suddenly rest seemed much less alluring. "I can rest when I'm dead," I croaked in a sleep-roughened voice. "And if I live, sleep is something I'm willing to give up indefinitely in return."

After the incident with Vaughn, I'd been extra wary of NIX. I supposed Vaughn might have just changed locations, but I thought it more likely NIX's cleaners had something to do with it. But they hadn't come for me or Zed, and I could only hope that meant they weren't going to. I'd questioned Bunny as subtly as possible, but he didn't seem aware of any danger to either myself or my family. I would have liked to keep watch over Zed constantly, but he would have grown even more suspicious, and I had other obligations.

But it made me think hard about how I would keep my family safe, because my team and I weren't the only ones in danger from NIX.

I ran to Blaine's house again, arriving drenched in sweat but feeling surprisingly good. I'd leveled up my Stamina twice.

A gratifying scene greeted me when I walked into the basement room I'd commandeered. Jacky and Sam were already there, moving furniture in. The windows high above were clean, and the extra light shining through them brightened the room.

Training mats covered a large portion of the cement floor. Weights and bands sat in one corner, and in another stood a swiveling upright cylinder of wood with rods sticking out of it all around, the kind I'd seen people training with in kung-fu movies. Large punching bags hung by huge chains from two big hooks in the ceiling. Smaller bags hung under the loft, and large mirrors had been attached to the long wall so we could keep an eye on our form while training.

Blaine stepped up beside me and said, "Jacky said you'd need these things, so I bought them and had them delivered last night. They've been unpacking the whole morning."

"You paid for this?" I asked.

"Yes. But it is no big deal. I have money, and you needed things that money buys. Easy solution."

I nodded. "Nice." The type of wealth my new ally had might come in extremely useful. Money created opportunities where none had existed before. I stepped in to help move the rest of the furniture to the upstairs loft and set up the training equipment. While we were working, Adam and China joined us, and Blaine ordered Chinese takeout for everyone, joking that he wouldn't be getting pizza delivered again for a long time.

I stuffed my stomach in silence, like the others, while Blaine watched in amazement. Something about being a Player seemed to ramp up our metabolisms so we were always hungry. When the hunger had subsided somewhat, I said, "We need to set up training regimens for everyone. Get stronger before the Trial."

With her mouth stuffed full of chicken, Jacky said, "I'm the best fighter here, so I'll be in charge of training and exercise."

I nodded. "Anyone else have something?"

China looked around, and then raised her hand. "I can teach everyone how to throw knives. And I don't know if it's important enough, but I do yoga and meditation, and it helps to increase Grace and Perception. If you want, I'd be happy to help with that."

I wasn't sure how useful that would be, but any increase in Attributes was a bonus, and I knew I for one could do with some relaxation. "That sounds great."

I looked to Adam and he snorted. "Sam of the Second Coming may have helped, but my arm's still fractured. Fight training's out for me. And I can't teach you guys to be smarter." He ignored Jacky's scowl and continued, "I can draw and do magic tricks. Not exactly something you guys need. But," he conceded, "I might be able to show you and the doc how my computer monitoring programs work. That way, in case I die you'll still be able to get updates."

Sam said, "I can't really teach how to heal people, but I could give some basic first aid and trauma stabilization training. In case something happened and I…wasn't there," he finished, obviously uncomfortable with the thought of his own death.

Blaine cleared his throat. "Umm…it would take years to teach you guys to do what I do, but I've got some ideas for things I could make to help you in the Trials."

I nodded. "Okay, wonderful. I don't have any skills to share that you don't already have, but I have ideas, and a plan for getting out of all this. I'm working with Blaine to figure out exactly what the things they put into us are. I'm still working on getting more information and figuring out fine details, but I'll share my plan with you all when I've got something more complete. If we survive till then, that is."

Jacky raised her eyebrows and pursed her lips. "On that note, I need to see everyone spar so I can figure out a good training plan for each of you. Don't use no special Skills, just your natural abilities. I don't wanna get someone killed." She glanced at China.

Adam and China both tried to question me about my plan, but I fended them off. I was still trying to figure it out myself, and my ideas and the snippets of things I'd learned hadn't formed into something solid I could share. Giving them hope was enough for now. If I explained what little "plan" I actually had, it might take that hope away.

After explaining what she wanted, Jacky paired me up against Adam, and Sam against China. The latter two went first, China dancing around Sam and throwing playing cards at him in place of her knives, along with darting in and "stabbing" him with them. He refused to attack her, but nevertheless failed to properly defend himself.

Adam and I were next. Despite the handicap of his healing arm, he seemed more than confident enough in his ability to fight me. "You're going down, Eve Redding."

I raised an eyebrow and grinned at him. "Go ahead and try." I was fully aware that I didn't know how to fight. And without my claws, I would be just a slightly uncoordinated girl flailing against a guy who'd been in his first street fight long before ever becoming a Player. So I steeled myself for pain and humiliation and tried to imitate his loose, ready stance.

Jacky grunted to herself, but I didn't take my eyes off Adam and the way he held his legs, arms, feet, and back.

He shot forward, I felt a tap on my chest, and then the world was tilting off its axis. I slammed hard into the floor, half knocking my breath out. I groaned and rolled over, ignoring a tap on my side as he showed me he could have kicked me while I was down.

I got to my feet, and readied myself. My subconscious had responded to my instinctual fear, and though I held my claws in, focus sharpened all my senses. I could smell the new plastic of the pads under my feet, my own sweat, and the scent of my opponent.

He lunged forward again without warning, tapped me on the

side of the head and the side of my left knee, and then kicked my legs out from under me.

I didn't lose my breath when I landed on my back that time.

He stretched out a hand to help me up, and a mischievous thought popped into my head. I didn't pause to think long enough to seem suspicious, but reached out my hand to him. As soon as I had a good grip on him, I braced myself against the floor with my other arm and swung my leg around low to the mat and fast.

His eyes widened as my leg made contact with his calf and I felt a flicker of satisfaction as he started to fall.

But then my grip on his hand was broken, and he half-jumped, half-twisted over my head and behind me, wrapped an arm around my throat, and squeezed. While not painful, it was definitely uncomfortable.

I tapped his arm twice and he released me. I grinned and turned to look up at him. "Sorry. I just couldn't resist."

Jacky started laughing. "You did well, Eve. Next time isn't gonna be so easy, I think."

Adam pushed his hair off his forehead. "No, it won't."

I stood without his help and prepared for his attack once again. A giddy feeling rose within me, a mix of fierce competitiveness and laughter. I breathed deeply and focused on him.

He lunged, and I followed each subtle movement he made, how far his steps took him, and where he slipped his leg behind my own.

The world tilted in a way that was becoming familiar as my feet were ripped from under me. He thrust his good hand at my face to smash my head toward the ground. It would have been a devastating move if there weren't thick padding below us.

I grabbed his wrist in both of mine and pulled my legs toward my chest as I fell, tucking my head forward so it didn't land first. When my back hit the mat, I slammed my legs forward into Adam's chest and pushed upward, using my grip on his arm to swing him over my head and smash him full length onto the mat behind me. As he hit, I released his arm and used my backwards momentum to flip onto my hands and knees. I crouched by his head and snapped my hand to his unprotected neck.

Everything was still except for his heartbeat thumping against my fingers, and after a moment I realized I was panting as if I'd just run a race. Somehow my claws were out, pressed against the skin of his throat. I stood, forced my claws back, and held out a hand to help him up. "Sorry about the claws. I got a little carried away."

He stared up at me, then slowly grabbed my hand and allowed himself to be helped up.

"Holy…crap," Sam said from the sidelines.

Jacky walked over and smacked me hard on the back with a grin. "Seems you're a bit of a natural. Quick to acclimate."

Adam started to laugh. "That was amazing. Let's go again."

After that, Adam wasn't so careless and didn't try to throw me again. Instead, he danced around and jabbed at me, light taps on various exposed areas that I knew would have quickly left me dead if he had one of his butterfly knives in his hand.

I tried to learn from his movements, and by the end of our sparring match we were both dripping sweat onto the mat, and I'd gotten a few taps of my own in.

---

"HEY, SAM," I called. "Do you think you could help me out? I think I tweaked my neck a bit." I rubbed the completely uninjured muscles.

He gave an innocent nod, "Sure," and followed me to a corner of the room. He put a hand on my neck, then shifted it around and frowned. "I don't sense anything. Where does it hurt?"

"It doesn't," I murmured to him in a low voice. Only China would have the hearing to make out our conversation, and a glance confirmed she was busy getting instruction from Jacky at the moment. "I just wanted to chat with you."

"What's wrong?" he whispered gravely.

"Nothing!" I chuckled. "I just wanted to talk about your Skill."

"Oh." That didn't seem to reassure him.

"I know there's something you held back when you were explaining. I respect your right to privacy, but as the team leader I can see some Game information on you, remember?" I smiled in what I hoped was a reassuring way. "Will you explain the Skill to me?"

His lips were white, but he nodded. "My Skill isn't strictly for healing. It's like a sick joke. Whatever I heal, my body assimilates and understands, to recycle as a morphed attack. And the more horrifying and twisted the injury, the better I learn it."

I stared at him for a few minutes. "So…that paralyzing saliva?"

He nodded.

"Show me," I commanded.

He hesitated, but placed his hands on the bare skin of my neck again. Almost immediately, my skin started to go numb. It wasn't the same as the feeling of the grub-pug's saliva. Sam's version made me want to scratch and claw at the numb patch till I ripped it away.

"Okay!" I urged, and he touched my neck again, returning sensation to my skin and stopping the torture.

"Wow," I said.

"That was mild. It gets worse. Way worse. This Skill is a punishment. I hate it." He glared at his hands. "I don't want to use it, Eve." He looked up to meet my gaze.

"Not even against monsters? You'd fight them anyway, right? That's a really great Skill, Sam, and if—"

"No! No, I don't want to use it. Just like with any Skill, it gets stronger the more you use it. I'll use the healing side, but as much as possible, I want to avoid making it even easier for me to kill someone. I won't use it."

I searched his eyes for a second and nodded.

"And…don't tell the others?" he added hesitantly.

"You're our *healer*, Sam." When he didn't pick up my meaning, I added, "And that's it."

He let out a sigh of relief, and we returned to the others.

Jacky set me up on one of the lighter punching bags and showed me a few simple combinations of punches and kicks she wanted me to practice until I could do them in my sleep. "Your fancy move back there might'a worked, but being efficient and effective is better than being flashy. When you've got these moves down by instinct, it reduces the chance of failure."

She watched me till I started to get the hang of it, and then showed me how to hit with my elbow. "The elbow can do a lotta damage at close range. At the point you're closest to the bag, start to add that into the combo." Once again, she watched me attack the bag. "You need practice with combat. But even so, I would trust you to fight at my back."

I grinned in surprise at the compliment, and used my shirt to wipe some sweat from my face. "You know, aren't you supposed to start off training me with basic blocks and evasion? Defense first?"

She laughed and cracked her knuckles. "The best defense is an overwhelmingly powerful offense, I always say."

With that, she left me to my practice. I alternated between starting the combo with my left and right hand, and repeated until my knuckles were raw and bleeding, my wrists wobbly and weak, and my shoulders felt like they were being ripped out of their sockets every time I moved my arms.

Sam placed a hand on the bag in front of my face to get my attention, and jerked his head to China standing on the mat. "Time for cool-down."

China told us to follow her lead, then ran us through some seemingly easy movements that were in fact anything but easy. Something like yoga, mixed with a martial dance. Each movement was slow and controlled, and she watched us all in the mirrored wall across from the mat, correcting our form when needed.

I was shaking like I had a car battery attached to my central nervous system, and was deeply relieved when China finally had us sit down. We folded our legs, laid our hands on our laps, and closed our eyes. As I breathed deeply, I became aware of the blood rushing in my veins, and the air entering and leaving my lungs. The sweat on my skin was cool, and I could feel the currents of the air moving around me. Heat radiated off my flushed skin in waves. I focused harder, and realized I could hear the others breathing. I could smell their sweat mixed with the piney scent of the cleaning liquid we'd used all over the place. Outside, the wind blew gently. I knew because it made a low, smooth noise as it parted and cut around the corner of the house above. I reached farther all at once, and something different happened.

My eyes were closed, but whiteness fogged the backs of my eyelids. As I concentrated harder, it solidified. My body hurt with cold and fatigue. I felt something come alert then, and then a sense of amazement. My wrists and ankles started to hurt, and I realized that my body was yanking against something, though I wasn't consciously moving it. The room around me shone with painfully bright light, and as my view changed, chunks of hair fell across my face and blocked some of it out. Dirty blonde hair, not my own almost black strands.

A deep, croaking voice spoke in a language I didn't know, but that seemed familiar all the same. Adrenaline built until I couldn't keep my concentration, and I felt my mind ripping away from that place despite something trying desperately to grab and keep me there.

My eyes opened and I jerked violently backward, an awkward half-shout bursting out of me. I looked around at the familiar base again, and held my hands up in front of my face, moving them deliberately. I was there. I was me.

The others stared at me, and Sam said, "Are you okay?"

"Cramp?" Jacky asked sympathetically, stretching her own forearms. "Stretch it out."

I shook my head. "No, I, um…" I swallowed and lost track of what I was saying for a moment when a Window popped up, telling me I'd leveled up Perception and Focus. "I had a mini hallucination, or maybe…a dream? I couldn't have fallen asleep in that amount of time, right? I saw a white room, and I couldn't move my arms and legs…"

"You're probably exhausted. You should go home and get some rest. We all should, actually. There's only so much our bodies can take in one day," Sam said.

My head pounded with a headache so strong it felt like something was literally pounding on the inside of my skull. "Yeah, you're right." I needed to be strong, not seem panicked and crazy. But I remembered where I'd heard that language before. It had sounded in my head when I was first made a Player. "I'm going to go get some juice. I think I might be a bit dehydrated." Hey, it was probably true, judging from the amount I'd sweated out.

Instead of getting a drink, I plunked myself down in front of Blaine, who was scribbling formulas onto the screen of a glass pad in tiny, scrawling handwriting. "I need you to figure out what they put in my head, and what it's doing to me. I just had a hallucination," I said.

He kept scribbling for a moment as if he hadn't heard me, and just when I was about to repeat myself, he stopped writing, put the pen down, and said, "Great! I have been wanting to do more tests, but the others all seem a bit wary of me, and I haven't been able to get a willing subject."

I rubbed the back of my neck, remembering the two sharp pains I'd felt as they inserted something under my skin. "They put something at the base of my skull, and something else a little lower down. From what Bunny's told me, one's a virtual reality chip, and the other is probably a GPS tracker. Can you get them out?"

Blaine pushed his glasses up and walked away to grab some weird device from his supply closet. He mounted its two halves on my shoulders, on either side of my neck, and fiddled around behind me.

I felt a warmth, and then he put something sticky on either side of my neck, picked up a smartglass tablet from the table, and pulled up what looked kind of like an X-ray on its screen, except I could see shooting pulses of energy moving along my spine and into my brain.

"Like you stated, there is one at the base of your skull, and one a little lower down." He pointed to two different spots of discoloration, then pinched and flicked at the screen, and the picture zoomed in to the base of my skull.

A little spider-like thing nestled there, except it had too many legs to be a spider, they were too long, and each of them was digging upward into the base of my brain.

I swallowed.

"I am assuming this would be the Virtual Reality chip. Of course, it is not fully integrated, but those tendrils likely extend into your visual cortex, which is what allows you to see the Game windows," he said.

"Can you get it out?"

"Not without risking serious damage to your brain and spine. It has embedded itself like a tick. Honestly, I doubt you will ever be free of it."

"Well, could you just kill it, then?"

"It is attached to your brain, and has a power source strong enough to control your visual cortex. If I were to risk doing anything to it, I could damage your brain beyond repair. I am not a neurosurgeon, Eve. The most I could offer you would be a signal blocker between NIX and your brain, but I would need some time to make it work."

I lifted my hands and sent a blank message Window to Adam using my new Command Skill, and the nestled spider let out a flurry of small bright pulses.

Adam sent me a message back, and it pulsed again.

—Is everything okay?—

-Adam-

"Did you just use the Game interface?"

I nodded.

"Well, that proves my theory." Blaine stood and returned quickly with another gadget, a bright smile on his face that kinda annoyed me, seeing as the situation was decidedly not cheerful.

Adam popped his head into the room. "What's going on?"

Blaine waved him over. "Oh, come look at this. We are scanning the implants NIX put into Eve. It is quite fascinating. Do it again, Eve," he said, stepping back and pointing a small curved satellite-like dish at me.

I sent Adam another message, and Blaine "oohed."

"Interesting. The lower implant, which is definitely a GPS, is sending out timed pulses to nowhere, but I can also see the data transfer between you and Adam. Each of the chips must have some kind of local area wireless technology built in. I wonder if we might be able to do some tracking of this data between you and Bunny." Blaine lifted his head over the device and grinned at me.

That, I could see the cheer in.

We spent the next hour doing little tests on Adam and I, and Blaine came to the tentative conclusion that he might be able to create something to block Game interaction from NIX, while keeping the localized access between me and my team. As for the GPS, it was also imbedded into my spine, but not my brain, and though he didn't want to try and remove either of the implants, he thought he might be able to create a localized shock that would render the GPS useless without much damage to the rest of me.

But he had no idea what might have caused the hallucination, especially as the VR chip wasn't connected to my auditory cortex, and I knew I'd *heard* things. He hypothesized my problem was too much stress and extended physical and emotional trauma, and seconded Sam's advice to get some rest.

After a while, our resident scientist sat down and began to draw diagrams and make notes to himself while glancing at the videos he'd taken through the gadgets on my neck.

"Do you need a ride home? You ran here again, right? I can take you on my bike," Adam offered. "I have a feeling you'd get a few feet past the door and collapse, in the state you're in."

My eyes widened at the offer. I must look even worse than I felt. But riding home while someone else drove sounded wonderful. No thinking, no moving. “Yes, thank you. That would be great."

“Okay. Wait here while I get my stuff.”

When we were alone, I turned to Blaine. “What plans do you have in place to keep yourself safe if you were ever able to save your niece and nephew from NIX?”

He stared at me from behind his glasses, but then his surprise faded away and he started to talk. We laid plans for a few minutes until Adam poked his head back through the doorway and told me he was ready to leave.

I stood up and made my trembling way to the door. I needed to rest, and then try for a repeat of the hallucination, if that was what it was. I could feel it was significant, and I needed to find out exactly *why* I believed that.

# Log Of Captivity 3

Mental Log of Captivity-Estimated Day: Two thousand, six hundred eleven.

I do not know how, but my master reached out to me today, as I have been doing to her, though the *blood-covenant* is still incomplete. She touched my mind, fairly *skin-jacked* me! It was only for a moment, and then she withdrew, but I am filled to bursting with these strange feelings I barely remember. Pride and happiness fill me, because I know she is in this way acknowledging our *blood-covenant*. A Matrix has accepted me, and I can only be selfishly grateful that she must be still too young to know the worth of her bond.

# Chapter 18

I wanted to find one law to cover all of living. I found fear.
— Michael Ondaatje

I SPENT the next few days worrying fruitlessly about Zed, sparring, endlessly smashing different parts of my body against the unfeeling sandbag till I felt like I would fall apart, learning how to throw knives and darts from China, and then trying to reach that hyper-aware state again. I gained points in Focus from trying so hard, but had no luck. I did level up and gain several other Attribute points through the sheer amount of work I was putting in, so my efforts weren't completely fruitless.

On the tenth day, we gathered in the base and waited for the Trial to start. I'd told Blaine about the video I'd taken of my teleportation and asked him to monitor and study our disappearance. We were attached to wireless biometric monitors and under the watch of high frame rate cameras. Tension filled every corner of the room as we anticipated what was to come, checked and rechecked our equipment, and tried in vain to relax.

Finally, after hours of my understandably fruitless attempts to meditate, the Boneshaker played. The five of us gathered together, and left together.

My knees tried to buckle under the sudden added weight after the transfer, but I was prepared, and controlled them. My stomach roiled, and I took a deep breath of the strangely flavored air.

We were all standing together, as we had been. I turned in a circle, looking around. Under my feet lay black, granite-looking stone, reaching far and unbroken in every direction until it met with what looked to be a waterfall reaching into the sky. It was almost as if someone had placed us upside down on a huge black penny, turned on the sink, and placed us under a running faucet. I squinted my eyes, but the light was dim, and I couldn't tell for sure if the substance that surrounded this huge black disk in a shimmering tube was indeed water.

It wasn't what I was expecting. There was no greenery, no buildings, no rioting mass of strong colors and strange shapes. Ahead was the familiar black cube that always welcomed us to a Trial, but with a little extra.

HERE YOU WILL BE TRIED, YOUR MEASURE TAKEN.
THE WORTHY WILL BE GRANTED THE POWER OF THE GODS.
TAKE YOUR PLACES ON THE BOARD.

Almost immediately, a timer appeared in front of my face, with a three-minute deadline. The other Players milled around the cube, speaking with despair tinged voices.

"What's going on?" I asked aloud.

Adam's voice was grim. "It's going to be an Intelligence type Trial." Something about his tone put a heavy stone pit in the bottom of my stomach.

Jacky nodded. "Every once in a while we get the mental Trials." She cracked her knuckles. "They're…hard." Her voice cracked along with her joints and her face was pale.

Sam breathed hard, studying his own hands intently.

I'd heard of mental Trials from the others before. There was often no Moderator, and the Players had to use clues and deductive reasoning to figure out how to survive and win. And there was usually a cruel twist of some sort. Needless to say, they were almost always a bloodbath, with higher fatality rates than any other type of Trial.

This was bad. Very bad.

I looked around for a clue to the cube's message, and noticed an aberration in the smooth stone ground. Circles about a meter in diameter were etched into the stone. They were bordered in complex, almost Celtic looking knots, and on the inward-facing side, small, ornate letters spelled out the name, 'Adam Coyle.'

"Adam!" I called. "This one's got your name on it." I pointed to my feet, then walked to the one directly next to it and saw my own name. "And this one's mine, I guess." Good, that was good. Adam had the highest Intelligence in our group, and I the second highest, after recent increases.

I turned to my team. "We'll make it through this, working together." I reached out and grabbed both China and Jacky by the hand.

Jacky squeezed back. "This isn't my specialty. Gimme a monster to fight any day, not puzzles and silence."

China took a deep breath and stood as tall as possible with her small body. "I won't die here today. I've still got to find Chanelle."

"None of us are alone." I squeezed their hands and met the eyes of both Adam and Sam, trying to instill confidence in my words. "Everyone!" I called out loudly, "Find the circle with your name on it, and get inside. Before the time runs out."

Slowly, the whole group of Players in that Trial obeyed. As soon as the last person stepped into their circle, the timer abruptly disappeared, and clear bars shot up around each of us.

I reached out and touched one, and found it warm and buzzing, but unmovable. There wasn't enough room between the bars to squeeze through. Which meant we were trapped.

Angry calls rang out at me from around the ring, as if I was responsible for this.

Adam tried to shake and rattle his bars in the cage next to mind, to no avail. He caught me watching and took a deep breath, pushing his hair out of his face. "I don't know what's going on. But this worries me."

I smiled. "That's okay. Neither do I. But we'll figure it out."

He cracked a small smile, and then another timer popped up in front of our faces, this time for thirty minutes.

The ground of my circle moved strangely, causing me to stumble. Then out of the opening it had formed, a small black cube rose up and sat at my feet. I bent to touch it tentatively, and when nothing happened, picked it up.

It was shiny and smooth, except for an infinity symbol on one side, and hairline cracks dividing the surface with curves and lines. I tilted the box back and forth and ran my finger over the surface, trying to see the cracks more clearly. They seemed to be geometrically shaped, not the random lighting branches of true cracks.

"It's a puzzle box, Adam," I said, as soon as the thought formed in my mind.

I tried to take a step to turn and face him, and I realized the floor had softened beneath my feet. I took a shuddering breath, and saw pretty ink-black hands curled around the bottom of my boots. The floor was grabbing me, and as I watched, the fingers wriggled, as if pushing out of the restricting stone, moving a bit further up my shoe.

"Adam!" I choked out.

He looked at me, and then followed my eyes down. "Oh, no." Though I couldn't tell exactly what was coming out of the ground underneath him, he swallowed. "A puzzle box," he repeated, focusing on my previous words. "Which means, logically, we have to solve it before the time runs out. I used to love these things as a kid," he said bitterly. "I had a Rubik's cube that I would solve over and over again."

"Will the skill translate?"

He laughed. "Damn. I hope so."

"The infinity symbol on the front, I'm thinking that might be the shape of the finished puzzle."

"Sounds good to me." After a few minutes of intense thought that drove me crazy waiting, he wriggled one of the corners. It spun away from the rest of the box, swiveling along with his fingers. Then, he started to twist in earnest.

I watched his intense concentration for a few moments and then twisted the same corner of my own box, hurrying to catch up with his movements. Staring at his hands, I mimicked him frenetically, always a few moves behind, until a few minutes later he stopped.

"I've got it," he said. In his hands was a twisting infinity sign, kind of like a double helix.

Just as I was about to make the last twist on my own puzzle, screaming erupted on the other side of the ring.

The boy opposite from Adam threw himself forward. The bars around his circle were gone, but that didn't matter, because the stone of his cage had risen up fully, and huge stone spiders and snakes rushed over him, holding him down and covering him, biting again and again.

The guy's screams gurgled, and finally fell silent. The stone forms seemed to sense his death, and melted back into the ground, the empty circle looking perversely innocent. Discarded at his side, his uncompleted puzzle had turned from black to red.

The silence permeated everything as we all looked at his silent form.

When I tore my eyes away to look back to Adam, I saw his bars were gone, too. But the floor of his circle had stopped attacking and solidified, whatever had been coming out of it suppressed.

He stared down at the looping double helix, expressionless.

"Adam," I said, my voice low.

He looked at me, his eyes wide. "I just killed him." He blinked. "I escaped the cage, and he was devoured by it."

I shook my head. "That wasn't your fault. That was a coincidence. And…even if it wasn't, you couldn't have known."

He ran his hand through his hair roughly, and then seemed to gather himself together. "Yeah. I didn't know. But everyone else does, now."

I bit my lip. "This is going to get bad." I was now doubly grateful that our whole team was on the same side of the circle. But maybe that wasn't coincidental. "We're a team, after all. Wouldn't do to have us killing each other," I murmured without thinking.

Adam nodded. "Yeah," he said, but was obviously distracted, looking across the circle.

I followed his gaze, and saw the girl directly across from me. The boy's body lay still on the ground in front of her. She frantically twisted her box's pieces around, glancing up at me every now and then.

Adam took an experimental step out of his circle. When nothing happened, he walked over to the bars surrounding me and wrapped his hands around them. "She's going to kill you, if you don't fix that puzzle before she does." His eyes were intent on mine, the dark brown irises looking harder than I had ever seen them. "You have to solve it, Eve. And you need to hurry."

I clenched the misshapen shape in my hand. "But…I'll kill her," I protested.

He reached through the bars, grabbing me by the wrist. "She's trying to kill you, right now, as we speak."

I looked at her.

She desperately twisted and turned the pieces. Around her feet, the stone had risen to form a low-hanging, bubbly cloud of blackness.

"She's afraid, Adam."

He closed his eyes as if in pain, then clasped my hand between both of his. "We're all afraid."

The ground under my feet shifted again, and I would have lost my balance except for his steadying grip on my hand. I looked down, and saw that faces were starting to pop out of the surface, along with the hands now crawling further up my leg. They looked familiar, too familiar, and then I realized they wore my own features, staring up at me with eyes of stone.

I started to tremble, and squeezed one of Adam's hands desperately hard with my own. The sight of myself in that black abyss moved something sick in the pit of my stomach, and raised the hair on the back of my neck. "It's like a nightmare," I whispered, my voice too shaky to speak properly. The light dimmed further with every passing moment, and the thought of being in the dark as the stone swallowed me made me want to slam myself against the bars until either they broke, or I did.

"It's our personal nightmare," he whispered back to me. "Each of these is different. Spiders and snakes for that guy, something else for me, and something else for you. Eve, if you don't win here, you're going to lose either way. She doesn't have to solve the puzzle for you to die. What do you think happens when the timer runs out?"

He looked down at the floor of my cage pointedly. "Do you want to be killed by them?"

I shuddered visibly, unable to stop myself.

The bodies pulled themselves out of the ground, inch by inch. Each face was my own, the arms and hands my own, but the *eyes*…

I slipped my hand out of his and squeezed the puzzle. My fingers shook, but I kept a good grip because I was too afraid to drop it to the ground.

Adam let out a deep, relieved breath. "Thank you. We need you to live, as much as I hate to admit it. With you gone, the team would dissolve."

I chuckled without humor. "I'm doing this for selfish reasons, believe me. And what's this, you, protecting the team? I'm surprised. I thought you'd resent being coerced into joining it."

"I see the value in what you're trying to create. And besides, don't you know by now that I don't do anything I don't want to do? I could have said no, when you asked."

I paused before the last twist, staring at the almost completed puzzle.

Then someone else solved theirs. Not the girl across from me. A guy. Across from him a woman, one of the very few adult Players I'd seen, tried to run, ripping out of the animated stone holding her. She got a few feet before the completely freed stone form knocked her down.

It was a giant muscular man, with a curly beard and hands like clubs. He straddled her, and hit her again and again until blood splattered outward with every blow. Until her face was unrecognizable, caved in.

I couldn't look away, couldn't move, throughout the whole thing. I wanted to, oh, I wanted to, but my body wouldn't listen, and so I watched.

The meaty, thunking…*squelching* went on and on, and the scent of blood and raw meat filled my nostrils.

She must have finally died, because the stone man melted away and flowed back into the circle. The only evidence he'd ever existed was the corpse lying in a puddle of blood in the middle of the ring of Players.

My own stone tormentors were grabbing at my hips by then, and I could swear they moved faster as they freed themselves further from the floor. My hands were slippery with sweat, despite how very, very cold I was.

So I breathed in through my nose and out through my mouth, ignoring the smell of her. I forced myself to calm down and focus, to ignore the terror and unyielding hands on my body. I closed my eyes and focused on the breath in my lungs, the sound of blood rushing through my ears with every heartbeat, and the shape in my hands.

I opened my eyes and twisted the last piece into place, staring at the girl. The *snick* of that piece sliding together with the others sounded like thunder in my ears. That last move, perfect and horrible. The puzzle was without any edges or discernable cracks, smooth and unending.

In her hands, I saw a shape almost exactly like my own. But the timer disappeared. The clear, warm bars were gone from in front of me, and I looked down to watch as the faces of my destruction melted and formed back into the floor, staring back at me as they sank. The stone beneath my feet was once again solid, harmless.

The girl's screams were loud, sobbing. She pleaded with no one, with everything, to save her, to spare her. The black cloud rose around her body, a swirling, amorphous mass. As each particle of stone touched her, it sizzled into her skin, and kept sizzling till it had eaten its way through.

Her cheeks shrunk in, and then her face collapsed as the bones melted away, her eyeballs sinking down and inwards without the support of her cheekbones.

I watched as her legs crumpled under her and she sank to the ground like a deflated balloon. Please, please, let it be over. Let it be done already.

But she didn't die. She just kept screaming, and screaming, and screaming.

And then she finally stopped, her body little more than a pile of burn-riddled skin wrapped around an oozing sludge. Her hand still held the misshapen, now red puzzle. Silence reigned.

My stomach revolted, bile rising up in my mouth. I retched onto the ground. "Oh, god…" I could not keep thinking about it. Could. Not. What was important right now was…the team.

Adam and I were okay, but what about China, Jacky, and Sam?

I stood and spit, then wiped my mouth against my sleeve. No time to be squeamish now.

Adam already stood by China's cage, resting his hands on her shoulders as he guided her through each twist and turn.

Two others solved their puzzles. One of their opponents screamed and cursed, spewing vitriol across the circle as some large creature I didn't look at long enough to identify devoured him.

But what interested me was the other girl who'd solved her puzzle, and threw away the twisting infinity symbol in horror. It flew through the air and landed, and then its color seeped from black to red, as if wounded.

The girl shrieked as the floor of her cage reanimated like the rush of a tidal wave. Huge twisting vines…no, snakes, shot out and caught her, slithering around and around, and then squeezing until bones crunched and blood seeped out from between their coils. Her opponent had died, too, not spared by the death of the winner.

Damn. Note to self. Do not throw your completed puzzle away. I stood beside Jacky's cage and reached for her. "Okay, what have you got?"

She ground her teeth together audibly, then forced out, "Nothing." She took deep breath. "I've been trying and trying, but I'm just making random moves. I dunno how to do this." Her voice broke on the last bit, and I could literally hear the creak of her knuckles as she clenched her free hand around nothing.

Stone men had formed from the ground, their reaching hands pressing lewdly into the flesh of her thighs and hips.

I grabbed her fisted hand between both of mine, passing warmth into her clammy digits. "You're going to be okay. We'll figure it out." Once again, I was reminded of the empty reassurance I'd given the boy. I would not let these words be empty. "Look at me, Jacky," I said. I had to repeat it before her terrified brown eyes met my own. I spoke clearly and slowly, putting weight into my words. "I won't let anything happen to you. I'm here now, and you're going to be okay. Believe in me."

She looked into my eyes for several long moments, and then nodded. Her body sagged as she released some of the iron tension she'd been clenching in her muscles. "You know how to solve the puzzle?"

"No, not quite yet." I could probably solve the puzzle from scratch again, but Jacky had changed the positioning of its pieces who knows how many times, so I couldn't go on memory alone. I needed to fully understand the puzzle. I was halfway to the answer from walking through the solution with Adam as guide, but not close enough to save Jacky. "But I'll figure it out."

I slung off the pack I'd prepared for this Trial, the contents of which were mostly useless, as we hadn't ended up fighting as I predicted. But I'd also stashed something extremely valuable in it, on the chance that I might need it. And I needed it now. I brought out a small pouch, and poured three unused Seeds into my palm.

Though I'd never tried it, I believed I'd be able to use them, even with a Trial in progress. If not, we were screwed. Adam was helping China, and after that would move on to Sam, who had seemingly frozen in fear and not made a single move with his puzzle box. By that time, the ever-ticking timer would have reached zero. Saving Jacky was up to me.

I held the first Seed up to my neck. "I wish I was more intelligent," I said, and it injected itself into me in that all-too-familiar way. I held the second Seed up to my neck, but paused before repeating myself, as something Vaughn had said played through my head again. The Seeds were wish-fulfillers. I debated with myself for a moment. Was it really the time to be experimenting? But if my hunch was right, it could mean the difference between Jacky's life or death. "I wish I could better visualize three-dimensional movement." It injected itself into me, recognizing my words for a wish, even if it wasn't for one of the thirteen Attributes. And for the third Seed, "I wish I had better pattern recognition and could make better projections based on said patterns." Splitting the last Seed between two wishes was an even riskier move, but I was all in on the high-stakes bet.

I stared at the puzzle in Jacky's hands and focused everything I had on it, waiting for the tingle in my brain to come and pass. I breathed slow and deep, imagining the possible moves and their countless different outcomes. I focused everything I had on it, and for a few seconds, I thought I understood.

I placed my hands over hers and started to guide her soundlessly in rapid-fire movements of the puzzle. I made a few mistakes, but realized in time to correct them without much time lost. I knew, finally, that the next turn would be the last. I paused for a moment, and then pushed against her fingers for the last time.

The bars surrounding her disappeared and I fell forward, wrapping my arms around her. I turned her so her back was toward the center and hugged her to my chest with my hands over her ears. She wouldn't see the price of her continued life, and maybe the screams would be muffled, too.

I watched for her, as Jacky's former opponent bucked in what was either defiance or maddening pain, as stone chains attached to his arms and legs literally ripped him apart. Drawn and quartered.

When it was done, I released Jacky and gripped her shoulders.

Her eyes let out a steady stream of tears, though she made no sound.

"You did well. It's over now," I said. I led her to stand together with China, who was also free, and turned to Sam.

Adam threw up his hands and turned away from Sam's cage, stomping back to us with a face twisted in anger and disgust. Our eyes met as he passed, and he shook his head once, a silent explanation of his anger.

I moved to kneel beside Sam, pressing against the buzzing bars.

Tiny hands were dragging him down into the soft stone, but instead of becoming frantic to solve his puzzle, he was holding his head in his hands as if trying to block out the world, hyperventilating.

"Sam. What's wrong?"

He raised his head, looking bleak and distant, as if he'd already lost. "I'm afraid. I'm so afraid. But if I give in, that person is going to die. I can't. But, it's too late for me now, already." He nodded as if consoling himself, but his face pinched together at the words and he panted faster. "There's not enough time left. It's too late already. I already made it. But I'm scared."

I reached through the bars and took his hand, as Adam had

done me and I'd done Jacky. I knew the comfort touch brought, and with that comfort, the increased willingness to listen to whatever the comforter said. To let them guide you. "Sam, I'm here."

He looked at me uncomprehendingly.

I squeezed his hand and rubbed it chafingly, trying to bring some heat back into it. "I'm here, and we're all here with you. I'm going to help you, if you let me. We need you, Sam. You're part of our team." It seemed he had given up any hope for himself. So maybe, I could push him to have hope for the good of someone beside himself.

"I can't. And it's too late anyway," he repeated, as if those were the only words in his head.

"That person? The one who you're protecting? He's trying to kill you. Right now, Sam, he is trying to kill you. And the only reason is so he can live. You know that's wrong. It's why you're refusing to try and win against him. Because you know it's wrong to sacrifice someone else so that you can live."

He relaxed. "Yes. You understand. I can't do that again."

"You can."

He stiffened again immediately, and drew back from me.

"You can, because we need you to. You can't do it to save yourself, but you can do it for me. For us." I squeezed his hand.

He took a sobbing, heaving breath. "Why are you doing this to me?" he pleaded. "Why are you making it okay for me to do what I know I shouldn't? I can't kill that guy. It's cowardly and wrong." His voice was firmer, but he hadn't taken his hand away from mine.

I continued rubbing. "It's wrong to kill someone else in cold blood. But this isn't your fault. You didn't ask to be a Player. The Game is forcing you to act in self-defense, just like it's forced the rest of us."

He shook his head, denying me, and closed his eyes.

Slight change of tactics, then? "It's also wrong for you to stand back and do nothing when someone needs you, Sam."

His eyes opened, blood shot and blue, and locked on my own. "What?"

"This isn't just about you anymore. You're not playing this Game by yourself. You are part of my team. A team of four others who are depending on you, and you…you're trying to take the easy way out."

"The easy way out?" his voice rose in indignation. "I'm trying to do the right thing!"

"No. The right thing to do is to live, to listen to me now. I'm right, Sam, and you know it. The team needs you, which means I need you to listen to me, and do what I say. The team is my responsibility, but as a member of my team, it's your job to follow me." Not my most subtle work, but I didn't have much time to convince him.

Luckily, he was terrified, and just selfish enough to hand over his responsibility, along with the power to command him. He focused on me as if I were his last lifeline. As if I were a piece of driftwood in a turbulent sea storm.

I nodded, giving him silent permission. "He is not pleading to be saved. He is not begging for mercy." I pointed to the boy across from Sam and spoke low and calm, trying to give my voice import. "He is trying to kill you, and it is not wrong for you to defend yourself. You will stop him from hurting the team."

He hesitated, and then nodded. "But it's impossible, Eve. There's no way. It really is too late." His face crumpled in the despair that comes from having hope for a split second, only to have it ripped away. "There's only thirty seconds left."

All around us, people in their cages were panicking, dropping their unsolved boxes, fighting with the liquid stone crawling up their bodies, and clawing desperately at the bars. But the boy across from Sam was still controlled, almost finished with his puzzle. He would make it in time. Shame he wouldn't live to see the benefits of his efforts.

I dropped Sam's hand and put my own on his shoulder. "There's hope, if you'll do as I say. Listen."

He nodded, and I gave him my orders, spewing them out quickly as the last seconds counted down.

His opponent completed his puzzle.

As soon as the bars disappeared, Sam ripped away from the tiny stone hands and threw himself forward into the middle of the circle, sprinting toward the other boy, who was also free of his bars. Childlike stone bodies followed Sam with unnatural speed, pumping their little legs in a blur.

I followed at a slower pace, ready to lend a hand if needed.

The timer reached zero, and as the arena erupted into a death circus around us, Sam smashed into the other boy. He wrapped his hands around the guy's throat and squeezed.

I expected the boy to fight back, but instead he jerked as if in surprise, and then threw himself backward and tripped.

Sam stalked forward calmly. When the downed guy tried to kick out, Sam grabbed his leg.

The boy started to convulse, shaking the leg free from Sam's grip.

So Sam just moved forward again and straddled the boy. He pressed his palms down hard and flat on the guy's stomach, where the shirt had ridden up and the pale skin lay exposed.

The stone children reached Sam and crawled onto his body, weighing him down and dragging at him, but he ignored them as if they didn't exist.

Sam's opponent shook and screamed, convulsing as if to wiggle free. His skin turned dark and started to split open in a million tiny spots as bloody crystals grew from beneath it, bursting outward like a time lapse video of ice crystals forming on the surface of a lake.

Sam kept pressing and pressing, shaking with effort. A drop of sweat fell off of his nose and dripped onto the boy, mixing with the bloody crystals beneath his hands.

Finally, the guy was still.

Sam grabbed the completed black puzzle from the dead hand and hugged it to his own chest. The granite boys pulling at him paused for a moment, seeming confused, and then melted away.

I let out a sigh of relief that my guess of the winning conditions had been correct. We needed to be in possession of a winning—black—puzzle. Solving it wasn't enough it we didn't keep it. Otherwise the girl who'd thrown hers away wouldn't have died. And the only reason to release the cages of both the winner and the loser was to give the loser a chance to turn the tables.

Sam sat atop the body, staring down at his handiwork.

I moved to him and placed a hand on his shoulder. "Sam."

He looked up at me, startled. His bloodshot eyes were blank and wide in the growing darkness, but then they seemed to focus on me, and his face twisted in sick anger. "You."

I frowned. What was wrong with him? "It's over now. Are you okay?"

"Don't touch me." He yanked his arm back and stood up, tripping on the hardened corpse as he turned toward the rest of the group.

I watched in bemusement as he walked away, then knelt to the body of the boy. His eyes were still open, and I closed them with my fingertips. He was warm, still, and I realized I'd expected him to be frozen. His stomach had two patches of normal skin, in the outline of hands, like a child had traced Sam's hand on the boy's skin. Around the outlines, blood crystals sprung up and outward, like magnetized metal shavings drawn towards a lodestone.

I touched them with the tip of my finger, and found them rigidly sharp, and still radiating the warmth from inside the dead body. I remembered what Sam had told me. He was the harbinger of death.

Sam, the healer.

## Chapter 19

And what constitutes evil, real evil, is the taking of a single human life. Whether a man would die tomorrow or the day after or eventually…it doesn't matter. Because if God does not exist, then life… every second of it…Is all we have.

— Anne Rice

I THOUGHT the Trial would end, but we waited for minutes on end, and nothing happened. The cube stayed still and gave no message. No instructions came to us, no timers appeared, and we began to grow worried in a whole new way. What if we hadn't completed the Trial properly, and weren't allowed to return to our lives?

Then I felt ripples through the soles of my shoes. The black stone turned white in the center of the Trial board, then rippled outward, changing color as it went.

"Get ready, everyone!" I called out, not taking my eyes off of the ground as I tucked my completed puzzle safely into a large pocket in my pants. When the ground beneath us had turned all white, threads burst upward from the rippling stone, thick and so fast I had no time to react.

They surrounded me in sheets so thick I couldn't see anyone else. I screamed for my teammates, but no one called back in response.

Within moments, thick walls of glowing strings enclosed me, twisting and winding together to create a large room, shaped like a smooshed ball. Helixes, columns, and bridges made of the strands filled the inside haphazardly, stretching from wall to wall and formation to formation.

I took a step around a random column, and the floor vibrated outward in a ripple of light and sound. I froze, not because of the unexpected reaction of the strings, but because of the huge woman crawling out of the floor.

She rose and detached herself from the string, standing almost twice my height, maybe twelve feet tall. Her body was made of black stone, and full of holes and strange facets. Tears flowed constantly down lines carved down the middle of each of her cheeks, as if eroded by hundreds of years of crying. She wore a crown upon her head, and had a beautiful, regal face.

She looked around, and then seemed to see and focus on me. "You. You are the supposed descendant?"

"Are you the Moderator?"

She barked a laugh. "I am no such thing, tiny one. In your language, you would call me the Oracle."

"My language? What language do you normally speak? What does an oracle do in the Game?"

She slashed her hand through the air to cut me off, and the sound it made was sharp and commanding. "I will answer no more questions. It is not the time for it. I am here to test you."

She moved to the side and plunged her hands into what looked like a birdbath standing on a musical string pedestal. Another stood across from it a few yards away. If there had been birds, I would have no doubt of their function. But there were no birds, and somehow I knew the pedestal's purpose was not so innocent. Her tears dripped down into the water like little diamonds. She moved her fingers within the water, and some of the strings connected to the birdbath spontaneously lit up and rang out with sound, causing a ripple effect that ran outwards, transferring to connected strings until it reached me and stopped, falling dim and silent.

A half-formed image of the Oracle split away from her. The shadow's movements caught the air, and its body created a beautiful haunting melody, a thousand different wind instruments harmonizing with each other. The sound of its movements mimicked the sound she'd played through the water. Though it was as large as her, and deliberately ponderous, a few gargantuan steps brought it in front of me. It slammed the back of its forearm into my chest, sending me flying backward.

I slammed into the threaded ground and slid, throwing out light and discordant sound with the friction. I saw the shadow disappear out of my peripheral vision, but she was already playing a new tune and creating a string-path with the birdbath.

My lungs shrieked in silent pain, begging for the breath that had been crushed from me. I cradled my torso with an arm, so, *so* grateful I wore the banded armor vest beneath my clothes. It had spread some of the impact, which perhaps was the difference between me rising again or being incapacitated by that single blow.

The new shadow was already on me then, and I didn't have time to lie around. I slipped by it, running back toward her original body. I couldn't breathe, and every movement of my arms shot pain through my chest.

Something caught me in the back and I smashed into the floor and slid once again, this time skinning my jaw and ripping my clothes.

The Oracle let out her barking laugh again, somehow still beautiful even in its sharpness, and I knew she had anticipated my movement. No other way would have allowed the huge, somewhat lumbering shadow to hit me.

This time, I stood up faster, and ran toward her before she could sic her after-image on me again.

The room was already filled with music, but I was quick enough, and lead with a low kick to her ankle, and then a hard sideswipe to the side of her knee.

Her leg buckled, but she didn't go down, and with a flick of her fingers, an ephemeral copy shot from her and blew me backward with a lunge and two palms smashing into my chest.

My body caught on a twisting double helix and bounced to the floor, facedown. This time I didn't get back up right away. I couldn't. I hadn't gotten a good breath since the first hit, and stars sprinkled around in the darkness creeping through my vision.

But I had to move, I had to, or the next one would kill me. I crawled to my hands and knees and scuttled behind the helix, gripping it to hold myself off the ground.

She was unfazed by my little attack. Tears still streamed down her face into the water and music poured out of the strings in ripples, moving my way. They were more complex that time, and two different paths played intertwining melodies, coming from either side of me.

I regained some space in my lungs, but two copies split from her, moving toward me in a pincer formation.

I needed to stop her from making more of them, so we could fight one on one. I needed to get her away from the pedestal. I shot forward between the two copies, but they were already moving to intercept me. I skidded to a stop and backpedaled furiously, but one had only been feinting my interception, and had slipped around behind me faster than I could change my direction.

I was falling backward towards its waiting fists. I slipped out my claws, wondering why I hadn't done so sooner, and in the space between one heartbeat and the next, plunged a hand into the strings of the floor, while pushing myself sideways with a foot.

My claws gave me the purchase I needed to twist my backward fall into crouching on my hands and knees. I tried to throw myself sideways between the two shadows, but a third one already waited for me to move toward it.

It grabbed me by the arm as I tried in vain to backpedal once again. With a twist, it threw me across the room like a stuffed doll.

My shoulder popped and crunched as the arm twisted, and I couldn't help my scream of agony, even though in truth my scream came from the horror of realizing I'd just been broken like a twig. The pain hadn't hit yet. No, it didn't hit till I smashed into the curve of the ceiling, bounced from it to a branching column, and smacked into the floor like a tenderized steak. The pain hit then, bursting outward from no specific point and flaring bright.

My eyes rolled back in my head, and I lost track of myself for a moment. When I found myself again, I allowed pure terror to take over. It overwhelmed the pain and stood me up, looked for the Oracle and her shadows through the blood in my eyes, and hobbled away from her to give me distance from my attacker, and maybe time to regroup.

The shadows had once again disappeared, but she was still playing more intertwining melodies, except with even more complex music.

I had no time, and no power to win against her. I took a quick inventory of my body. A definitely dislocated shoulder, possibly broken and screaming in pain from the weight of my pack's strap over it. Twisted knee. Fractured ribs, I was pretty sure. Cut on the head bleeding a lot, maybe a concussion. And lots of other small hurts, too many to count. All in all, the worst shape I'd been in yet.

I might die there. The thought slipped into my mind to feed my terror. No, no, no. I wouldn't die. Would not. Would. Not. I just needed to figure out how to beat her. She seemed to literally anticipate my every move, but that didn't mean I couldn't win. There had to be a way.

"Ah," I puffed. The Oracle anticipated my movements? "Stupid, stupid," I mouthed venomously at myself. By name alone, I should have realized the clue she gave me toward her power. I'd been treating this like the other Trials I'd been in. But this one was based on the mental faculties, not my ability to kill monsters. Why had I forgotten that?

But even now that I understood, how could I beat her if she could predict the future? Already the strings around me played in complex interweaving patterns, and soon the shadows would echo through the music. I wouldn't make it through the round.

An arc close to me lit up with a final smash of light and sound, and instinctively I thrust my good arm toward it. I touched my blood-covered fingers to the strands before the sound faded away, and in front of my eyes I saw an ephemeral image of my body dodging one of the Oracle's shadows, only to be hit by a hammer-fist from another. The ragged-looking girl's neck broke downward with a grinding crunch, and her skull caved inward from the impact.

The sound faded away, and with it, the glimpse into my future. "Hell, no." I wouldn't let that happen.

The shadows came at me, five strong. I dodged them as best I could with my body not working at full capacity. Each movement had my blood flowing faster and my focus deepening. No more panic, only a goal I would achieve, or literally die trying.

I felt Deja-vu in my next twisting dodge and knew my death swung down from above. But then I slipped, tilting backward as my legs shot out from underneath me.

My back smashed hard into the ground, but I received no broken neck or collapsed skull. I bucked and arched, bringing my feet right back under me, and slipped through the already-fading shadow's legs. I headed straight for the other birdbath, ignoring the Oracle, and her bell-tone laugh of surprise.

I reached it before her shadows could stop me, and plunged both my good hand and the one hanging limply from my ruined shoulder into the water. Blood mixed with the crystal-clear liquid in silky tendrils, and then my mind exploded like a crackling firework.

I understood how the cocoon-room worked, what each string

signified, and exactly how to play them to get the melodies I needed. Even so, my brain wasn't equipped to hold all the information, and pieces of the puzzle slipped into and out of focus as it strained to hold everything.

I breathed deep and focused on the blood in my veins, and then outward to the blood swirling in the water, and then the water itself. The focus helped, and I twitched my fingers, sending out an experimental thread of sound and tumbling light to meet one of the melodies she'd sent my way.

I knew what would happen even before the shadow actually followed my instructions, so I focused my energy on stopping the Oracle's other shadows from coming to remove me from my place of power and kill me.

In the water I saw all the moves she could have made, and all the ways I could respond and counterattack. At first, I played out only the strands of my future that would stop her from killing me. My waves met hers in just the right way to cancel out both sides, silence resounding where they met. But as I focused harder my brain bent with more dexterity to the task, and I began to send out preemptive strikes of my own.

We matched each other through a myriad of possible futures for a long time, long enough that I began to lose concentration. Each time I slipped up, I stopped her from killing me later and later. Soon I would be too late, and I would die.

I started to tremble with the effort of sustaining so many different fights, even if I was only thinking through them while standing still. I couldn't go on for much longer and she showed no signs of wearying. I needed a way to stop her from attacking.

The next strand she sent toward me was a simple, lilting thing.

I split a larger portion of energy than I could truly spare away from my other futures and played one strand of my own in an exact match. The sounds and lights playing on that thread synced to each other so exactly that they meshed, and as she tried to finish it, I pushed in another direction, continuing the music in an unexpected tumble, then let it fall into a soft silence.

She let out another laugh. "That's it, tiny one. Show me your worth."

I'd let the other futures slip too far from my control, so I pushed extra hard against them for a moment to buy myself some time. She pushed back, but not overwhelmingly, and strand by strand, piece by piece, I matched her melodies, taking them over and changing their course.

Finally, I wrested them from her control even as she began to play them, laying each violent attempt to rest. From there, it wasn't so difficult to play her as she was at that very moment, and draw her hands from the water in gentle contentment. I played docility into her as hard as I could, straining to my breaking point. The last notes were little more than a squeak.

I slumped over the water, shuddering and gasping. If there was more, I could not fight it. I had pushed for life with everything I owned, and nothing remained. Even as I thought that, I defied my own exhaustion, already gathering strength to match her next attack.

But she didn't attack. Her strange, stone mouth stretched in a soft smile, and the lines down her cheeks no longer flowed with tears. She walked to the middle of the room and knelt on one knee, bowing her crowned head to me. She raised her head, and her chest opened strangely, folding in on itself, creating a twisting slot. She was still, then, her eyes focused unwaveringly on me.

Nice. Why hadn't I gone straight for the second birdbath in the beginning? But I knew it wouldn't have worked in the beginning, because there had been no blood to mix with the water. It was something I understood in the way you remember understanding a complicated concept in a dream, and it slipped from me as I withdrew my hands from the small pool and lost its connection to understanding.

I shuffled to her, keeping a wary eye out for any sudden movements. "What now?" I wondered aloud.

She flicked her eyes downward, leading my own to the hole in her chest.

I pulled the puzzle from my pocket, placed it at the opening in her chest, and pushed. It slid in, but met resistance, so I twisted slightly, and it slid further, continuing until the last bit lay flush with the surface of her body.

With a small click, her chest folded inward once again, opening up to a large cavity about a foot wide. Inside were three piles of what looked to be silver loops. Small, medium, and large.

She whispered to me with a voice made from the splashing of spring water and wind across the tops of glass bottles. "You are worthy. These are my three gifts to you, that they may guide your path. May you walk through the midst of tribulation, and not waver from the way."

I frowned, said, "Umm, thank you… I guess." and reached into the space within her chest. I pulled out the smallest set of loops first. Each was bent strangely, and connected to the others in a chain. I placed the small and medium pile in my pockets, and the large loop in my pack of crushed and broken supplies, as it was too big to fit anywhere else.

I felt the Boneshaker begin to hammer into me without warning, and stared into her sad stone eyes as it carried me away.

# Chapter 20

People often believed they were safer in the light, thinking monsters only came out at night.

— C.J. Roberts

I CRUMPLED to the floor of the base, surrounded by my team, and ignored the level up window that appeared.

"You're alive!" China screamed, smashing into me and wrapping her arms around me. "Oh, we thought maybe you were dead, but you're alive."

She squeezed, and I let out a gurgling scream as my shoulder moved under the pressure.

Jacky grabbed China by the forearms and yanked her arms open and away from me. "She's hurt," she snapped. "Sam, come now. Fix her." Her finger pointed at me imperiously.

Sam sat beside me, stony faced, and placed his hands on my shoulder.

"I'm so sorry, Eve. I shouldn't have hugged you. I was just so excited," China whispered.

Blaine saw me and went pale. "Oh, my god. What happened?"

I laughed. "Got in a bit of a tussle. No big deal. Tell me what happened to you guys."

Jacky crouched in front of me and grabbed the hand of my uninjured arm. "The spider egg thing swallowed you up, and you were inside for a long time. We tried to cut through it and get to you, but nothing worked. Then the cube said congratulations on surviving, but you were still inside. We all pressed the button to return from the Trial, but nothing happened. Honestly, we were starting to panic a little, but then all of a sudden the song started and we were back here, and you were with us."

"Right before that, the cube popped up with one last message," Adam said. "No one else was paying attention."

"What—" I broke off and bit my tongue to stifle a scream as Sam did something with my shoulder that caused it to pop and grind. I went lightheaded for a moment, and had to take several deep breaths before I could think again. "Ouch. What did it say?"

"Eve Redding has been found worthy, and granted the blessing of the Oracle," Adam said. "It seems similar to the message when someone gets a new Skill, but worded differently."

"Interesting."

"What happened in there, Eve?" he said.

"I met...something. A huge, huge woman made of stone crawled out of the ground. She called herself the Oracle, and said she was there to test me. She could see everything I was going to do, and I couldn't win. But then I figured out how to play the same game as her, and beat her. She said I'd proven myself worthy and gave me these little silver chains. Then the Boneshaker started playing, and I was back here." What an extremely simplified version of events. It felt like everything in my life was spinning around in a tornado of pain and fear and the illusion of strength I'd tried to wrap around myself. I needed to grab hold of things before I could talk about what had just happened in more depth.

I squeezed Jacky's hand. "But I'm fine. How about you guys. Are *you* okay?" I let my voice soften on the last sentence, speaking directly to her.

"Yeah, because you saved me. Thank you. Words don't even cut it." She, squeezed my hand painfully, swallowed, and shook her head, blinking suddenly shiny eyes.

I nodded my understanding and smiled. "Good. And you, Sam? Are you all right?"

His face was pale from the injuries and pain he'd been absorbing from me, but his cheeks flushed at that. "I killed someone today. I took a life, with my bare hands, while you —*because* of you. Do you *think* I'm okay?"

Adam stepped forward and yanked on his arm, pulling Sam away from me. "She saved you, you idiot. She kept you alive when you were too stupid to stand up and save yourself. If not for her, you'd be dead."

Sam stood and yanked his arm away, still staring at me. "You didn't save me. You made me betray myself. You're a murderer. *I'm* a murderer." His voice broke on the last bit, and he choked off any more words.

I stood up to match him, feeling the sharp pain of my heart breaking for him. "No. I helped you choose to live. NIX made murderers of us all tonight. There was no other choice for us. Kill or be killed. If I'd let any of you die when I knew I could stop it, would I be any less a murderer, then? This is...horrible beyond words. I know it. But we can't blame ourselves. You can't blame yourself. If not for this Game, tonight would never have happened. We are monsters of circumstance, not of choice."

I knew the words weren't enough. Nothing external could absolve someone from guilt if they couldn't forgive themselves. And in truth, I called myself a murderer, too, just not aloud. "There's nothing we can do about this except get out of this Game. What happens if the next time, it wants us to turn on one another?" I looked at my team. "It won't ever stop as long as we're forced into the Trials, unless we die, or find a way to escape. So we've got to find a way, because I won't let any of you die."

I turned to Blaine, who'd watched the exchange with wide eyes from behind his glasses. "Please tell me you got something useful from monitoring the transfer."

"W—well, I'll have to examine the data more closely, but I think so…"

Sam clenched his fists and left the room in red-faced silence.

China smiled bravely. "We'll find a way."

I gave her a small smile of gratitude and started to hobble toward the bathroom. Sam had left before getting to my twisted knee, but hell if I was going to call him back and ask for his services now.

Jacky immediately slipped my arm around her neck and half-carried me, despite her smaller size. "What crawled up his butt and died?" She snorted. "And what the hell was that thing he did? Nucking futts, he turned that kid into one of those pretty rock crystal things. What are they called?" She looked to the others for help.

"A geode?" Adam supplied.

"It was a Skill," I cut in. "One he wishes he didn't have, for obvious reasons. Let's leave it to him to talk about, when and if he feels like it."

Jacky pursed her lips. "Just seems like he's been holding back on us. If I had a cool Skill like that—"

I shot her a look, and she clamped her mouth shut, pursing her lips. "Let me know if you need me," she said as she deposited me at the bathroom entrance.

"Thank you." I opened the door and limped inside. The mirror over the sink showed a face covered almost completely in blood from a cut at the edge of my hairline. My clothes were torn and bloody, and my skin was covered in scrapes and string-burn.

I struggled to take off my jacket, and paused in surprise when the door swung open.

Adam stepped through with a chair in one hand and a first aid kit in the other, and set the chair behind me. "Sit down."

I did, gratefully, and reached for the first aid kit.

He pulled it back from my reach. "Nope. You're in no shape to fix yourself up right now. Let me help you, since the self-righteous jackass didn't finish his job. Besides, I brought numbing cream." He held up the tube of numbing antibiotic ointment with a teasing grin.

"Hurry up, then," I said with a grin of my own. I was exhausted and in pain, and I'd take any break I could get.

He unwrapped some steri-pads first, and wiped my bloody face down with them till they came away clean. He did the same to the rest of my cuts and scrapes, squeezed a small bit of salve onto his slender forefinger and carefully applied it to the cuts, then bandaged them with a layer of camouflaging, second-skin patches. They would help me heal without scars and also disguise the events of my evening from my family.

His fingers were gentle, and I relaxed into the chair back and closed my eyes, letting some of the pain flow away. Salve, bandage, repeat, until my little surface cuts were all clean, numb, and hidden.

When he finished, I tried to stand up, but he held me back down. "I'm not done yet." He pulled out a can of numbing spray, pushed up my pant leg, and misted the bruise already forming on my shin from when I'd tried to kick the Oracle. "Feel better?"

"Yes," I sighed.

"You did the right thing today. With Sam, I mean."

"Did I?"

"Yes. We become what we need to, to survive. He doesn't understand that. Someday he will, or he'll die or cause someone else's death because he can't make the hard choice. But you can make those choices. That's what leaders do."

I thought I should put some strength in my spine, thank him, and leave. "Leader? Is that what I am? Because I don't feel like it. I'm flailing just as much as the rest of them," I said instead.

"But you don't show it."

"What am I doing right now, if not showing it?"

"I can handle it. Besides, I know that when the time comes, you'll do what you always do when it counts."

"And what is that?"

"You'll get your way."

We both laughed.

He sprayed the side of my face, noticeably avoiding eye contact. "I'll be the first to tell you when I think you're making the wrong decision. But as a leader, you did the right thing today. I understand that. I understand what you're dealing with. And I know you're not a stone."

What? Was he offering support?

He clamped his mouth shut then, and finished spraying. "Okay, all done. You ready to go?"

"Yeah. Uh, do you think I could get a ride? Home, I mean? I'd rather not go on foot, and paying a transport pod leaves records."

"Of course. Let me bring my bike around. I'll come get you when it's ready."

I nodded silently, and when he was gone, slumped into the chair. I took my link sheath out of my bag and slipped it onto my arm. "What a crappy day," I said into the silence.

—You don't look so good.—
-Bunny-

"I've heard that one before. When do I ever look good, after a Trial?" I worried for a second Bunny must have cameras in the base to be able to see me, but then I realized he was using the ID sheath. He must have been waiting for it to be taken from its protective spot in my pack.

—Are you okay?—
-Bunny-

I took a breath, and then another while my answer built in me. "No, I'm not freaking okay. Tonight, I killed three people! I—" I stopped myself, as I heard the resemblance to Sam's earlier reaction. "Do you know what the Trials are like, Bunny?"

—Basically, yes.—
-Bunny-

"No, not basically. Do you *know*?"

—I'm not an Evaluator. I don't follow my Players to the Trials.—
-Bunny-

"Let me tell you about them, then. I'll try to help you truly understand. NIX takes kids, children, sometimes ones even younger than China. They put them into the Trials, places where nothing but monsters live, with no explanation and no help. Everything within the Trial is designed to either terrify or harm you in some way. Did you know, in my Characteristic Trial, a little boy died in my arms? He must have been younger than twelve. Did you know that, Bunny? Did you?"

—No...I didn't know that.—
-Bunny-

"He was innocent. He did nothing to deserve this. Why would NIX do that to him? What kind of people could hold down a little kid and make him a Player, even knowing what it meant? That he could die in the acclimatization process, and that dying before becoming a Player might actually be the *kinder* option?"

Bunny didn't respond.

"What about what happened tonight, then? We were trapped in cages where the floor rose up in the shape of our nightmares. We had to kill the person across from us to be released, so that we could live. If neither of us was able to kill the other, then both of us would die. What could possibly be a good reason to do that to a group of kids? To *anyone*? Do you seriously believe there's some good purpose behind all of this? That they're doing it because they need to? That's what you told me, but I think you were lying. Bunny, let me tell you what the Trials do. They make us so desperate to survive that we'll do anything for more Seeds. We'll do anything to become less and less human, and further the course of this sick little experiment. We're like little ants in a terrarium to them. You watch us, and you monitor us, and you give us drugs to enhance our performance, and do tests to examine our behavior." My claws dug into the arms of the chair.

"Have you ever killed someone, Bunny?"

I waited a long while for him to respond.

—No, I've never killed anyone. But you're trying to say I *have* killed, through being a part of all this.—
-Bunny-

"You said it. You said it because you know the answer in your heart. You've judged yourself, Bunny. And I think—I think you've been found lacking."

—What am I supposed to do, Eve? I can't just stop being a Moderator. It doesn't work like that. I don't have anything to do with the Trials, I can't stop them and I can't help you through them. The most I can do is give you Quests in between so you can get more Seeds and protect yourself.—
-Bunny-

"You're lying again, Bunny." My voice was soft, but the words were hard, and as forceful as I could make them. "I and my team are going to escape NIX and its Game. You can lie to me, but not to yourself. And that's why you're not going to try and stop us. If you won't help, the least you can do is keep silent, and not get us caught and killed. Because then you *will* have killed someone, no escaping or denying it. And trust me, you don't want to know what it feels like."

I stood and moved stiffly out of the bathroom and to our resident scientist. "So what did you get?"

Blaine looked up from the screen in front of him. "How they are doing it is a bit of a mystery. Well, that is obvious. They are teleporting you like some science fiction film! They must know *exactly* where you are. The sensors picked up the anomaly instantaneously. But the algorithms that know how to keep you clothed, now those must be interesting…"

I'd lifted my hand to my neck. "They must use the GPS to teleport us. So when we short them out, they'll lose connection, right?"

"I would imagine so. Unless they have some other way of tracking your exact location, I do not see how they could possibly continue to do…whatever it is they are doing.

# Chapter 21

This horror will grow mild, this darkness light.
— John Milton

I JERKED from a nightmare into the afternoon sun knifing my bleary eyes. The light through my window cleansed my memory of the dream I'd been having like bleach. Except the dark stains of the nightmare remained, in the way I felt sick to my stomach, and my sheets, damp from sweat. A shiver swept through me, and every inch of my body ached. Every injury seemed to have bloomed into maturity during the night. I grabbed loose clothes that would cover as much skin as possible and snuck into the bathroom without being noticed.

After a long, hot shower, I looked at myself in the mirror. "God. That's going to be hard to hide." I could have easily passed for someone who'd just been in a pod accident. "Or fallen out of a plane with no parachute," I muttered to myself. Sam had healed the serious injury—my shoulder—and no more than that. I debated for a moment whether or not to put one of the Seeds I'd earned into Resilience. I had gained a record six Seeds from the Trial.

Instead, I snuck into my mother's room while she messed around in the kitchen making breakfast for the family, and took her makeup. I didn't know what I was doing, but we had similar pale coloring, and thirty minutes later I'd managed to cover up most of the bruising on my face. More liquid skin camo bandages over the cuts and scrapes, some powder to make them blend in, and I was ready. My face wouldn't stand up to scrutiny, but if I hung my now-dry hair over it and didn't interact with Zed or my mother too much, I might be able to slip by.

I passed by my brother on the way around the table, trying not to walk too stiffly.

My mom bustled around the kitchen, cooking with the commanding concentration of a conductor at a symphony.

"Whoa, Eve," Zed said.

I gritted my teeth as I wondered what had given me away.

"Did you get taller than me again?" He tilted his head and looked me up and down with a frown.

As children, we'd traded places for the title of "tallest" for years. It had been a bit of friendly sibling rivalry when we were younger, and in recent years, a title I gladly conceded to him. I had a model's height, if not one's thinness, but any taller and it would start to stand out as strange. My mother said our father had been huge, head and shoulders above other men. That was all well and good for Zed, but as a girl, I didn't *want* to be head and shoulders above other men. But, better that question than the one I'd been expecting. "No, I'm the same size. It's just that you're sitting down."

He considered for a moment, and then shook his head. "No, I don't think so. Here, let's go check." He stood and grabbed my arm to pull me to the wall where my mom had hung the piece of wood she'd measured us against. We'd moved house to house often in my younger years, so instead of a wall, she'd measured us against a flat panel of wood that moved along with us. At least one childhood memory wasn't left behind.

Though I managed not to jerk away from his painful grip on my left arm, which had suffered more than its share of abuse from the Oracle, I couldn't stop my wince of pain in time to avoid notice.

"What's wrong?" He said.

I looked slightly down at him and shook my head. "Oh, it's just a bruise." I smiled convincingly, I hoped. "No big deal. But I guess you were right. I've grown. Again." I nodded toward my old height mark, now at my eye level.

He frowned. "I've got some salve for bruises, if it's bad." Before I could react, he'd leaned over and lifted the end of the baggy sleeve of my shirt, exposing the bruise.

He paused, and then raised the sleeve higher, and higher still when the discoloration didn't end. He stood silent, staring at my completely exposed arm and shoulder.

I knew what he was seeing. It was a mottled mess of blue and purple from the top of my shoulder down, fading out to a strange yellow green around my elbow.

It looked like I'd been attacked by a semi.

His voice was low and forcefully controlled. "Just a bruise?" His brown eyes met my own silver-blue ones with scorn. "How did this happen?" His voice was louder now, and my mother looked over, gasping when she saw my arm.

She walked around the table and brushed her fingers lightly over the colorful area.

I was careful not to react to the pain even her gentle touch caused me. "What happened, Sweetie? I should call the doctor." She paused for a second with her hair shielding her lowered face, and then her voice came out, low. "Did someone hurt you?"

Zed latched onto that idea, his eyes narrowing. "Did someone hit you?"

I drew back from them both, pushing my sleeve down over my arm again and frowning. "God, no! What's with you two, jumping to crazy conclusions, going all over-protective on me?" I shook my head and gave a half smile. "I was riding my friend Adam's bike. He let me borrow it. He told me to be careful, but this bunny ran across the road, and I swerved, and I fell off. I'm completely fine, it just bruised really bad. That's all. It doesn't even hurt very much."

My mother backed off a bit, but her frown was still skeptical. "Are you sure?"

I rolled my eyes. "Of course I'm sure. It happened to me, didn't it? How would I not know for sure?"

She turned back to the kitchen at that. "Well, serves you right, you silly girl. There's a reason they require a license to drive a bike. One for a pod is *not* the same thing."

"I know, Mom. I was being stupid. No more joyrides for me, okay?"

She nodded and sat a plate on the table. "Damn straight."

I turned and sat, then started to load my plate with food. I was so hungry it felt like my stomach might turn inside out with the sucking need for sustenance. I ate till my stomach was so full I couldn't keep another bite down without throwing up, despite the censoring looks of my mother.

When I left the table to go back to sleep, Zed was still staring at me in silent, pointed anger. He didn't believe my little story about the bike, and he was making it obvious.

I ignored him, too tired to deal with it. I couldn't tell him the truth, so the only way to alleviate his suspicions was to continue steadfast in my secrecy and lies. At least if he thought I was being bullied or abused by my "friends," he wouldn't be on to the real secret.

To my surprise, he came to my room a few minutes later with a small jar in hand. “For the bruise,” he said simply.

“Uh, thanks,” I mumbled, reaching for the jar.

He shook his head. “Roll up your sleeve. I’ll do it.”

“That’s okay, really. I can do—”

He sighed exasperatedly. "You know I'm better at stuff like this than you. Just let me help."

I grumbled, but did as he asked, rolling up my sleeve all the way to my neck.

He sat on the edge of my bed and stared silently at my arm and shoulder again, his lips pressed together in a white line. But he didn't say anything, just dipped his forefinger in the jar and applied the salve gently to my skin, rubbing it in slowly with butterfly-light touches.

Almost immediately, I felt a decrease in pain of the areas he'd covered. I let out a sigh of relief. "You've got those magic hands. I'm sure all your future patients will love you." I still remembered my faint jealousy as a child toward Zed, who apparently was born with normal hands and feet, which my mother cooed over to no end. I'd, somewhat snidely, started calling his hands "magic," and it seemed to be true. Everything Zed touched flourished. My father had six fingers and toes, like me, but his parents hadn't chosen to have the extras amputated as a baby like mine were. I'd questioned my mom about my father a lot when I was younger, but she didn't like to be forced to remember him, and I learned to stop asking.

"I'm sure I developed this magic patching you up every time you got into trouble as a kid. Remember how many times you skinned your knees?"

I laughed. "I was so gangly and awkward! And you, my little brother, getting out the med kit every time and taking care of me."

"Someone had to," he grinned. "Or all those sidewalks and gym floors would have beaten you up mercilessly. It was like your knees were magnetically drawn to anything that could hurt them. I see things haven't changed too much." He raised an eyebrow at my shoulder. As kids, we would joke that whatever inanimate object I'd gotten my latest injury from had purposefully hurt me, and scheme ways to get back at it. Zed had deliberately tracked dirt onto the gym floor for months after I'd ripped the skin off the bottom of my feet running too fast on it.

"Don't worry, I'm much tougher now. If you think this is bad, you should see the tree I got into an 'altercation' with." I winked.

"A tree?" He shook his head and sighed. "Oh, Sis, you do stupid stuff sometimes."

"Tell me about it," I grunted, wincing as he rubbed a particularly sensitive part of my arm.

He stayed, rubbing salve into my arm and shoulder till his jar ran out, and we chatted and laughed like we hadn't in a while. Not since before the Game. I didn't realize how much I missed it.

---

I WOKE AGAIN to a light flashing in my face. I shuddered from the abrupt detachment from another nightmare. I never slept without them, now. What I'd thought was a light was actually a Window, sent from Jacky using the Skill gained by joining my team. There was only one word, but it made me throw myself out of bed and grab my shoes.

—HELP—
-JACKY-

I sent a response, asking what was wrong and where she was.

—I'M IN HIS OFFICE.—
-JACKY-

That wasn't useful, and she ignored my request for clarification, so I pulled up her location on the map using my Command Skill, snuck into my sleeping mother's room, and took the keys to her pod. I drove faster than I'd ever driven in my life, uncaring if an enforcer might see. Jacky may have been in danger from NIX. I sent another Window, asking what was wrong.

—I THINK HE'S DEAD. DEFINITELY DEAD--

## —Please come—
## -Jacky-

After that, I couldn't get any more out of her, and I gunned the pod till I reached the home for "troubled" girls. It was a large, fenced in detention center. She'd mentioned it before, but it was still strange to realize Jacky lived in a place like that.

I parked the pod in a tree's shadow and took a running jump at the barbed wire-topped fence. I held down the spiraling row of metal thorns with one hand, and crawled over. The nearest door into the building was locked. "Damn it!" I growled. I was wasting time.

I pinpointed Jacky's location on my map, and saw that she was in a room on the fourth floor. Its glowing window was visible from down below. "Okay, let's try this," I mumbled. I took off my shoes and unsheathed my claws, then walked a few yards away from the building. I sprinted toward the wall as fast as I could, and took a running leap at the last second, smashing into the concrete with my claws out.

I scrabbled and dug in desperately, and finally found purchase. I hung for a second as my still-healing body screamed out in pain, and then found a seam in the concrete for my toes to grip. Then I began to scale the wall, digging in my claws and gripping with my toes as I drug myself upward, till I made it to the window on the fourth floor.

Inside, Jacky paced back and forth, biting a clenched fist. An old, overweight man lay on the hardwood floor across from her, with his skull caved in, blood puddled around it like a red halo.

I ripped the windowsill away, squinting as glass burst outward into my face, then twisted the frame to the side and scrambled through.

Jacky gasped and took an automatic step toward me, her features sagging open in relief. But just as quickly, her eyes darted back toward the corpse, and she stopped herself. "I—I killed him.

It was an accident. I just...panicked." She bit down on her knuckles again, and shook her head wordlessly.

The old man wore a button-up shirt, and socks. No pants, no underwear. His lifeless hand clenched a fistful of shiny brown hair. Jacky's hair, ripped from her head.

Her shirt was torn, hanging half open and exposing her bra and stomach.

"What happened?" I asked.

"They're gonna send me to jail," she said in a low voice, letting her hands fall to her sides. "It'll be just like before, but worse because I'm older, and I've got a record, and he's the *warden*, and he's *dead*."

"Just like before?"

"My first foster family. Distant relatives of my dad, back here in this country. I was already beautiful, even as a kid. They had a son, older than me. They wouldn't believe me when I told them what he was doing, and he tried to...I hurt him, and I ran away. When the cops finally picked me up on the streets, my relatives said I was violent, that I attacked their son cause I was an animal.

The second home, it was the husband. The wife was nice. I told her, hoped she would help, yeah? But she was jealous, not surprised. She hit me with the rollin' pin she used to make biscuits. When they were asleep, I burned down the house."

"And then you came here?" I swallowed against the lump in my throat.

She shook her head and continued on in a soft voice. "After that, it was the streets again. I found another martial arts gym, like the one my father used to take me to. I cleaned the place at night to pay for lessons. And I used the lessons to fight. For money. That's where the enforcers found me again. I was still too young, and nobody died, so they brought me here. And it all started over again." By the end, she was drooping with cynical fatigue. "I just murdered the warden. I'm so screwed, Eve. I dunno why I even called you."

I strode forward and grabbed her by the shoulders, pushing

backward and forcing her to stand straight. "You called me because you knew I would help you. This time is different from before, because you're not the only one standing up for yourself anymore. You're part of my team, now."

"But I killed him. I murdered him."

"He tried to hurt you?"

"He tried."

"And he hurt others?" I guessed.

She nodded.

"He deserved it. You did the right thing, Jacky. And I'm not going to let you be punished for that."

She stared at me for a moment. "What are you going to do?"

"I'm getting you out of here. And you're never coming back."

"How? They're gonna investigate, and they're gonna figure out what I did. Even if I run, they'll find me, eventually."

"The first step is to destroy the evidence you were even here." They'd have Jacky's prints, and maybe even her DNA on file. "Give me a hand. He looks heavy."

We maneuvered his torso and head into position beneath his huge, antique liquor cabinet. I carefully removed Jacky's hair from his fist, and handed it to her. Then we toppled his liquor cabinet onto his already damaged skull, crushing it even further, with a satisfying crunchy squelch that was almost overwhelmed by the shatter of glass.

"One last thing," I said. "If he's got a liquor cabinet, he's got to have cigars." Already, the alcohol fumes burned my sensitive nostrils.

Jacky rummaged in his desk and came back with a cigar and an old-timey zippo.

"Perfect." I lit the cigar with some effort, stepped back, and paused as a thought came to me. "Jacky, is there anything you need in this place? We're not coming back."

"There's nothing. Nothing of my own anymore."

I flicked the cigar at the warden's head, and the room roared into flames. "Let's go. The fire will draw attention." I jerked my head to the window. I jumped first, and landed in a roll, but still lost my breath and felt the pain of impact all the way up through my body.

Jacky came next, slamming to the ground and sinking down into a graceful three-point crouch with enough force to make dust rise from the ground around her. Normally she would have grinned and bragged about being a badass, but she followed me wordlessly to my mother's pod.

"Where are you taking me?" Jacky asked.

"To our base. You're getting a room in the main house," I replied. I set the pod to semi-autopilot, since I was no longer in a hurry, and pulled up my Command Window to send a quick wake-up message to Adam.

—I'M AWAKE.—
-ADAM-

—GOOD. I NEED YOU TO DO SOMETHING FOR ME.—
-EVE-

—WHAT IS IT?—
-ADAM-

—HACK INTO THE SECURITY CAMERAS AND THE RELEASE RECORDS OF THE NEW LIFE HOME FOR TROUBLED GIRLS. THEY SHOULD STATE JACKY HAS BEN RELEASED FROM CUSTODY OF THE STATE, AS OF YESTERDAY, AND ANY INCRIMINATING EVIDENCE ON THE SECURITY CAMERAS FROM 12:00AM TO 2:00AM NEVER HAPPENED. CAN YOU DO THAT?—
-EVE-

—GIVE ME 30 MINS.—
-ADAM-

I let out a sigh of relief. "In half an hour, your records will reflect that you are no longer a ward of the state," I said to Jacky. "And the evidence you had anything to do with what happened to the warden will be either erased or burned away." The claw marks I'd made in the wall would be the only evidence remaining. Good luck interpreting that. I smirked silently.

"How?" she asked simply.

"You're not the only useful one on the team, Jacky," I teased.

She stuck out her tongue at me, but whispered, "Thank you." There was a kind of force behind those words, as she bound herself to me with chains of gratitude.

I set Jacky up in one of the many spare bedrooms in Blaine's house. He was enraged when I gave him a vague explanation of why Jacky would no longer be staying in the detention center, and was more than willing to house her.

Adam successfully completed his assignment, less than thirty minutes after my request, and sent me a message saying only,

—THE BASTARD'S BETTER OFF IN HELL. BUT NO ONE ELSE WILL EVER KNOW EXACTLY HOW HE GO THERE.—
-ADAM-

I stayed with Jacky till the morning, then left to replace my mom's pod before the sun had fully risen.

## Chapter 22

Nobody really cares about your existence, but they will pretend.
— Raja Molanthe

THAT AFTERNOON, Blaine presented me with his latest invention, through which we would find NIX.

I called the team together to explain the plan, and the preparation necessary to carry it out. "Blaine's got something ready for NIX. He's going to set up a drop to exchange his research for proof of life on his niece and nephew, and when it's done, we're going to follow the people who come."

Adam grinned, tossed a coin high above his head, and caught it behind his back without looking. "I knew it. That's the next logical step, after the doc told us about the drops. But it's quicker than I thought we'd be able to prepare."

I nodded and smirked. "Well, we'll be giving them an inferior product, of course. Why don't you tell them, Blaine? It's your accomplishment, after all."

Blaine stepped forward, "I have two things I've been working on at Eve's request." He held up a small silver disk. "This is the most efficient battery this world has ever seen. Well, except for the one you brought me," he nodded to Adam and me. "I created it based on the model from the Game. It is inferior, because I had to use the most similar known elements I could find. The original uses some previously undiscovered elements. Actually, it is quite amazing…" he visibly restrained himself from going off on an intellectual tangent. "That is beside the point. We will give this to NIX. The perfected product will be for us."

"What's the second thing?" Adam asked, doodling on the back of his hand.

I grinned wide at China. "You're going to like this."

Blaine held up a sealed vial of amber liquid in his other hand, "It's an antidote to meningolycanosis. That's what I dubbed the parasitic samples from NIX. The ones that infected your sister," he looked to China. I used samples of Eve's blood to do a series of tests, and found that the Seed organisms would fight off other infectious diseases with varying degrees of efficiency. But meningolycanosis, they completely ignored. The Seeds can't see them, and thus don't recognize them as a threat. So, I thought, *why not*? Long story short, it's because the meningolycanosis camouflages itself."

China leaned forward and gripped my forearm, without taking her eyes off Blaine. "But you figured out how to make it visible, right?"

He cleared his throat. "Well, yes. Unfortunately, stripping the coating off them creates a sort of acidic reaction. The Seeds can kill them, but they have a harder time dealing with and disposing of the acid. I'm working on a second step to the serum, that will neutralize the acid after stripping off the coating, but I haven't finished it yet. It's proving more difficult than I thought. However, when I have the completed serum, we'll keep it for ourselves."

I placed my hand over China's. "And we can use it on your sister."

Her eyes filled with tears as she looked at me, and Jacky smiled at us with approval. Even Sam, who hated my guts at the moment, gave me a grudging nod.

I felt the burden of their trust and expectations weigh heavy on my shoulders.

Both girls looked at me as if I was some great person, a trustworthy leader, a loyal friend.

I was not a hero. I was the leader of this team by necessity. My own necessity. My need to stay alive. Sure, I tried to take care of them, but it had nothing to do with being a good person. An intact, well-oiled, loyal team meant better chances for my own survival. Couldn't they see that?

But of course they couldn't. And so I took the burden of their ever-deepening trust, and hoped that I wouldn't have to betray it someday.

"I want to give us a couple days to prepare for this, but it's happening soon, and we need to be ready. Blaine will be working on the serum two-point-oh, and working with Adam and me on our preparations. Sam, I'd like you to help Blaine with the second step of the serum, since your abilities might give him a clue how to augment it."

He nodded immediately, "Sounds good."

At least Sam didn't have a problem taking orders from me, despite his resentment. "Adam, you're in charge of a tracking device. It's top priority. Also, let's see if we can't trace their response to Blaine's request for a drop."

"I'm on it," he said.

"China, if he's got the technical side down, you'll have the physical. With your Perception and Grace, you're the most likely to be able to follow someone organically without being detected. In case something goes wrong."

She bounced on her toes. "I can't believe this is happening! I'm so excited. We're going to save Chanelle, and we'll find a way to get out of this Game and the Trials, and everything's going to go back to normal. I can't believe it. I can't wait!"

I laughed, "Well, we need to find NIX, first. But at least it's a start. Jacky, you're our fighter, and you'll keep teaching us as you have been. Sound good?"

"Hell, yeah." She cracked her knuckles and her neck, all evidence of last night's ordeal gone, though I knew at least part of it was an act.

"Okay, then. Time to brainstorm," I said.

---

TWO DAYS LATER, I crouched in the corner of a field, behind the rusted shell of an old pod, watching as a large black transport vehicle pulled up to Blaine's sportier pod. Two men jumped out, scanned the field of tall grass and the tree line on the far side, and turned back to him. I could only be grateful they didn't have access to our GPS data, or we'd be given away. Blaine was still working on shorting it out safely, along with all the other projects he'd been spreading his energy among. In the meantime, he'd created a lead collar to wear around our neck, that mostly stopped the signal from transmitting.

"Whatcha got for us this time, doc?" The larger man said. He wore a dark blue shirt, and the other man a black one. Except for that, they wore exactly the same outfit.

I could have heard them faintly with my increased hearing, but the henchman's tinny voice came instead out of an ear bud tucked into my ear. It was connected to a small mic on the inner corner of Blaine's glasses, and the whole team had ear buds, just in case.

Blaine held up the energy disk cushioned within a Styrofoam bed, and a folder of papers explaining his research. The file was clipped on top with a simple metal clamp. Inside the clamp was a tiny tracking device, which Adam was monitoring with his computer.

"Just this," Blaine said. He sounded nervous, but I thought that was acceptable, given the circumstances. He was probably nervous every time he did this, even when he didn't have a group of Players hiding all around the field where he had set up a meeting with a secret organization.

They brought out a lock box and the Blue henchman opened the door, while the Black took the energy disk and file from Blaine and placed it inside.

There was a faint beep when he did so, and Blue and Black shared a look, and then turned on Blaine. "It says something's sending a signal."

"Shit," I hissed, and sent a message to Adam.

—TURN IT OFF!—
-EVE-

Blaine was stammering, trying to convince them that was impossible.

They took the vial and file out, and the box beeped again.

He grew more flustered.

—I SAID TURN IT OFF!—
-EVE-

—I'M TRYING!—
-ADAM-

Blaine held up a hand, as the two henchmen's expressions changed to promise violence. "Wait! I know what it is. I know what it is."

Blue henchman took a threatening step forward. "Well, what is it?"

Blaine pulled a pen out of his pocket and held it up. "This! It's a magnet pen. It's not sending a signal; it's just a magnetic field. The clip on the file's metal, and it's catching the magnetic field, sending out a disturbance to the box's sensors. Look, I'll show you." He walked to the back of his pod with the pen, and stuck it to the metal side. It hung there while he walked back to the men, buying us time.

"Try it again," he said.

Black henchman nodded at Blue, and Blue placed the file inside again. No beep.

I melted with physical relief, and heard Blaine let out a tiny puff of his own through the bud in my ear.

Blue henchman pulled off the clip and turned it around in curiosity. "All the same, we'll leave this," he said, tossing it into the dirt beside Blaine's pod.

—We're screwed.—
-Sam-

—I hope China's ready to do some tracking.—
-Adam-

The team sent me a flurry of messages. Adam had been unable to track the electronic source of NIX's response to Blaine without being detected, so we were forced to rely on physical means.

The disappointment was just starting to seep through me when I saw a movement in the tall grass beside the pods. Suddenly, a group of birds erupted on the other side of the field in a cacophony of squawks and flapping of wings.

The attention of both henchmen was drawn in that direction, and they put their hands under their jackets, reaching for their guns.

While they were distracted, China crawled from the grass, scrambled around Blaine's pod low to the ground, and grabbed the clip.

—What the hell is she doing?—
-Adam-

## —China's going for it!—
## -Jacky-

I itched to send her a message telling her to get the hell away, but I didn't want to distract her and get her, and thereby all of us, caught.

She slipped around behind all three men without them noticing and put the clip in the side pocket of a messenger bag sitting inside the open door of the transport pod.

Black turned away from the spot where the birds had erupted and scanned the rest of the field, while Blue stepped away to investigate what had scared them.

China had nowhere to escape. Just as the man turned toward her, she slipped underneath the black pod in one fluid motion.

She must have made some noise, because the man looked to the spot where she'd been standing, and then crouched to look under both pods.

But she'd tucked her small body into the underside of the pod, holding herself aloft in some indentation in the mechanics of the underbelly.

The man saw nothing, and stood with a shrug. His partner returned, shaking his head. "Probably a snake or something."

But I knew it had been China's command that had caused the birds to act as a distraction.

They gave Blaine a smartglass tablet, and I vaguely saw the faces of two dark-haired children pop up. Proof of life for his niece and nephew. He had a quick conversation with them that I tuned out in my worry over China's situation.

Then the men took away the pad, got into their pod, and drove away with China still hanging underneath.

Just before they turned a sharp corner on the small path, she dropped off and rolled into the grass.

Blaine got into his small pod and drove away, oblivious to the whole adventure of China's involvement, muttering, "Sorry guys. Looks like it failed. It's up to you now."

—Wait a few minutes, guys.—
-Eve-

I sent the message to the whole team. After I was fairly certain we weren't being secretly observed, and the men had put distance between themselves and us, I gave the okay to move.

China stood up and ran back to us without bothering to brush off the dirt and grass all over her. She was trembling visibly, but had the biggest grin on her face. "I did it. I did it."

Adam scowled. "What you *did* is almost get yourself caught. And all of us along with you."

Her grin slipped a bit, but she didn't back down. "I don't think we could have tracked them all the way there without the beacon. Following them in a car would have been dangerous, too. They're probably trained to look for a tail. Besides, I couldn't just let this chance go. Who knows when we'd get another? And every day we waste, Chanelle's still in there. Who knows how much time she has?"

Adam pressed his lips together, but pushed the hair back from his face with a sigh and ruffled her hair. "Well, you didn't get caught. You're okay, and that's the most important thing. But don't do something so stupid again, okay?"

She grinned and nodded, but there was an obvious lack of remorse on her face.

I couldn't help but laugh, and it felt good. It had been a long time since I last laughed for real, and the relief of our small victory made me feel lighter inside than I had since before I was a Player.

---

THAT NIGHT, we sat around the tables in Blaine's lab.

"Don't be such a lily, Sam." Jacky shook her head. "What did you think we were tracking NIX for? Like we weren't gonna actually *find* them?" Jacky snorted, more on edge than usual, because of what had happened with the warden, I assumed. The fire and his death had been on the news. All the residents of the juvenile center had escaped unscathed, except for the warden, and it was reported as a strange drunken accident. Whether the enforcers were investigating despite that, I didn't know. Time would settle both Jacky's mood and any suspicions, I hoped. If my claw marks in the side of the building had been noticed, I laughed a little at the enforcers' inevitable confusion.

"My sister is in there," China said simply, steel in her voice.

"Adam rubbed his fingers together, sparks jumping over his knuckles. "I want to go. But Sam's not wrong. It's dangerous to jump into this. You guys do remember that we all have a GPS chip embedded in our necks, right? They could have alarms set to go off if Players get too close."

"They might not," I speculated aloud. "They keep some Players who failed Trials there to research on. And if anyone but Bunny were actually monitoring us, they'd notice that we're in the house of one of their contractors-slash-blackmail-victims."

"Unless they know and don't care. Or they're keeping an eye on us secretly." Adam shot one of his sparks into China's side, making her jump, then grinned mischievously when she smacked the top of his head.

I rolled my eyes at them. "We need more information. That always seems to be the problem..." I rubbed the back of my neck, and sat up straight. "But we do have a resource on the inside, which we've forgotten about."

"You want to ask B—*him*?" Adam asked.

"Not overtly, of course. But if we could tease some information out of him, think how useful that would be."

Sam's eyes widened. "What if he realizes what we're doing?"

I leaned forward, my mind racing. "That's why we'll have to be careful. We'll slip the information-gathering into conversation secretly, and each of us will try for different pieces of the puzzle so he doesn't even realize everything he's told us."

---

CHINA WAS the one to end up getting most of the information we gathered out of Bunny. She learned more about NIX's physical and organizational structure, as well as some hints about security, all the while bonding with Bunny and subtly planting seeds of empathy toward our little team. She was amazing. When I told her so, she just shook her head sadly. "I just want us all to be safe."

From what we gathered of Bunny's knowledge, NIX wouldn't know if we snuck up on them, unless someone checked in on us specifically and noticed our location. This was least likely to happen late at night, because while Bunny had constant access to all the Players he moderated, he did need to sleep. And he did it on a fairly regular schedule.

So, late at night a few days later, after driving to a spot Adam had deemed suitably removed from NIX, our actual target, the team got out of the pod and spent hours in the government-property forest, circling in around the tracking beacon. We moved cautiously, and scanned for any electronic security devices hidden among the trees. When we found them, we marked a way around in their blind spots, and continued on.

Finally, we got close enough to see what we'd been working for so long to find. It seemed to be a huge compound, cut from the inside of the mountain cliff. The front side had windows and air vents cut into the stone face, little bright points of light or deeper dark in the night.

The back side was a bowl depression into the mountain, with a huge metal ball on a concrete tower shooting out of the middle, surrounded by mostly open courtyard and some smaller individual buildings. The walls were made of glass in places on the inside, and we could see people moving along the curved hallways. We had no way of knowing how far the underground construction went, but I had no doubt it was extensive. The inside had stairs running up the wall for convenience, while the other side plunged to rock, river, and trees far below. Because of the way the compound had been built, it almost seemed as if the ball tower was surrounded by huge stone walls made of mountain, like a king's castle or city of olden days.

Guards walked around atop the outside of the walls, on constant patrol. They carried large guns strapped to their bodies, as well as handheld radios and binoculars. The whole place was well secured, and easily defensible on all sides.

My team crouched at the top of a hill, hidden among the trees and underbrush at the base of a nearby mountain.

"This place isn't on any official map," Adam murmured. "We've definitely found NIX." He pointed to the river. "That runs through the bottom of the mountain they've built into. They must be using it as an energy source to keep this place running."

"What's that?" I jerked my head toward the huge ball elevated above the courtyard. Bands of different colored metals spun around it, in all directions, as if in moving orbit.

"No idea." He shrugged.

"I didn't expect NIX to be quite so…big," China said in a small voice. "How are we supposed to…?" she trailed off.

"Yeah. I hate to say it, Eve, but how does this help?" Sam asked. "Now we know more about them, but that only makes us more of a threat to them, and gives them a reason to kill us."

"They already try to kill us every ten days in the Trials, so not much has changed, then, huh?" Adam said.

"Sam, do you know what the casualty rate is for Players?" I said.

They were all silent for a few moments as the weight of my words settled on them.

"High. Over fifty percent. But once you've survived a few times, the survival rate goes up," he whispered.

"Does it? What about our last Trial? Even if every one of those Players had been able to solve the puzzle, *half* would still have died. Because that's what NIX wanted. They don't want us all to survive." I placed emphasis on every word. "Otherwise they wouldn't put us into the Trials. How long till one of us slips up and dies, or we're sent to a Trial where we're forced to work against each other? We can't keep this up forever."

He was silent, so I continued. "So, like I've said from the beginning, we need to escape. As soon as possible. And I've got an idea. I had an interesting conversation with you-know-who." I lifted my eyes skyward to indicate Bunny, without saying his name and drawing attention to our current situation. "He told me that when Players commit suicide, NIX takes them off the list of active Players—the ones that enter Trials."

Adam twisted onto his side to face me, the weaving tattoos on his arms making him blend into the darkness like camouflage. "I know you're not going to have us kill ourselves. So what's the plan?"

I grinned. "That's where you come in." I could feel the weight of everyone's anticipation for my next words. "It's only logical that they keep records of all their past Players, right?"

"Right."

"And as you-know-who's the only one that watches us enough to know who we are, if suddenly we disappeared, no one would notice as long as nothing drew their attention to our absence?"

"Probably not...but—"

"So, if suddenly Adam Coyle's status changed to 'dead for the last six months,' and somehow also happened to be the exact same information as Joe Schmoe, some random guy that actually did die, and already had the cleaners erase suspicion on him..."

"Whoa. That might actually work. Of course, they probably have tracking and audit programs in place to find discrepancies, at least they do if they're smart. And I'm sure they've got backups, too. But they'll likely be digital, for security purposes, and even if not, I'd bet there's a self-destruct protocol for invasion or takeover scenarios. But if I could write a program designed to spread like the zombie apocalypse and wipe out our real information and any traces that it had been changed...plus set off the backup self-destruct..." he trailed off, and lay in silence for a few minutes.

"I'm going to need to level up some more to be able to create something that robust. And I'll need a direct linkup. But I can do it. If I can get in there," he jerked his head toward the compound, "for long enough for the program to work undetected."

"I've got some ideas for that, too," I said.

# Chapter 23

We are what we pretend to be, so we must be careful what we pretend to be.

— Kurt Vonnegut

MY MOM CALLED us into the kitchen, and sat us down for a particularly fancy breakfast. She rubbed her manicured hands together with a mixture of excitement and nerves. "I've got something to tell you," she announced.

I bit back my smile.

"I've received a job offer from the marketing department of one of our sister companies. They're expanding into some products with high profit potential, and they want me to lead the team. They're willing to compensate for our relocation, and the pay is high enough—"

"Relocation?" Zed interrupted. "What are you saying?"

"The decision is already made, children." She met both our eyes challengingly. "It would mean a higher standard of living, less hours of work for me after the initial push, it's got a significantly better enforcer presence, and the school is top notch."

Zed looked to me for help.

Sorry, brother. I won't be giving a hand with this one. I shrugged. "I'm out of school anyway, so it doesn't matter to me."

My mother smiled and subtly relaxed. "There are some wonderful opportunities for secondary education, Eve, as well as job opportunities if you can't pass the entrance exams…"

Zed glared between the both of us and stalked out of the room, leaving the elaborate meal untouched.

My mother sighed.

"He'll come around," I said to her, piling my plate with his abandoned food. Wouldn't want any to go to waste, now. I snickered to myself.

"At least I have one reasonable child," she sighed.

I smiled at her around a mouthful of melon. If only she knew. If all went well, the others in my team with families to protect would all be having similar discussions. Blaine's wealth could create connections and opportunities seemingly out of thin air.

---

THREE DAYS LATER, the power went off as I was lying on the floor in the living room with Zed. I sat up in vague curiosity, and let the indirect sunlight through the window wash over my body in the now-darkened room.

"Power's off," Zed stated the obvious, putting down his school pad.

"I'm sure it'll be back on soon," I frowned down at the small chain I'd been fiddling with while quizzing him for his year-end test. I couldn't see well enough without the light, and obviously couldn't activate my Huntress Skill to improve my night vision while in a civilian's presence. "Probably just a rolling blackout."

But then I heard faint musical tones, and my insides started to vibrate harmony. "Oh, shit. Shit, shit, shit," I muttered, launching myself off the floor and sprinting to my room.

"What's wrong, Eve?"

"Uh, nothing!" I called back distractedly. "I just forgot I was going to go to a friend's house tonight. I'm late!" I grabbed the pack that I kept always prepared and nearby from my closet. I lifted the edge of my mattress and fumbled for the Seeds hidden within, tossing them into my pack. I barely remembered to strip off my link and toss it on the bed so it didn't get scrambled. "This shouldn't be happening. It's only been nine days, not ten. It's not time yet!" I hissed. Were the others going to Trial, too? Or was NIX singling me out, sending me off-schedule to see if I would die by myself? Before I had time to even put on shoes, my bones shivered me into my fifth Trial. I was understandably distracted, and didn't feel the eyes watching me in secret through the crack in my doorway. If I had, maybe things would have been different. But I didn't notice.

I found myself transported into mid-air and falling fast, and any thoughts beyond the moment quickly blew their way out of my head. I landed hard on a knobby brown tree limb, bruising my knees, scraping my hands, and half knocking the air out of my lungs.

I was sucking at the shockingly warm air, disoriented by the huge, huge distance between myself on the limb and the tawny ground far below, when a warning shout from above caused me to rear back, just soon enough to have my face smashed into the branch as something large landed on me from above.

My nose flattened, my bottom lip got caught between my teeth, and the little air I'd managed to retain after the first impact was forced from me.

"Oh goodness. I'm so sorry," Sam's voice came from above. "I just got transported right into the sky and fell on you. Are you okay? I'm going to move. Nucking futts, this is high." He'd obviously been picking up some of Jacky's language.

I twitched my fingers and nodded slightly, unwilling to respond further past the pain of my face and the sick feeling of fear you get when your lungs temporarily stop working.

Sam inched awkwardly off me and helped me to sit up. He put

a hand between my shoulder blades and started to cough, and I was suddenly able to pull in a small breath. I used that to fight for more, and finally said, "God. How many times am I going to get the air knocked out of me?" I gathered up the bloody saliva in my mouth and spit. Some of the pink liquid landed on one of the tree's knobs, and was absorbed immediately.

The knob unfolded, spreading large, pale petals wide as if seeking more moisture. The petals were almost translucent, and I could see my spit running through their veins, being sucked into the branch. As my bloody saliva traveled, the branches around me stirred as if in anticipation.

I raised my head slowly, and took in my surroundings fully. I was straddling a tree branch, probably a thousand feet above the desert ground. In the distance, reddish rocky buttes jutted from the sand, throwing a shadow towards us from the harsh light of the setting sun. Except for the stone cliffs reaching toward the sky and the patch of trees we'd been dropped into, everything lay barren. The sand stretched out for miles around us, rolling in hills and rippling waves like a dry ocean in the midst of a storm. The heat was enormous even all the way up in the sky, and the air below shimmered unceasingly, like a second layer of ephemeral water above the sand ocean.

Someone screamed as they were dropped from the air a few yards above us. They didn't catch on our level, and with each foot they fell, their chances of grabbing one of the ever-fewer branches decreased. They screamed all the way to the ground, though their voice grew thin and distant after a while. Finally, their body became just a bug-speck of red splatter, half buried by the sand.

The body lay there for only a few moments before something dark and tapered shot out from the sand, arced through the air, and swallowed the entire red-stained area, while disappearing back beneath the surface.

Sam shuddered. "Sand sharks. I've heard of them." His face was pale, despite the beads of sweat already plastering his hair to his forehead.

The trees around were thin and slender, with limbs reaching horizontally out of the trunks at similar intervals. Their pale branches wove together, making individual trees into an interlocking copse, with levels at each interval. The branches grew more plentiful up higher. I looked upward, and realized I couldn't see through the branches more than a few levels above my own. "You'd be able to walk around up there," I said.

Blood from my just-smashed nose dripped into my mouth when I spoke, and I instinctively spat again. The petals all along the limb beneath us unfurled, faintly pink with the blood.

I heard a sound overhead, and jerked my gaze upward.

The limbs above my head had shifted themselves to create a tunnel of visibility to higher levels. I didn't get a good look before they shifted back into place, but I caught the glint of reflective eyes far above. And I definitely heard the scratchy roar that followed afterward.

"Crap. Something's up there, Sam," I said. “Watching us.”

"But it hasn't even started yet! Where's the Examiner? Is this another mental Trial? Where's the cube?" He looked at me accusingly, as if it was my fault.

I let my claws out and scanned the surrounding trees with my improved vision. I could see better through the branches than he, and noticed the cube floating on the level above us. “Cube's right up there.” I didn't know about the Examiner, but I hoped to god this wasn't going to be a repeat of the last Trial. “Let's go.”

I found it easy to climb higher, and my lack of shoes helped me grip the bark. I helped Sam a few times, and we quickly reached the next level of branches. It still wasn't quite stable, but the chance of falling was less. I kept an eye toward the higher levels, but our growling watcher didn't reappear.

Other Players appeared below, popping into mid-air one by one, the rest of my team among them. We called them upward, and sat waiting.

A couple Players were talking about the early start of the Trial.

"Nine days? This is getting really short. It's like they're trying to see how far they can push us before we break."

"I remember when it used to be twelve," the other said.

I turned to Jacky, who had been a Player the longest of our group. "Do they do this often? Change the length of time between Trials?"

"Every four to six months it happens, from what I've heard and the shifts I've seen. But it hasn't been ten days for long. We should've had more time before it changed again."

Adam pulled out his butterfly knives and started to twirl them around in both hands with a distant frown on his face. "I wonder why they're doing that. Interesting."

"It is," I agreed.

After even more waiting, our Examiner, a baby elephant with the voice of a five-year-old, explained the Trial.

There was to be a battle between monsters, and we were to choose sides and fight in the battle. If we could stop the side we picked from being annihilated, or if our side completely defeated the other side, we won. If we didn't die, of course. "Yep, I think that's it. Good luck!" The creature said, letting out a comical toot through its trunk.

Out of the buttes in the distance, dark dots started to appear, jumping off the cliffs and flying in our direction.

I heard their distant roars. "Damn. It's started." I said aloud.

The branch under my feet jerked, as the tree it was connected to shuddered. Down below, the sand-sharks, as Sam had named them, were attacking the base of the trees, smashing into them and gnawing away at the wood.

Adam sighed. "And that's the requisite time limit. No matter what happens with the battle, as soon as they topple this structure, we're dead."

"So we just have to win before that, right?" Jacky said, and they all looked to me.

"Yeah. One group of monsters is a few levels above. I say we go up and see what we're dealing with." I spoke loud enough that the other Players could hear. None of them seemed to be low-leveled newbies, which I found interesting. That could be bad, if NIX thought only stronger Players would be fit for this Trial. The upside was none of them looked helpless enough to trigger my guilty need to protect them.

We started climbing, and some of the Players followed.

Each level grew increasingly thicker, until it was hard to squeeze through the dense weave of branches. A few levels up, a large slanted tunnel led up from our level to the next.

China and I both listened and smelled for anything or anyone on the other side of the tunnel, or traps within it, but noticed nothing, so we walked through.

Same thing on the next level, though there were huge piles of feathers, obviously used as beds or nests by something huge. On the next level we heard snuffling, soft growls, and the pad of feet walking around above.

The others looked to me expectantly, and with an internal groan at the danger, I waved them back and walked into the tunnel.

Light from the setting sun streamed into the opening, blinding me as I reached the end. I stopped before exiting and squinted out.

Something smashed into my back, and I stumbled forward. I immediately fell into a fighting stance, knees slightly bent, lips drawn back in a snarl, and claws ready to rip and tear.

This level was open to the sky, at the top of the little patch of trees. All around me huge, winged cats sat and stood and crouched as if ready to tear my guts from between my ribs. Each was as big as a medium-sized horse, and some were bigger.

One large, dark brown, heavily muscled creature lunged forward in a feint and roared straight into my face, its hair and feathers all standing on end. The force of the sound blew my hair back from my face like a wind tunnel, and almost forced me back.

Instead, I dug my toes into the woven floor and leaned into it.

When it was over, I wiped away the spittle that had landed on my face and tried to ignore the dizzying ring in my ears. "You sound like a kitten," I said. "Maybe if you took up smoking you could deepen that voice a bit." I knew it couldn't understand me, but if it had wanted to kill me, it would have attacked. It wanted to scare me, so I couldn't let any self-doubt show. I hoped it couldn't smell the fear, because there was nothing I could do to stop the emotion running through my veins and prickling along my skin.

Other cats around us leaned forward, eyes trained on me. A low rumbling growl started from one, and was picked up by the others, like the chant of an audience. They harmonized together until I felt like I was standing in a massage chair made of air and sound.

Behind me in the tunnel, Adam and Jacky were calling my name, and I heard thuds like they were pounding on the wood, for some reason unable to get through.

I was just about to attack, so that at least I could go down fighting, when a shadow blocked the sun and something plummeted out of the sky to the floor in front of me.

It was another of the creatures, bigger than the others, and with the more slender build that I associated with females. Its wings were spread wide and protective in front of me, and reached several yards in each direction. It roared back at the dark brown male, and stared down the others until they stopped growling and backed away.

She made growling sounds at them, mixed with coughs and the occasional yowl.

The male responded in kind, but then lowered his head and exposed his neck to her.

With that, she turned to me and licked my face. Her huge tongue rasped away the blood from my nose, along with the top layer of skin. Ouch.

She stared into my eyes for a moment, and I found the hair on the back of my neck raising as I realized the large orbs didn't have slanted pupils like a cat. They looked...human. Deep and clear and intelligent. Expressive.

The creature swallowed, and her eyes widened. She leaned back and roared joyfully into the sky.

The others looked at her, all at once, as if shocked. After a few moments of still silence, they leaned back and roared, too, screaming with all the power in their lungs.

I put my hands over my throbbing ears and cringed. "Ever heard of an inside voice?" I muttered.

The huge female returned to all fours and licked my face again, which was more painful the second time, then pressed her nose to my forehead as she stared into my eyes.

My brain felt like it was being punched through my skull, but I couldn't pull back, and then I started to see things. Pictures and clips of movement and sound and emotion.

I saw the group of winged cats as they lived, as if I was one of them, isolated from all others here in the desert, hunting the other creatures of this wasteland to survive, and trying to keep their race alive. They were a close-knit group, all related to each other in some distant way or another. They knew joy in each other and the hunt and the occasional child, and sorrow in their dwindling numbers, and hunger, and the sick-deaths of their hatchlings.

I saw images of the other creatures flying towards us now. Huge, scaled, with lumpy bodies and sagging skin. Carrion eaters and nest robbers. I knew of feuding with them over the passing of countless seasons, at first beating them easily, and then as the numbers of my family dwindled, with more difficulty. Less than a season ago, there had been a night attack, such as the one about to begin, and they had lost almost all their eggs along with the warriors set to protect the nests.

The group was weakened, and would lose this time. All the eggs would be destroyed, their children killed and eaten before ever knowing a world bigger than the inside of their shell. They would fail in their only purpose. I felt a sense of despair that made tears well in my eyes unbidden and roll down my face.

But then hope bloomed from her to me.

I saw my own face from high above, glaring at the snarling male. Flashing images of the one-eyed wildcat from my Characteristic Trial, humans dressed in strange clothes speaking a strange language, landscapes of beauty stretching out before me as I flew, an image of mold and putrid spores devouring over a patch of purity, and the vicious exhilaration of flying into battle with my brethren, ripping and killing and obliterating my enemies.

Then she pulled back, my eyes rolled back in my head, and I dropped to my knees. My vision tumbled and my stomach heaved, but I stopped myself from throwing up or falling over by taking deep breaths of the thin air and digging my claws into the wood.

Behind me, wood cracked, and cracked again. "We're coming, Eve!" Adam called.

"Stay alive!" Jacky ordered.

I took a few more deep breaths, then croaked out, "I'm okay," then again, louder, "I'm okay. They're friendly." I didn't know if that was exactly true, but they hadn't attacked me, which was the best I could say of any monster I'd ever met in the Trials.

The door broke, and throwing knives thwacked into the floor on either side of me, warding off potential attackers.

Adam rushed forward and wrapped his arms around me, dragging me backward to the mouth of the tunnel.

"Where are you hurt?" Sam asked, moving along with Adam.

China and Jacky moved to stand in front of me, a wall between me and my perceived attackers. China had multiple throwing knives ready in each hand, and Jacky's fists were clenched.

The cats stood still, watching us small, "threatening" humans in curious amusement.

"I'm never letting you go first again," Adam said. "Stupid. You're just gonna get yourself killed."

I rolled my eyes. "I'm fine. I'm fine, guys!" I called, louder. My pounding headache had seceded, and I struggled out of Adam's grip. "They didn't hurt me. Well, not intentionally, anyway. The big one," I pointed, "was just talking to me."

They looked at me in worried disbelief, and Jacky said, "They did something to her head. Fix her, Sam. I'll hold them off."

Sam stepped forward and laid clammy hands on my forehead.

I swatted his hands away. "Stop it! Okay, so she didn't speak English. But they've got some sort of psychic power. She showed me things. They're not going to hurt us, as long as you don't attack. They're just trying to survive, but they're about to be wiped out by those other twisted monsters." I flung my arm wide to encompass the mass of forms in the sky, growing ever closer.

The floor shuddered beneath our feet, probably from something the sand-sharks were doing.

"Guys, they're intelligent. And I want to communicate more with them. I can't do that if they're dead. We're going to fight on their side, against the attackers."

Jacky lowered her fists immediately and turned to face the group moving through the sky. "Damn. That's definitely the harder option."

The others looked between the two groups of monsters, and the winged cats preened and stretched their wings under the attention, showing off.

"Are you serious, Eve?" Sam said. "You're going to decide for all of us, just like that? What if I don't want to die? Because we're definitely going to lose if we do what you just said. They've got three times the numbers!" He pointed to the misshapen flying monsters. "And there's a whole other group down below, trying to topple this nest of gigantic, supposedly psychic cats! Why the hell would I follow you? You're focused on nothing but what you can gain, no matter how dangerous it is. Think about something besides yourself, for once. I know you don't care about what it *means* for someone to die," he said pointedly, "but my *life* is more important than your *curiosity*." He finished, out of breath and flushed from the force of his tirade.

I'd waited silently for him to finish, wondering how to handle the situation. Sam had an invaluable Skill, which had already saved my life, and I needed him around in case we needed it. But I could do without the open resentment, which had been hovering at various distances from his emotional surface since our last Trial.

I wanted to walk over to Sam and beat him into submission, the urge strengthened by the irritating ringing in my ears, but I ignored the instinct. It was sure to backfire.

While I was thinking, China surprised me by stepping forward. "You're a coward, Sam," she said calmly. "And you're mean."

He gaped down at her, just like the rest of us.

"Eve saved your life, because you were too afraid to give yourself permission to save your own. You made the choice to listen to her, and you were the one that killed that guy. No one blames you for it. You had to do it, and if you hadn't you wouldn't be here to help us today. But don't *you* blame *Eve*, because it's not her fault. You feel guilty, because you listened to her, and you think it was wrong. But she's never been anything but good to you, to all of us. She's helping me save my sister."

"She helped me when I needed her," Jacky added.

"Eve's always there to help us," Adam said, after a reluctant pause.

"She's given you a place to belong, and people who have your back," China said. "We all have your back, and you should have ours, too." With that, she spun away from him and climbed up the side of a tree-branch hill, then began to methodically dip the points of the knives crisscrossing her chest into a small jar of poisonous goo.

Sam was red-faced, silent.

I cleared my throat. "I'm not a perfect person, Sam. Sometimes I can be quite the opposite. But I know you're good, in your heart. You want to do the right thing. And if you listened to what their leader has to say, if you could see what she showed me, I think you'd want to protect them all on your own." I stepped forward and put my hand tentatively on the female's nose. "Could you show him what you showed me? Why you need help?" I didn't know if she could understand my words, but she watched intelligently as I brought my hand to my forehead where she'd touched me, and then pointed to Sam.

She gave a nod, and then turned to him.

He gulped, but stood still as she approached and touched her wet nose to his skin.

I turned away. "Okay, guys," I called loudly, knowing there were other Players on the level below, too cautious to come up after the series of threatening roars they'd no doubt been half-deafened by. "The attackers are almost here. I and my team are siding with the ones who live in these trees. The cats. They're friendly to humans as long as you don't attack them, but the ones that are coming aren't. Even if you're fighting on their side, they won't recognize that, and they'll attack indiscriminately. Your best bet is to side with the rest of us." I had no idea if what I'd just said was true, but we needed all the help we could get. And like I'd said, I wasn't perfect. Lying didn't cause a second of guilt.

The female drew back from Sam, and after a few moments of pale dizziness, he said, "I'll fight with you."

And that was it. We waited less than a minute for the others to arrive, as the trees underneath us shuddered and swayed subtly back and forth.

The flying enemy monsters looked like a cross between a Shar Pei dog with extra saggy skin, and a flying lizard. Their necks hung down in pink waddles, like a vulture's, and the wind blew a stench of rot from toward us.

All around us, the cats roared their defiance, and many leapt up to meet the attackers in the air, while others moved to protect the “cave” China stood atop. "Their eggs must be in there," I murmured.

The first of the wrinkled lizards made it past the line of defense, crashing hard enough onto the platform to cause everything to sway.

China threw a knife at it, and almost immediately it seemed to have trouble finding its feet. It collapsed in a twitching heap, and Adam sprang forward to cut open its throat.

Thick, dark blood oozed out, which the trees ignored, and Adam stepped back with a grimace of distaste, then wiped his knives clean on its hide.

There was a beat of silent waiting after that, and then everything exploded into chaos. More wrinkle-lizards broke through, and the Players and cats on the ground began to fight.

I found my claws useful, but the sluggish, thick lizard blood inevitably got all over my hands and arms.

All around me were screams, and the roaring growls of monsters, and the pink bloom of the trees sucking up the non-gunky blood of both cats and humans, but I didn't look. I had to focus on what I needed to do. I found myself forced to the edge of the platform together with Sam, and was just finishing off a monster that he'd brought down with his crowbar when a small dark blur whizzed past my cheek.

I looked behind me, and saw a wrinkle-lizard drop to the ground with a knife in its eye. It had been about to bite down on my head.

China nodded acknowledgment to me, and then turned to continue throwing at other targets.

"Whoa, that was close," I said to Sam. But almost immediately, I heard a roaring shriek right behind our backs. I started to duck and twist, but something large and sharp caught me on the shoulder, lifting me and ripping my flesh. I flipped into the air violently, spinning around like a tossed toy soldier. I turned in midair so I could see the huge creature that attacked me and land on my feet to fight back. I could feel the heat of the putrid breath coming out of its open maw.

A cat barreled into the monster from the side, huge teeth ripping into its neck and taking it instantly out of play.

I relaxed for half a heartbeat. Then I realized I had been tossed out too far, there was nothing beneath me to land on, and that I would end up a dark smudge on the canvas of beige a thousand feet below. I stretched a hand out, but I was too far away to reach any of the branches.

I turned to look at Sam, insanely wanting to apologize.

But he was not horrified, for once, not hesitant. His teeth were bared in effort, and he was lunging toward my outstretched hand. Moments before it would have been too late, his hand closed around my clawed fingers, crushing them with the force of his grip.

Then I was stopping, wrenching my hand and wrist and elbow and shoulder. It was the same side I'd been attacked on, and I felt a strange tearing on the already injured skin of my shoulder. Warm blood ran down, pooling in the curve of my neck and running down between my breasts and over my back.

Sam grunted with the force of gravity on my large body, and I saw that he only had a grip on the platform with his other hand.

"Eve!" Adam's hoarse shout filtered through my ears past the rushing of the blood in my veins and the wind pushing on us.

I ignored him. This wasn't the time to be reassuring Adam that I was okay. It was the time to be focusing on making sure I *stayed* okay, stayed alive.

Sam's fingers were slipping.

I tried to breathe deeply and stay still. "Sam, you need to swing me back and forth. I'm too heavy for you to pull me up. If you can get my trajectory far enough inward, and let me go, I'll be able to catch myself on the level below."

He shook his head minutely, desperately, straining too hard to talk.

I clenched my teeth. "You can do it. There's no other way for us. You can't hold on much longer, and when you slip we're both gonna die." I grabbed onto his wrist with my other hand, and began to wriggle myself back and forth, like I was on a swing. If I'd been a better person, I might have told him to drop me. I knew his grip wouldn't last much longer, and my movements were making it harder for him to hang on. If he fell when I swung inward, I likely wouldn't be able to save him like he'd done for me. But I wasn't a better person, so I didn't even consider saving him. Like he'd said, I was selfish. He was the only one who came close to realizing just how selfish.

I looked down to try and time my release, but could only gasp in helpless fear when he grunted out, "Sorry," and we began to fall.

# Chapter 24

Time held me green and dying
    Though I sang in my chains like the sea.
    — Dylan Thomas

I LOOKED DOWN, down, and down. There was nothing below us for so far. I vaguely heard my name shouted again, but both Sam and I were screaming too hard for me to listen. My stomach had started to try and rise through my chest when my fall stopped abruptly and unexpectedly, for the second time in the last half hour, this time on something warm and scratchy.

Sam landed half on top of me again, twisting my ankle strangely underneath his weight.

Underneath me, the passing wrinkle-lizard we'd landed on bucked sharply at the unexpected weight of us on its back. It was barely big enough for its two unwelcome passengers, and I dug my fingers into the skin of its back, holding on for dear life.

Sam grabbed onto my leg with one arm and clenched a handful of lizard hide with the other.

I met his terrified eyes and couldn't help but laugh. "This

wasn't quite what I had in mind when I said drop me onto the level below, but I guess it'll do. Good job."

He shook his head, lips pressed together in a white line, as if to keep from throwing up.

The creature beneath us shrieked angrily, flapping hard as it struggled between staying afloat under the extra weight and throwing us off.

I started to inch forward, drawing myself toward its shoulders, handful by handful of skin. My right shoulder screamed out in pain, begging me to stop, and I left a shiny trail of blood on the brown and green skin of its back, but I kept going until I reached the base of its leathery wings.

I sat up cautiously, wrapping my legs over its huge back and squeezing. I looked around breathlessly and took our bearings. We were swinging back around to the trees again, luckily not too far from where we needed to be.

I felt its wings strain to lift us higher and saw where the creature's eyes were focused. "Hold on tight!" I blurted out, ducking down between the flapping wings.

Seconds later the creature smashed into the bottom of the top tree level, crushing and scraping its back along the myriad branches. It dropped away, shaking its head, half-stunned by its own maneuver.

I sat up and looked back.

Sam was still holding on, hanging off the side and looking both surprised and terrified.

"Just hold on!" I screamed above the rush of the wind. I turned back and grabbed onto the strange lumpy growths on the sides of its neck, squeezing hard and pulling. I hoped they were sensitive, and not just there for decoration. I was right.

The creature stiffened and jerked, causing Sam to cry out in alarm.

But it angled its flight toward the side where I applied the most pressure, as if to try and relieve the pain.

I didn't know how long it would work, so I pulled harder and faster, and the creature followed the direction of the circular protrusion on its neck. I guided it upward, swung back around to the trees, and crashed us hard into the middle of the platform, almost hard enough to flip me forward and off the creature's back. But I wrapped my arms all the way around, and somehow stayed on.

It struggled to its feet, tossing its head back and forth and flapping its wings experimentally. I could feel that it was about to take off again. "We can't have that, now," I said, pressing my face into the side of its head, where an ear might be. "But I also can't just get off and let you attack me. So..." I hugged its neck and gripped, similar to something I'd seen Jacky demonstrate, and twisted with all my strength.

The neck snapped around, and something broke with a loud crunch. One of the bulges on the side of its neck popped, and a small red organ spilled out, pulsing like a heart and hanging by a few fleshy cords. The creature slumped gently to the ground and collapsed, never to move again.

"I have to kill you," I concluded, though it couldn't hear me anymore. I climbed off, and saw three wrinkle-lizards attacking a single cat guard in front of the eggs' hatchery.

Sam was fighting with another lizard already, but seemed to be holding his own.

I leapt forward to aid the outnumbered cat, feeling somewhat numb, and attacked one of the lizards. Claws to the neck seemed to be the fastest way for me to stop them, but they were quick and vicious, and it took me a few moments to bring my opponent down.

By the time I'd done so, more lizards had joined the other two, and they finished off the guard.

He let out one last gurgling roar before he died, calling for backup, but the lizards were already into the hatchery.

Large eggs sat nestled into beds of fur and feathers, and the blooming flowers of the tree were clipped above them, so that blood spilled down onto their shells. The surfaces of the eggs were pockmarked, and they drank up the dark red liquid as it touched them.

The first lizard inside grabbed the nearest egg and bit down on it. The hard shell punctured its gums, but it ignored the irritation, and bit down again on the newly exposed, half-formed kitten within.

The kitten's limbs flailed uselessly, and then it was swallowed with a bobbing jerk of the lizard's head.

More lizards entered in a frenzy after that, some stomping the eggs, some biting like the first, and some just swallowing them whole.

I threw myself at the nearest lizard, righteous rage nearly blinding me. I fought quickly and viciously, but there were too many, and I was too weak.

But then the cats' leader smashed into the mouth of the hatchery, so big she scraped against the walls of the entrance.

She flailed around with her teeth, wings, and legs, ripping lizards apart left and right. For a second I felt relief.

But more enemies came, and the floor beneath our feet was now pitching back and forth like the deck of a ship during a storm. Between my mindless attacks on the lizards, I saw glimpses of the outside. Corpses lay everywhere, and almost the whole platform had bloomed, the bloodsucking flowers a dark red now. But despite the amount of dead lizards, they kept coming, and there were no reinforcements arriving on our side.

The cat leader and I were pushed toward the back of the hatchery, despite our best efforts, and more and more of the unhatched kittens were killed. My stomach filled with despair and heartbreak.

They might have been cats, and monsters of a type, but the female had shown me they were people too, with feelings and lives to be lived. And the eggs were babies, being killed before they even had a chance to experience those lives.

Even I would do anything to stop tragedy like that, when it was happening right in front of me.

The female used her wing to knock me behind her, then took a huge breath and let out a roar like nothing I'd ever heard before. It literally knocked back the lizards filling the front of the hatchery, stunning them with its force.

She spun then, using her claw to cut through a piece of the wall. A flap swung open, and she pushed me through before wriggling in and securing it again with a thick branch across the back of the newly revealed swinging door. She pushed past me toward the back of the hidden room, where an egg lay on a bed of feathers the same color as her wings. Blood dripped down onto it from one of the tree's clipped blooms, like the others. She nudged it gently, then scooped it up in her wing and held it toward me.

I lifted my hands, and she dropped it into them.

Behind me, the lizards were attacking the door, and I knew they would be through soon.

"Is this...your egg?" I asked.

She stepped forward and pressed her nose to my forehead again. A burst of pain followed, and I started receiving her message. It was like a dream this time, me thinking and moving, but at the same time watching myself and knowing it wasn't real. I had the understanding that I must take her egg, the thing most important to her in the world, but also important in a different type of way that I couldn't understand. Maybe it was next in line for the cat-leader throne? I watched myself wrap it in protective arms and fly far away, though I knew I didn't have wings and it was meant as a plea to leave this place behind and protect her child.

She stepped back quickly so that I wasn't incapacitated by the aftereffects of our communication.

I wrapped my arms around her egg and nodded. "Got it."

She nodded back to me, then turned to the back and ripped open the wall of the hatchery. I stepped out, and she followed for a few steps, making sure I wasn't attacked.

I sent a Window to the other members of my group, telling them to retreat to the lower levels as quickly as possible, and headed that way myself, screaming loudly for any other Players to follow, if any were still alive. I knew I was pretty badly injured, and my ankle kept trying to collapse under my weight, but I could barely feel the pain.

China arrived the quickest, holding two branches in lieu of her knives, which had apparently run out. Her cheek was bleeding and she had an already swelling black eye, but other than that she seemed fine. She sagged in relief when she saw me, and I realized she must have thought I died when I fell off the edge.

Sam and Jacky arrived next, both of their eyes widening when they saw me, and then Adam. Adam was bleeding from a deep slice along the palm of his hand, and had blood finger-painted across his face, like Native American warpaint. All of them were injured with varying degrees of severity, but at least they'd all made it. Most hadn't.

"Eve, you're hurt," Sam said, reaching a hand out to me.

I shrugged it off. "Everyone's hurt. We don't have time for that. Come on, we've got to get out of here."

I led the way, running as fast as I could with the surprisingly heavy egg, my pack and my unreliable ankle. We descended faster than we'd risen, and when I turned around to check, I saw that a few other Players had made it in addition to my team. That was good.

When we reached the cube, I saw the count of each team's forces. Two columns separated "TAILOS" from "RETCHIN," and had a number of monsters still alive. The tailos had a much longer list of Players than the retchin, but the number of tailos was dwindling quickly, decreasing even as I watched.

I reached out and placed a hand on the cube, which pulsed but didn't respond further. "I've got an egg. One will live, though the rest may never see another day. One will live. The tailos will not be annihilated." I hoped to god it would let me through, accepting the unorthodox winning conditions I was providing.

The cube pulsed, and then the words across the screen changed.

CONGRATULATIONS ON SURVIVING THE TRIAL!
EVE REDDING HAS GAINED THE UNHATCHED EGG_

With a series of cracks and shudders from down below, the tree started to pitch sideways.

"No time, hurry up!" I snapped.

The cube complied, skipping ahead to the return message.

DO YOU WISH TO RETURN FROM THE TRIAL?
YES / NO

I slammed my hand onto "Yes," and wrapped my arms tight around the egg.

Sam leaned forward and put his hand on my back. "What's your address, Eve?" he shouted.

I frowned at him, but rattled it off. "Why?"

"I'm coming for you, okay? Just stay alive. I'll be there soon."

Then I returned, riding on the vibrating melody of the Boneshaker.

---

I COLLAPSED onto the beige carpet of my room, the tailos egg rolling out of my arms. I was suddenly freezing, and noticed the stars floating in front of my eyes, and the blackness creeping in from the edges of my vision. I let out a shuddering breath, and the pain I hadn't felt before hit me like a tsunami. I looked down over myself, and saw the blood staining my clothes dark, and felt the frantic beating of my heart as it tried to pump what little blood was left inside me around fast enough to keep me alive. "Damn," I whispered.

I fumbled at the pack on my back, pulling the half-shredded strap out of the wound the retchin lizard had given me. "I'll need a new one," I said inanely, speaking to myself as a way to keep my eyes open. I dug clumsily for the pouch I'd stuffed inside it before the Trial.

When I shook, three Seeds rolled out, two landing in my hand, and the other bouncing off and rolling away to the far corner of the room, under my bed. I ignored it, and held both Seeds to my neck at once. "I wish for more Life," I said. They shot into my veins, and within a few seconds I felt some strength return, and the edging black behind my eyes was pushed back. Only then did the Game notification telling me I'd earned seven Seeds pop up. Waiting to see if I'd live, I thought caustically. I fumbled the large, sturdy tailos egg into my pack.

I sent a Window to Sam, telling him I'd be at the base of the tree in the community park behind my building. He couldn't come to my house, into my room. Not without sparking my family's curiosity, and thus alerting them to my situation.

No, I needed to meet him somewhere else. So I pushed at the window latch till it broke, too exhausted to use fine motor control. I tossed my pack over my good shoulder, crawled out onto the tree, and looked down onto the manicured grass below. But then suddenly the world twisted like a marbled ice cream cone, and the green changed to the grey-blue of a smoggy summer sky. My pack floated strangely around to my front. I could see the sparkling stars, even though it was daytime. I was pondering this enigma when everything went black.

I woke up on the ground, with a gasping, white-faced Sam bent over me with his eyes closed, pressing his hands into my sternum, between my breasts.

My head was resting on something warm and supple, and I felt the familiar sting of a Seed injecting into the skin beneath my jaw.

"Are you groping me right now, Sam?" I whispered, and then started to cough.

He gasped again and opened his eyes.

A barrage of muddled and overlapping exclamations assaulted my ears, and suddenly my vision was filled with the faces of my team leaning in around me.

China took the Seed from my neck, and handed the empty shell to Adam. He added it to a handful of other empty Seeds and put them in his pocket.

"Did you guys...use your Seeds on me?"

He scowled down at me, also pale faced. "Well, we had to, you idiot. What the hell, Eve?"

I was taken aback. "What?"

"How could you let this happen to yourself?" He clenched his hands at his sides, for once not twiddling his fingers.

I gaped at him, at a loss for words as a couple seconds of silence passed. "Um, it wasn't on purpose, trust me." I quirked my mouth in as much of a smile as I could muster.

His pale face reddened in anger. "Yeah, we saw that."

"I'll pay back the Seeds to whoever gave them up," I muttered, moving my hand a tiny bit as I prepared to sit up.

"Nobody's worried about the Seeds!" Adam snapped, grabbing my forearm and holding it, and me, down. He turned to Sam. "I know what you did. That wound was meant for you! If you hadn't stepped out of the way, or if you'd at least moved her with you..." Adam's long, dexterous finger trembled as he pointed it accusingly. "You may be angry at her, but what you did is inexcusable."

Sam flinched visibly and swallowed, looking down at me with a sick expression. "It wasn't intentional. I mean, I just—I just dodged. I saw the retchin coming and I moved. I didn't know it'd end up hitting you instead. I swear, it was an accident. I would never, never do something like that on purpose."

Jacky scowled at him. "You shoulda taken that hit. You woulda healed from it just fine."

He opened his mouth, but was cut off by Adam. "Bullshit, you didn't do it on purpose. How *convenient.*"

What was going on here? "Adam. Stop it. All of you." It was news to me that the creature had been aiming for Sam, but it made no difference to the situation.

Adam turned to me and opened his mouth angrily once more, but I cut him off before he could continue. "Sam wasn't at fault.

We may not always agree, but he's never done anything to make you distrust him so. If he didn't want to be here, be part of this team, or wanted harm to come to me, it wouldn't be too hard for him. Look at him. He looks like he got drowned. If he wanted to hurt me, he wouldn't have jumped off the side of the tree tower to save me, risking his own life in the process. He wouldn't be here right *now*, and I wouldn't be alive."

Adam knelt beside me, but didn't touch me. "If not for him, you wouldn't have *needed* saving, or be hurt this bad in the first place."

My breath hitched as I struggled for air, and Sam turned his attention back to my chest as I spoke. "What if he hadn't been there to dodge, and the monster had actually aimed for me in the first place? I just got the accidental swipe. And except for an apparent fall out of my own backyard tree, I'm barely hurt at all."

Adam sputtered, his eyebrows raised. "Barely hurt? Have you seen yourself? You look like a zombie!" He was shouting again.

I chuckled. "Well, thanks. Tell me I look like shit. What a great way to make me feel better."

He gaped at me as if I was crazy.

I actually felt fine, if a little weak. I moved to sit up and prove it, and screaming pain erupted from every inch of my body with the force of a sonic boom. I blacked out again.

# Chapter 25

She's mad but she's magic. There's no lie in her fire.
— Charles Bukowski

I WOKE up in Blaine's house, on the little bed in the closet attached to his lab. An IV bag dripped into a tube attached to my arm.

China leaned forward and smiled at me brightly. "You're awake!"

I frowned. "Guess I passed out again."

"Yeah. Sam healed you up as best he could, then we brought you here. We sent your mom and brother a message from your sheath saying you were staying the night at a friend's house. Hope that was okay?"

I raised an eyebrow at my mother's no doubt pleased excitement that I actually had friends to spend the night with. "Yeah. They're already a bit freaked out at my suddenly booming social life, but it'll be fine. It's not like they'd ever suspect the truth."

China giggled, a surprisingly young sound, and I was reminded again of how difficult it was to live life like this. And how much it had to have aged her, that I only heard sounds like that from her on the rarest occasion.

"What time is it?"

"It's late afternoon, Sunday."

"Whoa. I slept over eighteen hours?" I lifted my arms to push the covers back, and winced as the movement woke the angry wounds covering my body, especially my back.

She shot over and pressed my forearms back down into the bed. "No moving! Blaine gave you something to let you sleep. You shouldn't even be awake right now, but your body keeps adjusting to the dose and metabolizing the sedative faster and faster. I'll go get him, and we'll up the dose again."

"No, no. I don't want to sleep any more. There's a lot to be done."

"You are not to move from this bed," she commanded imperiously, drawing her small frame upright and towering over me with her hands on her hips. "Is that clear?"

I stared at her for a moment, and then leaned my head back into the pillow. "Okay, but could you at least get me my pack? I won't move from the bed, but my mind can still work, even if my body doesn't, right? I have a puzzle I need to solve."

She hesitated, but when I gave her a puppy dog look that was as pitiful as possible, she relented, and brought my ripped and blood-soaked pack to me.

After checking to make sure the dark red-brown egg was okay, I dug out the silver chains I'd gotten from the Oracle, and started to fiddle with the smallest one, the one with the fewest rings, as I'd done every chance I got since she'd given them to me.

There were eleven bent links in the chain, and I had the idea they were a puzzle that would hold together if I could just figure out exactly how they fit. I knew they must be important, but the way to bring out whatever hidden potential they had was still a mystery to me. It was quite frustrating. But, since when had I let a little thing like that stop me?

I slept again for a few hours that afternoon, and woke again at night.

Sam sat beside me this time, looking thoroughly exhausted. "Hey, how are you doing?" he said, smiling weakly.

"Peachy keen," I responded along with a sarcastic smile.

"Well, that's a lie," he chuckled. "But you're going to be okay. In fact, you got quite a few extra Seeds, so once you're mended and the ones you lost along with all that blood have replenished themselves, you'll be better than ever."

"Thanks."

He leaned forward as if he wanted to grab my hand, but settled for smoothing down the edge of my blanket, instead. "I hope you know, I didn't—I didn't let this happen to you on purpose. I would never do that. I mean, I was angry at you, and to be honest I still am. But it's really just anger at myself, because I let you convince me to kill that guy so I could save myself. I wouldn't ever try to take revenge, or anything—anything like that." By the end, he was whispering.

I slipped my hand out from beneath the cover and patted his own lightly. "I know, Sam. I didn't think you would. I know you better than you think, you know. We're not so different, in some ways."

He raised his eyebrows at that, but didn't respond, and after a few more awkward moments, left me for some work in the lab with Blaine. Apparently everyone was busy preparing to carry out my plan for NIX. At the door, he stopped. "I'm not brave, Eve. I told you before, I'm not the person you want at your back in a fight." He left.

With no one there to stop me, I made my way out of bed by increments, and moved to a seat at one of the chemist tables. I'd been fiddling with the Oracle's puzzle for a few minutes before Blaine, Sam, and Adam, all working in intense silence, noticed my presence.

Adam tried to tell me to lie down again, but I waved him off.

"I'm fine. I'm sitting down, and I'm not straining myself. There's no need to coddle me."

"You said something similar the last time we spoke, if I remember correctly. And then you tried to move and passed out," he said, deadpan.

I raised a challenging eyebrow at him. "Yes. That happened. But I'm staying right here, in this seat, and you're not going to stop me."

He returned my challenge with a glower, but bit back the words he obviously wanted to say, and returned to typing away furiously.

I took a measured breath so as not to stretch my back with the movement, and returned to messing with the puzzle chain.

Blaine noticed, and moved over to peer at it. "What is that?"

"I don't know. I got it in the Intelligence Trial. The Oracle said it would guide my path, and I think it's a puzzle, but I've got no freakin' idea how to make it work. I need to figure it out, because all this not knowing is dangerous. I hate it."

He held out a hand. "May I?"

"Sure." I dropped it into his palm, and he took it to a microscope.

After a few minutes of silent inspection, during which he turned the links around and examined them from every angle, he sat back and returned the chain to me. "It's a puzzle ring. The bands join together around your finger, designed to come apart when you take it off. This one has minuscule grooves and protrusions, so unless you match all the bands to each other exactly, they won't join. It's quite complicated. Impressively so. You said you got that in the Trial?"

I nodded, speechless at his quick understanding of something I'd spent many futile hours on already. I bent my head to study the bands, trying to see the imperfections he'd spoken of in their surface.

"Interesting. I have some ideas about the place you go to when you're transported away..."

I jerked my head up as I remembered, and interrupted him. "I've got something else you might want to take a look at. It's in my pack. Will you get it from the closet?"

He brought the pack to me, laid it gently on the table, and opened it.

The egg lay inside, clearly visible, and as big as a cantaloupe.

"Good thing it didn't break in the fall." I almost shuddered at the thought.

Blaine removed it reverently, holding it cupped between both hands. "What is it?"

"It's a tailos egg. The tailos are…big cats with wings. And I think they're telepathic. Its mother gave me the egg to protect. It's probably the last of its kind."

He blinked, staring through thick glasses at the heavy, porous, blood-crusted orb. "You brought back an unhatched…Trial monster?"

"Umm, yeah?" Suddenly the idea seemed questionably dangerous.

"If I'd known you could bring them back, I'd have had you bring me more. I could be dissecting them right now!" He flicked it with a finger, leaning close to listen.

"Well, usually the monsters are quite…large. We can only bring back small things, things we can kind of wrap ourselves around. And besides, I don't even know if they could survive in this world."

He sat the egg down on the table and scurried away, then came back with a tube of gel, a stethoscope like device, and a series of small metal hammers.

"Whoa, you're not going to try and crack it open. I promised the mother I'd protect it. If it's still alive, being born prematurely could kill it."

"Relax, I'm only going to do a sonogram."

He spread the gel over a patch, and then placed the pad at the end of the stethoscope into the gel.

Some gel ran down into one of the pores, and a tiny but forceful puff of air from inside sprayed it away and onto the table.

My eyes met Blaine's, and Sam and Adam joined us at the table as the air filled with a charge of excitement.

Blaine chose the smallest mallet, and tapped gently on the shell. His eyes widened, and I had to resist the urge to rip the stethoscope-thing's tips from his ears when he said, "It moved. Something's alive in there."

"Let me," I said. I put the tips in my own ears, and tapped gently on the shell. A sloshing wriggle came from inside, along with what might have been an irritated squeak.

My face stretched in a huge grin, and I reluctantly gave up the stethoscope to Adam and Sam.

Blaine was frowning into the pores, and scratching at the dried blood on the surface. "I wonder if it's cold. Should we incubate it? What temperature, though, and for how long?"

I thought back to the tailos hatchery, and slid off my chair, making my way to Blaine's supply closet while they were too focused to notice me. I grabbed a handful of scalpels, and made my way back. Then I took the stethoscope back from Blaine, put the tips in my ears, and ripped open the packaging of one of the scalpels.

"Whoa. Be careful there. I thought you didn't want to hurt it," he said. "Cutting it open isn't any better than cracking it. And either way, a scalpel isn't the tool for the job."

I ignored him, lifted my left wrist above the egg, and cut a slice into the side, away from my veins, but deep enough so the blood flowed well.

Adam gasped, and then slapped the scalpel out of my hand while the others were still gaping at me.

He clamped a large hand around my bleeding wrist, and pulled it up to elevate the cut. "Get some blood-clotter and some bandages. Wait. Sam, just heal her."

Sam moved to obey, but I pulled weakly at Adam's restraints, and scowled. "Stop it, you two. The tailos eggs drink blood. I was just giving it some. Look."

The blood that had made it down into the pores was being sucked up, and when it was gone, I heard more wriggling from inside, and a definite squeaky sound.

I pulled my arm away from Adam, and let more blood drip onto the egg.

It continued to suck up the liquid until Sam put his hand on my wrist and stopped the bleeding.

"You just lost a crazy amount of blood. Now is not the time to be slicing open a vein to feed some cat egg," Adam said.

I laughed, and then realized that I did feel a little lightheaded. "Yeah. You're right." I nodded to Sam. "Thanks."

Sam nodded, and the slice healed to a raw pink patch of skin before my eyes.

Blaine had watched the whole exchange in avid silence. "It drinks blood. And you said the adults are telepathic?"

"Yeah," Sam responded. "They don't use words, but it's like they push sensory input and feeling right into your brain."

"And they're good. I mean, they're pretty vicious, but they don't attack any and all humans indiscriminately, and they have families and…a culture," I added.

Blaine blinked owlishly. "You guys realize what this means, right? There's a sentient, communicating race in these Trials. One that's never been seen on Earth."

"Well, at least not for a long time, right? What if…have you guys ever heard of a gryphon?" I said. "They're not the same, but…what if there's some sort of connection? And some of the places we've gone, it's like an ancient city of ruins. I mean, what about that energy cartridge, Adam? There's something…more, going on here. There's something missing, something we don't understand."

Blaine sighed wistfully. "I wish I had access to the Trial world. I'd love to get my hands on everything you guys keep telling me about. The technology of a futuristic society…it's incredibly exciting."

"No," I said. "You don't wish that. If any of these speculations are true, then it's pretty damn amazing. But that doesn't negate the fact that the lifespan of a Player bears some resemblance to the lifespan of a fruit fly. It's short. I'd give up all the 'excitement' in a second, to live an ordinary, miserable life here on present-day Earth till I was old and pollution-wrinkled."

There was a silence, and then Blaine handed me a bundle of unopened syringes. "At least don't cut yourself open. Use these instead."

Adam snatched the syringes away, glaring at him, and I left the boys to bicker and went back to sleep.

---

—We'll be ready.—
-Adam-

I NODDED to Adam's reassurance, though I knew he couldn't see me, and packed another box into the back of the huge transport pod my mother had rented. My back twinged with the movement, but I was careful to keep any hint of pain off my face.

Zed stared at me not-quite-secretly from the corner of his eye as we passed each other, as he'd been doing for the last few days.

"What?" I snapped. I was hungry, tired, sweaty, and stressed out about both getting my family to safety and the team's plan for NIX that evening. Needless to say, my level of patience had taken a flogging. "You're irritating the hell out of me."

"*I'm* irritating *you*?" his eyebrows raised, then lowered into a scowl. "I'm worried about you, Eve."

"Well, stop. I'm fine! Better than fine."

"What happened to you the other night? You disappeared without even saying anything."

"Didn't Mom tell you? I messaged her. I stayed the night at my friend's house. And what does it matter? I don't have to report my every move to you."

His fingers squeezed dents into the box in his arms and he glared at me silently for a few moments. "Why are you so freaking obstinate?"

"I'm not the obstinate one. You don't have to be involved in every aspect of my life, Zed. Stop thinking something has to be wrong just because my life is changing for the better. I'm getting tired of having this same conversation over and over."

"Eve, I *know*—"

My mom stepped around the pod and dusted off her manicured hands, which had somehow managed to stay perfect through the packing and loading of almost our entire house.

Zed cut off whatever he was about to say.

"All done now, children. I'm going to make a last pass through the house. Say bye to your sister and get in the pod, Zed. You're driving this one." She tossed him the keys.

She and Zed were moving to the new location ahead of me. I'd be following them soon, I hoped, and we could resume our mostly normal lives. Free from the Game and NIX, though I knew I'd feel the need to look over my shoulder for the rest of my life.

I sighed and softened my expression. "You don't need to worry about me. I've got everything handled, I promise." I stared into his eyes, trying to make him believe.

He said nothing, but after a few long moments, his own stubborn expression morphed to something I couldn't quite read, and he gave me a hug.

My mother came back down, satisfied the only things left were mine, and they left for the safety of the new home and life I'd created for them with Blaine's help. A life away from NIX and its influence.

# Chapter 26

Who overcomes
By force, hath overcome but half his foe.
— John Milton

I CROUCHED JUST outside the line of NIX's security, with my team behind me. I was tense and sick with fear. I wished we could wait, but NIX implemented a shift rotation every couple weeks, and it was the best time to slip in unnoticed. If I could have waited till the next rotation, I would have. An operation like this should be the work of weeks or even months, not a couple weeks. But in another four days, we'd be going back to the Trials, and I wasn't sure we'd all *live* till the next shift rotation. Plus, by working day and night on almost no sleep, we'd somehow managed to get everything ready. No matter what happened tonight, we'd all be leaving the city in less than twenty-four hours.

Even if I hadn't given the go-ahead, China would never have waited. Her whole focus was on saving her sister, and she would be there that night whether I wanted her to or not. I'd tried to at least convince her to stay behind to carry out our plan B, but she'd found a way around that, too. I had to admit her sonar-like senses would be invaluable to us on the inside, if she could focus on the mission at hand and not just her sister.

I motioned with my hand, and we crept around to the side of a large military transport pod, properly keeping to the path of disabled motion sensors and cameras that Jacky had created, with Adam's guidance. Once behind the pod, we stood up, and strode forward with Adam at the front, as if we knew perfectly where we were going and had every right to be there.

My hands felt cold with sweat, and I hoped the uniforms we'd mimicked held up to casual inspection. We had no guns, because they were too strictly regulated in our country, and though Blaine had the money to get pretty much anything off the black market, there wasn't time to prepare them. In addition to that, China was too small to be a guard, so we'd put her in a different type of uniform. A uniform of the Players NIX kept, probably for experimentation. I only hoped that she wouldn't rouse suspicion, as long as she was with us, and had instructed Sam to keep a firm grip on her at all times, as if she was a prisoner under our guard. If things got complicated, she would be our backup access key to the captives. Bunny hadn't contacted any of us in a few days, probably because of the last accusing conversation I'd had with him.

We moved to one of the doors, and Adam held up a little device to the security pad there. After only a few seconds, it beeped, the pad flashed green, and a click announced that the door had unlocked itself. Adam opened the door and threw a grin over his shoulder. "Got that little trick from an online acquaintance. Quite useful."

We stepped through the doorway into a well-lit hallway, with small cameras positioned at regular intervals. We wore military caps, like many of the other guards, but the real protection was a little powder Blaine had given us in gleeful excitement, like a kid unbearably eager to have their gift opened. The powder gave off only the slightest sheen to the naked eye, and could be disguised as the shimmer of a woman's foundation, or a light misting of sweat.

But to a camera, our faces looked like a thousand beaming facets of light, and completely unrecognizable.

Blaine hadn't been idle for a moment, working like a crazy man to meet all my demands.

As we walked, I started using the Game interface. "Bunny," I said. "Stay still, and listen to me. Don't make any indication that we're talking. Check your map for my location." Before he had the time to send a response, I continued. "You're going to keep silent and let me do what I need to do. If we get caught, I'm going to know whose fault it is. And I'm going to come for you. I know where you are. I'm watching you, just like you've been watching us." That last part was a bluff. Blaine's tracking of our chip data only showed direction and distance from the person we were messaging; I didn't have access to any cameras.

"When they go crazy trying to figure out what happened, you're going to keep all of this a secret, because you're part of it. If you say anything, they will wonder why you never reported us earlier, when we were planning all of this. And if you try to say you didn't know what we were doing, they might wonder what use they have of someone so incompetent. By now, I hope you've grown a better understanding of exactly how much mercy NIX has."

—What R U doing, Eve?—
-Bunny-

"I'm escaping. If you interfere with that, your employers won't be your only problem. So you'd better sit tight and pretend you're clueless."

Jacky knocked out the first lone guard we saw with a chop to the back of the neck, took his ID sheath, and locked him in the supply closet that Adam located with the map he took from said ID sheath.

Then we were on our way properly. Largely due to the obsessive reconnaissance China had been doing, we had a good idea where everything was already, but the detailed map of the inside was necessary to move within the maze-like compound. We passed other guards, but none paid much attention to us or our ward, China.

A few minutes later, Adam held up a hand at an extra-securely locked doorway. It still stood no chance against Adam's little gadget, and after a few tense moments when China notified us of footsteps coming our way, we slipped in to the unlit room.

It was a room full of glass-circuit servers, stacked one atop the other on shelves that reached from the ceiling to the floor and stretched the span of the room.

Adam set up his computer and connected it to a random port. "We're in!" he said.

Jacky had just given a triumphant chuckle when the room lit up, light shining from all the glass, into every shadow.

I jumped about a foot, I'm not ashamed to admit.

And I wasn't the only one.

Adam looked up quickly, but then back down to the keyboard his fingers were literally blurring over. "It's just an acknowledgment of access. And...uploading."

The glass-circuits and screens on the walls started to give off a beautiful light show that almost looked like splashes and beams of light fighting against each other.

Adam grunted almost as if he was in pain, and moved his hands from the keyboard to the sides of his computer, where he'd modified it to have holes to the inside just the size of his fingers. He closed his eyes and let the sparks start to jump from his skin, communicating directly with the computer.

China was biting her nails, looking between Adam and the hallway outside through the window cut into the door.

Sam said, "I don't mean to interrupt, but is everything going okay?"

Adam snarled at the computer. "It's freakin' fighting me. It's adaptable. Every time I get past it, it tries to push me out again. If I get kicked out even once, it'll be too late. So please let me concentrate." He took a deep breath, and let it out, and I knew he was activating his Hyper-Focus Skill. His sparks jumped even faster, and the sound turned into the buzzing of a live wire, each zap indistinguishable from the others. His curly hair rose around the sides of his cap eerily, static making it twist and turn as if it was alive.

"The lights are visible," China said.

My heart gave one sick thump in my chest, and I whipped around to the door, which had a window to the outside running right through the top half of it, just as the handle turned.

It swung open as if in slow motion, and Jacky, who'd been next to the door, stepped quickly behind it, putting the metal as a barrier between herself and the guard.

The guard. His eyes took in all of us, in the mainframe computer room, one frantically buzzing with electricity.

---

I TRIED TO RELAX, and leaned against the shelves behind me. "Hi. Doing some testing in here. Hope we didn't alarm you."

He frowned. "No one's authorized to be in here."

I nodded. "Yeah. That's what we're testing. The security system's resistance to intrusion during a nonauthorized time frame. You weren't notified of this?"

He shook his head.

I sighed and lifted my face to the ceiling. "How many times do I have to send out notification to get anything official done around here? This is ridiculous. Your C.O. probably has the memo somewhere in his computer, unopened. What happened to compliance training? God."

He frowned, hesitant but still not convinced.

Maybe I just wasn't that good of an actor.

"I've never seen you before. Where are you from?" he asked. But instead of staying locked on mine, his eyes began to travel over each of us thoughtfully. "I've never seen any of you before."

"Of course not." I raised an eyebrow. "We're not stationed here. It's just a routine audit."

His eyes stopped for a moment on China, who was staring at him intensely. He looked first at her face, then at her uniform, the only one different from ours. "Why do you have a Player in here?"

He didn't allow me to answer the question, instead pulling back and waving to what I assumed must be his buddy, while lifting his radio wristband to his mouth to say something to someone on the other end.

We never found out who that someone was or what he was going to say to them, because Jacky punched her hand through the door window and grabbed the wristband, snapping it off and crushing it. She swung around the door and punched him in the face, then pulled his instantly limp form into the room.

"Don't kill him," I snapped as she reared back. Just in case.

She grimaced, so maybe that had been a good idea on my part. Instead, she struck the back of his neck, and his eyes rolled up and back.

That move was just as cool, every time.

Unfortunately, she couldn't undo the guard having alerted his buddy, who kicked the door open wide, gun at the ready. She dropped like a rock, kicking both feet out in front of her and taking the second guard's legs out from under him, while I knocked up the barrel of his gun and ripped it out of his hand so that he couldn't shoot us.

I heard the distinct crunching sound of the guard's trigger finger breaking, and grimaced. Not pleasant. But also not something I felt bad about. Anyone who was a part of NIX deserved that, and more.

The guard flipped over and gained his feet again right away, much more of a challenge than his partner. I doubted a normal soldier could have stood against us for even as long as he did. But he was no match for both Jacky and I. I wondered if Seeds were at work in the fighting skill of the guard.

He went down, but the radio at his wrist crackled again.

"Reinforcements on the way. Report your status, Decker." When no response came, it crackled again, "Status report, Decker!"

I turned to Adam. "You've got to hurry. We don't have much time."

He was breathing hard by then. "We can't hurry," he snapped. "Data only transfers so fast, and if the program doesn't have time to finish properly, we might as well not have come here in the first place."

I took a deep breath, trying to calm the piece of bubbling lava inside me that reacted to my fear and tension, and pushed my claws back into my fingers. "Jacky, China. Time to implement Plan B." Jacky nodded and ripped a storage port with built in WiFi from her back pocket and shoved it into the slot on one of the fallen guard's ID sheaths. It would forcefully override the locks and open all the doors in this section of the compound, thereby setting off a slew of other alarms. In a few minutes, the anti-fire system would engage, drenching everything nonessential in water, and sucking the oxygen out of non-water-friendly rooms.

"I need to know when the reinforcements get close, China, and how long we have till they get to this room."

Plan B was to create widespread chaos, and slip around and away, undetected in the midst of it.

She nodded silently, pale skinned and round-eyed. Her fingers were curled into white-knuckled fists, but she uncurled them deliberately and cupped them behind her ears to increase the amount of sound she could capture from the specific direction she wanted, like the ears of a dog or cat. After a few moments, she said, "Now. I hear them."

"How long?" I asked, pulling on the steel-fingered gloves I'd brought to hide my possibly identity-revealing claws.

"A minute?"

I turned to Adam. "You've got thirty seconds to get out of the system. Everyone get the charge sticks ready."

He growled, but gave no other response, and twenty-eight seconds later he said, "Now!"

We all pressed the charge sticks into our necks, a couple inches below the VR chips, and gave a heady jolt to the tracking devices embedded under our skins.

The lights stopped abruptly as he disconnected his computer.

"Did you do it?"

"Of course," he tried to smirk, but looked too afraid and strung out to pull it off. "You know who I am, right? I always perform. Ouroboros is in motion. She'll eat every bit of the surveillance from the last few days, along with everything for the next fifteen minutes, till she's devoured her own existence. Along with any trace we ever existed."

"Good job. Let's go." We left the room and ran down the hall, just slowly enough for China to be able to run at the forefront and still listen at the same time.

The holding area was in a different section of the compound, but China thought Chanelle and Blaine's remaining family would be there, judging from snippets of information she'd gotten from listening to the guards' conversations. If we could get there and take Chanelle, Blaine's niece and nephew, and some other random decoy prisoners and test subjects without being noticed, we had set up getaway motorcycles and rent-a-pods all throughout the nearby forest. Untraceable back to us, of course.

Honestly, I would have left at that point without Chanelle and Blaine's niece and nephew. If we could just get out, we'd be off free. But I knew China wouldn't come, and I couldn't exactly leave her to be caught and tortured by NIX, likely leading them back to the rest of us.

Adam guided us toward the lightly trafficked connecting hallway that would lead us directly to the holding area. We turned the corner into a lounge-type area. It had a large wall-to-wall window looking out over the edge of the mountain we were dug into, onto the river and forest beneath.

Just in front of us stood a tall, thin man, cutting off our route of escape. He smiled thinly. "Well, well. What have we here?" He breathed deep. "I can smell the fear on you. Real fear, felt so often and so recently it's become part of your blood. I haven't smelt a guard like that here. Let alone four of them, together with a Player."

"Oh, no," China said, her voice calm, which only made her fear more plain.

# Chapter 27

You monsters are people.
— Jacqueline Santiago

CHINA GRABBED me by the sleeve and tried to force me back, away from the man.

"What's wrong?"

She shook her head, never taking her stare off him. Her eyes were wide and filled with a kind of blank terror. "We need to run, now. He'll crush us."

Jacky didn't seem to hear her, confident in her own abilities. She rushed him. As soon as she got close, she was blown away. Literally. She smashed into the window, and spiderweb cracks spread from where her body had hit, branching outward as her body seemed to fall in slow motion to the ground.

China whimpered. "They're coming from behind. And up ahead. We need to run. He's a snake…I can feel it, Eve. I can tell."

Jacky got up, gaining her feet again with stiff movements, and my mind struggled to comprehend this stringy man's strength and speed.

I could hear the pounding of feet behind us, too, even through the blaring of alarms. "What can you tell?"

A tear slipped down her face. "We're going to die."

I straightened. "We're not going to die. We just need to get past him. There's still time to move forward before we're boxed in."

Adam rushed forward as Jacky came from the thin man's side. He zig-zagged back and forth, trying to use his speed as a distraction, but was stopped by a bony flash to the gut, and retched bile onto the floor as he hung suspended, bent over the snake's fist.

Behind us, footsteps skidded to a stop, and I turned my head to see a gasping, rumpled man take the situation in. "Oh my god," he said, meeting my eyes. "Seriously?" he asked, as if he knew me.

What? I opened my mouth to question him, but the group of guards turning the corner behind him diverted my attention. They pulled him back, behind the first line of bodies, as if to protect him. Their guns immediately lifted, but then they saw the snake-like man, and lowered them. The ones in the front line edged backward to increase their distance from him, jostling the ones behind them.

Well, that wasn't good. Just who was this snake?

Sam spun in a circle, looking trapped. "What do we do?"

"We move forward." I gripped him by the arm to steady him. "We do whatever we can, whatever we *have* to."

He stared at me, and then shook his head. "No. I know what you mean by that. I'll help us get past him, but I'm not going to hurt another human being. And I'm not using my Skill. Not again. Besides, aren't we supposed to be incognito? My Skill's pretty distinctive."

I grimaced, but was distracted when Adam's back knocked into my foot as he skidded to a stop across the floor.

The snake man smiled. "I think I'll play with you for a while, until it's…*safe* for the guards to take over."

Adam groaned, and behind the man, Jacky was holding a now injured left arm close to her body.

My claws had slipped out without conscious thought in

response to the threat, luckily hidden by my gloves, and as Adam rose from the ground we all prepared to fight. I sent a reminder to the team.

—Keep any of those distinctive Skills hidden, just in case.—
-Eve-

Adam took out a collapsing baton from one of his many pockets and with a flick, sent electricity crackling through it. It wasn't a stun baton, just normal metal he was using to disguise the origin of the electricity.

I jumped forward this time, with Jacky coming in from the back, Adam beside me, and Sam moving around to the side. China held back, but the few throwing knives she'd managed to hide on her person were out, and ready to back us up. The guards made no move to stop us, instead watching the scene with unnatural silence.

I thrust one gloved hand forward, aiming for his eyes. My other hand was ready to smash my claws into his gut when he instinctively protected his face, but he didn't even blink.

Instead, he unflinchingly grabbed my outstretched hand and whipped me around like a rag doll.

I felt the gashes in my back rip open again as I swung around and flew into the window. More cracks spread outward, mixing with the ones Jacky's body had created. The urge to scream in pain might have been overwhelming, if my lungs had any air with which to do so. I stood again despite that, and when the black dots cleared from my eyes, saw that the others had fared no better than me.

Jacky was crouched on the floor, blood dripping from her head. She kept trying to get up, but as if drunk, couldn't find the balance to stand and kept falling back to her one good hand and knees. In any other situation, it would have made a hilarious sight. This was not that situation. Our best fighter, down. And I couldn't help but remember when the same thing had happened to Chanelle.

Adam was trying to help Jacky up, and Sam was standing back and clutching a broken wrist.

China threw her knives at our opponent with just enough delay to keep him focused on her, while drawing out the time for the rest of us to recoup.

He dodged every one, weaving and bending his body like the hero of some kind of Asian martial arts movie.

Okay, so obviously we weren't making any headway like this. And in the meantime, things had gotten even worse. Another group of guards had come up the hallway leading away from the windowed room, and we were boxed in.

—Sam, I know you've got qualms about hurting others, but we could really use your help here. Maybe you could paralyze him? Kinda like the grub-pug poison you healed me from?
Or something else you can't see from the outside. His heart, or lungs...—
-Eve-

—What!?—
-Sam-

—He's gotta be a Player. We'll kill his GPS, take the body.—
-Eve-

Sam glared at me and snapped, "*No.*"

I ground my teeth and snapped back, "Then at least make yourself useful!"

"I am!" He held up his already healing wrist and laid his other hand on Jacky's neck.

I'd never wanted a gun quite so badly before. Ah. I eyeballed the groups of guards plugging both exits. A forced breath and a few sprinting steps later, and I was in front of them. I ripped a gun out of one of the guard's unsuspecting fingers, and turned to shoot at the snake. I got a few rounds out before the anti-theft system recognized that I wasn't the proper owner and locked the gun.

The snake man flexed his fingers open wide with enough strength that they almost bent backward, and the bullets veered around him, smashing into the wall behind him, and barely missing Adam's head.

Adam's eyes widened as he looked back to the hole in the wall, and then met mine for a moment that seemed to last forever.

I felt like we both had an 'oh crap,' moment of understanding, and then time started moving again at a frantic pace. Time to escape while we still lived. But there was nowhere to run.

My eyes caught on the hairline fractures running through the window, and then looked past them to the dark line of the river rushing far below. I dashed toward the window and slammed the butt of my stolen gun against it as hard as I could. The force of the impact made my hands go numb and my bones hurt, but the cracks spread, and I turned to Jacky. "Help me."

She nodded, for once without her cocky grin, and grabbed a sturdy looking coffee table on her way to me.

The snake waggled a finger. "Oh, no, kids. Don't be getting any ideas now."

Adam picked up two chairs and threw them at him one after the other, and the snake was distracted for a moment, long enough for Jacky to smash through the first layer of glass, and then the second. The wind whipped along the cliffside and slipped into the room, ruffling my clothes with the force of its passing.

Then the program we'd plugged into the system kicked into the next stage, and the ceiling dropped water down on us in a distractingly heavy torrent.

She looked at me, and I nodded, and then sent a Window to the team with barely muttered voice commands. "Down him, then get out. There's a river below." I focused on widening the break enough for a human to pass through it, as they turned all their energy to distracting our opponent. I could hear them fighting, even through the spraying water and screeching alarms, but I didn't turn, and tried not to imagine the loss of my fighters.

When the opening was large enough, I turned back to the room. Sam was standing beside Jacky and clutching his arm, but hers had been healed enough that she could lift it at least.

The snake had a huge grin across his face. It twisted his features grotesquely, as if his cheeks were made of putty. He still hadn't moved from his place.

China crouched beside me, picking up sharp pieces of glass.

"I'm sorry, China. I doesn't look like we're going to be getting Chanelle today," I said in a low voice, knowing her Perception was high enough to pick up my words.

"She's strong. She'll survive until we find a way to come back for her and Blaine's family." She clenched her jaw, as if to deny the possibility of any other outcome. And then she looked at me and nodded, as if I was the one who'd suggested such an unlikely happy ending.

I turned my attention to the others, unable to face her optimism and the reflection of that idealized version of me in her eyes.

Jacky faced off with the snake warily, making no move to attack. Her gaze flicked to mine, and I jerked my head to the broken window.

China threw the shards of glass at him, two at a time. Three quick volleys, quicker than even my eyes could see.

The snake's mouth twisted in surprise, but he smashed them out of the air, actually disintegrating them into fragments that exploded away from him. The little crystal dust pieces mixed with the wind and pouring water and whipped around.

Not a piece reached him. But they did distract him, and then China, Jacky, and Adam shot in all at once from three different directions, moving in low to the ground and aiming for his legs, while Sam threw a decorative plant at his head. They took him down, and his forehead smashed against the edge of a splintered coffee table.

"Hurry!" China screamed, pointing out the window.

They didn't hesitate or try to finish him while he was down, instead running or limping toward me as quickly as they could.

Sam made it first, jumping even before my nod and quickly disappearing into the darkness below.

Jacky was next, though she waited a few seconds to hear Sam's splash in the water below, and jumped far out into the empty air to ensure she didn't have an unfortunate meeting with the cliff or rocks at the edge of the water below.

China waited to jump next, but I saw that Adam was limping badly and moved to go help him.

I'd wrapped his arm around my neck and almost made it to the window.

China was about to jump, leaving only Adam and me in the room, but she froze, and then turned around to look behind us.

I turned my head to see what had made her stop.

The thin man had risen, and was walking toward us. His face seemed to almost glow from within. Not with actual light, just a terrible power.

Behind him, the soldiers had their guns out and pointing at us, but for some reason weren't firing. Instead, there was again a general scrambling as they all tried to back up into the ones behind them.

He raised his fingers to his forehead and took them away bloody, then looked at me.

I flinched.

Adam grabbed my arm, as if to protect me, and pulled me closer to the edge. "Jump, China!" he snapped.

The snake raised a hand, and the hair on the back of my neck rose in a burning instant, screaming at me to run.

Adam's other hand snapped out to grab China, but she'd stepped forward out of his reach, screaming, "NO!" at the top of her lungs.

Then Adam's arms were wrapped around me, and he was pushing me backward, jumping out of the window and taking me with him, his body a shield between me and the thin snake of a man.

But China.

China's body crumbled and twisted and fell apart, wringing her head around to me as Adam and I launched outward through the air. Even the air and water around her contorted, an instant twister mixed with squirts of blood.

Her eyes met mine, and held for a long, long time. And then her broken, mangled body was falling, taking her face with it.

The man grimaced in distaste at the mess of her corpse, and I heard his murmured, "What a waste," through the rushing wind and now distant seeming sirens.

I vaguely noticed a commotion from one of the groups of guards, as the rumpled man who'd run up earlier strained forward and they held him back.

But we were falling, too, downwards. I was surprised that my stomach could still protest at the plunge, trying to rise through my mouth in vertigo, even with what I'd just seen. Or maybe it was trying to leave *because* of it. I didn't know.

I stared up at the stars as we fell, our sky with only one moon floating through the heavens, and tried to figure out if she'd still been alive when her eyes had met mine, or if he'd already killed her, and she was just still on her feet for that last second.

Then I smashed into something hard and cold, and Adam's body above mine pushed me down into the blackness.

# Chapter 28

God kills, and so shall we; indiscriminately … for no creatures under God are as we are, none so like Him as ourselves.

— Anne Rice

ADAM DRAGGED my half-senseless body out of the water downstream, then bent me upside down over a boulder, like a kid about to get whipped over their father's knee, except he pushed hard on my back instead.

Water spewed out of me, and he did it again.

Once the water was mostly gone, I gasped for air, and spewed some more on my own, throwing up a bit in the process. I shuddered and coughed, crawling off the rock and retching into the pebbly sand until he helped me to my feet. We started to run toward the nearest escape point.

Behind us, spotlights were pointing from the compound and scanning the river and the bank, so we hurried. If we were to be caught…I shuddered.

We made it to a motorcycle stashed in the woods earlier, and he helped me on behind him, then navigated away through the darkness, clear-headed enough to remember not to turn the vehicle's lights on.

Jacky had warned us of that, along with suggesting the muffling pads around the engine.

I held on tight, my mind too dazed to thank Adam for saving me, not once, but twice.

In my head, the gruesome scene replayed itself over and over. I whispered, “No, no, no,” pressing my head into Adam’s back and closing my eyes. But my mind wouldn’t listen to me, and I was unable to stop seeing it—her eyes, her body, and the man’s little grimace of distaste. Her body crumpling limply to the ground, no longer in the right shape to support itself. Her eyes.

Adam drove for a long time, till we were out of the woods and into town, and then took a long, circuitous route, which we'd laid out beforehand to make sure we weren't followed.

We arrived at the base last, and when we entered Blaine's lab, everyone's eyes swiveled to look at us.

Blaine looked drawn out and weary, so I knew he'd been told of our failure to save his family.

Jacky let out a relieved breath and stood up. "You took so long, we were worried." She leaned to the side to try and look around us. "Where’s China? Didn’t she come with you?"

I choked.

After a few moments of silence, she asked again. "Where is China?" But this time, her voice had lost the higher pitch of excitement and relief.

"She's dead," I managed, stripping my claw-concealing gloves off. "That man..." My throat convulsed, and I couldn't force any more words out. My knees threatened to buckle beneath me, and I forced them to straighten and hold. I couldn't let the team see me so weak. They needed someone strong, especially now.

Blaine flattened his palms on the table, and stood. "What is she saying?"

Adam stepped forward. "China...was killed. He was able to do things, inhuman things. Skill-type things." He pulled up his shirt and fake uniform jacket, showing us the skin of his back. It lay swollen and dark purplish-red in artistically strewn swaths, where the membranes of skin and blood vessel had been pulverized. The edges of that twisting force had just licked at his back. "I was lucky," he said, his voice rough. He cleared his throat and clenched his jaw, blinking back tears.

The snake had been a Player, a powerful one. I'd known NIX had Players, but I'd thought they were more like captives or test subjects. He'd been on their side.

Sam shook his head, staring at the marks. "No, no, that doesn't make any sense. Why would he kill her? China was just...a kid. Completely innocent."

The full force of my emotions turned on him and started to spew out of my mouth. "But he did! He was too strong for all of us, and he killed her. While she was trying to protect us, protect me. He reached out his hand, and she turned into an ice cream swirl. He. Killed. Her!" I was screaming by the end, my voice hoarse and something of a half-growled warning shriek, like one of the Trial monsters.

They all leaned back with wide eyes, and I realized that my teeth were bared and my claws out in an explicit threat. I closed my mouth, and willed the swirling burn inside me back down.

There was silence then, and Jacky opened and closed her mouth, then started to cry. Her tears lasted only a few moments, and then she turned on Sam. "You shoulda stopped him," she snarled. "You're the only one who maybe coulda, and the only one who refused to try. You coulda done what you did in that puzzle Trial, turned him into a crystal-thing. China coulda escaped with us if you took him out."

He paled and stepped back as if she'd hit him, but didn't rebut her words.

"Did the mission work? Do they know it was you?" Blaine asked. What he meant was 'Are they coming after you? Is my family in danger?'

"Adam did his job," I said, "There's no record of us or

anything relating to us, and we shorted the GPS chips. But they've got her body. They still have her body," I repeated. "And they've still got Chanelle, and your niece and nephew."

"What does that mean?" Jacky asked.

"It means we're all in danger," Blaine said. "Eventually, they'll figure out who China was. And they've got people imprisoned, but with the wrong information. They're going to notice, and they're going to realize what we did. Somehow, they're going to connect this to us. Maybe through Bunny. Just because you don't have any records in their system doesn't mean you're safe. We're not safe."

"How long do we have until they figure it out?" Sam asked.

"My program had an ouroboros clean up code. There aren't traces of tampering in the system, other than the empirical evidence of those three with all the wrong information. The computers won't give us away. Our downfall will be some person, someone who remembers their real information, and knows who Blaine is," Adam said.

"So we just have to go back and get them, right? If we can finish the plan, and take away any evidence that connects to us, we'll be safe, right?" Sam perked up a bit, with a kind of desperate plea in his eyes.

Jacky snorted. "China won't be safe. It's too late for her. And how the hell do you think we're gonna get back in, after what just happened?"

"We might make it in, but we'd never leave again. Especially not with Chanelle and the other two," Adam said.

Sam deflated, and returned to staring at his hands.

"Their names are Kris and Gregor," Blaine said, low.

Adam paused, then nodded. "Sorry. Kris and Gregor. But it's only a matter of time before they connect all this to us. It's not like they're just going to let it go and write it off as bad luck. If there's something to find, they'll find it. And us."

"So what do we do?" Jacky looked to me.

"We run," I said. "And we hide. If they don't know where we are, they can't use teleportation to take us to the Trials. So at least there's that." It was a small victory, considering. Why didn't I feel better about it?

I smelled our defeat in the air, saw it in the curve of our spines, bowing under the weight of fear and loss.

Sam clenched his fists, and muttered, "We were so close."

"Blaine already had a more fugitive-style escape plan, since we wouldn't have been able to make NIX forget about him just because his information disappeared. None of us were planning to stay in this city anyway," I said. "We were already going to run. We'll just have to do it a little more...seriously." Desperately. My voice felt dead, and I steeled myself to get through the next few hours of planning. I was shaking, shivering. I didn't feel cold, but maybe I was, because I was still damp from the river, and I couldn't feel my fingers.

"I'm not running," Blaine said. "I can't just leave the kids to NIX's mercy, especially if they were to think the reason for keeping them alive as hostages just ran away."

Adam sighed. "You don't know what they'll do to you."

"But I have to take responsibility for my actions. I helped you because I wanted to save the kids and hurt NIX any way I could. Well, we failed. I can't just run away from that burden."

"That's your choice to make, Blaine. And I think you're a good man for making it. But the rest of us aren't in your situation. I'd rather not face NIX ever again, and I'm definitely not going to wait for them to come to me," I said.

He smiled. "I wouldn't expect you to. And I'll still help you to get away. I just won't be coming with you."

I sat down at one of the tables, and called for a blanket, some coffee, and Sam's Skill to help my re-wounded shoulder. I was settling in for a long night. I couldn't be weak, couldn't let my body or my mind fail me and the team again.

---

A FEW HOURS of planning and discussion later, I'd grown even more frustrated and irritable, and every second I half expected agents from NIX to break down the door to Blaine's lab and take us all. Either that or call us up to tell us they'd taken our families, too, and were holding them hostage. I could only be grateful I'd had the foresight to move them to safety, away from any memories those at NIX might have of them. I hoped desperately it had worked. But now I had put them into more danger.

I wondered if I should go ahead and tell them everything, so they could be on their guard if I weren't around to watch their backs. But what if that made things worse? They could both be stubborn and reckless, especially Zed. My pack in the corner started to vibrate and lit up, distracting me from my thoughts. I'd put my ID sheath inside and left it at the base, so in case something went wrong NIX wouldn't be able to use it to identify me.

I retrieved my pack, and the ID sheath from within it. It was an unknown caller. The call went to message when I didn't respond, but after only a few seconds, the person on the other end redialed. I answered, sending a warning look to the others to stay quiet. "Hello?"

"Eve?"

"Who is this?"

"It's Bunny. Listen, everything's going crazy—"

"How do you have this number?" I demanded, my heart racing. If he knew, NIX new, and we were screwed.

"I...I just happened to remember it. Listen, this is a secure line. They don't know I'm calling, and I don't have much time. They don't even know I know who you are."

"Why are you calling me?"

"Just listen! Everything's in chaos here. The whole place is on lockdown because some unknown people with Seed augmentation broke in, but they don't know who you are. They know you had Seed augmentation, so they know you're probably Players, and they're going to find you using the next Boneshaker, if they don't get any other leads before that."

I shook my head. "But we killed the GPS. How would they

find us? They can't use the Boneshaker without knowing where we are."

"That's what I'm trying to tell you. I figured out what you did. Tried to cut yourself off from NIX's access to you, escape the Game? I mean, it was smart, but I heard them talking. They said as long as you're alive and have any Seed material from our facility in your body, the Trial will take you along with the others. They're going to run scans on the Shortcut, the huge metal ball-thing above the courtyard. At the moment of transfer, it's going to show them where all the transfers are coming from. They'll track all the ones they know, and the ones they don't must be you guys. They're worried you might be Players from an unknown entity and in that case they won't be able to track you. But you are one of ours. So they'll find you."

Disappointment sucked the strength from me. "What? I—I thought..."

"I thought so, too. When I realized what you'd done, honestly, I was so glad for you, but then..."

Suspicion flared. "Why are you telling me this?" I stared blankly out at the others sitting around the table, who stared at me with almost identical expressions of horror.

"I couldn't go along with it any more. What you said to me before...I realized it was true. And when I saw you guys fighting in that room, and then what happened to China, I—I just couldn't, not anymore."

"You were that guy?" I'd thought the guy who ran up and got shielded by the soldiers looked at me with familiarity. Now I knew why. Because he'd had access to every waking and sleeping moment of my life for the last few months, except for the Trials.

"If they find out, I'm screwed. But I had to do something to stand up to them."

"How can I trust you?"

"Well, there's no way to...*prove* it, but does it matter? If I was trying to betray you, you'll know soon, because they'd be tracking this communication signal right now, and you'd have an army crashing down around your ears in a few minutes. But you won't."

"That doesn't mean I can trust you. This could be a trap."

"So don't trust me. But I'm here to help, if there's anything I can do. Look, I've got to go. If you need to contact me, call me and hang up. I'll get back with you as soon as I'm able."

The line went dead.

I dropped my ID sheath back into my pack and sat down again at the table. "You guys heard all that, right?"

Adam dropped his head into his hands. "It was all…for nothing. The Trial is coming again in four days, and along with it we're going to be caught by NIX. We've only made things *worse*."

I felt hollow. All of it was my fault. I'd gone to China and told her about her sister so she would agree to help me. I'd gathered the rest of the team and convinced them to help me try to escape from the Trials. I hadn't forced China to stay behind, even though I should have kept her safe. I hadn't forced her and the team to wait till NIX's next shift change so we had more time to prepare and grow stronger.

The only thing I'd accomplished was to get China killed, and put the rest of us on NIX's hit list. So much for my promise not to regret my actions ever again.

"We have to get as far away from here as possible," I said. "So far that they won't be able to retrieve us, even if they do know where we are. And we have to keep moving, so they can't pinpoint our location from Trial to Trial. If you've got family we sent away, you might want to talk to them. It could be a while before we get the chance again. Don't alarm them. We don't want our faces on the news when we disappear and for someone at NIX to notice them and happen to remember we used to be Players. If we can, we want to keep our families safe."

"We'll have to come up with some other story, then," Adam said.

---

EARLY MORNING, after a long night without sleep, I called my brother to give him a reason why I'd be disappearing, and to say goodbye. Instead, everything fell apart.

"What?" I growled across the connection.

"I'll go join Mom later, when you do. I used your bed last night, since you weren't here and mine's gone. Hope you don't mind."

"Weren't you supposed to drive the moving pod?"

"Err, yeah. Mom was livid." He snorted. "But she makes enough to afford a driver, now."

I stood up, my chair scraping on the ground as I pushed it away from the table. "You should have gone with her. You need to leave, Zed."

"Why?"

I ground my teeth together. "Cause that's the plan. There's stuff waiting for you there. Are you just going to leave Mom to deal with everything? What about the summer programs you were going to enroll in? You should go, Zed."

"I don't think so. We need to talk."

I strained to keep my claws sheathed. "I'm going to be home soon. Stay there." I disconnected the call and quickly explained the situation to the others.

"It's dangerous to be seen going home," Adam warned.

"I don't have a choice," I snapped.

"At least change your clothes first. You've got blood on you."

I nodded. "I'll be back in an hour. Get everything ready to go." I dressed as inconspicuously as I could, covering my face like a paranoid film star. As I made my way back to my house, which I'd scheduled to be sterilized of any trace of living inhabitants later that day, rage bloomed in my chest like a flower whose infinite petals just kept spreading open. How could Zed be so willful? Didn't he know how much danger he was putting himself in? Undoing all my hard work to protect him.

As I opened the front door of my house, even my anger couldn't keep me strong. Of course he didn't know. I stepped through the entrance in silence. My strength had been grated away, hour after hour, and I felt like a creature of trembling tendons and hollow bones. My thoughts had the fuzzy distance that came from extreme fatigue.

I moved to the doorway of my room, bracing for an additional weight to land atop the wobbling burden already crushing me.

Zed sat on the side of my bed, hands clenched in front of him. He looked up at me with bloodshot eyes, obviously not having slept. "Hey." He smiled at me gently. "You don't look so good. Wanna sit down?" He patted the edge of the bed beside him, as it was the only piece of furniture left in the room.

I didn't know what to say. Instead, I just stood there in the doorway to my bedroom, staring at him. Anger, I could deal with. Accusations would strengthen my backbone long enough to get me bluffing through the conversation. Even threats would have been preferable. At that moment, compassion slipped through my defenses like a burrowing weasel.

There must have been some hint in my face, because he said only, "Oh," then stood and wrapped me in a hug.

It was so surprising that it startled a tear right out of me. One, and then another. Then I was sobbing, being nasty and slobbery and unwashed all over him, but he didn't seem to mind.

Finally, I calmed down and pulled away from him. I wiped my face on the bottom of my shirt, beyond caring about propriety at that point.

He led me into the room and sat me down on the bed, one fist still clenched tight. "You're in trouble," he stated, voice calm.

"No, no, I'm really not, Zed. You don't have to worry about me." After crying so hard, and all that had passed since the last time I slept, I barely had the strength to keep sitting up. But I couldn't leave him fretting about me when I disappeared for what might be the rest of his life. "You're way overprotective." I rolled my eyes. "I haven't slept in a while, my body's tired from working out, and I…I'm probably not going to see you for a while."

"What do you mean?"

"I got an offer from the foreign relations branch of enforcers. If I join their training program as a recruit right out of high school, I'll get the chance to travel the world, have adventures, get more schooling, all while getting paid. It's a wonderful opportunity." I tilted my head to the side and smiled as cheerfully as I could. "I think I'm going to accept. I realized I'm going to miss you and your stupid overprotectiveness. That's why I started blubbering like a sea cow." I elbowed him playfully.

He stood and started to pace back and forth. "Don't lie to me, Eve. I *know* you." He reached the far wall and turned to stare at me.

Maybe at one point that was true, I thought. But who I was had changed over the last couple months. He didn't know me, not any more. I didn't say any of that, but I saw the recognition of it in his eyes, and realized how sad this must all be for him. We'd been so close before the Game. We looked out for each other. But all of a sudden, with no explanation, I'd started distancing myself from him, cutting him out of my life. And he could never know why.

"You look so tired you might as well be wearing panda makeup, you've got dried blood behind your ear," he nodded when my hand flew to my ear, giving me away. "And you're so freaking scared, all the time now."

I opened my mouth to protest, but he held up a hand and talked over me. "I've listened to you pretend everything's okay, that you have everything under control, over and over now. But whatever's going on, it's obvious you're *not* 'handling' it." He took a deep breath, clenched his fist, and said. "So I have to force my help on you." His fist opened to reveal a Seed.

Even as my mind was stuttering for a response, an excuse, he did the one thing that could make everything that had come before seem like a trivial test of my ability to hold myself together.

Before he even had the, "I wish I was," out of his mouth, I'd lunged across the room toward him. But I didn't make it in time to stop him from saying, "like Eve," and clenching his fist around the Seed.

I clamped one hand down around his wrist hard enough to force his fingers loose, and used the other to slap the Seed out of his grip with stunning force.

It flew across the room like a bullet and left a dent in the wall.

"Ahh!" my brother screamed, yanking back and cradling the hand I'd slapped. "What the hell!"

I ignored him and pulled his hand forward, inspecting it for a small incision that might soon be gone. Sure enough, even as I watched, the small puncture wound disappeared, knitting itself back up so quickly and so flawlessly I might have believed it a figment of my imagination if I hadn't experienced it so many times before in my own flesh.

# Chapter 29

Part of my soul I seek thee, and claim thee my other half.
— John Milton

"NOW, whatever you're caught up in, I'm part of, too," he said.

"What the hell did you do!" I screamed.

"I saw you, Eve. The other day when the power went off and you disappeared. And then you reappeared, hurt. Bad hurt. You left your link here, though. So I used it to access all your files stored in the cloud for the last few months, since you started acting strange. You tried to hide those videos, I could tell. Even a password. But I've known your favorite password for years…" he trailed off and took a deep breath, frowning.

Rage overwhelmed me for a moment, and I wanted to punch him. I'd been trying so, so hard, and he'd just ruined it all. Instead, I forced him to the bed and made him sit down. "How did you get the Seed?"

"That marble thing? You dropped it when you reappeared." He plopped a hand on my shoulder, eyes drooping. "You don't realize it, but you can't fix everything alone. Now you don't have a choice. Whatever that was I just did, you'll have to let me in… Whoa," he blinked in disorientation and swayed on the bed.

"You're okay," I muttered, scrabbling with inept fingers at my link.

"I'm not feeling too grlll…" he slurred, and then his eyes rolled back in his head.

"No, no. Stay awake. Don't pass out, Zed!" I slapped his cheek, but it had no effect, so I turned my attention back to my ID link and finally managed to dial the number Bunny had called me from. My hands were trembling, and when I heard the first ring I forced myself to hang up and wait for him to call back. I shook Zed, slapped his cheeks, and yelled at him, but he lay unresponsive. "They'll take you to the Trials too. No, don't do this to him," I pleaded.

My ID sheath rang only once before I picked up Bunny's call. "Bunny! Please, help me. Don't let this happen to him. I'll do anything, just help me!" I said, basically sobbing by the end.

"Calm down. Speak clearly. What's going on?"

"It's Zed, my brother. He took a Seed. He saw me use one right after the last Trial and found one of mine and he just made a wish and took it and now he's passed out and I'm so afraid." I took a deep breath. "He can't be a Player. I'll do anything, just please, tell me how to stop this. He doesn't deserve this." I breathed hard, waiting for his response.

"Eve…once the wish is made, there's nothing to be done. If he's been injected, it's already spread through his system. The acclimatization process is already starting. There is nothing I can do. There's nothing anyone can do. But…"

"What?" I snapped. "But what?"

"He would have been tested, too. If he's not a Player already, I can only guess that means he doesn't have the compatibility gene. Which means he's in serious danger."

"Explain."

"NIX chooses candidates that have the highest chance of

surviving the acclimatization process the body has to go through to adapt to its first Seed. You were chosen. He wasn't."

"Are you saying he's going to die? No. No, he's not."

"I'm sorry," his subdued voice said.

It barely reached my ears, as I was too busy throwing Zed's limp body over my shoulder. I thanked the Seeds wordlessly for making me strong enough to carry him, at the same time cursing them for daring to touch him with their taint.

I made it back down to the pod I'd arrived in unnoticed, and stuffed him onto the empty back seats. Then I took the driver's seat, sent a Window to Sam, and floored the acceleration pedal on my way back to the base.

Sam and Blaine met me at the door and helped to carry Zed in and lay him in Blaine's lab.

"Keep him alive," I said. "He took one of my Seeds and it's killing him. So you two need to keep him alive."

Blaine hurried around the room, grabbing monitoring equipment and bags of IV fluid from their storage places, while Sam bent over Zed with one hand on his head and the other on his chest.

Sam closed his eyes for a few minutes, and then said to me, "I won't let him die."

I wondered for a moment if that was a promise he could keep, then shook the thought from my head. Sam could work miracles, literally. He would save my brother, because if he didn't I would kill him.

He said, "I can't stop the process that's been started, but if I can heal him fast enough and for long enough, I think I can keep him strong enough to survive it."

"You *think*?"

"I—I will. And Eve, I just want to say, I was wrong. Wrong about everything since the Intelligence Trial. I feel so responsible." His voice broke on the last bit, but his eyes didn't waver from mine.

I gave him a half smile. It was all I could afford without

cracking into a quivering mess. "I can't judge. I've screwed *everything* up."

---

THE WHOLE TEAM had gathered in Blaine's lab, watching Blaine and Sam work as I paced back and forth anxiously, asking how Zed was doing every five minutes. We'd postponed our departure a few hours to let the two work on him.

Finally, Sam took one last frustrated breath and snapped at me to leave. "The Seed is attacking his body on a cellular level. Keeping him stable is very difficult. It takes a lot of power and concentration, and you're making it harder."

I clenched my jaw, but then Blaine laid a hand on my shoulder. "He'll be fine even if you don't stay here and watch over him. We know what we're doing. Especially Sam. Go, get some rest."

I nodded and left the room after one last look at Zed. Instead of going to lay down, I went outside in my bare feet.

Early afternoon sun shone down with determined strength, and the lack of smog in the air around Blaine's remote property was noticeable in the subsequent lack of burning sensation in my nostrils. I dug my toes into the pleasantly cool grass and breathed deeply. Just as I had begun to force some tension out of my muscles, my ID sheath rang with Bunny's secret number. I picked up immediately.

"They've got your face," he said.

"What?"

"Your face, they've made drawings from the witness accounts. I've been sticking my nose in as much as possible without getting noticed, and I heard they're calling in some guy that monitors Players with potential. Apparently you were on the watch list because of some Bestowals, which are special accomplishments in the Trials. If anyone can remember any of your information from looking at the drawing, you're screwed, Eve."

"I thought you were the only one who watched us?"

“I thought so, too. But you stood out, did well, and apparently it drew attention.”

"Crap."

"Yeah. If they figure out who you are, and they will, I think, then they're going to know I've been keeping your identity a secret. I'll be screwed, and I'm not going to be able to keep you safe."

"God. They're going to question you." I crouched down and buried my head between my knees.

"I won't tell them anything, I promise."

"You can't promise that. What if they torture you?" It wasn't really a question, and he knew it, too.

"I'm sorry, Eve," he said after a long pause. "I never wanted it to turn out like this."

"Yeah." I couldn't keep talking to him. I needed to be alone. "I've got to go, Bunny." I hung up before he could respond, stood, and walked barefoot into the forest surrounding Blaine's mansion.

The news wasn't so crushing. They would have found us all, sooner or later, I knew. But it added a pressure just a little too heavy to bear, on top of all the rest.

I walked under the weight for a long while, forcing my legs to bear the grueling burden that had built up over my never-ending day. Finally, I stopped, and let it all out in a scream that ripped through the woods around me like a ravenous beast.

Birds exploded out of their nests in terror, and small things chittered and squeaked as they raced away through the underbrush.

I screamed and kept screaming, pushing everything within me out into the air till my mind was a ringing, empty place. Then I crumpled to the ground and flailed at the dirt and decaying leaves with my claws, ripping at it so I didn't cut into my own flesh.

I opened my mouth in a straining, silent scream, flexing my muscles as I lost control of everything I'd been holding back for so long. Barriers inside creaked and cracked and broke, and everything slipped away from me.

Then something within the aching emptiness reached out to me. It enfolded me, wrapping around and holding me together with warmth and darkness.

I shuddered and sank into the comfort.

It spoke to me, but I couldn't understand.

I shook my head and my concentration slipped from the sound.

Hesitantly, warmth pulsed acknowledgment of my hurt, a feeling rather than words.

I shook my head again. I wasn't hurt, not really. I was just broken, defeated. Like a small beaten animal.

It questioned. Who hurt me?

I remembered Zed's eyes as he passed out from the Seed, the snake-man and China, the Trials, and the masked duo at the beginning who'd started it all. NIX had done this to me. NIX had broken and destroyed me.

Anger seeped into me then, and along with it, strength. It showed me what it was like to crush my enemy with power enough to lay a blanket of dread and reverence over all who would oppose me.

The feeling was wonderful. But I was weak. I couldn't even save one person from NIX.

It gave me the solution. Become strong.

It was simple. So simple. All along I'd been going about it wrong. The only way to defeat a huge power was with an even more overwhelming power. Fear was the most effective tool against my enemies. Along with that understanding, more strength flowed into me, and the warmth bound me tighter and tighter till I opened my eyes and saw the forest around me.

I lay in a fetal ball at the base of a tree, and I was alone. I sat up slowly, feeling as if I might fall apart if I moved too quickly. But inside, a burning mass fed strength to me.

Hours must have passed, because the light was different, fading and yellow as it slanted through the leaves above. I stood and looked around. At my feet the ground was scored and gouged, and there was dirt under my nails, but no sign of anyone else.

I took a cavernous breath and let it swirl in that ball of heat within me, then blew it out. "Time to plan," I said aloud, and typed Bunny's number into my ID sheath. When he called me back, I said, "I need to restore Chanelle, Kris, and Gregor's info into NIX's database without NIX knowing. And you're going to help me."

# Log Of Captivity 4

Mental Log of Captivity-Estimated Day: Two thousand, six hundred twenty-nine.

The lacerations I tore into myself trying to escape throb. I felt her come close to where they keep me captive, and I struggled to join her as I know she wished, but I failed. I failed to go to her side, and she was hurt. She reached out to me in pain later, and I, useless as I am, was only able to give her my anger as fuel. It is the one thing I have in abundance. She grabbed it like a true *warrior-queen,* and rose again. She grows quickly, even without my help. Thank the gods, for if she were weaker, I would be the first *blood-covenant-champion* to let their master die before even meeting her.

# Chapter 30

Do not go gentle into that good night.
— Dylan Thomas

I SPOKE with Bunny for a long while, brainstorming and asking questions while still keeping my newfound goal hidden from him. He may have been willing to help when I and my team were innocent, helpless victims, but I didn't know if he'd ally himself with a wolf baring teeth in his direction. When I was ready, I sent a message to the group asking them to gather for a meeting. Then I headed back through the darkening forest, planning my persuasion.

They were all sitting, waiting for me nervously when I arrived back dirty-footed and somewhat disheveled.

Before talking to them, I went to Zed's beside and bent over him.

He was breathing shallowly, and sweat beaded up on his skin. An IV needle pierced through his arm and fed fluid into him.

Sam cleared his throat. "He's stable," he said. "I'm checking on him every ten minutes, but the Seed seems to have moved past the first stage and I'm just waiting for the second to start."

"And you can handle it when it does?"

"I will keep him alive through this, Eve. I promise." He drew himself up straight, and looked me in the eye with more steel in his bearing than I'd ever seen.

I nodded. "Okay." I turned to address the whole group. "I've got a new plan."

Adam leaned forward. "Oh? A better way to hide from NIX?"

"No."

He tilted his head to the side, and the rest of them just gave me blank looks.

"The old plan isn't going to work," I continued. "It's only postponing the inevitable. Soon they'll be tracking us through the Trials. Even if we somehow manage to keep surviving through them, how long before we're too badly injured to escape afterward? NIX may not have our information, but they have my face, and maybe some of yours, too. And soon—"

"What?" Sam's faced paled and he interrupted.

"Bunny contacted me earlier and told me they had sketches from the witness statements of my face. Someone outside of the Moderators was keeping track of me specifically, and they're going to recognize me."

Adam shrugged. "Well, that sounds bad, but..." he paused and frowned. "Oh. They'll be tracking us through the cameras. If they know our faces, they might not even need to wait for a Trial to try and get us. They'll just have to find us in any monitored area. Which means we'd have to stay away from civilization in general..." he took a deep breath. "Which means we're going to be hard pressed to lose them after the Trials, because satellite imaging will be on us and we'll have to be creative to escape its eyes. It's not impossible, but..." he trailed off again, and lapsed into glowering silence.

Blaine adjusted his glasses. "But is not the point of all this to buy yourselves time? It's not like you can just give up. Either run or sit there waiting for them to come for you. Even if there are some unforeseen difficulties, it does not change the situation."

"Buy ourselves time? Time to what? Keep running? Always be looking over our shoulders, living in fear? You have Kris and Gregor to consider, which I understand, but nothing is going to change if we don't force it to. The situation can only worsen with the playing board the way it is now. We're screwed, either way. But," I paused, "There is a third option."

They stared at me in confusion, as I'd been saying the opposite only hours before.

I took a deep breath before continuing, "We take pre-emptive action. Rather than letting NIX control this, we change up the rules a bit."

"What do you mean?" Adam said.

"I mean, I want to do more than figure out how to escape being Players in the Game. I want to completely stop NIX from coming after us."

"And…how do you propose we do that?" he asked.

"We attack. We crush them." I turned to Jacky. "Didn't you tell me once that the best defense is an overwhelmingly powerful offense?"

Her eyes widened, but then she leaned forward and clenched her hands together, fingers entwined so hard they turned white. "Hell, yes. That sounds wonderful. I'll go wherever you decide, but if it's to fight, hell yes. Payback."

While Adam was looking at her incredulously, Sam spoke up. "I'm with you, too, if you can think of a way to make it work." He rubbed at his worn and tired face. "I've been afraid to really fight for a long time, because I don't want to be…a murderer. And it's way, way too easy for me because of my Skill. But from now on, I'm going to fight properly, whether it's a suicide mission or not. Some people, those people at NIX…they deserve to die. If I'd realized that sooner, maybe someone who was innocent would still be alive." He looked around self-consciously, and we all knew who he meant.

Adam gaped at him next. "Are you freaking serious?" he spat. "Have you forgotten what happened the last time we fought with someone from NIX? I haven't. I've still got internal bruising! We were totally outclassed."

Blaine nodded. "He is, I must say, correct. You barely escaped last time, and China was killed less than a day ago. You are not thinking clearly, Eve. Understandable, with the tragedy you've just been through. Maybe you should sleep for a while. NIX will be on the alert for any attacks. The one reason you made it as far as you did is the element of surprise."

"An element which is now *lost*," Adam said. "And not only are we too weak to go against them, we no longer have a way to get stronger, now that the Game interface and our location are blocked from NIX. No more magically appearing Seeds, remember? There's no way in hell I'm ever going back there. In fact, I plan to stay as far away and as hidden as possible."

Sam had paled as Adam spoke, but he didn't take back his statement, and Jacky only rolled her eyes in derision at Adam.

I smiled. I hadn't expected it to be so easy. I'd thought Jacky would be with me, because she was the type to jump into any fight with glee, and lately she'd been hero-worshipping me. But Sam? A surprise, there. "Any other concerns?" I asked, looking at each of them. Once they laid each objection out, I could find a way to shoot them down all at once.

"I caution you against this path of action, Eve. It is illogical and reckless. And I fear that it would endanger those still held by NIX," Blaine said.

"Other than the fact that you're being *stupid* and reckless, no. I think those two things should be reason enough," Adam added.

"Okay, good," I said. "Blaine, I want to fix Kris, Gregor, and Chanelle's information in NIX like it was never erased. That will give them some protection, and it might keep you safe too."

Adam interrupted, "How are you going to do that?"

"Well, you're going to help me," I smiled. "Bunny's on the inside, and he's willing to access the computer system for us. It wouldn't have to be too fancy. Just something so any erasing we did won't be noticed at first glance."

Blaine beamed at the possibility of protecting the kids. "Oh, wonderful! If Adam can get the program ready, I can send the data through to the Moderator's link device."

"Good. That'll keep those three safe. And yes, Adam, we're not strong enough right now. In fact, we were blown away in terms of power. And we won't be getting any more Seeds. But you know that new Seeds aren't the only way to get stronger. They replicate organically if your body displays a need for them. Like muscles. That's where our spontaneous Attribute level-ups come from."

"That takes *time.* Which we are decidedly lacking right now," Adam ground out. "Didn't you just say running wouldn't work? Your 'plan' doesn't avoid that. The amount of training we'd have to do to face that superhuman strength...we'd be running forever, trying to survive the Trials while organically leveling up."

"Exactly." My smile was a sharp thing full of menace I didn't bother to try and hide. "Which is why we need to create more time."

Jacky pursed her lips. "I know you've got a plan, Eve. But I dunno what this one is. Explain, please."

"If you've noticed, when we are in the Trials, much more time passes there than what the clock says when we return. In fact, it seems to be about five times as much. Plenty of time to train ourselves uninterrupted."

"You want to stay there, after the Trial is over," Jacky inferred. Her voice was low, scratchy.

Sam stood up and laid his hands on Zed's chest, took a deep breath, and shuddered as he began to heal again. "What if we get trapped?"

"What if we get *killed*?" Adam snapped, scowling at me.

"Getting trapped shouldn't be a problem. I've talked to Bunny about it. Getting killed is a real possibility. But in our current situation, it's not so different than if we stayed in the normal world."

Sam sat back down. "I'll go."

Jacky nodded. "Me too. I'm not a yellow-bellied coward."

Adam stood up, sparks jumping along the dusting of hair on the back of his arms up to his head. "This is idiotic, Eve. You're leading them into danger, just like with NIX. I've supported you in the past, but I'm not going to agree to this. I won't die just because you hate NIX so much you want to find a way to get back at them, and I won't go with you and watch you do it, either. I'm going with the original plan, the one with the least risk to my life." He started to stride way but stopped and turned back. "And I hope you all come to your senses and stay with me. You're the leader, Eve. The team needs you to *lead* them, beyond your desire for revenge and panic for your brother." Then he left, disappearing through the doorway, though his angry footsteps could still be heard.

I sighed. I'd have to keep working on him.

Blaine took off his glasses and rubbed them briskly. "This is not my decision to make. I am not a Player, so I couldn't go even if I wished. But I do have a lot to lose if you screw up."

"You also have a lot to gain. Freedom from NIX, for both you and the kids."

"I trust that you're not leading all of us to our deaths or a life of being test subjects—or enslaved scientists, in my case," Blaine said. "You must have a plan, knowing you. What is it?"

"I want to hit them where it hurts. *Everywhere* it hurts. A multi-pronged attack that will make them recognize us as a poison they don't want to touch with a ten-foot pole. And if I can't escape the Game, I want to destroy it."

# Chapter 31

Whenever a thing is done for the first time, it releases a little demon.

— Emily Dickinson

A COUPLE DAYS LATER, Zed finally woke up, startling both me and Sam, who'd fallen asleep at his bedside. We were in a small village off the coast of some city whose name I couldn't pronounce, hidden from NIX's watchful eyes as well as possible.

He looked around blearily and croaked like a chain-smoking frog.

Sam rushed to get him some water, while I helped him to sit up.

"He's awake!" I said loudly, letting the others know.

Zed gulped down the liquid and handed the cup back to Sam. "What's going on?"

"You were sick, really sick," I said with a grin so wide I felt like my lips might split. "But you made it."

He frowned. "What was I sick with? I feel like crap."

"You..." I trailed off. How exactly was I supposed to explain this?

Jacky moved to stand beside me, and grinned. "You've just been initiated into a super exclusive club."

"You injected yourself with something, remember?" I said.

He nodded. "Yeah. One of those glass balls you use."

"Those are called Seeds," Sam said.

"Do you remember a few months ago, when I was so sick?" I asked

"Yeah. Is that what this was?"

I nodded. "The Seed is...something that changes your body on a cellular level. Little microscopic organisms go in and change things, according to the wishes you make when you use the Seeds. And using the Seed makes you a Player." I paused to swallow past the lump in my throat.

Adam picked up the explanation for me. "We're all Players. We've all taken the Seed and survived. Well, except him," he pointed to Blaine. "He's just got beef with the people behind all this. And rightfully so. They took his family and blackmailed him into helping them. The rest of us just hate them because of the Game."

"Wait, slow down, I'm lost. What does it mean when you say you're a Player?" Zed said.

Jacky butted in again. "It means you're a kinda super human badass now."

Adam rolled his eyes. "Sorry, but the other side of that is you're teleported away and forced to play in a death game every handful of days."

Sam shook his head at the both of them. "Guys, you're kind of horrible at explanations. You're being confusing and frightening by turns." He turned to Zed and said, "Hi, I'm Sam. I'm a member of your sister's team. This must all be very confusing."

Zed nodded at him in relief, "Yes, it is." He looked to me. "Please, someone just start making sense."

"When I got sick that time, I wasn't actually sick. Not in the conventional sense. There's a secret organization called NIX that forces people to play something they just call the Game. They do that by injecting us with a Seed, a tracking device, and a virtual reality chip. Since you did it to yourself, you only have the Seed. But you'll still have to go to the Trials. When you saw me disappear, that's what happened. It's basically teleportation, as far as we can tell. Or maybe time travel. Every few days, that happens to us, and we reappear at something called a Trial. Basically, it's a test of our ability to survive using the abilities we gain from the Seeds." I continued trying to explain for a few more minutes, with the others interjecting periodically.

At the end, Zed just stared at me. "I feel like I'm dreaming."

A laugh bubbled up from my stomach. "You're not dreaming. But I remember when I thought it was all a crazy hallucination, too. That changed quickly enough. Here, let me show you." I looked to the others. "Quick demonstration?"

Jacky nodded and picked up the ceramic mug Zed had drunk from.

She squeezed, and the handle crumbled away in her hand. She held out the dust for Zed's inspection, and then blew it into the air, creating a little cloud of floating particles.

Which Adam then poured little sparks of electricity through until it looked like a cutely menacing storm cloud.

Then I allowed the now-familiar feeling of power to roll through my veins, turning my fingernails into thick, slightly curved claws. Looking down, I saw that my toes had changed a bit, too. The joints and bones of my foot seemed to have thickened and spread out, and the nails had grown pointed. "That's new," I said, using my superior balance to raise my leg straight up from the ground to show the others.

"Fascinating," Blaine said, leaning in. "You say this had not happened before? I would love to spend a little more time examining your transformation..."

I rolled my eyes and gave him an exasperated smile, then turned to Zed, whose eyes were wide enough to show the whites.

I picked up his hand and ran my index fingernail across the palm.

He yanked the hand away, and stared up at me in horror as blood started to bead along with scratch. "What the hell?"

"It hurts, right? I don't know if it's true, but they say you can't feel pain in a dream. Plus, I needed to set something up for Sam to show you what he's capable of."

Sam took Zed's hand gently, and within a few seconds, the scratch had transferred to Sam, and in a few seconds more it was gone.

Blaine wiped the blood off Zed's hand with a cotton swab, and moved away to examine it at the nearest microscope.

"This is insane," Zed said. "You guys are all...mutants?"

There were a few seconds of silence, and then we all started to laugh. I chuckled at first, and then noticed Zed's surprised confusion and started to laugh even harder.

Jacky's immense strength deserted her under the effects of her mirth, and she sank to the ground, snorting like a pig on every inward breath.

Finally, I was able to open my mouth without laughing. I wiped my eyes and said, "Yeah, kinda like that."

---

ZED HAD GONE BACK to sleep as his body fought to regain strength, and I lay on a pallet in the large room we'd rented, working on the smallest puzzle ring the Oracle had given to me. Technically, I should have been sleeping like the others, but I felt a constant pressure to do something to give us all a better chance at survival.

My weary eyes grew a sort of tunnel vision, allowing me to see the irregularities in each band's surface. I'd slipped it over my left forefinger because without something to hold onto and wrap around, the bands kept slipping apart.

I'd found that my claws were better suited for the finesse

required to fit the bands together. I could use their tips like tweezers, instead of the clumsy flesh of my fingertips.

After a long, intense period of fiddling, twisting and turning, and matching protrusions to grooves, the last piece of band matched up with its companions, and the shiny ring became one solid piece.

I made a fist and pumped it in the air. Finally, I'd finished it!

Then, the ring seemed to come alive, grabbing at my skin, sliding down, and shrinking around my finger till it fit snugly. It pierced inward and injected into me, just like the Seeds.

YOUR NON-SENSORY PERCEPTION HAS INCREASED

The window hung in front of my face, prompted by the sensors of the now local-access-only VR chip still embedded in my skull.

I stared at my hand in a mixture of curiosity and horror.

Then the seizure started, and all curiosity slipped away. Pain ruptured my consciousness, and my eyes rolled back in my head as my body flailed on the couch.

There was only pain and flashing lights behind my eyelids for a while, and then I started to see things in the lights. Most of them passed too fast or were too strange for me to understand. Blood, yellowing teeth, mold growing over a sick child's cheek, and a dizzying rush of sensations and images that I didn't catch but which filled me with fear and the sick feeling of decay and ruination all the same.

Then, it settled down, and I saw a huge mountain towering above a beautiful land filled with dark-rippling fire. I stood on the mountainside, and knew that at the top sat power unimaginable. Then the ground trembled beneath my feet and my perception changed like a child that looks up at the sky and realizes they are about to fall off the bottom of the world. I understood the power dwelt not at the top, but beneath me, and I stood on a gargantuan body only pretending to be a mountain.

I woke up then, but still my physical eyes did not open.

Instead, I lingered in a body not my own. A man's body, and his thoughts, and his world. A vague part of me realized that I was dreaming of being someone else, but the other part of me was too caught up in the sensation of the moment to care.

I looked up at the moons, showing through the still brightening morning sky. I stood at the top of a small grassy knoll looking out over a lake. This place, at least, still lay untainted. I smiled, and lifted something over my shoulder with a strength I'd never experienced in my real body. I wanted to protect this land, my land, and my people. I turned then, and saw a face peeking out at me from behind a tree. A beautiful girl grinned at me and my heart filled with happiness.

Then I woke up, gasping and looking up at the peeling-plaster ceiling of our rented room. I rolled off the couch onto my hands and knees, choking and gulping back sobs. Tears dropped rapidly onto the wooden boards between my hands, and I shook my head in confusion. I felt a deep-seated sense of loss, heartbreak almost, as if something precious had been ripped away from me.

I sobbed as quietly as possible, but someone placed a cool hand on my back in comfort. I jerked away from it, and looked up to see Adam.

He knelt beside me on the floor and just rubbed my back silently.

After a while, the sobs calmed down, and I wiped my face. "J—just a dream," I hiccupped. I doubted the truth of that. The ring puzzle had given me a vision, but the second part had been different. It had a kind of mental scent to it, which I'd felt before. It smelt the same as the time I'd been expanding my senses under China's tutelage, and had felt like I was somewhere else, and the same as when I'd been in the woods at our base, breaking under the pressure. "The crazy thing is, it was k—kind of a nice dream."

"Sometimes those are the hardest. When you wish they were real, and then have to wake up to reality," he said quietly, the soothing hand still on my back.

That wasn't quite it, but I didn't have the desire or the energy right then to try and explain what had happened, so I just nodded. "Sorry I woke you," I sniffled.

He shook his head. "I was already awake. It's one of the side effects of the Seeds augmenting my body. I just can't sleep as much as I used to."

"Oh."

"You should go back to sleep, though. Come on," he waved me back up onto the pallet and pulled a light blanket over me. "I'll stay with you until you fall asleep."

"Adam..."I said hesitantly.

He smirked. "I'm not going to tell anyone you were crying like a little girl, Eve. Just turn over and go to sleep."

I wrinkled my nose and turned my back to him.

He rubbed my back soothingly, over and over till I fell asleep, but all I could think of was that feeling in my dream, that happiness.

---

ON THE NINTH day since the last Trial, Blaine drove us all into what remained of the real countryside. We thought the Trials would be nine days apart from the last one on, but the exact time the Boneshaker would start was a tension-causing mystery.

I sat next to Zed, berating myself that he was seated in this van, facing this fear along with us, because of me. "I should have never let this happen to you," I murmured.

He turned to me in surprise. "Let this happen to me? You didn't have anything to do with it. Well, except..."

"That you did this for me. Right? You did this for me, and if I'd been more careful, hadn't left that Seed, hadn't let you know anything was wrong..."

"You mean if you'd lied and kept secrets from me better." He clenched his jaw.

"Yes. Exactly! No matter what, I should have kept you safe and separate from all this."

"And then I'd go about my life blissfully unaware and happy? Is that what you think? That's not how it works. If I didn't figure it out now, it would have happened eventually. Or maybe I'd never understand, and just go about my life wondering what happened to you and why you disappeared. That's not what I want. You didn't cause this. I chose this."

"You didn't know what you were choosing!" I hissed. "Not knowing is better. It's better than knowing because you're forced to live it!"

"If you'd told me, I'd have known! And I would still—" he cut off as the Boneshaker started to play, reverberating through us all. "What is that?"

"The Boneshaker," Jacky said grimly. "It will get loud."

Adam grunted. "At least it's better than listening to you two bicker," he said to Zed and me.

"Better step on it," I said to Blaine.

He nodded, and started to accelerate past the point where the pod beeped an incessant speed limit warning and started to shudder lightly.

Sam gripped the seat beneath him and took a deep breath. "Are you sure this is safe?"

Blaine frowned. "It should be safe?"

"*Should* be?" Sam's grip tightened more, and he looked out the window at the blurring scenery as the pod shot down a straightaway.

"Yes. Whatever teleportation device is being used for the Seeds and to take you to the Trials, from what I can tell it takes into account the movement of your body and neutralizes excess kinetic energy. So, you should be fine."

"But you don't know."

"Well," Blaine cleared his throat, "I do not have access to the technology, so it is technically just speculation. But I am rarely wrong, and the speed should help to mask your signal from NIX when you go. They will still find you, but it might take a minute or so longer."

"That's not much time, guys," I said. "So we need to finish this quickly so Adam and Zed can return and get away before NIX comes for them. We've got the upper hand this time, because they don't know we know how they're going to track us."

As the song grew louder, I swung the large pack on my lap around to my back, and wrapped my arms around Zed.

Across from us, Adam did the same, so Zed was as covered by our bodies as possible.

Because Zed wasn't officially a Player, Bunny couldn't add him to my team, and thus we needed to forcefully take him with us to the Trial, so I could make sure he was safe.

A few seconds later, the pulse slammed through the pod, and all of its passengers popped into the Trial.

Zed's eyes were closed, and I stepped back from him in case he threw up, keeping a hand on his arm to stabilize him against the dizziness. He opened his eyes warily, but they grew wide as he took in the world around us.

We were on a white-sand beach under a tree with drooping leaves that looked like cocoons. We'd been deposited about a mile from the base of a colossal mountain that seemed like a lot of flat-topped buttes and mesas gathered together and stacked into a tiered tower. Huge waterfalls came from openings in the rock faces and spilled down from the top, which was obscured from view by the thick clouds of mist that rose like a veil of waves all around the mountain and coalesced into a sight-blocking layer higher up.

Multiple vast lakes cut through by what seemed to be randomly shifting sandbars reached out from the base of the mountain in all directions and spilled out into rivers that cut through the lush land we stood on. The sun shone bright even through the clouds, the colors were deep and richer than any I'd seen except in the Trials. For the first time, I thought this place had something which I, living on Earth, might be envious of.

But that thought was quickly replaced by a mix of tension and watchfulness, because I remembered this view. In fact, I'd seen it the night before, in the painful dream I'd gotten after the Oracle's first gift had been solved and injected itself into me.

"It's beautiful," Zed said, taking a deep breath of the invigorating air. "And it smells like it comes out of a scent bottle. An expensive one. I've never seen water so beautiful."

I grimaced. "Yeah. Wait till the water turns out to be acid. Or better yet, a paralytic, so you drown peacefully if you try to take a swim in it." I wiggled my bare toes in the sand, suddenly rethinking my decision to forgo shoes on my "mutated" feet. Yeah, they'd be in the way when my claws slipped out, but my boots offered great protection.

He took a step back from the water's edge. "Really?"

Jacky walked over and poked a finger in. When nothing happened, she took the finger out, sniffed it, and then put the tip in her mouth. "Just water," she said. Then she started to convulse.

Sam lunged forward, grabbing onto her face with his hands, ready to heal.

Zed sucked in a breath, eyes wide, and both Adam and I tensed in horror.

Jacky stopped twitching, and pulled back with a grin on her face.

Sam frowned in confusion. "I can't feel anything, I don't—" he cut off, and his eyes widened, then narrowed at her mischievous look. "You were faking."

She snorted a loud laugh. "Sorry. The idea popped in my mind, and I couldn't resist."

I let out a loud breath, along with the rest of the team. "God, Jacky! Get away from the water. You scared me half to death."

She pursed her lips and walked back to us, then turned to look up at Zed, her mirth sliding away. "That was a joke, but it was in bad taste, no? Because here, it would more likely be real. And maybe I did just eat poison, and it's only waiting, like a cat in the bushes, to strike me."

Adam spun in a circle, his eyes taking everything in as he

scanned for danger. "It's beautiful here. And it's just as dangerous as it is amazing. Don't do anything without testing it out first, or watching someone else do it without dying."

We'd been deposited close to the cube this time, so we waved the other Players over as they arrived. As always, I checked for children. When one appeared I stiffened for a moment, until a group of older Players gathered around her, obviously protective.

I nodded to them in acknowledgement and allowed myself to feel relief. Zed would be enough to protect today.

Jacky gathered up her spit and loudly shot it into the sand.

The ground started to tremble underneath our feet, causing gentle ripples in the otherwise glassy water.

We all took a collective step back into the cover of the trees.

"What did you do, Jacky?" Sam said, looking a tiny bit sick.

Her eyes widened, and she shook her head mutely.

Zed imitated Adam's scan of his surroundings as the shuddering grew more pronounced.

"Guys, you remember that Intelligence Trial? The one with the puzzles?" I said.

Sam stepped closer to the rest of the group, starting to scan the surroundings as well. "Who could forget? Do you think this is another one?"

"I don't know. But that's not the point. Do you remember when I got caught in that string-room-thing with the Oracle?"

"Yeah? We never saw this Oracle, but I remember the cube said you got some sort of reward for that."

"Puzzles. Last night, I solved one of them." I held up my left hand to show the ring. "It turned out to be some sort of Seed. It increased my Perception, and made me pass out. I had a...dream. Maybe you'd call it a vision. Because I saw this place. Except I saw fire falling from the sky. I mean, it looked kinda like fire. But also like water. And it was dark. And the mountain was alive."

Adam stared at me, nonplussed. "Why didn't you say something?"

I bit the inside of my lip. "What would I have said? I had a weird, freaky dream and saw all this stuff I can't explain, most of which I can barely remember?"

He nodded slowly, "Yeah. If you said, 'Hey guys, I just got injected by this strange Seed I got from an intelligent Trial monster, and then I passed out and had a weird dream-slash-vision. Just thought you should know,' that might have been nice."

I scowled. "Well, if I'd known this was going to happen, I would have."

"Umm, guys," Sam said, "is this really the time?"

We fell silent, waiting for something to happen and throw us into action.

Shortly after that, one of the tree's cocoon leaves started to wiggle.

I grabbed Zed's arm and drug him away from it.

The team moved with me, each of us scanning our surroundings in a different direction so nothing snuck up while we were distracted.

The cocoon unfolded, and an ancient looking old man emerged from within, hanging from his head, which sprouted brightly colored feathers in lieu of hair.

He dropped to the sand with a *pop*, and steadied himself with a cane. His back bent like the curve of a fruit-laden tree branch, and he smiled at us kindly out of a face with no unwrinkled spot.

"Hello, children. I see that you are all here, and appear to be ready."

At least it wasn't an Intelligence type Trial. From all our combined experiences, the Intelligence types never had Moderators.

When there was no response, he continued. "Very well then. That volcano," he pointed with his cane, "is about to erupt. To win the Trial, you need to capture some of the fire and bring it back to me. Inside the Cube are the containers for that. Everyone please take one. And be quick about it. We don't have much time."

He continued to speak as the Cube doled out clear glass bulbs.

"Point the end toward some of the flame and snap the seal. It will suck inward and seal the fire within."

"Is that all?" someone asked.

His eyebrows drooped over his eyes, along with the feathers on his head. "You must survive, too. That is enough."

The ground gave a rolling heave, and a booming wave of sound followed, forceful enough to almost knock me off my feet. The clouds around the mountain were writhing, but I still couldn't see above them to the tip of the volcano.

The feather-headed old man reached upward with is cane and prodded the tip of the leaf-cocoon.

It reached down and wrapped around his body, then drew upward along with the other branches and shrank in close to the trunk. It shivered, then settled, color changing to a dark gray that spread out from the trunk to the tips of the cocoons.

One of the Players rapped their knuckles on the tree. "Stone," they announced.

All around us, the other trees started to pull their limbs in close and do the same.

Adam ran to one of the cocoons and patted on it, trying to get it to open, but it pulled away unconcerned and stiffened as its color leached away. He turned to me and shook his head in futility.

Something started to fall through the clouds. Something flickering dark and light, and heading our way.

"Uh oh," Jacky croaked.

"Fire," I said. In my dream, the land for miles and miles had been covered, cleansed by the flame. "There's no outrunning it."

I looked to Zed, whose eyes reflected the light of the flickering sky. I willed the panic down and started doing mental calculations. In less than two minutes the fire would reach the ground. Since there was no way to escape the mountain's spewing wrath, we needed a way to weather through it.

The trees around us curled up and turned to stone in ever widening ripples. “Find us a place to take shelter,” I snapped to the group, already racing toward the still-green trees. If the Moderator was hiding in one, I knew they could keep us safe. I launched myself at the side of the tree, used my momentum to take a few more steps upward, and grabbed one of the folded green leaves. With a firm grip, I used gravity and my feet pressing against the trunk to rip the leaf off. It ripped away from the stem with a milky white spray and started to calcify even as I fell to the ground. Once it was hardened I couldn't unfold it, and I tossed the useless thing to the ground in frustration.

I repeated the process, but this time snapped the leaf as if I was airing out a dirty rug before the gray spread through it. It straightened and hardened in that position, a makeshift leaf umbrella against the coming firestorm. I dropped the stone leaf at my feet and moved on to the next green tree. When I'd used up as much time as I could, I turned and sprinted back to the others, snatching up the huge leaves I'd harvested as I ran.

I pulled up a map Window through my Command Skill and followed the moving dots on it to the rest of the team. Adam was leading the others over the lake, across the sparse sandbars rippling a path through its depths, toward a large rock jutting diagonally out of the water. I followed them out into the deeper water, each lunging step splashing the crystal clear liquid up and out.

Zed looked back to see me, relief loosening his face.

A dark shadow moved across the water in the corner of my eye and drew my alarm. "There's…something in the water," I screamed, gasping for air.

They immediately started to move faster, but the resistance of the water impeded their movements, while the shadow raced toward them. They would not arrive quickly enough.

My heart crashed around in my chest, and the sick feeling of fear and helplessness made me want to scream. I pushed myself harder and started to catch up with the group, but I knew the creature, slicing toward them like a bullet, would reach them first.

I threw the leaves like Frisbees towards the rocky overhang, slipped off my pack and hurled that, too, and then turned to intercept the creature. I inserted myself between the team and the approaching monster with only seconds to spare and jumped as hard as I could. I blocked off everything in my mind but the monster. My body twisted in the air and I brought my clawed left hand down first, thrusting into the water as the monster passed beneath me.

I caught a glimpse of the legged, spiky-spined shark in the second before I thrust my hand into the lake and hooked my claws into it. They tore through its thick, rubbery skin, just behind the head, and continued tear as its momentum forced my hand along the body. I realized it was going to rip itself free in a frenzy of pain and anger, so I curled my clawed fingers inside even harder and wrenched, swinging my other arm around. That hand slammed into it right above the tail, and then we were both under the water, and it was thrashing around with a strength I had no hope to match.

My claws ripped free, and I saw only huge, curved teeth in the opening of its tube-like throat before it was on me. I sliced my pointed fingers through the water as quickly as I could, and slammed my right hand into its jaw right behind the mouth to throw off its toothy aim. With the other hand, I raked across its murky black eyes, slicing them open.

It tried to get away then, but I dug the fingers of my right hand in even farther, far enough to clench them together on the inside of its throat cavity. If it left, it was taking me with it.

With my left hand, I continued to thrust, holding my hand and fingers straight and compact like I was going to karate chop it, but using my claws like daggers. They allowed me to pierce easily, and I did so, again and again, stabbing indiscriminately.

The volcanic fire started to hit the top of the water and fall down, un-dampened by the liquid. A piece hit the creature's torso and evaporated some of its flesh into a flashing, dark mist. I prayed none fell on me, because I was too busy fighting the monster to focus on anything else.

My lungs burned and my arms weakened from lack of oxygen,

but the creature finally slowed, having lost too much blood to continue. I ignored my exhaustion and searched desperately for the surface of the water, disorientated after the shark's mad, blind flight. Luckily, we were close. If not, I'm not sure I would have made it.

I burst through the surface with a gasp, and only after a few breaths of air cleared the blackness from my eyes did I realize I was still holding the huge creature in a death grip with my right hand.

Blood dyed the water, splashing into my face and rolling over my head as the fire rained down, all around me. If these creatures were anything like the sharks of Earth, others would come soon, and I knew I didn't have the strength to fight them. If I didn't get incinerated first, that is. But as I tried to remove my forearm from the monster's throat, I realized I was stuck. Somehow, the corpse had tightened around me, and something hard pressed together around my wrist. I couldn't release my fist to make my hand small enough to slip through the entrance wound, and so the huge bleeding beacon was stuck to me.

With a single sob of exhaustion, I started trying to swim back to the rock overhang with one arm, dragging the shark like monster. Water kept finding its way into my mouth and nose as I struggled to stay afloat.

I heard indistinguishable shouting on the shore, and then Adam calling out to me. I looked blearily upward to Jacky holding a huge length of rope in her arm. I was too winded to shout acknowledgment, but she threw it anyway, spinning her body and releasing the rope so that it flew in a wide arc through the air, unwinding as it went.

It landed in the water not far from me, and I grabbed on with just enough time to wrap the loop around my shoulders before they started hauling me forward. I sliced through the water, the rope never losing tautness, and was soon being grabbed by the hands of my team.

I coughed, spitting up some water, and then collapsed onto the warm sand beneath me. Someone grabbed me and drug me, shark and all, under the protection of the jutting rock and hardened leaves.

Behind me, I heard the wet sounds of slashing and stabbing, the evidence of my team fighting the monsters that had followed me.

After a while, the fighting died down and I regained some of my energy.

Adam leaned over me and pried at the flesh gripping my right hand. He let out a shuddering laugh. "I thought you'd lost the arm, because you weren't using it to swim. I thought..." he trailed off.

I smiled weakly. "No worries. My arms don't come off that easily."

Jacky knelt beside me and gave me a quick visual inspection, letting out a sigh of relief only when she didn't find any wounds. "You are *loca*. We thought for sure..." she stopped herself. "You were under for a long time."

"I'm just glad you guys kept an eye out for me. If you'd given me up for shark bait, I don't know if I'd have made it back."

She scowled. "You'd definitely be dead, stupid. If not for me and my crazy good tug-o'-war skills, no?" She sniffed and pursed her lips.

"Thank you. Now stop bragging," I said, giving her a light smack on the arm.

Zed finished helping Sam use the rock leaves to create a barrier around the opening of the scoop-cave we were all huddled in. He knelt beside me, his dark eyebrows pulled down in a horrible scowl. But when he saw me lying there, his eyes started to fill with liquid.

I frowned and shook my head. "Zed, everything's fine. It's okay. This is no big deal, I promise. I've dealt with much worse."

He shook his head and bit his lip hard, as he worked to push down the tears. "Is this...what you've been doing? Stuff like this, is what you've been going through?"

Adam cut away the shark that was gripping my hand, and gently slid the appendage out of the carcass.

I flexed my stiff fingers and muttered, "Thanks," then turned to Zed. "This is why I didn't want you involved. This Game runs on fear and death. But if one of the team needs help, we help. Like I helped stop the monster, and everybody helped me just now."

He pressed his lips together and clenched his jaw.

"Are you hurt?" Sam asked. "Do you need my help?"

"I'm fine, just a little winded," I said.

When I stood up, Jacky gave a whooping cheer and flipped the bird outward, to everything that was making our little makeshift hiding place quiver and shake.

We stayed huddled up under the rock as the world rumbled around us for what seemed like hours. Finally, things seemed to settle down, and I tentatively shifted one of the leaves covering the opening and looked out.

Fire no longer fell from the sky, so I removed the leaf and crawled out, climbing up the rock for a higher vantage point. Except for the large landmarks like the mountain and the water down below, the landscape was completely different.

The lakes had spread and changed shape, and the greenery on the shore sprung from the sand, a riot of brightly colored blooms sprinkled among the transformed vegetation. The only things that were the same were the cocoon trees that had turned to stone. Mist from the mountaintop was quickly spreading to create dark clouds, but for the moment the sand sparkled clear and bright, reflecting light from the water and the sun. Here and there, patches of dark flame shone, rippling shadows as they burned a new land into existence.

# Chapter 32

Into this wild Abyss/ The womb of Nature, and perhaps her grave--/ Of neither sea, nor shore, nor air, nor fire,/ But all these in their pregnant causes mixed/ Confusedly, and which thus must ever fight,/ Unless the Almighty Maker them ordain/ His dark materials to create more worlds,--/ Into this wild Abyss the wary Fiend/ Stood on the brink of Hell and looked a while,/ Pondering his voyage; for no narrow frith/ He had to cross.

— John Milton

WE HURRIED to grab samples of the last of the flames before they burned themselves out, and brought them back to the feather-headed Moderator, who had survived, protected by the stone trees.

He took the bulbs from us and secured them in a padded briefcase. "It gladdens my heart to see you alive," he said. "May your strength lead you on." He turned and walked into the trees and sprawling bushes till his hunched form disappeared from sight.

The Cube popped up with its usual message.

DO YOU WISH TO RETURN FROM THE TRIAL?
YES / NO

I stepped forward, a shaking finger hovering over the cube surface. I pressed, "No," and let out a breath.

IF YOU DO NOT RETURN NOW, YOU WILL NOT BE ABLE TO UNTIL THE NEXT ALIGNMENT. ARE YOU SURE?
YES / NO

I picked "Yes."

Jacky went next, and Sam after her, both repeating my actions.

I turned to Zed and Adam, who would both be staying on Earth. "I guess we'll see you guys in about nine days, your time. Good luck." I bit the inside of my lip, wishing things could be different, and I didn't have to worry about the two.

Adam ran a hand through his hair, pushing it back from his face. "Ah, damn it. With things like this, you leave me no choice, Eve." He stepped forward and quickly chose the option to stay in the Trial world, rather than return to Earth. "If I leave you alone with these two," he flicked his fingers to Jacky and Sam, "how can I trust you'll survive? I have to be here to watch your back, especially when you keep putting yourself in dangerous situations."

"Hey!" Jacky said. "I… Well, I'd be offended, but I'm just glad you decided to stay. We're a team, and we should stick together, no?"

Zed stepped forward and pressed "No," too, but I grabbed his hand in a crushing grip before he could confirm his selection.

"What the hell do you think you're doing?" I hissed.

"I'm going to stay, too. I can help you, Eve. I want to be here." He wriggled his hand in my grasp, trying to force the issue. "Just let me stay and help."

I thrust him back hard enough that he stumbled, and growled, my claws fully extended. "You're not staying."

He steadied himself and stepped forward again. "This isn't your choice to make. The whole reason all this happened is because I wanted to keep you safe. There's no way I'm going to just watch you go into danger and not do anything to help."

My heart clenched, because I knew I'd be saying the same thing to him in this situation. But I also knew what would hit hard enough to make him stay away despite all that. "I don't want you here, Zed," I said clearly.

"You want me to be safe, I know. But it's no safer if I go back, now. Adam was supposed to be with me, help protect us, but now it will be just me and Blaine."

"NIX doesn't know you exist. I want to keep it that way, and I'll need you on the other side as a point to return the team to next time. And it's not just that I want to protect you by keeping you out of this Trial. You're weak," I said, stepping forward and poking him in the chest with my claw. "If you stay, you're going to put me and my team in danger. We'll have to be looking out for you every step of the way. If I needed your help, I would ask for it." I took another step, pushing him backward and glaring at him with every ounce of malice I possessed. "I don't need your help, and I don't want it. So please, do as I say and quit making trouble for me."

He stared at me for a moment, searching for something in my eyes that I made sure he didn't find. "O—Okay. Are you sure?"

"I'm damn sure. Now please, hurry up and go back so we can get on with it." I pointed toward the Cube.

He moved forward, and with one last glance back to me, he selected the option to return to the normal world and popped out of existence.

There was a moment of silence, and then Jacky let out a low whistle. "Damn, that was vicious." She laughed ruefully, and clapped me on the back.

Sam pinched his lips together. "She was doing what she had to, what needed to be done to get the job done. It was the right thing to do."

"Sam, my boy, you're coming 'round." Jacky clapped him on the back with a laugh, hard enough that he stumbled forward.

I took a deep breath and turned toward the mountain. It stood towering over the land like a giant. "In my dream, there's something important up there. Who's up for some rock climbing?"

Of course, the sky chose that moment to start a torrential downpour.

---

WE DOVE FOR COVER, but it seemed to be ordinary rain, aside from how much of it there was. It dried up quickly, and I realized it had put out the last of the fires.

We made our way to the base of the mountain, wary of shark monsters, but either they had all died or they were in hiding, because none showed up to attack us.

When we reached the base, I looked up, my eyes tracking the side of the tiered mountain up, and up, and up. "This is gonna be great training, guys," I said, wiggling my still bare toes in the sand and adjusting the straps of my heavy pack on my shoulders. I extended my claws and tested them against the rock. They made satisfying scores in the surface. "Jacky, we're going to need your rope again. I want us all tied together, but leave some slack in the line so we're not all tugging on each other. I'll go first and cut hand and footholds with my claws so you have something to hold onto. We're going to go diagonally across the rock surface, moving in zigzags. We'll stop once we reach the top of this first section and reassess. Don't slip, it's still wet from the rain. Got it?"

They all nodded silently, though Jacky was grinning and clenching her muscles, Sam was looking up at the mountain in apprehension, and Adam seemed to be absorbed in his own thoughts, his eyes constantly scanning.

Thus, we started a climb of many days.

A plateau topped each butte, each its own little ecosystem with water either falling down from above or springing out of the rock side, and most containing different things trying to kill us. In just the first few days we encountered more than enough danger and hardship to last a few Trials, and grew stronger at every turn. When we weren't fighting against our environment, Adam spent his time quizzing us, and teaching strange theories and complicated math we'd never need in real life. But they stretched my mind in new ways, and I found, to my surprise, that we could level up the mental Attributes spontaneously. And in another surprise, my Beauty also leveled up spontaneously. I could only guess it was because I was so much more fit than I'd been before the Game. My Physique was a high level, and the two things obviously went together. I had no mirror, but I could feel cheekbones instead of vague pudge on my cheeks.

A sucking-mud swamp gave Jacky a chance to practice her Skill when we chose that plateau to rest on for the night. It was safe enough as long as we didn't walk into the mud. Anything that touched it would be sucked down as if some huge monster was slurping at it through a straw. Jacky played in the mud until she gained the finesse to control her body's adherence to the law of gravity to the point that she could float through it. She also liked to use her Skill to reduce her gravity while we scaled the mountainside like spiders, grinning cockily at the rest of us who grew tired while climbing with huge packs on our backs.

Another plateau held what seemed to be a fruit orchard, a notion that was quickly disproved when Jacky ate some small, bright cherries, and Sam had to heal her when she started to asphyxiate. She smiled euphorically while choking to death, after which Sam had an idea, and ate a few himself. When I snapped at him, he reminded me of his Skill. Every time he healed something, his body grew a natural resistance to it. But at the same time, it also grew the ability to replicate that damage, slightly augmented. He was hoping to add the berries' effects to others of the same type he already had, and create a harmless, painless paralytic ability, which he could use to fight.

On another plateau, swarming bugs camouflaged themselves

expertly until we had settled in for a meal from the food we'd brought with us in our packs. Then they came after us in sheets and waves, biting and clawing and wriggling at us until Adam sent a jolt of electricity through the damp air. They smelled like roasted almonds covering the ground with their crunchy carcasses.

But my biggest concern was actually our food supply. If my calculations of the time in-Trial versus the time in the real world were correct, we would be there for about forty-five days. We were pushing our bodies hard, and like I'd wished, we were leveling up many of our different Attributes through old-fashioned hard work. But that also meant we were eating like ravenous hyenas, and would run out of food within days, despite having filled our packs to the brim with little else.

Ten days into our climb, I was sitting the early morning watch against danger and contemplating our situation. I groaned and rolled my shoulders, then pushed up from my rocky perch to stretch my sore and stiff muscles. I felt like I'd gotten only a few hours of rest. Sleep was difficult with the luxurious damp stone mattress, the insects, my grumbling stomach, and the constant worrying at the back of my mind that I would need to get up and fight at a moment's notice.

Water was a nonissue, seeing as the stuff was everywhere, even in the group's shoes, in our blankets, and hanging heavy in the air. But delicious and energizing as it was, it had no calories. We would run out of food in a day or two, and I'd already noticed the others self-rationing to try and make it last. Doing that would only make it harder for us to get stronger. "We're going to have to acquire a taste for monster," I muttered. "Hope it's edible," I sighed. The sad thing was, I wasn't joking.

I sat down on the edge of large rock ledge we had made camp on and looked out into the darkness of the trees and heavy jungle-like foliage that covered a large portion of this plateau. I let the familiar feeling of power roll through me, allowing my eyes to pull in light through the fog cover from the bright, milky thick stars and the single moon hanging low in the sky at that time of night.

Adam walked over, holding a glowing bulb on a stem, a makeshift light bulb created from a carnivorous plant he'd ripped the leaves and teeth off of. With a tired sigh, he plopped down beside me and shot me an excited grin. He wasn't wearing a shirt, since the night was warm and the bugs had mostly dispersed this late. The intricate design of his tattoo had spread significantly since the last time I'd seen it, having crawled up his arms and started to reach across his upper back.

I wondered how he'd done that to himself. A mirror? "Have you been up all night?" I asked in a low, hoarse voice, and then coughed and cleared my sleep-scratchy throat.

"I'd been doing some work on augmenting my program to help get past NIX's security again. It'll be more powerful, more robust. They won't know what hit them. I just wish it wasn't so humid here. If I'd known, I would have brought some cooling gel."

"That's funny, because when we went into the Trial, you were still saying you wouldn't be coming with us. What would you have needed cooling gel for?" I raised my eyebrow, suppressing a smile.

He looked away with an embarrassed half grin. "I may have been having second thoughts."

"That's great, but you should be sleeping. Your watch was over hours ago."

He shook his head. "I need less sleep now, remember? Unfortunately, the less sleep I get, the less I seem to need. It's gotten to the point where I can barely sleep five hours straight. So I figured I'd be productive. And I don't just mean with the program." He smiled in excitement, a rare expression on him.

"So what have you been doing?" I raised a curious eyebrow.

"I," he paused for effect, "have been practicing with a new, absolutely awesome Skill. This is going to blow your mind."

I grinned, unable to help being infected by his enthusiasm. "Show me."

He nodded and pulled out a large berry from his pocket. We'd found them a few days before in the poisonous fruit orchard and dubbed them inkberries both because of the instant-staining, abundant black juice they provided, and their bitter taste. Adam had gathered tons of them. He crushed the berry into the palm of his other hand, letting the dark fluid pool in his palm.

"Wait," I held up a hand. "You're about to show me a new Skill, right?"

He nodded.

"So…I seem to recall you jumping on me when I revealed I'd solved the Oracle's puzzle and had a strange dream that turned out to be prophetic."

He bit his lip, obviously understanding what I was getting at.

"But you got a new Skill," I said. "Something obviously of interest to the rest of the group, and you kept it a secret? When did you get this awesome Skill?" I teased.

"The desert Trial. And before you continue, I didn't tell everyone partially because of all the other important things going on, and partially because I didn't know how to use it properly. It's taken a lot of practice to get to this point. And it's kind of… personal. I haven't shown anyone yet. "

I grinned at him, "I'm just messing with you. And I'm honored that I get to see it first. So hurry up and show me!"

He tilted his fingers toward the stone between us and let a drop of ink slide down onto it. He frowned fiercely, his eyes locked onto the dark liquid.

It moved, seemingly of its own accord, spreading out into thin lines and blobs on the stone.

I caught my breath in surprise, watching as the ink moved eerily, forming the easily recognizable image of a giraffe.

He let out the deep breath he'd been holding. "I'm not used to drawing in front of other people."

"Whoa," I whispered, eyes locked on the cute creature. "You just drew that with your mind. Awesome! Can you do it with your eyes closed? How far away can you be from the drawing for it to work? I'm assuming you could do words, too, and not just images.

Adam, that could be *extremely* useful," I rattled away, my mind already spinning with possibilities.

Then, he took another deep breath and whispered, "Animus."

The ink climbed out of the rock, the giraffe poking its head and neck out, then lifting itself with a hoof on the stone and pulling the rest of its body upward.

My eyes were as wide as they could go, and I definitely wasn't breathing. I'd seen a lot of fantastical things, but this was new.

The giraffe was a thing of ink and air, black and clear, and three-dimensional. It sniffed curiously, and then started to move around.

Adam blew on it, and it flattened its ears under the relatively strong onslaught of wind and seemed to glare at him fearlessly before running around to hide from the artificial gusts behind my knee.

It peeked its head out from behind my protection, almost tauntingly. After a few more seconds, it disappeared, disintegrating into clearness and falling away on the air. Where it had been, there was no trace of ink, no flat drawing on the ground, no anything.

"Adam, that was amazing!"

He grinned, self-satisfied and smug.

"Can you do other animals? How big can they go? Is that the time limit on them?"

He chuckled at my rapid-fire questions. "I can do anything I can draw, and they have the personality traits I'm imagining when I create them. A real giraffe would probably be scared of me if I leaned over and blew on it. I can go bigger to a certain degree, but it takes a lot of concentration, and the Skill isn't very strong yet. I haven't tried to animate any words yet, and I can't animate something far away from me. I haven't tried to do it with my eyes closed yet. And right now, the time limit is twenty-one seconds.

"You know," he continued in a low voice, "I think one of the tailos made it happen. We fought together, and I'd used some of the monster's blood like warpaint in the heat of the moment. I was just angry." He shrugged, looking away in embarrassment. "The tailos seemed interested in it and my tattoos, and when he died, I wiped some on him, too. A useless gesture, you know? I just wanted…to let him know I thought he was a great warrior, and that he wasn't alone. And now I've got this ability to make my drawings come to life for a few seconds." He smiled again, less cocky and more melancholy.

I was about to ask for another demonstration when I heard a snuffling sound from the direction of the jungle. I grew absolutely silent, pushing my slightly enhanced eyes to their limit as I peered into the shadows. The fog was heavy, as it always seemed to be, and it obscured things in the darkness even more.

Adam slipped out his knives, which had gotten a great workout from all the battles we'd been through lately. He, too, scanned the dense foliage.

I saw movement and the tip of a snout and shouted, "Attack! Incoming from the trees," over my shoulder, not taking my eyes off the tree line.

Behind me, my sleeping teammates jumped awake at the same time monsters poured out of the deeper darkness into the edge of the sky-lit clearing.

By the time we had eradicated them all, the sun had risen, and everything from our camp to the tree line was covered in blood and dead monsters.

I had Sam cook up a haunch of one of the monsters and sample it. If his body gained any Resistance or anti-poisoning Skill upgrade from it, it wasn't safe for us to eat.

His eyes widened in surprise, and he took a bigger bite, juice dripping down his chin.

We all stared at him avidly, our stomachs grumbling jealously and our mouths watering at the smell of cooking meat.

"Well," Jacky snapped, "Can we eat?"

He nodded. "It's safe. And it tastes freaking amazing."

---

A WEEK LATER, we neared the top of the mountain and stopped on a small plateau to rest, eat, and prepare before we faced whatever power was making the hair on the back of my neck rise up just from being close to it.

By my estimate, we'd only been gone from the real world a little over three days. But to us, it felt like we'd been climbing for seventeen days. The air was thinner near the top, and the water ran fresh like nothing I'd ever tasted. The bottled water companies in the real world had been ripping us off. Fresh mountain springwater, my ass. Everything from the monster meat to the misty-yet-scantily oxygenated air here seemed designed to make us stronger, pushing us to our limits.

We pulled out food from our packs, all stuff that we'd hunted and gathered on the way up, and sat down in a circle.

Adam gave everyone's meat a quick zap to warm it up, and we all took bugs, fruit, or a tasty smaller animal out and set it in the center of the circle to share among the group.

Difficult though the ordeals of the climb had been, the team had changed for the better, growing not only in power, but in the sort of deeper confidence and comradeship that came from making it through hell together.

Sam let out a deep sigh and rolled his shoulders. "I've been wondering, what happened to Bunny? We didn't make plans to save him."

"I did make plans," I said. "By now, Bunny's told NIX some of the things he knew about us, with some key differences between his story and the truth. Keeping Zed a secret, and that we died here, or committed suicide by Trial, to name a few. Most of what he knows doesn't matter for our safety anymore, but they'll think he's on their side so he'll be safe, and we'll have a man on the inside when we go back."

Sam nodded with a thoughtful frown. "So, what's the plan? For right now, when we reach the top, I mean," he asked me.

Jacky took off her gloves and dug into a comically large drumstick. In her hands, it looked like a barbarian meat club. "We go up there and destroy the enemy, no?"

He rolled his eyes and passed her his flask of water. "That may be your plan, she-hulk, but the rest of us would like to act in a way that's going to get us through the fight still alive."

She jostled him with her shoulder and took a swig of the water, no longer so averse to the touch of the boys, when once she could only stand to touch them if she was inflicting violence. "She-hulk? What're you spewing out of your ass? For some reason, it doesn't smell good..." she cracked her knuckles, play-threatening him.

He leaned back so far as he pretended to cower in fear that he fell off the rock he was sitting on.

While Jacky was busy pointing and laughing at him, Adam took a handful of inkberries from his pocket and crushed them in his fist, which was perpetually black-stained lately because of all the practicing he'd been doing.

Well, maybe not so much *practicing* as entertaining the group. Jacky begged for a show almost every time we stopped to rest, never-endingly delighted to see his creations come to life.

The drops of ink running from his fist burst into action almost before they even hit the ground, spreading into a cute, flowery meadow that looked like it came from a children's book. Small animals played among the flowers and peeked out from behind rocks.

Jacky's laughter sobered, and we all focused on it, what we'd been doing forgotten.

The fairytale meadow sprang upward, and then a small form pulled itself over an invisible edge, climbing into the frame. It was a comically muscular creature, broad-footed and club-fisted. Veins popped from its arms, and it had a small hunchback and no visible neck. Atop the body sat Jacky's pretty face, twisted in anger.

"It's a she-hulk," I gasped, already holding back a laugh.

Mini Jacky-hulk roared, shaking every blade of grass and petal in the meadow and causing the animals to freeze. She beat on her chest like a monkey, and then stomped forward. The animals leapt away, keeping a safe distance from her and her crushing hands and feet.

Real Jacky's eyes were wide as she watched her counterpart go uselessly berserk, lumbering around the meadow in circles as the more nimble creatures teased her.

By the time Adam's Animus Skill wore off, he was struggling to hold back laughter, and the rest of us were gasping on the ground, unable to breathe past our hilarity.

"That…is not…me!" Jacky finally got out, suppressing a smile of her own.

I wiped the tears of laughter from my eyes. "Of course not," I said. "Those rabbits *never* would have escape you!" I fell back into laughter while she scowled at me, and then finished my quick meal while the team continued to joke amongst themselves. I'd grown closer to them than ever. Though I wished I could say I wasn't so weak, I feared for what might become of them if my plan didn't work.

Whatever was up above was powerful. Likely the most powerful thing we'd ever encountered.

When I was ready, I took a few deep breaths, focusing on my heartbeat, and slipped into the hyper-aware state that had once been so difficult to achieve. I'd been practicing, sometimes even in the midst of climbing the mountainside. It was getting easier and easier, as though perhaps solving the ring had given my ability a boost, but I still hadn't been able to reach out to that other presence again. It worried me a bit, though I wasn't quite sure why. Maybe because I didn't like the unknown, especially when it could be important to my survival.

When I threw my senses out, I was almost blinded by an aura that assaulted every sensory channel. After completing the ring puzzle, the smallest gift from the Oracle, I'd gained a vague perception of something new, an energy that couldn't be seen with the naked eye, but that flowed through all of my team, brightening when we used our Skills. But here, that was overwhelmed by power seeping from the rocks beneath, thrumming in the air we breathed, and sliding through the water around us. But overpowering all of that was a large mass above us.

It was unmoving, planted in the center of the caldera we'd have to descend into once we reached the lip at the top. It had roots longer and thicker than I could see, and all around it were smaller points of strength.

I gathered my seeking senses back into my body and opened my eyes.

The others were all watching me intently, the layer of mirth wiped away as they waited for news of the coming danger.

"Well, that vision was right. Whatever's at the top, it's powerful. Very, very powerful."

"Powerful enough to defeat NIX?" Jacky asked.

"If it could be used as a weapon, I don't see how it could fail to defeat them."

"But that's just it," Adam said. "What *is* it? How do we know if it's going to be useful for us? Or even something we can take back?"

"I'm…not sure," I said. "It's so strong, it sort of overwhelmed my senses. I could only get a vague idea of where it is. I couldn't tell what it was."

"How do you know this is safe, Eve? I mean, some Trial creature gives you something that makes you have visions of the future, but not before trying to *kill* you. What if this is just its way of finishing the job?" Adam asked, ever the pessimist.

Sam looked between Adam and me, taking deep, slow breaths to keep himself calm despite Adam's words.

"Adam, something's going on that we don't understand, here. That Trial monster you're talking about was…intelligent. It talked to me. Yeah, it tried to kill me, but it was just a test. When I proved myself to it, it gave me its blessing and wished me well. And what about the tailos? They were telepathic, sentient beings!" I patted the side pouch of my pack, where the tailos egg was nestled. I had brought syringes in my pack, and fed it frequently.

"You said yourself you think one gave you the Animus Skill. Consider the possibility that not everything here wants to kill us indiscriminately."

He let out a sigh. "Fine. We're already here, anyway. If you think it might be the answer, I'll follow you," he said, but then he muttered something under his breath that sounded suspiciously like, "not *everything* may want to kill us, but ninety-nine percent of everything seems designed to do just that."

# Chapter 33

Yet from those flames
    No light, but rather darkness visible.
    — John Milton

I CROUCHED down on the edge and looked over into the steep, huge bowl cut out of the top of the mountain. Clear blue water bubbled and steamed like a witch's cauldron. It spewed up from nowhere and spilled out through cracks in the rocks, no doubt creating the numerous beautiful waterfalls that dropped for so long before feeding into the lake below. Submerged beneath the water, orange and red spots glowed hot, and caused the water to bubble more furiously around them. Large flat stones broke up the surface of the whole caldera. We'd have to cross on those to get to the middle.

I still couldn't figure out what was in the center, though I was squinting right at it. Steam rose up from the water there, with huge wafting clouds making a shrouding column so thick I couldn't see through it. "That's where we need to go," I pointed." But I felt other points of power, too. There might be monsters lying in wait. Or traps of another kind." I fed my armored vest a few extra drops of blood to make sure it was ready, though I kept it unfurled all the time at that point.

After a few minutes to psyche ourselves up, stretch muscles, and sharpen knives, we left our packs at the top and started the descent, jumping from ledge to ledge along the inside wall. Before coming to that Trial, I may not have been able to make those jumps, but I'd grown stronger.

When we reached the bottom, gathering on one of the flat stones, the water around us started to splash as if it noticed our presence.

"That's disturbing," Sam said, stepping away from the edge of our platform.

We jumped forward, moving from stone to stone, farther toward the center and the tower of steam. The heat grew more oppressive, and even the stone beneath our feet burned.

I was glad for the toughness of my feet, which had increased over the past two weeks of going around without shoes, but jealous of the protective boots the others wore.

The water became more and more frantic as we moved farther, and suddenly one of the red-orange spots below us shot up from the depths. It burst out, steaming with the sound a drop of water makes when you drop it on a too-hot pan.

The first thing that came to my mind was that it was a rock and lava golem. It was humanoid, with a featureless lump for a head, and limbs of rock held together by flowing lava. The second thing that came to my mind was that it was damn scary.

Jacky just happened to be on the edge of the platform it arose next to, and it caught her pant leg with a swipe of its rocky hand. She kicked it in the head hard enough to make the stone crumble, and it fell away from her into the water, leaving a smoking hole in the fabric of her pant leg.

Almost immediately, it recovered and shot to the surface again, this time climbing onto the rocky platform.

She squared off with it and started to fight, carefully avoiding the lava-flowing parts of it and crumbling away it's rocky limbs and head. One solid roundhouse kick to the abdomen cracked through its chest, and the thing collapsed into a steaming pile of rock and quickly cooling lava. "Go for the chest!" she called.

The water started to boil and jump even stronger all around us, and more lava golems shot upward. I bit my lip at the number, but noticed that there were no more red lights shining up from the bottom of the water, so at least there wouldn't be more than one wave of the creatures.

We started to attack, making surprisingly short work of them. We'd gotten stronger. A lot stronger. I was grinning cockily when the crushing sound of a lot of water crashing down blew past us, and a huge wave rolled out of the bottom of the column of steam, rushing out in all directions. "Damn," I said, the grin erasing itself instantly.

There was nowhere to run, and nothing to hold on to except the rocks beneath our feet.

"Jump when it reaches you!" I called out, and followed my own advice. I came back down into shallower rushing water, but the depth and strength of the tail end were still enough to knock me off my feet, and it was scalding hot.

I grabbed onto the edge of the platform and managed to pull myself back up after a few moments of spluttering. I was looking around to check on the others when something grabbed my foot. I had less than a second for the alarm to sound in my mind and to look back before the clear, watery fist yanked me off the edge and down into the water.

I kicked and struggled to swim away, but my efforts had no effect. When I looked down, I saw nothing, but I could still feel the fist around my ankle.

It pulled harder, dragging me down fast and far enough that the pressure of the boiling water began to feel uncomfortably strong. Finally, it stopped pulling and released my ankle, but before I could swim away, something wrapped around my torso and pressed against my face, pinning my arms to my sides and pushing against my nose and mouth, trying to force the burning water into my lungs.

I bucked and wiggled, but the liquid creature only swirled around me more strongly, completely dominating against my clumsy underwater maneuverings. Bug-eyed, I felt the air being squeezed out of me, and knew the burning panic of a person who's about to drown.

Then Jacky shot by like a rocket, ripping away my assailant and setting me free.

I swam toward the surface and sucked in a breath of air along with a little water. I choked and started to cough, but my head cleared and I was able to swim to another of the platforms. I spent a few seconds clearing my lungs and letting the dizzying heat of my skin cool, careful to keep away from the edge of the platform.

When I stood and looked down, I saw Jacky shooting around the water like a superhero, decimating vague watery outlines left and right. She'd burst out for a breath of air every minute or so, then dive back in.

Above, Adam was still dealing with the remaining rock and lava golems, and Sam fought by his side with his crowbar.

A roaring crackle sounded from the direction of the column of steam, and out of its center burst a ring of that strange light-and-dark fire. The fire separated, and pieces of it formed into bird-like shapes and flew out in all directions. They eyed us on the ground for a few moments, circling overhead, and then one made a dive for me.

If not for Sam's screamed, "Don't touch it!" I would have counterattacked with a rake of my claws or a kick as it went by. I skipped out of the way instead, teetering on the edge of my platform for a second.

The water below me bubbled and burst upward in a vague humanoid shape, arms reaching for me.

Jacky shot out of the water, spearing through its chest with a single punch, and crushing a fistful of harder clear liquid within her fist. "Gravity Skill comes in handy," she gasped. "I can go side to side, if I just pretend that way is down. I got the water. You can handle these, no?"

I nodded. "Thanks for the save. We've got this."

She took another deep breath of air and shot downward, feet first.

I moved to Sam and Adam, jumping along the stone platforms and avoiding the swoops of the fire birds. "What's wrong, Sam?"

"Anything they touch gets…unmade." He held up his crowbar, which was missing one end.

"How the hell are we supposed to stop them, then?" I moved my eyes to the sky, scanning for signs of an attack, which would be especially dangerous since all three of us were together.

Adam lifted his hand, then, and shot a bolt of electricity at one flying dangerously close to us.

It jerked at the hit, then seemed to burn out of control and devour its own body. A few chunks of flame hit the water and sank still burning, but soon extinguished themselves.

"I guess that's how," Adam said. "I hope I've got enough power for this." He slipped a cylindrical energy cartridge from his pocket. "I've been saving this for an emergency. I think this qualifies."

He lifted his free hand. Another bolt shot from his fingertips, crackling outward through the damp air and hitting two targets at once.

"You handle them," I said to Adam. "Sam, you and I are going to go take care of the source of our problem." I pointed toward the billowing column.

He stifled a groan and adjusted his grip on his shortened crowbar. "Lead the way."

My chest had a strange tightness in it, because something big was moving within the mist and steam of the column, and I could feel it in the air. As we moved closer, the humidity made it hard to breathe, and I started to cough and worry about being steam-cooked, like my mom used to do with vegetables and chicken.

But then a huge arm made of stone and water swung, clearing

a swath of steam. Another gargantuan arm swung, and almost hit me as it passed. More of the obscuring mist cleared, and I saw the colossal torso of a woman, literally rooted to the mountain. She had distinct features cut into the stone of her face, and more graceful arms and torso than the smaller golems.

Bright, clear water ran over her body and connected her limbs, and also filled the large cavity in the center of her chest. It seemed to completely defy gravity, and maybe a few other rules of physics, too. Right where her heart might be if she were human floated a small object, suspended in the glimmering water. Fire burned in lines around her base, and the stone near it ran a bright liquid orange.

She saw us then, and sound came out of her with the slow booming of a rock avalanche. Somehow, I vaguely understood it. "Bugs, you dare to come before me? I am not so weakened as to fall," she said. Then she brought down her palm in a flat arc to smash us as if we were insects.

---

I PUSHED Sam into the water and jumped out of the way onto a platform just far enough away to avoid her hand. The force of her slap caused the water all around to jump higher than my head. It reminded me of a child playing in the bath, slapping the water's surface and making it splash. "Except you're not that cute," I grunted.

Sam rose pink-skinned from the water and I grabbed the end of his crowbar and helped him back onto the platform. "Really? Push me into the water?" he gasped, dripping.

"I made sure you didn't get hit."

"Well, couldn't you have just yelled, 'Run,' or 'Jump,'" instead?"

"What if you hadn't reacted in time?" I shrugged. "This way I was sure. The chest seems to be the weak spot. I'm going to make a run for it."

A few running leaps brought me to a platform close to her base, which looked like hips growing into the mountain's core. Another leap brought me to her waist, where I used the claws on my hands and feet to scurry up the rock of her body like a spider.

I'd just reached the chest and was extending a clawed hand towards the water filled chamber that held her "heart" when I was brushed off. I went flying, my whole right side where I'd been hit feeling like I'd slammed hard into a stone wall, which I guess technically I had.

My Skills let me twist around to land on all fours, thankfully onto a platform. I dug the claws on all four limbs into the stone and gouged strips out of it, but I still had enough momentum from her swat to slide off the edge into the scalding water. I scrambled back out of it, gasping in shock at the temperature. No wonder Sam had been perturbed. A few minutes in there and he'd have been cooked like a lobster. Creatures who I suddenly had a lot more sympathy for, by the way.

Sam ran around her base in a circle, whacking the stone with his crowbar. It barely even chipped her. He tossed it away and positioned himself behind her, putting a hand on her in an attempt to use his Skill.

The mountain-slash-woman scowled in frustration for a minute, then unhinged her water-jointed arms and twisted them backward, over her head.

Sam stepped away from her, and a nice chunk of her base, crystallized and sparkly, crumbled away with him. He ducked her swing and made it a safe distance away from her on the other side, so that it looked like we were playing a doomed-to-fail game of monkey in the middle.

But then she roared, and out of her burst another wave and ring of fire. Almost immediately the water golems popped out of the water, sliding around half submerged on water tails like a snake, and the fire creatures looked bigger and fiercer.

"We have to stop her," I called across the caldera to Sam.

The mist veil had cleared, and I saw that the other two were still busy fighting their respective golems. It was just us, and we didn't have much time before she multiplied again and the amount of golems became insurmountable. I flexed my claws and whispered, "I won't lose here," to myself, and sprang forward to attack the thing again, as Sam did the same. This time, I crawled up to her shoulder to hack and gouge at the joint there, trying to break off her arm so she'd lose some of her attack power.

Any piece of her rock I broke loose was immediately replaced with the glass-clear water, and I didn't know if my actions made a difference.

Once again, I saw her other hand racing toward me, but this time jumped out of the way, landing on her collarbone, at the base of her neck. I thought I was safe, and was surprised when the shock of her hand's impact with her shoulder shook her whole body like a large earthquake, sending me falling down her chest. I tried to claw my way to a stop, but her other arm came around and smashed into me again.

She was moving faster than she had before, almost as if she were waking up, or maybe warming up, judging by the heat radiating from those huge stone fingers when they smashed into my ribs and arm from the side.

This time, I landed in the water and shot a good few meters into it before slowing and starting to pull my way back to the surface.

When I reached it, barely escaping a water golem, I climbed onto a steaming platform and coughed and shuddered as my head swam from the heat and lack of oxygen combined.

I looked up, only to see one huge stone hand throw Sam spinning end over end across the caldera like a skipping stone. He looked like a rag doll when he hit the water bouncing. He was stopped by a firm bodily meeting with the far wall, and sank into the water unmoving. I flinched at the sight, and hoped with all my might that he was all right. I wasn't sure how he could be, though. Not after being thrown like that. He was our healer, and without him the aftermath of this fight didn't look so good.

I sent a Window to Jacky to help Sam, but in my worry over his survival, I was distracted. I noticed far too late the feeling of a huge hand rushing down toward me as the air swirled noisily with the force of its movement. I tried to roll away, back into the water, but knew that I wasn't going to make it. The shadow from above was already darkening the stone, there was no way.

But then there was Adam's voice, shouting "Animus!" above me, and a huge gust of wind as something collided with enough force to create a shock wave.

I looked up and saw that the beautiful tattoos of his arms and shoulders, which he'd so painstakingly and lovingly grown, were holding both her arms in place. They had sprung from his flesh huge and thick, and were rooting him to the ground, and her to him, in unmovable knots.

She brought her full weight to bear, trying to crush him into the ground along with me, even as he held her still. The sound of stone grinding on stone filled the air.

He looked over his shoulder to me, sweat and wet dripping hair hanging over his face. "Move!" he screamed at me, his voice raw and shaking.

I sprang to my feet and started running as fast as I could, digging my toe claws into the stone for more grip.

Adam's Animus Skill must have gotten stronger, but I knew I didn't have much time until that tattoo disintegrated into the air, and she flattened him, crushing his bones and internal organs beyond repair.

This was the perfect chance, maybe the only chance, and I needed to stop her immediately, before it was too late and he died.

I sprang up, clawing frantically at her chest.

She felt me moving, I know, and tried to pull back to brush me off or crush me again, but Adam held her in place even as I felt her stones tremble under me in the effort to pull back. His control of her must have been difficult, because I heard another hoarse scream from him.

But she didn't move, and I reached her chest cavity and

plunged myself into it with all the force I could muster. I shot through the water, grabbed the black, blob-like heart floating in the water, and held it to my chest with all my might. I burst out the other side, and was falling, falling, and then crashing hard into a platform.

I looked up and saw that she had started to tip backward, the direction she must have been pulling when Adam's tattoo disappeared.

That was wonderful, because she wouldn't crush him out of sheer momentum now. It was horrible, because she would crush me instead if I couldn't get out of the way.

So I ran, leaping from stone to stone like a football player hurdling opponents, her heart tucked tightly to my chest. When the shadow from her back started to grow dark around me, I jumped into the water, slicing downward like an arrow.

The force of her impact still shook me hard enough I thought I might lose the air I held in my lungs, but I was safe, and able to swim under her and out to the surface.

—I made it. Make sure Adam's okay.—
-Eve-

I knew what it must have looked like when the creature fell onto the spot where I'd been, and I didn't want any of the team to worry about me. Adam was the main priority.

I spent a little while just breathing and cooling down, and then held up the heart I'd taken from her chest cavity.

It was a black, shimmering mass, sort of like what the Seeds looked like except for the color, and about the size of a basketball. It flowed around my hand like what I'd seen the water of the creature's body do, and seemed to notice my inspection, because it started to ripple.

"Oh, wow," I whispered. "Treasure. I guess the Oracle was looking out for me, after all."

I STOOD up and started to limp across the basin of that huge bowl cut into the top of the mountain, skirting the fallen creature. The water had succumbed to the force of gravity and flowed away from the body, so it was only a few ginormous rocks lying still on the ground, but they were still somewhat terrifying

The substance around my hand, the woman's heart, was so dark that my eyes seemed to fall into it, and yet it shimmered light back toward me. As it flowed and rippled around my hand, having attached itself to my fist, I couldn't help but think it both the most beautiful and terrifying thing I'd ever seen. Something about it gave off the feeling of a writhing sea of darkness, despite the points of light and energy that swarmed through it.

Jacky had helped Adam to a seat on the ground next to Sam's motionless body. The two conscious ones drew back noticeably from the substance on my fist as soon as they caught sight, and then looked at it closely for a few seconds, which didn't alleviate all of their hesitation toward it.

Jacky was pale, wet, and shivering despite the heat radiating from her surroundings.

"Is he...okay?" I asked, looking at Sam.

She pursed her lips. "He's alive. For now. I dunno what to do for him. I really hope he can heal himself."

"Yeah. That's probably why he's sleeping. He needs to focus all his strength on healing himself." I laid my free hand on her shoulder. "You sit down. The fight's over. You did good."

She stared at me with an expression I couldn't decipher for a few moments, and then gave me a half smile. "Thank you."

Adam waved at me from his seat on the ground, looking pale. "I'm fine, too. Just a little worn out from saving you from a huge crazy rock monster. Who also happened to birth little elemental minions every other minute. No biggie. Thanks for asking." His eyes were red and bloodshot from straining so hard the tiny vessels broke under the pressure, and his voice was hoarse from screaming.

I smiled. "What, you mean that was hard for you? I think you should be asking me if *I'm* okay. I just defeated the monster that gave you so much trouble."

He chuckled, and then started to cough. "So glad you made it in time, though. Otherwise I'd be a pancake."

"But...what about your tattoos? I know how long you must have spent on them, how much effort. They're gone."

He held up his newly bare arms and looked them up and down. "It was pretty bad-ass that I did that, huh?" He pulled his knees to his chest and coughed again. "I'll draw another one. Even cooler, this time."

I bit the inside of my lip and nodded, then went to grab the packs from the rim of the caldera. I awkwardly fumbled the bedrolls and blankets from within the packs with the hand not covered in goo, and helped get camp set up in a smaller niche in the rock side, being careful not to jostle Sam when we moved him. I forced us all to eat something, and did my best to feed Sam some broth made from meat and bone juices. It was kind of hard with only one hand free of the black substance, but the others were in no condition to help me. They'd really given their all in the fight. I thought I might have a couple broken ribs, and I'd definitely have full-body bruising from being swatted and tossed around, but I could still function.

When everything was as settled as I could get it, I looked over Sam's sleeping body for obvious injuries. They were everywhere, and told me nothing. So I sat down next to him and closed my eyes, laying my hands lightly on his body like he did whenever he was going to heal someone.

"Nucking futts," Jacky said. "Can you do that? Heal him like he does us?"

I opened one eye. How awesome did this girl think I was? "I'm not a healer. But I might be able to tell if there's anything wrong inside."

"Oh." She drew back and nodded, wrapping her blanket tightly around her shoulders.

I slipped into the hyper-aware state with a bit of a struggle. I was so tired, and my body hurt. It was hard. My mind struggled to focus so much Perception energy in one small place, but I was able to get a vague idea of his injuries. "He's healing himself," I said, opening my eyes and drawing my hands back. "It looks pretty bad in there, but I think, I *hope*, he can handle it. I don't know what to do to help him."

Jacky rested her forehead on her knees. "He better make it. He…is such a trier. He tries harder than anyone I've ever met. Cares so much."

"He doesn't deserve to die," Adam said.

I sighed, and then gave myself a mental slap on the cheeks. Sighing didn't fix anything. I looked at the mass of strange goop still attached to my right hand and had an idea. "Guys, I want you all to stay tucked away in here, hidden. I'm going to do something potentially very stupid, and I'd like you all at a safe distance when I do."

Adam's wet hair had plastered itself to his head and all down his face, he looked half flushed and half pale, and altogether like crap, but he forced himself to his feet. "You need backup if you're doing something stupid."

"You're in no shape to be my backup," I said gently, putting a hand on his shoulder to push him back down.

"True! Better yet, how about you just don't do anything stupid? That would be awesome." He read my expression and muttered, "Guess that would be too much to ask for."

I turned away, looking back toward the still form at the center, and all around at the water that had ceased to flow. "I'm either crazy, or I'm a freaking lionhearted genius," I said to myself. I moved towards the she-mountain corpse. "Why not both?"

# Chapter 34

...a dark
Illimitable ocean, without bound,
Without dimension; where length, breadth, and height,
And time, and place are lost.
— John Milton

I WALKED over the stone chest of the fallen boulders and stopped at the now empty cavity within it. With my free left hand I reached for the substance on my right. It reached out part of itself as if to meet my hand, which made me pause. I made a pinching motion in the air, and the smaller glob formed into a separate mass, connected to the whole of itself with only a thin string. I grabbed the smaller portion and pulled, and it separated easily, and then started to flow around my left hand.

I hesitated a bit, and then put some of the baseball-sized globe on my left hand back into the bigger mass surrounding my right. I then dropped my left hand into the empty air of the chest cavity and shook a bit, making it clear that I wanted the substance to detach and thinking hard about it doing so.

It slipped off the end of my fingers and hung in the air for a bit. Then the shallow water beneath the cavity began to flow upward to it, surrounding the small ball with an ever-thickening layer of clear water.

"I'm giving you back some of you heart," I murmured. "Be good and don't attack me when you wake up."

After a while, the chest cavity was filled, and the she-mountain stirred, seeming to take a deep breath, though I doubted whether a rock could even need to breathe.

I chose that time to retreat to a suitably safe distance and waited for enough water to gather in and around the creature so that it could move once again. I sat down and waited, hoping desperately that I hadn't just done the stupidest thing since my birth...besides stopping to help that traitorous guy who allowed NIX to give me the Seed in the first place.

The rock and water woman sat up and looked around in bewilderment, then down at me, sitting cross-legged on the stone below her with the majority of her heart flowing happily around my right hand. "You..." her voice came out weaker than before, but still a crashing rumble.

"Hi," I said.

"You have restored my physical form?"

I swallowed down the lump in my throat and tried to sound confident. "I've got a few questions. I hope you can be friendly, otherwise I'll have to take it back."

She threw her head back and her chest shook up and down with a roaring, breaking, booming sound.

It made me tense up for a moment before I realized it was a laugh. Then I had to wonder if her being amused at my threat was really a good thing.

She lowered her gaze to me. "Confident, for such a puny little thing. All right. I have decided not to kill you. You have gained my interest. Who are you?"

"My name is Eve. Who are you?" I decided I didn't need to

remind her again that we'd just beaten her. I didn't know that we could do it again, so I didn't want to start a fight.

"I am the Goddess. The one that came before, and was formed."

"I don't understand. What does that mean?"

"I am the formless mass, the void," she tilted her head, as if I should get what she meant.

I shook my head. "Also, you're a volcano." Time for another line of questioning.

She boomed again. "I have taken many forms, and I carry many now. This form is one of my branches, constrained to physical form. It pleases me, for now, though the order of it changes my power as it must channel through those constraints. But it allows me to easily cleanse some of the land."

"Cleanse it from what?"

"The sickness that is not my child. The abhorrent."

Yeah. Still not understanding. "What is this place?" I gestured around me. "I mean, obviously this is a mountain. But the whole thing? What is this planet?"

"The small ones call it Estreyer. Or they did, the last time I was among them."

"So it's not Earth, then." I'd suspected. I mean, two moons in the sky was kind of a dead giveaway.

"There is earth." She nodded. "Also sky and water and wood and much else."

"Right…" Was this the language barrier? I thought I could understand her words, the way you know what someone's saying in a dream by instinct even when they're making an unintelligible jumble of it, but something seemed to be getting lost in translation. "Okay, then. Are there other living beings, ones like me?"

"Yes, though they disappear along with the rest."

Perhaps she meant they disappeared when they teleported back to the real world. "Have you heard of NIX?"

"The night was born of me." She made a fist at my confused look. "You do not understand, even though you are the one asking me. And your deficient communication method confuses me, as well. What use have I for speech? Be done with your questions, tiny one, for I grow impatient with this."

"Do you know what the Trials are?" I tried.

"Your kind supplicates before us in hopes of gaining power. Most fail. Many die. You are the first to gain my interest in a long time. To come after me when I am weakened, you are bold."

"This power you speak of, it's the Seeds, right? I've never seen this black type before, but I've got something similar." I pulled out a Seed I'd reserved for an emergency and showed her.

She drew backward and sniffed in pointed offense, hard enough to make my hair flutter around my face. "My power is nothing like that flesh-power. Do you know nothing? Why is one so ignorant even here!" Heat started to radiate from her, and the water swirled faster along her body.

"I meant no offense. I just don't understand the ways of this world, or what's happening to me."

She settled as fast as she'd grown angry, giving me a wry smile. "Well, I cannot expect a head as small as yours to understand all that I do. The thing you hold, it is from a mixture of lower powers, focused on the physical. It is not a higher power, like me."

“A higher power…like this?" I held up my hand, where the dark substance swirled excitedly.

"You hold a part of my strength, condensed. Holding it here within me,” she pointed to her chest, “is what allows me to hold the physical form you see before you. It is not a power of the flesh."

"So what would happen if I…consumed it?"

"You seek to gain my patronage and ascend?"

"I don't know what that means. There are some people I need to fight back against, and I have to be strong. I don't know if you know who the Oracle is, but she gave me a gift, and the gift gave me a vision of this place. I think it might have been leading me to you."

"The Oracle? Hmm…perhaps…" she trailed off. "If you take

that, it will likely kill you. At best it will change you. You have given power to your body. My power will do that, too, but it will also change the void of you, your center…ah, I have not the words for it. But you will probably die instead."

"And if I don't die?" I stared at the huge Seed, something in my abdomen tightening up.

"You will surely die. My heart is too much for a puny bug like you, amusing though you may be."

"What if I only took a little?"

She laughed again. "So greedy! I like it. Perhaps your body could contain a small amount. But as with all power, it likes to grow, and mine especially. Perhaps someday it would rip you apart."

I continued to stare at its shimmering blackness, reflecting the yellowing light of the setting sun. "How soon would it be?"

"Eventually," she answered unhelpfully. "You would trade time for power?"

"Without power, I have no time, and neither do those who I care for. How much Seed can I take?"

"Not much. You are small."

I nodded, and sent a Window to the others.

—I'M GOING TO TAKE A BIT OF A RISK, NOW. IF I DIE, PLEASE HEAD BACK ON YOUR OWN. IF YOU ASK HER NICELY, THE MOUNTAIN MIGHT BE WILLING TO GIVE YOU A HAND GETTING OUT OF HERE.—

-EVE-

I ignored the Windows and shouts that came back at me. A couple motions and the thought of what I wanted made the black goop form a normal Seed-sized ball, which I popped off. I held it in my hand as it flattened itself to me and started swirling in little tendrils between my fingers.

Then I opened my mouth and let it run inside and down my

throat. It tasted like…the taste of something beyond the sensory range of my tongue.

It hit my stomach, and started to spread outward from that pit inside me.

There was pain, and more pain, and then the expanse.

---

I KNEW FORMLESSNESS AND CHANGE, as the shore knows the endless ocean. I slipped in and out of fevered dreams my brain couldn't comprehend when it knew what I was, but fell into wholeheartedly when the burning chaos gained the upper hand. My body's fight was an ebb and flow of power as it struggled to maintain itself against the Seed, which tried to make me one with the sea.

I was not myself for a while, and then I started to draw back, folding and squishing in on my body in an agony of pain. The endless ocean that I'd been part of slipped away from me, but I was left with a portion of it folded in the back of my mind.

When I woke, it was full night, and I did not know where I was, or who I was. This did not bother me until my mind started to gather together, and I realized that it should. Then I was frightened, and scrambled to regain my memories and control of my body.

Then I saw the stars shining bright and as thick as if a child had dumped out a bucket of glitter on the canvas of the sky, and it snapped together.

"So you are awake."

The sound blew through me, shaking me even from the inside. It hurt, as if I was one big bruise.

"Yes." My voice felt strange, but I couldn't remember why.

"I am glad. Though it is curious that I should be worried for one so small and fleeting."

The rest of the black Seed was gone from my right hand, once again floating within her chest. I probably should have been at least slightly worried by that, but the notion never crossed my mind. "I feel strange."

"Of course. You are different than you were before."

That made perfect sense to me, vague as it was. "I lived. Am I powerful now?"

"What is your name?"

"Eve. Eve Redding. Don't tell me you forgot so easily."

She leaned forward and touched my chest with the tip of her huge stone finger. "You are my progeny. I welcome you to the existence of power, child god Eve-Redding. May you go without chief or ruler, free and wild."

I could hear in the way she said it that she'd missed the concept of a first and last name, but that was fine. "May the waters without light flow unfettered," I replied, the words coming unbidden from that space in the back of my mind. It seemed like a good idea to respond in turn to her formal blessing.

She smiled and let out a deep humming sound, which was slightly more pleasant and easy on the ears than her usual repertoire of avalanches, exploding bombs, and earthquakes. "I go by many names, and my real name cannot be spoken with a tongue, or heard with ears. But in this form, you may call me Behelaino. Now go to your subjects. They have been mewling for you, and step on my patience. In the morning, you will begin your training."

"Training?" My ears perked up.

"Yes. You must train your puny body to contain and channel the drop of Khaos, if you are to live. Now, go." She pronounced the "K" and "H" separately, but I was pretty sure I understood what she meant.

Chaos? Is that what I'd swallowed? When she put it like that, it didn't sound so good. Right dangerous, in fact.

---

I TURNED AWAY from Behelaino to go check on the others, and

was surprised by a Window popping up. Blaine and Adam had done some complicated things with "double encryption and spiked firewalls" that I didn't understand, but which allowed the VR chips to work, and the team to use them amongst each other, but blocked NIX from any access. Not that they would have been able to reach us here, in the Trial world. Estreyer, I reminded myself.

YOU HAVE GAINED THE SKILL "—NAME UNKNOWN—"
WOULD YOU LIKE TO NAME THIS SKILL?
YES / NO

I chose "Yes," and named the Skill "Chaos."

SKILL "CHAOS" HAS UNKNOWN CLASS.
WOULD YOU LIKE TO ASSIGN A CLASS?

On a whim, I dubbed it "Godling" Class. Then I pulled up my Attribute Window, out of curiosity. I knew I'd been getting a lot of spontaneous level ups lately, but I hadn't checked my stats.

PLAYER NAME: EVE REDDING
TITLE: TEAM LEADER(3)
CHARACTERISTIC SKILL: SPIRIT OF THE HUNTRESS, TUMBLING FEATHER
LEVEL: 38 UNPLANTED SEEDS: 2
SKILLS: COMMAND, CHAOS

STRENGTH: 13
LIFE: 20
AGILITY: 19
GRACE: 17
INTELLIGENCE: 16
FOCUS: 15

BEAUTY: 10
PHYSIQUE: 11
MANUAL DEXTERITY: 9
MENTAL ACUITY: 18
RESILIENCE: 12
STAMINA: 18
PERCEPTION: 17

MY ATTRIBUTE LEVELS were much higher than the level I held might suggest, due to all the hard work my team and I had been putting in. But it still wasn't enough. Hopefully the new Skill would be helpful. "Display Skill Window," I murmured.

CHARACTERISTIC SKILLS

TUMBLED FEATHER (KINETIC CLASS): INCREASES GRACE AND AGILITY. IMPROVED SENSE OF BALANCE AND MOTION. SKILL EFFECTS WILL EXPAND AND STRENGTHEN WITH PLAYER IMPROVEMENT.

SPIRIT OF THE HUNTRESS (SPIRIT CLASS): INCREASED GRACE, AGILITY, PERCEPTION, FOCUS, PHYSIQUE, AND STAMINA. NAILS EXTEND AND SHARPEN ON COMMAND. GREATER CHANCE TO LAND ON FEET AFTER A FALL. AGGRESSIVE TENDENCIES INCREASE. SKILL EFFECTS WILL EXPAND AND STRENGTHEN WITH PLAYER IMPROVEMENT.

SKILLS

COMMAND (MUNDANE CLASS): ALLOWS LEADER ACCESS TO THE TEAM MANAGEMENT WINDOW.

LEADER CAN COMMUNICATE WITH TEAM MEMBERS THROUGH GAME WINDOWS, SEE LOCATION OF TEAM MEMBERS ON TEAM MANAGEMENT MAP, AND IS ABLE TO ACCESS BASIC GAME INFORMATION OF TEAM MEMBERS. MAY ADD ADDITIONAL TEAM MEMBERS AT HIGHER LEVELS OF COMMAND.

CHAOS (GODLING CLASS): UNKNOWN—PLAYER USE DATA WILL BE GATHERED TO SUPPLEMENT LACK OF INFORMATION.

"OH, *THAT'S* USEFUL." I shook my head and continued on, slowly. My team was already out and waiting beside the small niche where I'd left them. There'd be no sleeping with Behelaino's voice assaulting their eardrums.

Sam stood on his own two feet, though a bit the worse for wear.

Adam was the first to hug me, wrapping his arms so tightly I literally felt my painful ribs creak, despite my body's Seed-enhanced fortitude. He smelled like sweat. Hell, we all probably did at this point. "I'm really glad you're okay." But his relief quickly turned to outrage. "How could you do something so stupid!"

I drew back. "It wasn't stupid. It worked. Which means it was genius! I took a new type of Seed from her, the thing that was powering her physical body. I'm probably going to be strong enough now to take on NIX. We got what we came here for, essentially." I turned to the others. "It worked."

"Probably? Is that worth endangering your life, and ours too, for that matter? What if it hadn't worked?"

"It did work. And yes, it is worth it. We don't have a lot of options, Adam." I forced my surprisingly instantaneous anger back. "That's why we're here in the first place. We grow strong, or we die. When you think about it like that, I made a pretty simple decision."

He took a deep breath and let it out again. "You're right. I was just…tense." He stepped back and moved to the little niche in the rock wall, setting out food.

Jacky grinned hugely and moved to hug me next.

I held up a hand. "Don't crush me, okay? I'm feeling a little tender."

She laughed and crushed me anyway. "You're awake. I didn't know when you'd get up, and that crazy creature wouldn't let us go to you! I was getting ready to go over there and kick its ass again. But now you're here, so you spared me the trouble." Despite her bravado, the slight tremble in her voice let me know how worried she'd been.

I refused to feel bad, though. I'd done what needed to be done, and if feelings would be the sacrifice for power, so be it.

Sam threw his arm around me, and walked with me toward the small camp area. "They told me what happened when I woke up. I couldn't believe you'd done something so crazy. Eve…" he murmured, "You can't go dying on us. We need you. The last three days, it hasn't been fun."

"Three days?" I gasped. "Wow. No wonder you guys were so worried. But I was just sleeping it off. I'm fine, and believe me, I'm not going to give up my hold on life voluntarily."

Only when we sat down to eat from a smorgasbord of strange foods, which apparently Behelaino had supplied them with while they waited, did I realize how absolutely starving I was.

I gorged myself until my stomach was literally distended, and then had just a little bit more.

Adam brought out the tailos egg. "Figured you might want to see to this thing." He placed it tenderly in my lap. "It's been making sounds for the last couple days. I think it might be close to hatching."

I laid my ear on the dark, pocked surface. "Or maybe it's just hungry. Unless one of you fed it, it hasn't eaten in a couple days."

I fumbled in my pack for one of the syringes Blaine had given me, and quickly drew some blood from my arm.

The egg sucked up the blood as I gave squirts into a few of the pockmarks. But then it started squeaking even louder, and after a few minutes, the baby tailos moved inside its egg with enough force to rock back and forth in my lap.

The other three gathered around, watching with avid curiosity.

When the first crack appeared in the surface, Adam gave a hiss and bit down on a knuckle, maybe the most excited I'd ever seen him. "It's hatching. I told you, it's hatching!" He nudged Sam and Jacky, as if to make sure they knew, even though they were watching just as wide-eyed as him.

The first piece of shell broke off, clattering to the ground. After that, the rest was short work.

A creature small enough to be cradled in two of my hands struggled out into my lap, pieces of shell sticking to its back. It let out a croak, coughed, and then let out louder, scratchy mewl.

"A baby tailos," I whispered in awe.

It had the body of a baby wildcat, except for the fragile little wings covered in matted fuzz attached to its back.

It mewled again, and Adam reached out to clean the pieces of shell off its sticky body.

It snapped at his fingers with sharp teeth, and gave a hilariously pitiful attempt at a growl.

Adam gripped his bleeding finger, which Sam reached over to heal without conscious thought. "Wow. Vicious little creature." Adam scowled at it, and licked the blood off his already healed digit.

Jacky laughed delightedly and clapped her hands.

The tailos cub looked up and met my gaze. Its eyes still had the blue sheen of a baby, but I thought they might be green when it grew up. It licked its chops and mewled at me, louder.

"Aww, he's just hungry," I said. "Do we have anything tender for him to eat?"

While Sam moved to get food, Adam raised an eyebrow. "That

thing doesn't need something tender. Have you seen its teeth? I thought babies weren't supposed to have teeth right away. And how do you know it's a boy?"

"He's a warrior cub. Of course he'd have teeth," I said approvingly, scratching at the cub's head. "And he just kinda seems like a boy. That's the impression I got from his mother when she gave him to me."

Sam handed me some chunks of meat, careful to keep his finger out of reach of the tailos cub, which sniffed pointedly at his food-filled hands.

I took it, and fed the cub bite after bite, which it didn't bother to chew at all.

A glimpse of its mouth showed primarily canines, so that made sense.

When it had finished one handful, it licked at my empty hand with a rough tongue and mewled at me pointedly.

"Hungry. That's good, means he's strong," Jacky nodded approval.

"What should I call you?" I said to the creature. "Hmm? Do you have a name? Can you do that telepathic thing like your mother?" I touched a finger to the tip of its nose, and it jerked back in surprise, and then let out a large burp, which seemed to surprise it even more.

We all laughed at its comically wide-eyed, slightly alarmed expression.

The cub looked around at us for a moment, and then mewled in affront.

"Okay, okay," I chuckled. "Birch it is. We'll just say we named you after the mighty tree."

"I wish China were here to see this," Sam said suddenly.

We all fell silent, the sadness pushing out the happy atmosphere.

"Me too," Adam whispered.

Jacky angrily knuckled away tears. "I'm gonna make them pay. I swear it."

I swallowed the lump in my own throat. I felt like I should say something, but I didn't know what, so I just said, "Me, too."

I fed Birch until his stomach was even rounder than my own food-stuffed belly, and then fell asleep with him tucked in the crook of my arm, my organs and bones aching and burning as the Seed I'd taken continued to fight against me.

# Chapter 35

I am the creator and the destroyer, I am he that defines all worlds. I bring life to the lifeless, I rain death on all that lives. My judgement is supreme. I encompass all things, I am the progenitor of good and evil. I created sin, I cause its every pain. Hell is one of my works. I am the source of all gods. I create gods on a whim, I destroy gods with a thought. I am man.

— Craig Smith

WHEN I WOKE up again with a hungry Birch pawing and licking persistently at my face, another whole day had passed. I fed my new little companion and stuffed myself, too, but this time resisted the urge to fall back asleep.

I left the sleeping area and saw the other three on a new stone-floored area of the caldera, fighting against golems. For a second my muscles tensed and I berated myself for trusting Behelaino, but then I realized they were sparring.

When I asked, I found Behelaino had created the golems on Jacky's request, to help them train, and as a distraction from boredom while I slept. She'd also created stone pathways for us to walk through the water on, so we didn't have to go hopping around the slippery platforms.

I left them to their sparring, but took Behelaino's attention for myself, sitting cross-legged at her base. Birch followed me, curling up in my lap to sleep off the huge meal. After only a day he was walking, though it was more like a stumbling wobble than anything.

"Disorder naturally runs free and resists control," she rumbled at me. "While this is as it should be, if you allow it, you will die. You must learn to enforce order. That is the way of life."

"Okay, so how do I do that?"

She drew back and tilted her head. "Well, you mold my power. Guide it, rather than allowing it to run freely through you."

"Okay…but how?"

She frowned, head still tilted. "How?" she repeated. "Can you not feel it?"

"Feel it? I don't have some instinctual knowledge of how to channel power, if that's what you mean. Can you explain from a human point of view?"

She huffed, blowing the hair back from my face. "I am not the God of Knowledge, how would I know the training of a mortal to a godling?"

"I thought you'd done this before?"

"Yes, many years ago, but that one was different than you. Definitely smarter. I did not need to teach them what to do with something so natural."

The heat of anger burned up in me, but Birch woke up and gave a scratchy little growl in Behelaino's direction. The cute threat startled both her and me, and my anger slipped away. "I'll try to figure it out. In the meantime, maybe you'd like to continue your sparring with the others," I said.

Her growing irritation seemed to have dissipated as well, and she smiled, but said, "If I must. I'd be embarrassed if my godling was seen going around with such followers. They must grow stronger before you leave."

I let the insult slip past with a bit of effort, and took a few deep breaths, forcing my mind into the hyper-aware state. I focused on my own body, ignoring all outside distractions.

I slipped deeper and deeper into my own body, looking closer and closer, till I could see my cells struggling and dying against the onslaught of the Seed. I healed at an accelerated rate, but even the best healing power wouldn't be enough without being able to stop the constant attack. I tried to focus my will and calm down the erosion, but while I could control a few of the strange Seed organisms, the countless others went on unchecked, and if I took concentration away for a moment, the stilled Seed pieces would be right back to their destructive ways.

I opened my eyes when Birch stirred on my lap and began to pester me for food again.

"You did not succeed," Behelaino said before I had a chance to say anything. "I could feel it. I cannot teach you how to control it, but once you learn, I will train you to do it better, faster, and in different ways."

"If I can figure it out," I mumbled back, feeling defeated and so very, very tired.

I carried Birch back to our little camp spot and fed us both again, giving only lethargic responses to my teammates' conversation attempts, and went back to sleep.

The cycle of eating ravenously to power my body's healing, trying futilely to control the Seed, and sleeping as if I was a newborn babe continued for days. I grew increasingly frustrated and irritable at my failure and the constant pain, enough that the others started to avoid talking to me or getting in my way. The only one who didn't feel the lash of my tongue was Birch, but he was just as snappish as I toward anyone who wasn't me.

Enough time passed that I felt insidious doubt that I would ever be able to control the Seed, and would die from my reckless consumption of it. I walked along the rim of the caldera's lip, taking in a view like no other, in glimpses when the stretching clouds below and all around cleared momentarily. The land stretched away beneath me, so far that I could see the curve of the planet.

Birch followed behind me, tentatively letting his wings catch the wind. They were still more fuzzy than feathered, but he'd grown significantly in the time since he'd hatched, and was the size of an adult cat, with all the playfulness and body shape of a kitten.

My claws slipped out involuntarily as I paced back and forth, and I resisted the urge to yank at my own hair in frustrated rage. Tears prickled behind my eyes, and I choked on my own fear. I focused my mind inward, pushing past the emotion with some effort, and begged wordlessly with the Seed to listen to me, to stop attacking me.

It didn't listen, and so I screamed. I opened my eyes and screamed again, all the rioting emotions within clawing out through my throat. As I did, a strange power burst from me along with a dark-tendriled smoke, and the slippery rock at my feet turned to sand.

I stared down in amazement, unblinking, as the little grains slid off the edge. The wispy black smoke had dissipated almost immediately, and left me feeling empty. Then the rock crumbled and started to fall away beneath my feet, taking me with it.

My stomach lurched at the sudden change in velocity, but already the tumult of conflicting emotion in my mind was back, and stronger than before. My body convulsed with pain, and I blacked out as the wind of my fall brushed against my cheek.

---

WHEN I WOKE, Adam sat beside me, redrawing his tattoo with inkberries, wincing as he embedded the dark liquid into his skin. This design was even more intricate than the last one, twisting up his arm in fractal knots. It reminded me of bindings, holding any broken pieces of Adam secure beneath his skin.

Perhaps I should get some. I was falling apart, too, and could use something to help me hold it together. I giggled at the thought, causing him to break concentration.

He smiled. "You're awake." The smile slipped away almost immediately, morphing into a stern look I'd seen before.

"Yes. And let me guess, you're upset because I was reckless and hurt myself."

He sighed. "Birch gave this crazy yowl when you fell—he's awesome—and Jacky caught you. It's just lucky you fell toward the inside, rather than down the mountainside. Otherwise you'd be dead right now." He stared at me somberly, his eyes searching my face. "What happened? Sam said you didn't hit your head, but you passed out, and there's this crater and cracks in the rocks above where you fell."

I cleared my scratchy throat, and he handed me a flask of water without looking away. I drank, and said, "I got the new power to work for the first time. Or rather, I kind of lost it up there, and suddenly I'd destroyed part of the rock where I was standing. Then it was like all the different emotions went full volume, all together, and I just…passed out. It's the Seed. It's… chaos, Adam. Behelaino…she told me she's formlessness and the void, and I have that inside me. I don't know how to control it. Even now," I broke off, swallowing the sudden and furiously strong urge to cry, "I feel like I'm vibrating apart into a million pieces."

He stared at me for a second. "When I was a kid, I had some trouble…coping." He looked down to his hands, idly rubbing his fingers together.

I clenched my teeth, holding in an unexpected surge of anger. He was going to tell me he knew how I felt, try to sympathize with me? How dare he? He knew nothing, had never experienced something like this. What advice could he give me?

"My dad drank…*drinks*," he corrected. "But back then my mom was still alive. He'd get angry and do these little clever, hurtful things. Sometimes, those can be harder to take than the physical pain."

My anger slipped away, replaced by a burning shame at its existence only seconds before.

"I'd get angry and sad, and it would all get to be so much I just couldn't handle it. I'd hole up in my room, screaming into a pillow and punching the headboard of my bed." He rubbed his scarred knuckles absentmindedly, and was silent for a while.

"Adam," I whispered, unsure what to say, but he began talking again as if he hadn't heard me.

"My mom found me one day, like that, just kind of…unreachable. She pulled me onto her lap and rocked me for a long time, until I calmed down. Then she taught me a way to help control all the negative emotions when things got overwhelming. She told me to make a house in my mind, and in that house, to make a room. In that room, to make a box, and in that box, to put the things that were making me crazy. If I felt ashamed, she told me to think of the thing that had made me that way, acknowledge it, and then put it in the box. Then to cover the box and fill the room with things that made me feel confident and proud and safe, so that the shame wouldn't be as loud. If you put the bad feeling in a room made of bad things, it'll stay hidden, but it starts to fester and poison you secretly. That's why you hold it with its opposite."

He took a deep breath, and met my eyes again. "Maybe you can do that with this new Seed. Take it and lock it up so it can't keep making you crazy." He gave me a pointed look, and a small quirk of a smile.

"Maybe," I said. "At this point, I'm willing to try just about anything."

With Adam's serene voice guiding me, I made a house with many rooms waiting to be filled. I chose one of the rooms, and put the sea of chaos within my body and mind into a small wooden box made of silence. I locked it, and put the box in a chest made of stillness. I left them in the middle of my room made of serenity, and closed the door. Then I built a towering wall of protective stone all the way around the house, because it made me feel safe.

I opened my eyes, and then closed them again almost immediately, moving my concentration inward in a different sort of way, checking on the Seed within my body. It was still there, spread throughout, but it no longer pushed so strongly against the natural order of my body, and other than relief, I had no overpowering emotion coursing through me.

I was exhausted by the intense mental effort, and fell asleep again, with a muttered, "Thank you," to Adam.

The next day, I told Behelaino of my conquest, and she began to instruct me in the use of my newly contained power. She was a hard taskmaster, constantly impatient and fickle, and my body was still weak from its extended battle. Learning even a modicum of control was grueling. According to Behelaino, I was also singularly untalented.

"You must leave soon," she said to me a few days later.

"Yes. The Trials will be starting soon, and then I will go back to my world. There's not much time left," I said, sparring lightly with a man-sized tornado of jagged pebbles and steam she'd made.

"I have not much control left. My strength replenishes by the day, and I struggle to hold it in check so that you and your subjects do not die. I cannot continue to do so for much longer," she rumbled.

I frowned, and released a short burst of my new power, scattering and disintegrating the twister with a poof of fleeting dark tendrils. I quickly clamped back down on the Chaos, locking it up again before it could attack me in a frenzy of sudden release. The effort exhausted me. It would be a while before I could use the Skill again, though I was getting better compared to fainting the first time. "You're regaining the strength lost from when you… erupted?" She'd hinted as much a few times before.

"Yes. If you do not take some distance from this place, your lives in mortal form will be gone, your energy mixed with my own. Prepare your subjects to travel. If this Trial does not take you when you have said it will, you will need to run. I have grown…*fond* of you, and would like you to live on."

But it did take us, shortly afterward. When the Boneshaker

started to play, a cube formed in front of us, and we were given the option to go to the Trial or not. Behelaino could somehow tell. "You do not bear my power in vain, Eve-Redding. May you go free."

My eyes met the gaze of her face's swirling orbs of water and held, and then my team and I were snapped away to a Trial. For the first time since my first Trial, I felt no overwhelming fear.

# Chapter 36

A child weaned on poison considers harm a comfort.
— Gillian Flynn

AS I'D GUESSED and hoped, Zed was there, so we could protect him. When he saw me, his face lit up, as happy as I'd ever seen him. But instead of rushing forward to hug me and make sure I was alright, he hesitated, and his eyes searched mine.

I was puzzled for a moment, and then realized what was going on in his mind. I remembered the last time I'd seen him, and the things I'd said. So instead of waiting for him, I stepped forward and wrapped him in a crushing hug. He wheezed from the force my strength could now create, but when I pulled back, he was beaming. "I'm glad you're okay," I said. "And…you know, those things I said—"

"You wanted to keep me safe," he interrupted. "I know. Sometimes we do things we shouldn't, trying to keep each other safe. Must run in the family," he said pointedly.

My eyes widened in surprise, and I finally let go of the last bit of anger I'd been holding against him for taking my Seed. "Yeah. I guess we do."

He nodded, but I knew that even if all was forgiven between us, it would be a while till the wounds healed and things were back to normal. Maybe they would never be back to normal. And that was okay, too.

After the Trial, which seemed designed to test our speed, dexterity, and endurance, the team returned with Zed to the normal world, wrapping our arms around him in a kind of bulky group hug in the hopes that he'd take us with him to the point where Blaine was waiting with an escape route.

It worked, and we all piled into Blaine's dark-tinted pod, ignoring the queasiness that came with teleportation. He peeled away. We were in some network of mostly empty underground tunnels, which he navigated with ease.

My eyes had adjusted to the dark, so when the pod burst out into the brightness of day and merged with flowing traffic, I flinched and lifted an arm to block my face.

Zed, who was sitting beside me, did the same. When we'd had time to adjust to the brightness, he turned to me. "You seem different."

Jacky grinned and poked her head forward from the backseat. "Yah. That's because we're bad-ass strong now."

Sam, on my other side, sighed and leaned his head back against the seat. "Training in Hell will do that to you. But I never realized before how bad Earth stinks. I'd gotten used to the freshness."

"No," Zed shook his head, "that's part of it. But there's something else, too."

Adam flicked me a look from the front passenger seat, which I pointedly ignored.

Zed looked from Adam to me. "What is it?"

I shook my head. "We just have a lot more experience with danger than we did before. We've become veteran Gamers, kind of in the space of nine days. It's been a lot longer than that for us. That disconnect is probably what you're sensing."

"How long were you over there for?"

"About six weeks."

He nodded and let the questioning go, but the frown on his face said he wasn't quite satisfied. He was more sensitive to lies and evasion, after everything that had happened. "Well, you're crazy, crazy powerful now."

I couldn't blame him for being suspicious, but I didn't know what to say about the Seed I'd taken, or how to explain it, and I didn't want him to worry. But I felt a small twinge of guilt, and decided to elaborate anyway. "I also have a new…Skill-type-thingy." I made vague hand motions meant to play down its importance rather than explain.

He perked up with interest again, but I gave vague answers, and kept the true danger and side effects to myself.

The others knew the truth, more or less, but they wouldn't go against my word.

Blaine took us to a hotel suite, which he'd paid for using a fake ID link. He had some lab equipment set up, though not even close to the realm of the laboratory in his basement.

When I let Birch out of my backpack, where I'd firmly ordered him to stay hidden, still and quiet before the Trial, Blaine went into a state of frenzied, ecstatic curiosity, and lamented that he didn't have better equipment to examine the animal. Birch even bit him when Blaine tried to touch his wings, but the scientist seemed even more excited by that, asking a series of questions about him and the Trial world that I was too tired to answer properly.

Luckily, Adam was more than happy to rave about my new monster companion. He adored the little tailos, even though Birch seemed to know it, and bullied him mercilessly. Every time Adam got close, Birch swatted or made coughing sounds at him. And when Adam tried to feed him scraps of meat, Birch always deliberately nipped his fingers, too. It was obvious the tailos found it all great fun, and for some reason Adam only liked him even more.

After a few hours to rest and recuperate, I woke up while the others still slept and sat down with Blaine and Birch to satisfy his curiosity and my own. While I kept up a constant stream of petting, praise, and reassurance toward the sleepy cub, Blaine took samples of his various bodily fluids, fur, and feathers.

"Give me an update on the real world," I said. "What's been happening while we've been gone? Have you been able to safely avoid NIX?"

Blaine spoke without looking at me, intent on his samples of an alien life form. "Yes. We have been a step ahead of them the whole time. However, if not for my…especially wide skill set, that would not be the case. Everything we buy is on untraceable credit, and I've put some additional measures in place to avoid recognition by the satellites or cameras. It is not perfect, though. I may be a genius, but I am only one person, and they have resources most people can barely imagine."

"That can work against them, too. They may be big and powerful, but they're also secretive. They haven't let the world find out about them. It'll end up being just one more incentive for them to decide we're more trouble than we're worth, no matter how much power they have. Have you made any progress on verifying their method of teleportation?" I asked.

"From the feedback on the monitoring system, it seems your hunch was right. The sphere device in the courtyard of NIX's compound is in control of the Boneshaker. I still do not understand how it works, unfortunately. I cannot block it."

"That's okay. I know another way."

He was silent for long enough that I thought maybe he wasn't going to continue the conversation, but then he said, "What do you think the chances are? That you will be able to pull this off, I mean? This commitment you have made to all of us, it is quite… large. Save my sister's kids, free the rest of the team from the

Game, strike a blow to NIX and force them to leave us alone afterward… Can you do it?"

"Blaine, there's only one answer I can give you. I won't allow a future in which I fail. I'm going to keep everyone safe."

He pulled out a syringe and pierced my arm, drawing blood. "What if you cannot? What if NIX is too strong for us, even now?"

I suppressed a small surge of anger at his doubt, recognizing it for the emotional volatility born of my new power. I hadn't been to my mental room of peace for a while, and needed to visit it and tend the box within. "I won't fail. You may see something new in that blood when you examine it, Blaine. I asked about what's happened here, but I haven't told you about our little trip yet."

We talked for a couple hours after that, exchanging information and more plans. Though I wasn't willing to accept aloud the possibility of a second defeat at NIX's hands, I still made plans to keep Zed far away and safe in the event that I was wrong. I was cocky, yes, but never let it be said that I didn't learn from my mistakes.

## Log Of Captivity 5

Mental Log of Captivity-Estimated Day: Two thousand, six hundred forty-two.

She is back again, though she was gone long enough I worried myself to distraction. I have tried to reach her, and though I can feel our *blood-covenant-bond*, I cannot touch her. She has adapted some sort of *warrior's-technique* to protect her mind. I am grateful that she grows strong, but I feel her coming close to this place of *two-leg-maggots*, and I worry that she will attempt to find me again. It is shameful that my child-master must save her *blood-covenant-champion*. But my *mother-lord* would approve of her.

# Chapter 37

They shall have stars at elbow and foot;
    Though they go mad they shall be sane,
    Though they sink through the sea they shall rise again;
    Though lovers be lost love shall not;
    And death shall have no dominion.
    — Dylan Thomas

I SAT on the mountainside behind the bowl of NIX, which I'd just realized was similar to Behelaino's tip, only less defensible and harsh. A map of NIX floated in front of my face, and I'd shared it with Jacky and Adam, who sat on either side of me. We were going over the plan for our attack, and reviewing the myriad variations we'd come up with, in case of surprises.

The sun had just risen, and its cleansing light was almost harsh despite the early hour. We would come at dawn instead of in darkness this time. I let the wind whipping along the mountainside rush over me as I contemplated what was to come, willing my victory into existence.

—We're ready.—
-Sam-

I'd sent Sam around to the other side of NIX with Blaine. Sam would be able to heal the hostages if needed, so that everyone would be in condition to escape without being a burden. When they were finished, Blaine would take off with the kids and Chanelle, and Sam would come back around as backup for my group.

Bunny, now officially our man on the inside, had unlocked a door for them. Blaine would be going for the prototype of the electronically powered armor suit he'd given to NIX first, which would augment his fighting ability and hopefully allow him to hold his own while they broke Chanelle and the kids out.

Zed and Birch were on their way out of the country, to a place that would be safe if the unthinkable happened. Not that any place would be truly safe, if Zed had to keep going to the Trials, especially without our protection. I'd wanted Blaine to go with him, to keep him safe and out of the way, but he'd refused to leave Kris and Gregor to anyone's protection but his own, and insisted he could be useful. Zed would have to do his traveling alone, because as much as I hated it, in truth I couldn't spare the manpower to go with him. I'd left Birch with him, since the cub needed protection as much as he did.

I had a quick image of China dying, but this time it was Zed's eyes staring back at me. I clenched my fist. That wouldn't happen. It wasn't an option.

The ground of the huge courtyard rumbled below, and a hole in the ground dilated open. Three heli-pods rose from it, their blades making a deep *thwump*-ing sound. I watched them rise slowly, then head away at top speed. Whatever NIX was doing, it would just be a distraction from us, something to slow down their reaction speed a little more.

I rose and took another deep breath, feeling a ball of something cold and hard in the center of my chest. All or nothing, now.

"It's time," I said to the two next to me, as well as sending the words in a Window to Sam.

I adjusted the armored vest straps over my chest, pricked the back of my wrist, and fed it a few drops of blood. "Armor in place?" I asked the others, and received positive responses.

They were all wearing the impact absorbing body armor that Blaine had been so proud of developing when we first met him. I preferred my armored vest for the top, but I'd taken the leg covers. Unless we were shot in the head, or with a high-impact round from a tank, we wouldn't die from bullets. They would still hurt like hell, though, so the plan was to not get shot.

"Let's go," I told everyone, and started to lope down the mountainside, letting gravity accelerate my descent.

Jacky and Adam moved to my right and left, slightly behind me, so we ran in an arrow-like formation.

The guards noticed us before we reached the base of the mountain and the dirt road leading to NIX's only gate, a huge, double-doored thing cut into the side of the wall. No side entrances or sneaking for us this time.

They pointed their guns at us, and someone shouted for us to stop, raise our hands in the air, and identify ourselves.

I slowed, and Jacky and Adam slowed with me, but we didn't stop. We reached the road and walked on it, heading straight for the gate.

When we got closer, a guard called down with a megaphone, "Stop right there! One more step and we open fire!"

I stopped and looked up at the guns pointing down at us a couple hundred feet in both directions from the top of the wall. "Jacky," I said.

With only that, she crouched down and sprang up again, shooting over my head and toward the wall like she'd bounced from some epic trampoline. Combined with her Skill, gravity in the normal world was just low enough to allow her to make such a move. She screamed as she went, a screech of excitement and aggression, and tucked her arms around her head to protect it from any bullets.

She needn't have bothered, because the guards were too stunned by her inhuman jump to aim or shoot at her.

By the time they recovered, she'd already disarmed and knocked out four of them. At least I thought they were unconscious. They may also have been dead.

The others turned and started to shoot at her then, but it was too late. She used their fallen comrades as shields, and continued to take them out, moving forward unstoppably. Using the distraction she created to our advantage, Adam and I moved forward. A few seconds of him fiddling with a keypad beside the huge gate, and it unlocked with a series of loud metal clicks. The doors rumbled open, and I stepped confidently through into the courtyard, Adam at my side. I unsheathed my claws and sank slightly lower into a fighting stance.

I was quite aware of the theatrical effect of all this to anyone watching. That was precisely the point of a show of force, wasn't it? Cue the epic music.

From the glass walls facing the inside of the courtyard, people in different uniforms and lab coats stood, looking down open-mouthed. The panic hadn't hit yet.

Piercing alarms screeched through the compound, and the guards in the courtyard started shooting.

The bullets were aimed for our chests, rather than our heads, but we still dodged to try and avoid them.

Adam's eyes met my own, and I gave him a nod. He shot off toward the concrete column forming a trunk topped by the huge, metal sphere in the center of the courtyard, while I moved toward the nearest guard. Adam would break through the concrete and jack into the twisting mass of wires within to gain retrograde access to NIX's computer system, and thus their whole base, along with all their top-secret information.

My claws sank into the guard's shoulder and ripped down, immobilizing the limb. I yanked them out, grabbed his gun, and smashed him in the side of the head. Lights out. I twisted and swung my leg up, slicing my toe claws across the back of another guard's neck, and knocked him out, too.

I tossed the guns toward center of the courtyard. Guns were useless to me, since my DNA didn't match the guards,' and I wanted the weapons as far away from my opponents' access as possible, just in case. I moved onto the next person, and the next, until blood splatters stained my whole body. Earth made me feel light, after all the time spent in Estreyer, and I didn't hesitate or try to spare the guards I fought. I wasn't actively trying to kill them, but if it happened, I wasn't going to cry.

The air seemed to ripple with the force of all the alarms going off, and shouts and screams of pain filled the air, with the occasional burst of gunfire and booming crunch. A bullet barely grazed my left arm, and another hit the armor around my thigh.

Up above, Jacky was almost finished with the whole top of the wall, having disabled or killed most of the guards, and disarmed the mounted anti-aircraft gun stands.

I'd almost finished with the resistance on the ground level of the courtyard, and I saw Adam send a few distracted lightning bolts at a few guards who had slipped past me to attack him.

Only a minute or so had passed since the first bullet flew, and so far we were dominating. Of course, that's when the electronic doors all around the courtyard slid open, and soldier-types in full body armor and shields poured out.

"Damn," I said, watching as they moved into formation. These guys were not only better equipped than the normal guards on the walls and the randoms milling around the courtyard, they were prepared to fight people like us.

They moved in formation, the front line holding shields, while the center pointed guns the size of rocket launchers at us from safety. A soldier from the door closest to me tossed out a small metal pipe. As it arced through the air, it started to smoke, letting out billowing clouds of yellow gas.

I sidestepped and made sure not to inhale, but within seconds each little team of soldiers had thrown multiple smoke pipes, and the yellow fumes began to fill the courtyard. A whiff of it, and my head felt a little lighter, my couple wounds a bit less distracting. I noticed the soldiers were wearing small air filters over their mouths, and lenses over one eye, no doubt to allow them to see through the sedative clouds.

"Bastards," I spat. "Don't breathe it!" I called to Adam and Jacky. I back-stepped as far away from the smoking canisters as possible and took a deep breath. I crouched low to the ground, digging in with both my hands and feet, and scrambled to pick up the canisters while holding my breath. I threw them past the soldiers, back through the open doorways through which the defenders had come.

I'd been quick enough with a section of the courtyard, but I wasn't lightning-fast like Adam, and I didn't get to the other half fast enough to mitigate the smoke profusion.

Still, at least some of the air was breathable. And any of the guards I'd downed before wouldn't be getting up again in a "surprise!" kind of way.

The soldiers in the front row of one group bent to a knee, and the row behind them started to shoot. I darted to the side to draw their attention and bullets.

—Almost through!—

-Adam-

It was imperative to keep him protected till he could accomplish his part in my plan. I sprinted forward, straight toward the shooting soldiers. Their bullets bruised me as they punched into my body armor. I jumped over the crouching first line of shield holders, and slammed feet first into the shoulders of a gun holder near the edge. I knocked him out of formation, and scrambled around behind him in a single movement. I couldn't use his gun past a couple bullets before it would shut down on me, so I snapped his neck and held him up, with my arms wrapped around his body. My fingers moved over his, and used his gun to spray down all his comrades. While I was at it I took out a few from another group not too far away.

It was a good start, but there were too many of them, and only one of me.

Already, more bullets were spraying at me from all around, and other groups turned their guns toward Adam.

"Shields!" I screamed.

He ripped little scraps of paper off the pin on the side of his pants they were attached to, and Animated them. Three broad, ink shields sprang up around him, protecting him from the sides and back. He had less than a minute before they ran out.

I slammed my back into an empty section of the wall, holding onto the soldier and using him as a meat shield from the bullets. I continued to shoot back, but I wasn't able to move from behind him without getting shot, and I knew I wouldn't be able to protect myself for long, let alone Adam. The smoke was clearing, blowing away in the breeze, but I saw more soldiers coming, lining up in the hallways leading radially out from the courtyard. Backups already arriving.

The only positive was we weren't taking fire from above, too.

Which also meant Jacky should be finished with her first assignment. "Jacky!" I said under my breath, sending it in a Window.

—ON IT.—
-JACKY-

A few seconds later, something plummeted from the top of the wall into the midst of a group of soldiers like a meteor fallen from space. The impact alone knocked them off their feet, and then Jacky stood up from her crouch and attacked. They didn't stand a chance.

When they were finished, she moved onto the next group. Her moves were like a crushing dance, kind of beautiful to watch, even as I thanked God she was on my side. But even she wasn't enough.

My commandeered gun ran out of bullets. "Damn it!"

Adam's shields would be running out any second.

Time for me to step it up. As it was, I hadn't been very awe-inspiring yet. I didn't want to use my trump card this soon, but I could still make a difference. I thrust the quite dead soldier forward, and hoped the bullets aimed at me would follow him. In half a second I'd flipped around and was scrambling up the wall, finger and toe claws punching into the cement. A couple rounds punched into my back, but my armored vest repelled them with little more damage to me than a painful bruise. I reached the top in record time, and was more grateful than ever for the days and days I'd spent leading the others up Behelaino's mountain.

Imitating Jacky, I dashed around to the other end of the wall and took a running leap off of it, onto the shoulders of a soldier.

Some of the group had noticed me coming, but they were packed too tightly in their defensive formation to evade an attack from that unconventional route. The soldier crumpled under my weight, and I used my claws to slice into either side of his neck. The blood splurted out like a crimson sprinkler.

I wasn't as good as Jacky, but she didn't have claws, nor my Tumbling Feather Skill. I jumped and spun and sliced, hitting with my elbows and my knees, cutting with my hands and feet.

## —Got it!—

### -Adam-

Seconds after Adam sent the message, the center of the courtyard lit up. He had one hand plunged into the bare, twisting, coiling wires, and the other stretched outward as if it was trying to escape the pain of the current. Electricity jumped and branched out from him like a tree made of light.

I closed my eyes, remembering the last time he'd done something like this.

Sure enough, bright whiteness exploded, loud enough to send me rocking backward and cause me to slip in the pool of blood I'd created.

I opened my eyes after a second to be sure it was safe. My eyesight was a little dim and spotty, and my ears rang, but I made out Adam still standing in the center of the courtyard. He was the only person on his feet.

All around, charred bodies had fallen to the ground, selectively electrocuted while he avoided the rest of the team, keeping us safe.

The hair on the back of my arms lifted, though I wasn't sure if it was from the smell of cooked human, or from residual electricity dancing through the air.

I stood up, and saw Jacky throw a crispy soldier off of her, and get up, too. She rubbed at her eyes and groaned, obviously having failed to close them in time.

Adam sagged against the wires, and took his hand off of them.

I took a few steps, making sure I had my balance, and then saw soldiers within the hallways crawling to their feet. He hadn't barbecued them.

—Close the doors, Adam.—
-Eve-

I could barely make out my own voice giving the command, so I knew he wouldn't be able to hear anything, seeing as he was literally in the center of that lighting boom.

He shook his head and straightened, and started to tap away at a screen embedded to his side among the wires.

Two seconds later, and the doors slid shut, ignoring the panicked soldier's attempts to keep them open.

"How long?" I sent him in a Window.

—It won't be opening from the inside. They'll have to blast their way through. So maybe five minutes?—
-Adam-

I crawled up the side of the sphere's concrete support to the grated maintenance ledge that lay around the top.

The sphere stood in front of me, pulsing with a faint hum of energy. Lines covered its surface, a bit like the patterning of the Seeds. All around it floated orbiting rings moving at different angles, like a way more complex version of the belts around the planet Saturn, but of different sizes, orientations, and made of strange metals unlike any I'd ever seen.

"So this is it," I said aloud. The thing that NIX used to send us to the Trials, and to track us when we went, even without the GPS trackers in our necks. I pressed the tip of my claws to its surface and walked a few steps, making tiny scratches in the metal. The sound of it rang out like a long and continuous crystal bell.

I looked out, and saw people pressed up against the glass wall some of the inside hallways, staring out at the scene we'd been making. I smiled at them, and waved a bloody, claw-tipped hand.

The alarms stopped, as Adam crackled away with electricity down below, and only in their absence did I realize that they'd been sounding the whole time.

In the silence, I took a deep breath and screamed at the top of my lungs. "Send out your leader!"

Jacky jumped up beside me, shaking the grating.

"Glad you could make it," I said, grinning.

She pursed her lips, fighting against a smile of her own. "I was busy. Didn't you notice?"

"I noticed you taking forever with those guards. And then getting buried under Adam's lightning barbecue."

She was grinning full out now. "*Me* taking forever? I remember finishing my area, and then coming down to help *someone*, no?" She gave me a pointed look. "And I may not have a flashy power like you two, but I make up for it in other ways." She flexed her bicep and wiggled her eyebrows.

I laughed. "Hmm...how about a demonstration?" I patted one of the gently moving rings that orbited the sphere.

"My pleasure." As we'd planned beforehand, she began to pound on the sphere and its rings, varying kicks and punches.

It shuddered on its stand, and some of the rings jammed up on each other when she forced them out of proper orbit.

I added blows of my own, though they had nowhere near the impact of Jacky's. My claws were useless here, too soft to cut through the metals.

"Have you got the name yet?" I asked Adam.

"Almost...okay. I think it's Nadia Petralka," he called up to me.

"You *think*?"

"It is."

I called out again, "Commander Petralka! Come to me!"

From beside me, Jacky paused in her attacks, and said, "Isn't she trapped inside along with all the others? What if she's trying, but she can't get out here?"

I shrugged. "She'll come out once they finish blasting down the doors. I'm sure they've already started. And in the meantime, we can put on a little more of the show. I still haven't gotten to bring out my party trick, remember?"

Jacky opened her mouth, "Ah...are you going to do that, now?" She stepped backward.

"Yes."

She nodded, and stepped back again, getting as far away from me as possible while not going so far around the circle that she got in front of me. "Should I get down?"

"You should be fine. I can control it." I raised my hands toward the sphere, as if I was getting ready to push it.

She looked from my face, to my hands, and then down to the ground.

I sighed. "Fine. Go down if you must."

She nodded, let out a sigh of relief, and jumped off the edge to safety.

I looked around again, and saw some people pounding on the glass, impotent and silent behind its barrier. I turned back to the sphere and took a deep breath, closing my eyes. In that room of serenity in my mind, I opened the chest of stillness. The box of silence was leaking black mist at the edges, which alarmed me.

As if sensing my disturbance, the misty tendrils wriggled and thickened.

I grabbed that small bit of Chaos and threw it outward, into the real world, right at the sphere. Even as the metal screamed and buckled, the sphere rocking on its stand and letting out heat as its molecules rubbed against each other, in my mind I was slamming shut the chest and locking the door, lest the rest of my power escape.

I looked at the partly damaged sphere with satisfaction, and then screamed again, "Nadia!" My voice was strong, despite my spinning head and legs that were threatening to buckle. A mixture of Chaos-enhanced rage and fear kept adrenaline in my veins, and me on my feet. Using the power took a lot out of me. I heard glass breaking behind me, and turned back to see a group of people jumping out of the window into the courtyard, kind of like my team had done the last time we were here.

It was a group of younger people, dressed in a uniform quite different than the soldiers.

I smiled wide. "Players." The last time we'd done reconnaissance on the place, we'd thought maybe they were captives, or possibly test subjects. It'd been beyond us to consider someone who'd been forced into the Game, willing to cohabitate with their oppressors. But I knew them for what they were, now. "Why, hello," I called down to them. "I don't suppose one of them is Nadia?" I directed the question toward Adam, who was standing shoulder to shoulder with Jacky, facing off against the advancing group.

"No," he said, clipped.

"Then I'm going to warn you," I called down to them. "We're not here for you. Go back, and we'll allow you to live."

They didn't stop, and the hair on the back of my neck rose as rage at being ignored and a healthy dose of wariness both washed through me.

The Player at the forefront, a shorter girl with spiked pixy cut hair and a hooked nose, laughed aloud. "You were looking for the Commander? Sorry, scag. I can't make the same promise to you. None of *you* will be leaving here alive." She pointed two fingers from each hand at Adam and Jacky. "Two on one. Take them down. I'll handle the giant." She jerked her chin up to me.

I raised an eyebrow. "Now, that's a bit hurtful, don't you think? I'm just a little taller than the average—" I cut off as she shot off the ground like a rocket, slamming into me and knocking me off the platform.

# Chapter 38

It was like this blackness that crept into the corners of my life until everything was grey and dirty. My insides felt burnt out, like if you cut me open, all you would find would be smoke. No heart. No bones. There was nothing left, just the anger. It followed me everywhere. It sat on my bed and watched me sleep and when I had to eat, it looked at me across the table.

— Tanya Byrne

THE PIXIE PLAYER slammed me into the far wall hard enough that my body armor rippled with the attempt to protect me. Something cracked. I wasn't sure if it was me or the concrete wall, and I didn't know which was more likely.

She stepped back, and I slid to the ground, coughing out little puffs as I tried to regain my air.

I caught a glimpse of Jacky and Adam, fighting wildly with their backs to each other.

Before I could move, the pixie girl stepped forward again, and slammed her foot into my stomach, further winding me. She ground her flat-heeled boot into me, and brought down a fist for a quick punch in the temple.

When she pulled her fist back again, I grabbed her foot and bucked upward, slamming my bare feet into her chest, while simultaneously pushing and twisting at her foot.

Her much smaller body flew backward, but she followed the force of my throw, twisted, and landed on her feet, sliding backward.

That was okay, because it gave me enough time to stand up again. I tackled her before she stopped sliding, claws out. I expected them to sink into the soft flesh of her sides, but instead they slid harmlessly forward, and I ended up in a kind of awkward body roll with her.

I used the momentum to tear myself free, and jump back. I stayed in a limber crouch a safe distance from her, claws out and ready to slice, though I now had doubts about their ability to actually do so. Was she wearing some sort of body armor beneath that uniform?

Then her skin turned gray and scaly, rippling out across her neck, hands, and face from underneath her clothes. Literal armored skin.

"Sorry, scag," she sneered. "Your little claws won't work here."

I grinned, and lunged forward, my right hand aimed low. At the last second, I shot two fingers from my other hand at her eyeballs.

Her face twisted in alarm as my "little claws" came within millimeters of her unprotected eyes. But she threw her head backward, dipping her upper body recklessly toward the ground.

My claws missed her eyeballs and scraped across her gray-scaled forehead harmlessly.

She turned her dip into a backflip, and grinned at me again.

To our side, Adam shot off bolts of lightning toward his and Jacky's four opponents. The arcing electricity caught two of them, and Jacky and he were on them instantly, he with his knives, and she with her fists.

It was my turn to grin. "Looks like this isn't going too well for your friends, huh?"

"Don't worry. When I'm finished with you, I'll go help them out."

"For that to happen, you'd have to still be alive at the end of this."

"Like you're going to stop me? Honey, it's obvious you don't have what it takes."

I smiled at her, straightening from my crouch. "There's a whole other side to me that you haven't seen yet, *Honey*." I stepped forward, taking a deep breath with every footfall.

Her mouth tightened, and I saw the moment when she grew wary and decided on a preemptive strike. She shot forward a millisecond later, but I was already jumping to the side.

Her eyes widened as she realized her miscalculation, but by then she was in motion, and it was too late.

I grabbed her by the arm and spun her around, throwing her into the side of one of the buildings in the courtyard.

As her face whitened in pain—I guess that armored skin didn't protect her internal organs—I walked toward her again, breathing deep and concentrating.

She made it to her feet and climbed up the side of the building, hoping to buy time or gain an advantage with the height, perhaps.

I jumped and grabbed the edge easily, and from there it only took half a second and a grip on the concrete with my toes to make it onto the roof.

But of course, me coming up after her is what she'd planned for. She was already shooting forward as soon as I'd planted my feet.

There was nowhere to go but back down off the roof, and I threw myself backward to avoid her attack, lifting my arms in a defensive stance. I was too slow.

She stopped abruptly an arm's length in front of me, and

slammed both of her palms forward, carrying all the energy of the full body dash she'd just aborted. Her hands smashed past my half-formed defense like it wasn't even there, and crashed into my chest.

I watched as if in slow motion as my vest sank into a perfect impression of her small hands, then rippled outward like the surface of still water after a pebble is dropped into it. My body flew up and backward, bowed forward around the point where she'd hit me. My lower back slammed into the side of the grated walkway around the stalled metal sphere. I flipped backward, tilting around the axis where I'd hit, and slid along the grating. I clawed desperately at the platform, twisting and sliding to a stop. Damn.

I tasted blood in my mouth, and gaped soundlessly in shock as the pain hit me. But I grabbed onto the sphere and pulled myself up.

She was still standing on the roof down below, panting hard. Her eyes widened in surprise when she saw me rise.

This wasn't the first time I'd taken a beating or been thrown around like a rag doll. I wouldn't be taken out so easily. I fought the black spots behind my eyes and the desire to pass out, and tried to force my lungs to expand and take in air again. They ignored me for the moment, but I was sure they'd listen eventually. If they didn't, I'd pass out, and if that happened it would all be over, and this would be for nothing.

So I sucked harder.

She jumped forward in that inhuman way that I'd only ever seen Jacky do, and landed in a crouch on the platform a couple yards from me. She stood, and smiled when she saw my condition, blood dripping from my mouth, a hand pressed to my chest, and barely able to stand.

Desperation raged in my chest, and I screamed at myself wordlessly. I could not be defeated here. After all that I'd been through, and how close I was to accomplishing my goal, I couldn't lose here, just because I was weak. I'd always been weak, and my enemies had always been strong, but that hadn't stopped me before. I was supposed to be stronger now.

She stepped forward and threw a punch toward my stomach.

I watched it coming, still screaming inside for my body to move, to attack, to win.

Then, everything *snapped.* The world slowed down as my whole being overloaded. Every thought slipped temporarily out of my mind except for the sight of her bringing forward a fist to smash into my body, and my raging denial of my possible loss to her.

I stepped forward to meet her fist, grabbing it with my clawed palm, just so.

She was moving as if through water, her expression just beginning to change from cocky into something else as she saw into the depths of my eyes.

With one shallow breath and a sleepy blink, I unleashed Chaos.

I had very little control over my new power this time, and it roared out of me with the force of a hurricane. I slammed her into the sphere, staring into her eyes, my hand still clenched around her fist.

Visible ripples radiated through the air, her gray skin, her bones, her blood, her organs, and out into the sphere, which screeched again as the metal moved and buckled under my power like undulating water under the force of a storm.

She screamed the scream of being separated from herself, as her insides bucked and bubbled and burst. It was a horrible sound, reverberating through my bones and echoing from every surface in the courtyard.

Then her bleeding eyes rolled back in her head, and she went limp.

The overpowering storm of rage in my head hadn't calmed yet, and I wanted to continue hurting her until she died, if she hadn't already. I wanted to keep smashing her like the bug she was, until her body was nothing but an unrecognizable lump of flesh and blood and bone.

But I took my second breath, a gasp this time, and released her fist and my power.

# Chapter 39

Hello, darkness, my old friend…I've come to talk to you again.
— Simon and Garfunkel

THE FIGHTING down below had stopped, as everyone still standing looked up at me with wide eyes.

In the sudden silence, my knees almost buckled from the backlash of my attack. My head spun as the rage and triumph tried to take over again, and I was as tired and hurt as if I'd just fallen out of a plane with no parachute. If no one had been watching, I would have fallen to the ground and let my consciousness slip away. Using Chaos twice in such short succession should still have been impossible for me.

But this was neither the time nor place for weakness, so I straightened and put on a mask of calm confidence. "You will concede defeat," I called down to the still conscious attackers below, "or I will come down there and destroy you all."

They raised their hands, and the three that could still move backed away from Jacky and Adam. The other was unconscious, and didn't look like he'd be waking up any time soon.

A muffled boom sounded from down below, and then one of the concrete doors burst open, rubble flying as an explosion ripped it apart.

A uniformed woman stumbled out, ignoring the surprised call of, "Commander! Wait!" from behind her. Metal stripes glinted on her shoulder.

"Is it her?" I called down to Adam.

"Yes," he said.

"I am Commander Nadia Petralka," she shouted. "Please, stop now. I've come, like you requested."

"Do you know who I am?" I asked, again running my claws over the surface of the damaged sphere.

She nodded, but her eyes were drawn to the downed girl at my feet. "You're Eve Redding, one of our highest ranked Players. Stop what you're doing. There is no need for further destruction or violence."

I frowned. "You say that, but you people are the ones who started all this. And suddenly, when it turns out you may have taken on the wrong opponent, you call for peace? I warned her to leave us alone if she wanted to live."

"Is she...dead?" Nadia Petralka's voice threatened to waver, and she clenched her jaw instead, keeping a calm face.

I reached down for the pixie girl's throat, and Commander Petralka took half a step forward, hand lifting, before she seemed to remember herself and abruptly stopped.

I smiled down at her, and found an erratic pulse in the girl's neck. "She's alive. I'm not sure for how long, without medical attention."

"She's just a girl. She doesn't have anything to do with this. Let her go, and we can talk."

I laughed. "Why would I let her go when you so badly want her to be safe? She serves double duty for me, as a bargaining chip and a ticking clock. It couldn't be more perfect if I planned it myself." Wow. I sounded like a comic book villain.

Her mouth tightened, and she snapped her ID sheath link

straight, turning it into a flat screen. "You want something, and I want something, Eve. Maybe those two things don't have to be mutually exclusive." She held up the screen toward me.

On it, I saw the small figures of Sam, Blaine in his mecha suit, and two smaller children and a blonde girl surrounded by people with guns. Sam and Blaine were in protective stance, the three rescuees placed between them.

—We've been caught. There must have been people waiting for us. I'm not sure if we can fight our away out or not.—
-Sam-

Sam wouldn't have waited to tell me, so Nadia must have been apprized of their successful capture just moments before I was. But then again, she was probably expecting it. I suppressed any outside reaction to the news.

"It was a nice try, Eve. But did you really think we weren't keeping tabs on the Rabbit group Moderator? He was sneaky, sure, but opening that door was kind of a giveaway. It's too bad you didn't all come from that direction. We could have captured you immediately, and none of this," she gestured around to all the bodies and general destruction in the courtyard, "would have had to happen."

I raised an eyebrow. "So you got a couple of my team. I let them attempt the rescue for their own satisfaction. A kind of reward for the work they've done. In fact, it has no bearing on my larger plan." I stood up, looking down at her. "And do you really think you could have captured us all? Do you realize the situation you're in?" I sent a quick Window to Sam, telling them to sit tight and not do anything stupid.

I could still save them. They may be caught, but they weren't captured, and they weren't dead. "Do you know what my teammate below me was doing, besides just shooting those spectacular lightning bolts? He was gaining access to your computer system. The whole thing. Including the whole slew of data and the records of what you've been doing. In five seconds, we could have that streaming to every link in the nation." I pointed to the girl collapsed at my feet. "I've got a hostage of my own." Then I put a hand on the sphere. "And this thing that you use to send us to the Trials? A few more pushes from me, and it'll be nothing more than a crushed lump of metal. Do you think you can win against me?" I shouted down.

She paused for a moment, and then smiled slowly, an expression that chilled my blood. She waved her hand in the air. "You've done spectacularly. Truly. You've got a higher score than almost any Player before entering NIX. And I'm particularly curious about that Skill you just used. But did you think we'd just allow you to run wild? You created some leverage to get what you want. I've done the same."

A familiar thwump-thwump-thwump sound headed our way, filling the sky. Soon after, three heli-pods came into view, and sank to the ground of the courtyard behind Nadia.

My heart sank in my chest.

The heli-pod in the center's belly opened up, and three men stepped out. Two of them held my brother restrained between them, and the third held a gun to his head. Zed's mouth was covered, but when he caught sight of me, he renewed his struggled and muffled shouting, till they kicked his legs out from under him and forced him to the ground.

Birch was being held in a soldier's arms, and when he saw me, he began his little scratchy roaring again, and managed to struggle free, racing out of the heli-pod.

"Your brother," Nadia said. "From what I know of you, that's an awful big bargaining chip of my own."

How dare they? My tenuous control on my temper slipped, and I grabbed the gray-skinned girl by the back of the neck and jumped down from the platform.

Soldiers rushed up to Nadia Petralka's side and pointed their guns at me as I strode forward, dragging the girl, but I ignored them, looking instead to the ones that still held Zed. "If he gets hurt, I'm going to disembowel you. Literally." I said to them.

I continued to move until I was close enough to smell the commander's skin and feel the warmth of her breath. I could see the beat of her heart from the pulsing in her neck. I dropped the girl unceremoniously at her feet.

Nadia Petralka's eyes followed downward with concern, but I stepped forward those last few inches, until I could look down right into her face, almost nose-to-nose, and brought her attention back. "You have no idea the hell I've traveled through, the things I've done. If you want to deal in threats, I should let you know that I've got the bigger gun. What do you think I've been doing this whole time? That power that you want so desperately for yourself, the power of a god? I've got it. And if you cross me, I will annihilate you, and NIX, everything you've ever worked towards, and everything you've ever loved." I looked pointedly to the pixie girl, who shared Nadia Petralka's hooked nose, and probably shared a father, as well. "So if you want to deal in threats, think again." By the last bit, I was literally snarling into her face.

She swallowed, but didn't back down. "It doesn't have to be a threat. If you cooperate, none of them have to get hurt. They're still alive as a gesture of my goodwill to you." Commander Petralka looked down to the girl at our feet. "Take her down to medical!" she snapped at one of the guards whose gun was still pointed at me.

I smiled in my head, but kept it from my face. "You want to talk? Talk." My hand darted forward and grabbed her by the neck, claws just barely piercing her skin.

To her credit, she reacted immediately, bringing one arm up in a sweeping gesture to knock my hand away, and thrusting the other one forward towards my stomach. The hand she attacked with shot a dart forward from beneath the cuff of her sleeve.

I twisted, perhaps a bit unnaturally thanks to my Tumbling Feather Skill, and avoided the dart, releasing her neck for a second to grab her other arm by the shoulder. I shoved sharply forward and down, pushing her off balance, and brought a knee up into her lower back, riding her fall down to the ground. My free hand found the back of her neck and kept her face ground into the dirt, while I twisted her other arm up behind her in a very classic move.

No one shot me or my brother, likely because my attack happened so quickly, and their commander was in danger if they made the wrong move. A guard stepped forward, gun pointed at me, but I raised a hand and he stopped in his tracks.

"Let me return your gesture of 'goodwill,' Commander," I said. "One of my team you've got surrounded down below has a healing Skill. We'll be going down to see him, and he'll see to the girl. Of course, feel free to keep your men with guns on them," I added caustically.

She stared at me for a second, and I knew she understood my meaning. The girl's life, which she obviously cared about, would depend on my team, and therefore, on me. If Nadia tried to pull a trick, she'd pay the price. She nodded stiffly.

"Jacky, you stay here and guard Adam, make sure none of these buffoons tries anything that'll get them painfully killed," I said. "Adam, keep an eye on things. If something…untoward is attempted, you know what to do."

Adam nodded at me with a smirk, and patted the side of the exposed wiring. "Got it." He hid his stress well, but I could see the tension in the tightened skin around his eyes.

"Zed, you're coming with us," I said.

Nadia tried to protest at that, but I spoke over her. "Lead the way," I said, clamping a clawed hand on her shoulder. "You really don't have as many options as you seem to think, nor as much authority," I murmured to her, and with a pause as she seemed to think for a moment, she acquiesced.

---

ZED STRUGGLED AGAINST HIS CAPTORS, and Nadia waved a hand at them to release him. "I'm sorry," he said once he reached me. "I couldn't do anything. I know this ruins everything—"

Jacky gave him a quick blow to the back. "No worries. We can keep you safe, especially now that we're all together. Eve says the word, and we finish destroyin' the place, then bust the hell outta here." Zed followed me and the Commander, and I gave him the most reassuring smile I could. "This won't take long."

Birch mewled at me, but stayed with Adam and Jacky as I asked him to do.

Commander Petralka led the way through the concrete door they'd blasted open, looking back once to take in the scene of destruction and carnage. "It's going to take a lot of time and money to fix all the damage you caused. The Shortcut alone..." she sighed. "Not to mention the loss of life."

I noticed a familiar face watching from the windowed halls across the courtyard.

Vaughn grinned and threw me the victory sign, forefinger and middle finger spread in a V. So that's where he disappeared to.

—I'm coming to get you, Sam. Be ready, just in case.—
-Eve-

"What's a few lives lost, to you? It's nothing new," I said, turning away from the courtyard and pushing on her neck to move her forward.

She shot me a look of controlled ire, and turned her face from me, heading farther into the hallway. "Every life is my responsibility. Whether they die in the Game or defending our base, it's still on my shoulders. Whatever you think, I'm not running from that fact. But I realize there is a greater good at stake, and a reason that we are willing to sacrifice a few, in the hopes that we might save many. In the prayer that we might save us all." She was muttering by the last bit.

I stared at her back and snorted, and then edged both her and

I closer to Zed. Getting separated from her might not be a good idea. Any attack on us would be a possible attack on the Commander, if we were close enough together. I started to mentally track our route and the necessary security passes in my head, in case I needed to leave again, without a guide. The three of us continued down into the ground, and I caught glimpses of things through the occasional door window, some more interesting than others.

One small window looked into an immense room that seemed to be a mix of mechanical workshop, laboratory, and hangar. I saw what looked to be a jetpack on one side, huge glass tubes of colored liquid that looked like the cloning tubes I'd seen in movies on another, and a smaller sized attempted replica of the teleportation sphere in another.

I slowed, and stared, just taking in the crazy.

What really caught my attention was the plane at the back. At least I thought it was a plane. I'd never seen anything quite like it. It was a gray so dark it would look black without the bright spotlights shining at it from every direction. It looked kind of like what an airplane might look like if it was actually a stingray-shaped crustacean. Or made of a giant crustacean monster's hollowed out shell.

"Yes. Quite the oddity, isn't it?" Commander Petralka said. "We'd never seen anything like it before, either."

"This is your top-secret lab, right? Where are all the people, the scientists?"

"They evacuated, Eve, along with physical documentation of their work up to this point, and anything else they could carry. They were on their way out of here as soon as the alarms went off. Without being able to monitor you properly, we weren't exactly sure of your plan. But I believed you'd survive your little "excursion," even if no one has stayed there and lived before, so I didn't let down my guard. From where the Rabbit group Moderator was tampering around, we thought they might be at risk."

My eyes darted around, catching on Zed, who was almost stiff with tension, but whose attention was focused bull-doggedly on her. I pulled away from the window, and continued on. I was struggling to keep mental focus, exhausted from my earlier display, but it wouldn't do to reveal that to the enemy. "What did you mean earlier, when you talked about my score?"

We turned a corner, and stopped at a door, which Nadia opened by pressing her thumb to a fingerprint pad. "The Game is more than just the Trials," she said. "You know you're all being monitored?" When I didn't respond, she continued. "Of course you do. You managed to slip out from almost all our avenues of observation. You're only the thirty-fourth to ever do so. But the point is, we keep tabs on you because your actions outside of the Trials are also part of the Game. Your reactions to the situation, the danger, the artificial stimuli, the almost inevitable isolation...it's all part of a calculation. A score. A ranking, if you prefer." She stopped at the next door and swiped a card from within her jacket pocket, gave a full handprint scan, and a retinal scan.

The door beeped sharply when I stepped through behind her, but she said, "Allow guest," and continued walking till we reached an elevator.

I looked back at the door closing behind us and caught a glimpse of my reflected face. The whites of my eyes had turned blood red, every little vein and capillary burst within them. The light blue of my eyes stood out against them creepily.

She was silent while we sank downward, and we stepped out of the elevator into a hallway, so deep inside the earth I could feel the weight of thousands of tons of dirt pressing down, pushing the air against my skin. It almost felt as if there was a buzzing in the air, electricity just about to snap, something just about to happen. It was strange to realize that I was walking through where NIX kept their prisoners, that people were being held, trapped, in the rooms around me.

Blaine, Sam, Chanelle, and a couple of kids who looked like Blaine were there, surrounded by a circle of people with guns pointed warily at them.

"Hold fire," she told them, and they shuffled, but didn't take their eyes or their guns off me or my team.

I stepped forward, my hand still on Commander Petralka's shoulder, and broke through the circle.

Sam let out a visible sigh of relief and relaxed his grip on Chanelle, and Blaine stood, his mecha suit unbending from its protective crouch over the children. But Commander Petralka didn't relax, and one of the guards threw a look down the hallway, the type of look you throw over your shoulder when you're alone at night and you think someone might be following you to your pod.

The hair on the back of my arms rose, and that feeling of being on the edge grew more palpable. "What's down the hall, Commander?"

"My guards are worried about more of your little surprise attacks," she said.

"She's lying," Zed interjected, before I could say anything.

I turned to him in surprise, and he met my eyes with confidence. "Something important is down there, its on all their faces, in the way they're standing."

I looked around, and saw that he was right. "We like important things, don't we, Adam?" I said aloud, for the benefit of the people around me. I could have just sent him a Window, but this way they knew he was watching.

—Yes. I'll start looking.—
-Adam-

"Let's do some exploring," I said, and Commander Petralka winced subtly, as if in pain, though I hadn't dug in with my claws. That made my teeth-baring smile grow just a little larger. I pushed her forward, and my teammates and her guards followed. The tension quivering in the air grew stronger, and stronger again as we passed through one last security door.

"Commander…" one of the guards spoke up, fingering the trigger of his gun.

"Stand down," she snapped, as I wiggled my claws against her already slightly bleeding skin. "It's too late already."

## Chapter 40

I am alpha and omega, the beginning and the end. I am the creator and destroyer of worlds.

— Eve Redding

I KNEW the details of that moment would remain forever clear in my mind. I stepped forward and looked through an observation window. A giant was tied up alone in the middle of a large room, connected to tubes, wires, and machines, and enough straps and shackles to confine a large elephant. The metal slab he lay on was tilted forward, so that we could see his whole body, half-standing, half-lying on it.

"The window is a double-sided mirror, triple paned and bullet-proof. He can't see us or get to us." She said.

I felt uneasily as if she was saying that mostly to comfort herself. A couple steps brought me close to the window, which had little wires threaded all through it.

Even bound, I could sense his terrifying strength, and a strange sense of *other*-ness that caused all the small hairs on my body to stand up even more in alarm. My skin was crawling with unease, but not abhorrence.

He didn't seem that different than us, if indeed quite a bit larger than the average human. In fact, he was almost beautiful, lying there with his eyes closed. Long dark lashes fanned out on his cheeks, a contrast to the dirty, probably once-blonde hair that hung down matted and tangled, past his face and his equally unkempt golden beard. It had grown bushy and wild in whatever amount of time he'd been held there. Dark circles lay under his eyes like those of a raccoon, standing out against his pale, drawn skin.

His eyes snapped open, looking right into my own.

I jumped, and my heart smashed in a quick burst of fear, trying to punch its way out of my chest. I stared back into his eyes, wondering if he could see me through the glass despite the woman's assurance to the contrary.

I *knew* him.

His skin was no longer bronze and healthy, his body no longer looked as if it held the strength of ten men. Despite it all, I knew he would reign down terror and destruction that would make my own look like a child's tantrum if he were ever freed. I had dreamed of him, living in his skin. I'd never heard his voice, and yet I knew its sound. We stared at each other for a long moment, until Petralka said, "This. This is what stands against us, coming to destroy us."

Something changed in him, then. His upper lip lifted away from his teeth in a snarl, ever so slowly. Then he went berserk, roaring and heaving at his bindings. He strained until his face turned red, snapping his teeth at us.

An alarm started to go off, and a milky white liquid ran through a tube from one of the machines, into his neck. He weakened and calmed, but still stared out from his incapacitated body with malevolence.

I stepped back from the window, and turned her to face me.

“What are you talking about?” My fingers trembled slightly with fear, but she didn’t seem to notice, too shaken herself.

"They think they're gods," she said. "And compared to us, they might as well be. Which is why we're creating gods of our own."

Blaine shook his head, his eyes slightly vacant as his mind went to work. “This is absurd…” he muttered, except his tone of voice showed how alarming he found it, so his words weren’t comforting.

I opened my mouth to keep questioning her, but shook my head.

—Adam, I’m sure you’re seeing this. I need information. Everything and anything. Who is he?—
-Eve-

—Already working on it. I’ll send the info to Petralka’s link.—
-Adam-

It didn’t take him long. I had Sam strip off Commander Petralka’s link and straighten it out so the screen was flat and visible to all of us, and soon after, a video expanded atop its plastine surface.

The video was blurry, shaking as something small and indistinct flew across the screen. “What’s happening?” Zed asked, peering at the image.

“We weren’t sure at first, either. We thought maybe it was debris in the upper atmosphere, or an unauthorized mission from another country.” Petralka said, some of the tension gone from her as she stared raptly at the screen with the rest of us.

The next clip was clearer, though the image was still bad. Something gray shot through the sky far above a line of tall buildings, dipping out of the worst pockets of smog clouds every few seconds. The next was even clearer, and showed the strange plane slicing through the air, avoiding the shots and missiles of the fighter jets racing after it.

The dark grey aircraft flipped up some of the joints on its tail end, dipped one wing, and turned on a dime to shoot back at them. They fell out of the sky like fiery spitballs.

"What is this supposed to be?" I asked, having a feeling I already knew the answer. That aircraft wasn't like anything I'd seen on Earth before today. But in the last few months, I'd been introduced to a lot of things I'd never seen before. In Estreyer, the Trial world.

The Commander was staring at the screen intently. "This is the first recorded and verified alien invasion of Earth. We're calling it Breach Zero."

There was a huge, silent explosion across the screen then, as something hit one of the ships and blew up. The blast seemed much too big and violent for the relatively small size of the ship. When the shock wave reached the recording camera, the video cut out in a short burst of static, and another clip took its place.

"The attempted air strikes, seven years ago..." I trailed off as my mind whirled.

"P.R. had to put some sort of spin on it. Something the public could understand, something they could deal with. Terrorists have always been great news. And the outcry allowed us to put more defensive measures in place against the real threat."

On the table's huge screen, men in hazmat suits, machine guns in hand, walked toward the downed alien ship. The camera was obviously attached to someone's faceplate, because it dipped up and down with every step, and swung dizzyingly when its wearer looked around. The picture was grainy, and static kept rolling across the screen as if someone was waving a large magnet close to the camera.

But I could see clear enough as they pried open the side of the hatch with a large machine and inched inside, their weapons at the ready. The cameraman stepped inside after them, and the view dipped and swung as he maneuvered the makeshift entrance. Inside, the gray walls rippled, shining like silk, but hardened instantly at the touch of one of the suited men. There wasn't much left loose, but what there had been was strewn about. A small tree with orchid-like flowers was bent in two, leaking sap onto the floor, and vases filled with colored sand had tipped and broken, spilling their contents.

They walked farther in, and saw a small dead animal on the floor. Its mouse-like body had been crushed under a piece of fallen furniture, its bushy tail sticking straight up in the rigor mortis specific to its species. There was nothing like it on Earth, but I recognized it as one of the rare semi-friendly creatures from Estreyer. A lump in my throat was making it hard to breathe, but I kept watching.

The cameraman moved past the creature as someone else bagged it in a vacuum sealed hazmat pouch. They moved into the cockpit, or command center, or whatever you wanted to call it. In the back of the room a large metal sphere hung from the ceiling, with floating bands of different colored, different shaped metals orbiting around its axis.

"The Shortcut," Commander Petralka said. "Kind of a goofy name, but when one of our scientists figured out what it did, he started calling it that, and the name stuck."

The strangely designed controls in the front of the cockpit were abandoned, and when the cameraman stepped farther in, the body in front of the metal sphere came into view.

On the floor lay a giant, beautiful blonde man with shoulder length hair and a golden beard, trimmed neatly. He was laying on his back with one arm underneath his body, and one leg twisted oddly. He had obviously been injured and fallen, and seemed to be unconscious.

I remembered the force of the explosion and amended my assessment. I would have decided he was dead, if I hadn't known he was sedated in the room next to me. I felt sick.

Then the video cut, and it was the man again, this time bound and chained and locked on a huge metal slab in the center of a room. The camera was high above, at an angle, as if it was placed at a corner of the ceiling. The man had wires and patches and tubes running all over and piercing into him. His eyes were closed, but I knew he couldn't be dead, or they wouldn't have restrained him so.

A much smaller man in a white coat came in with a clipboard and poked him in the side with a metal rod.

The man—was it a man? He woke in an instant, and I saw the spark of electricity jumping from the end of the rod as the man in the white coat jerked it back.

The giant looked around, straining against his bonds, roaring at his attacker with enough force to send the normal-sized man staggering backward. His huge muscles bulged and strained, and then the shackles around one wrist started to bend, twisting both the metal clamp and the slab it was melded down onto.

Before he could rip the arm free, armored men burst into the room from doors in each of the walls and started to shoot him with little darts that I supposed were tranquilizers, while ushering the white-coated man out.

The giant ignored the darts in his skin for a few moments, shaking his head in rage and continuing to strain against his bonds. But as soon as the men were gone from the room, the doors closed again and thick gas started to pour from holes placed all along the outside of the walls. He was half obscured, but I could see him slump and fall back again to the metal slab, senseless.

There was another clip of him, snarling at a camera held at a lower angle, as if by a human. "My people...will kill...you all!" he snarled in English with a strange lilting accent.

The video clip cut off, and this time no other replaced it.

"I find myself completely astounded," Blaine murmured, which solicited a snort from Zed.

"The last one was taken a few months after we downed his ship and captured him. It seems his race is significantly intelligent, to learn our language so quickly. Or maybe I should say his species?" Commander Petralka, who I'd almost forgotten about, shrugged beside me. "Breach Zero hit most major military facilities around the world. We're fairly positive it was only a scouting mission. A test of our responses."

She chuckled bleakly, and turned away from the link. "Unfortunately, we failed that test miserably.

I listened to her silently, but stared back through the observation window at him, for once at a loss for words. This changed things. My plans had been decimated by this revelation, the same as if NIX had shot one of those ship-downing nukes at them. I was listening almost absently, scrambling to come up with a way to get what I needed out of all this.

"Almost all of their ships escaped unharmed as we scrambled to do something, anything, to counter their attacks. We destroyed a couple of ships, but managed to take this one mostly intact, along with some of their technology, like the Shortcut. After that, every single nation of the world banded together military resources in preparation for the coming war."

"War coming, when?" I asked.

"Soon. Less than a year. Maybe less than six months. We've got a rough idea of when the ones that escaped will be bringing reinforcements. That is, if none of the other ships had some different form of FTL communication or transportation that we don't know about."

"FTL, meaning faster than light?" I asked, even as Blaine opened his mouth to no doubt ask the same thing.

"Yes." She opened the security door blocking off the rest of the hallway. "If it takes them as long as we estimated to make the round trip. It all depends on how quick to mobilize military forces they are. Let's hurry back to the surface. Your healer has a job to do."

I motioned to Sam to keep an eye on her, and took one last look at the sedated man and followed her with the rest of my team, and her visibly uncomfortable guards, reluctant to be trapped alone down there with him. Excuse me, it. Funny how they looked like us, except bigger. What were the chances of that, two races looking almost completely alike, on two different worlds in an infinite universe? I'd bet my life the odds were beyond miniscule. And if I went with the plan forming in my head, I literally would be placing my life on the line.

Blaine herded the three defenseless captives he and Sam had rescued, and Zed fell into step beside me, silent but watching Petralka and her guards intently.

I gave the three rescues a quick once-over. Chanelle was staring blankly ahead and following Blaine meekly, looking worrisomely catatonic, while the two smaller children were huddled together, and though also silent, showed obvious signs of tears and not a small amount of jumpiness. What had they gone through, while we tried to find a way to save them?

"And you're sure reinforcements are coming back?" I asked, turning back to Commander Petralka.

She stopped and stared at me for a moment, then continued walking and talking as if I hadn't asked such a stupid question. "We have permission to enforce a mandatory draft from the citizenry. Kind of like martial law, except no one knows about it yet, unless they're part of it."

"Like me." I followed her onto an elevator, which started a long, dark descent into the heart of the earth.

"Yes." Her lips twitched at the look on my face. "The Constitution and human rights? Is that what you're thinking? Those don't mean as much as you might think in the face of our extinction as a species."

"Some would say the life of an individual is worth as much as the life of the masses."

She snorted. "That someone would die along with the masses when these things come back. They're different than us."

"You're drafting soldiers to fight an alien invasion," I said. "How crazy does that sound?" I laughed humorlessly. "But why do it like this? It seems counterproductive to actually gaining a fighting force. You take kids, basically, with no military inclinations, and leave them to their own devices. Why not allow volunteers, or recruit from within the military, or at least cultivate them and train them from the beginning?"

"We're looking for a certain type of person," she said. "We do recruit from within the military, if the genetics are right. We found out early on that the Seeds weren't compatible with a large majority of the population. Only people with a certain gene sequence can adapt. The survival rate is higher in younger people, which is why we aim for them. And the Game is designed to create a specific type of person. We are looking for people who will adapt, and fight, and survive against horrifying odds. The type who can make it without someone holding their hand," Commander Petralka said.

"Do you need to kill half of them to do that?"

"The Trials do create strong people. But you're right; I wouldn't use them if I didn't have to. We need the Trials, because the Seeds we can manufacture on our own are sub-par to what the aliens have. The Skills are beyond our current technology. But we don't create the Trials. They're entirely an invention of those creatures. The aliens are violent and horrifying in nature, and their games reflect that. They worship their 'gods' through them, and are rewarded with power." She stared at the restrained and sedated man.

"You send children into these 'violent and horrifying' games. What does that make you?"

"It makes me someone who's willing to pay the price. I'm not heartless. But I'm strong enough to do what needs to be done, even if I have to carry the weight of the dead on my shoulders." She knocked my hand away from her shoulders, and went back through the blown up security door into the courtyard, scowling.

I would have grabbed her again, but I needed some space to think, where she wouldn't be analyzing my every twitch. Her justifications were bullshit, and I knew it, but it seemed like she might actually believe them. But except for figuring out how I might use what I was learning against her, my focus was on the verbal confrontation I was about to initiate.

Zed sidled up beside me, and whispered under his breath, "She was lying earlier, when she was talking about the Trials."

"What?"

He shook his head, lips pressed together. "I don't know what about, exactly. But I could tell, she was lying. She's not being completely truthful, trust me on that."

And I did, but it didn't matter, except that it might make negotiations harder. "Well, that's no surprise," I muttered back.

—Guys, I know we all saw that. I'm going to take a drastic change in course. I can't leave, now, but if you want to, you still can.—

-Eve-

I got a barrage of Windows back, as if they'd all been waiting for that moment.

Sam sent me an apology for failing in the mission and getting captured, Jacky told me they were ready to come down and break me out if something had gone wrong, and Adam sent me a suspicious query about what was going on.

When I emerged through the destroyed doorway into the light of the sun, Jacky and Adam let out a simultaneous sigh of relief.

The armor-skinned pixie girl was lying on the ground motionless, but Sam rushed over to her and touched her head. His eyes widened, but then he looked up and nodded at me, communicating that she would live. Commander Petralka's shoulder slumped a little, then straightened again so quickly I wouldn't have noticed if I wasn't watching her. "We have to have soldiers that can match them," She motioned to the Players still watching from the windows lining some of the courtyard.

"People like me," I said.

She stared at me for second, surprise showing through the

mask of calm she'd regained. "People like you, Eve. I'll admit. You've gone the furthest of almost any Player before entering NIX. Was that Skill before truly a Bestowal? How did you get it?"

"I took it," I said, making it clear by my tone that I was unwilling to elaborate further. I gave her a large smile. "And why don't we stop playing this game, Commander?"

"You want to escape the Game," she said heavily. "You want me to just let you go, with you knowing what you do?"

"You shouldn't make assumptions, Commander. You've misjudged me," I said, and stepped closer when she frowned in confusion. "You mentioned being able to understand how the aliens work by looking at their Trials." I paused for dramatics. "I know how you work, because I've seen what the Game uses to motivate Players. Whatever fancy reasoning you want to spout for your actions, it's obvious you understand two things. Fear, and greed."

She stared up at me.

"I showed you what there is to fear from me, but it wasn't enough to sway you. It only served to fuel your greed instead. That's too bad, but it's okay." My smile was full of teeth and triumph. "Because your greed *is* enough to sway you. You want my power, and you've already proven you're willing to do whatever it takes to gain it. And I'm going to give it to you, whether you like it or not, because you're going to meet my conditions for doing so. I'll be staying here, with the other Players you deemed worthy enough to join your forces, rather than stay part of the ignorant cannon-fodder."

Her eyes widened, and she blinked a couple times, obviously thrown for a mental loop. Then, she regained her composure, and her eyes narrowed just a bit, with what I thought was calculation. "You think I'd take you in, after this?" She waved her hand to encompass the courtyard, and all the literal and figurative damage we'd done.

"You allowed this to happen, in part," I denied, shaking my

head. "These goons weren't even shooting at our heads. Please, spare me the false incredulity."

She shook her head in chagrin, and a little self-derisive amusement. "You're sharper than I gave you credit for."

"That's okay. I aim to continuously surprise."

"But why do you want to join us? If I recall correctly, I was only a few minutes ago that you were attacking and threatening to expose our cause to the world."

"I could care less about the aliens," I said. "I'm not interested in saving the world. But I am interested in keeping all of us safe."

"Safe, by joining NIX?" Adam interjected, raising an eyebrow. But he was subdued enough I thought the rebuttal was more his token role as devil's advocate.

I met his gaze for a moment, and nodded at him subtly. Adam was smart. Maybe he'd figured out what I was doing. "Safer. If we don't want to join, we need to destroy them. But destroying them doesn't stop the Estreyans from coming. What it does is reduce the power Earth has to fight back. From what I understand, they're the only real defense the world has. And I don't work for free. There are a few other things I want which I think they might provide."

Commander Petralka's mouth twitched, and I was almost certain she was hiding a smirk. Good, let her think that she was in control.

"I want my team to be privy to the hiring negotiations. Along with everyone else watching," I said, jerking my head to the increasingly packed glass hallways.

"Let's not make a production of this," Commander Petralka said, frowning. "You said you had conditions. What are they?"

"My first stipulation is my brother," I said.

"We'll let him go. He'll not be in danger from us," she agreed, nodding vigorously.

"That's not what I mean. Of course you'll let him go. What I need is for you to remove him from the Game."

"Eve, please don't do this," Zed said. "I'll be okay. I made the mistake. You don't need to sell your soul to fix it."

"I'm not doing this just for you, Zed. Stop being so conceited." I threw him a nonchalant wink, which only made me realize how much my eyeballs were starting to hurt.

"What are you talking about?" Nadia said.

"My brother got his hands on a Seed. He doesn't have the genetic marker needed to be compatible with them, but luckily I've got a pretty freaking amazing healer. However, because of the way the Trials work, my brother is forced into them, even though he's not a Player. I want you to fix that. I want him to have a normal life."

Nadia seemed lost in thought for a while, then said, "Was it...just the one Seed?"

"Yes."

"And he doesn't have the genetic marker? Amazing. I can't guarantee anything, but there might be a way to slowly release the particles and filter them out of his blood. I can't do that for the rest of you," she added. "It's much too late. We'll have time to get him clean, until we can get the Shortcut fixed."

"The Shortcut isn't my concern. If I have to, I'll stop it for good."

"The future of mankind depends on us!" she snapped. "What kind of life will the boy have, when Earth is destroyed by--"

I stared her down, and she stepped closer to our group so her voice wouldn't travel. Not that it would matter if one of the Players listening from up above had extremely high Perception, unless the glass was made out of something special.

"How will your brother fare in an alien invasion from the species that created the Trials, without us here to do anything to stop them?" she continued, as if she'd never cut herself off in the first place. "Especially being as weak as he is?"

"Good points, Commander. I guess it's up to you to make sure I never have to make such a difficult decision."

Her nostrils flared. "We will do everything we can to remove the Seed from your brother. Is there anything else?"

"Quite a bit, actually." I nodded. "Those of my team who wish to join me in NIX will be allowed to."

"That shouldn't be too hard to accommodate, though they may be a bit behind the other recruits."

"If they do not choose to follow me, you will let them go, no repercussions."

She clenched her jaw, but nodded sharply. "Okay."

"I assume you have leadership tiers among the others, if you're training them like soldiers?" I continued without waiting for her response. "I will keep my position as a leader, for those who will follow me. I won't accept being under the command of some random person, no matter if I'm a new recruit or not. And the same for any who follow me."

"Slightly unconventional, but doable."

"You will release Kris and Gregor," I jerked my head toward the two children, "back to their uncle, Blaine Mendell. Who I also consider part of my team. All stipulations for the team extend to him. Those conditions also extend to Bunny the Moderator. I'm sure you know who I mean, though I don't know his real name."

"I do."

"Chanelle Black," I said simply.

The girl was lying on the ground beside Sam, but if the first part of the plan had gone according to plan, the antidote to the "wolf" bite should already be working in her system.

"She's yours, too" Nadia said, anticipating my demand.

"Yes."

"I think it's my turn to lay out terms for our agreement, now." When I only raised an eyebrow, she continued. "You will follow orders like all the others we've taken into the fold. If you want to join us, act like one of us. You will be assigned training classes, and will be expected to attend, and perform to the best of your ability. Any disruption will be punished as if you were anyone else, and you are responsible for controlling the actions of your team, if they decide to join. If they do not decide to join, I want them fully aware that your wellbeing is tied with ours. I wouldn't want anything…unfortunate to happen."

I'd expected no less, but behind me, there was an angry stirring from my team.

Jacky clenched her fists threateningly. "You know what I always say, Eve. The best defense is an overwhelmingly powerful offense," she muttered.

"And one last thing," I said, raising my voice a little to draw Commander Petralka's attention back to me.

"Only one more?" she said sarcastically. "Why, please, go ahead."

"The man who killed China Black. You will give him to me, too."

Jacky guffawed and pumped her fist.

Both of the Commander's eyebrows rose. "I understand you must feel some bitterness, but I assure you he's been thoroughly reprimanded."

"Oh, really? Reprimanded?" The sarcasm was clear in my voice.

"Yes. He was demoted, and put under supervision, among other things. What happened was unfortunate and unnecessary."

I laughed. "What he did is unforgivable."

"He is a valuable asset to us, and though a bit unrestrained, he's proven his loyalty. You, however, are even more of a loose cannon," she spread her hands to evidence the courtyard, "and you show a distinct lack of allegiance to anyone besides yourself and your little team. I won't trade his life for your gratification. If I were to execute everyone who'd ever killed anyone else, you'd be on that list, too."

"Indeed, I would," I said. I decided to let it go. The argument, that is. The snake man would find himself painfully dead at my earliest convenience, no matter what she said. "Okay."

She searched my eyes for a moment, and then nodded, too. "Okay."

Someday she might learn not to trust me if I acquiesced so quickly. If I didn't screw up, it would be too late for her by the time she learned better.

She turned her back, but I still kept the savage grin I'd been holding back spread across my face. I may have won, but you never knew who was watching, and it wouldn't do to reveal too much.

# Log Of Captivity 6

Mental Log of Captivity-Estimated Day: Two thousand, six hundred forty-three.

She is a *two-leg-maggot.* When she attacked and the *screams-with-no-mouth* began to wail, the others of her kind gave me the seed of the poppy to force my tranquility, so that I would not damage my body again. Though her mind was walled off, I sensed her draw near. She stood on the other side of the glass, and fool that I was, I did not even notice her true nature. I thought only of my eyes meeting hers. Then the *most-abhorrent* and she began to hold discussion, watching me as if I was some fascinating bug. I am in *blood-covenant* with a *two-leg-maggot.* I am a halfwit. I thought my suffering complete, no pain not inflicted, no humiliation ignored, nothing pure undefiled. But the gods play a crueler game.

# Chapter 41

Who shall tempt, with wandering feet,
The dark unbottomed infinite abyss?
— John Milton

I SAT atop NIX's wall, staring out at the murky evening sky. In Estreyer, the stars would just be coming out.

Birch lay on my lap, carefully grooming his paws and sharp kitten-claws.

The rest of the team was down below, considering their options. I'd left them to make their own individual decisions.

"It might be just you and me," I said to Birch, scratching behind his ears.

He grunted at me and continued grooming himself.

After the team had seen the contents below NIX, we'd talked, and I'd laid out the reasons why I was staying through a Window to those who could see it, with instructions not to reveal the information, which was more than just bartering for Zed's life, and the team's freedom.

"So NIX continues to exist, we stay safe one way or another.

And you want other people able to do the fighting, so maybe we won't have to," Adam said aloud, skillfully holding a second conversation with me, out of notice.

—Do you really think this creature is so important?—
-Adam-

"Uh, yeah. Exactly. Plus, we'd have access to more Seeds, and targeted training."

I was routing his conversation to the others, so the team members with a VR chip could see both sides of the conversation. Unfortunately, for those who didn't have one, there was nothing I could do to make them understand without revealing things to the monitoring devices NIX was no doubt smothering us with.

—I can feel it. I know that sounds strange, but the Oracle gave me the vision of Behelaino that indirectly led me here, and along with it she leveled up my non-sensory Perception. I feel like he's important, and if I leave, there won't be another chance to come back.—
-Eve-

"And in exchange for this, they keep us under their thumb and watchful eye. They control us."

"They think they control us," I'd corrected, giving them all a quick grin.

—This is an infiltration. But the negotiation I had with the commander was valid. Anyone who wants to leave can do so. I will stay, and my presence will shield you from reprisal.—
-Eve-

Zed had started out frowning down at the table, not meeting

my eyes, but as the dual conversations continued, he'd gained that strangely intense focus again, his eyes flickering from face to face. He wasn't privy to the secondary conversation, but I thought he might be aware of its existence. I'd need to find a way to talk to him, soon.

Blaine and Bunny hadn't been to the Trials before, and so the revelations down in the depths had come as quite a shock. Both the scientist and the awkward-in-person Moderator seemed too overwhelmed to respond. And Blaine had his surrogate kids to worry about.

"I know what I have to do," I said. "I'm worth enough to keep NIX off your backs if you decide to leave. Think about it, and whoever's with me, meet me on the wall. I'm kinda tired. Gonna watch the sunset."

And so there I sat, alone, thinking about distant suns and the wind of change.

"Heya!" I heard from down below.

Jacky waved up at me, and started walking across the court-yard to me, the others following on her heels. All of them.

I grinned and waved back, then turned to watch the red and purple streaked sky fade out as they came to join me.

Birch turned around in my lap, and let out a whine.

"What's up?"

He leaned forward and started to lick my upper lip and nose, his tongue coming away dark red.

I drew back from him and brought a hand to my nose, taking away bloody fingers. "Just a nose bleed. No big deal," I said, laughing past the fear.

He nuzzled up to me and started to lick my neck, whining more insistently.

I felt the blood drip out of my ear, and saw it land on his muzzle.

He whimpered again, and licked more frantically.

I tilted my head back, tore a strip of my sleeve away, and used it to wipe away the blood spontaneously dripping from my nose and ear, then took a Seed out of my pocket. Commander Petralka had given them to me upon request, as a sort of signing bonus for joining NIX. "I wish I was more Resilient."

I took a deep breath, and then lifted Birch up to my head and had him lick up the rest of the dark red smears from my face and neck. "This is a secret, okay?" I said, staring seriously into his eyes. "The others can't know about the side effects of my new power. They think I've got it under control. No one can know, or we won't be safe anymore."

He let out his little scratchy growl, and I laughed. "I know you'll protect us. But it's still a secret."

I turned my head to the side, where my team had just walked up the steps on the inside of the wall. I waved them over, and they settled in beside me to watch the muted sun of Earth leave us behind.

CONTINUE READING for an excerpt from *Seeds of Chaos Book II: Gods of Rust and Ruin*, coming August 2017!

**If you enjoyed this book, please take the time to leave a review on Amazon or Goodreads. It doesn't have to be more than a sentence or two, and it really does make a difference. As an independent author, I rely on *you* to get the word out about my books.**

**Want to get an email when my next book is released, or when I'm running book giveaways and contests? Sign up here: http://bit.ly/SeedsofChaosNewsletter**

# Sneak Preview: Gods of Rust and Ruin

**Blurb:**

*My name is Eve Redding. They call me the godkiller.*

I was dying. Slowly being destroyed by the power I had worked so hard to obtain. My team and I were trapped within NIX's web of lies and manipulation, and even my allies couldn't be trusted.

Deep below, the alien called out to me like a beacon, and I decided to forge an alliance. As they say, the enemy of my enemy is my friend.

I SAT UP ABRUPTLY, choking on my own blood. I jerked out of the little cot tucked into the side of the wall and spat the liquid onto the floor in a dark splatter. The heavy iron taste in my mouth added to the terror of the nightmare I'd been yanked from. My claws slipped out and I sliced through the empty darkness, lashing out at a nonexistent enemy.

A second of flailing later, I got control of myself. I was alone.

The only enemy attacking me was also the thing keeping me alive, now that I lived within NIX's compound. The Seed of Chaos made me powerful enough to be valuable, while literally eating away at me from the inside.

I gagged and coughed, trying to staunch the blood flow with one hand while fumbling for the backpack shoved underneath my mattress with the other. The only light in the room came from the small diodes of a couple of sleeping electronics, but it was enough for my augmented eyes to see. I pulled out a small pouch and fumbled for one of the large, marble-like Seeds within. "I wish I was more Resilient," I mouthed almost soundlessly, pressing it to my neck. I was long past flinching at the pinprick. I sighed in relief as the Seed injected its contents into me and took hold, stopping the bleeding.

Birch, my little monster-cat companion, woke, either from the noise I'd made or the smell of my blood dripping everywhere. He let out his scratchy little meow, the sound lilting upward at the end in an obvious question. He hadn't yet displayed the ability of his late mother to share thoughts through touch, but he was far from stupid.

"I had to take a Seed," I muttered to him, my voice low in case something was listening. "I was bleeding again, but I'm okay now."

Birch bumped me with his head and licked at the blood on my forearm with his prickly tongue.

I withdrew my arm before his tongue accidentally removed the top layer of my skin, and moved to the shower in the tiny bathroom stall. I was the only one of my teammates with private quarters. The others were sleeping in a small barracks-like room across the hall from me, stacked two bunks high. I'd glanced at their room the night before, and then promptly passed out from exhaustion onto my own private little cot.

Behind me, Birch grumbled and moved to licking up my blood from the cold hard floor. He had a somewhat disturbing penchant for raw meat and blood. Especially my blood.

I turned on the water at a temperature most kindly described as "scalding" and let it wash away the sticky red residue, along with the lingering creepy feeling from my nightmare. I'd been waking up with nightmares, *from* nightmares, for a while. But they were getting worse than ever before, and I rarely went a night without them.

Sometimes, it was the monsters of a Trial coming for me, ready to rip me apart and dance in my entrails. Sometimes, it was the last time I saw my team member China, as the light went out of her eyes and she died. And sometimes, the nightmare had no form. It was the creeping mass of decay and putrefaction devouring everything in its path. A shudder, a feeling, a smell.

When I exited the shower, Birch had finished cleaning all the blood from the floor. My sheets and pillowcase still glistened with the dark liquid, but luckily they were black. I took them back into the shower with me and cleaned the synthetic material as best I could. No one would know what had happened.

Birch called to me from the doorway to the shower, his meow still scratchy from sleep.

"It's getting worse," I murmured.

The cub padded past the open shower door and under the spray of water, then licked my knee and peered up at me with his green human eyes. Water splashed down on him and his translucent second eyelids closed sideways for protection. He spread his downy wings to better catch the warm water. "I'm afraid," I whispered, knowing that he couldn't reveal my secret, and the rushing water would cover any other surveillance that might have slipped through my search. "The Seeds aren't working as long as they used to."

The Seed of Chaos grew continually stronger, as Behelaino had warned me it would. I just hadn't thought it would happen this *fast.* Every time I was forced to use it, it grew stronger, but being able to display it was the only thing keeping me--and the team--safe.

The meditation technique Adam had taught me helped control Chaos, too, but I could only do so much without more Seeds. A lot more. Without them or some other way to heal myself, the outcome was obvious. I had wanted to keep my condition a secret, but I would need to reveal it to Sam, and hope that he could help me until I could find a way to fix myself.

"I'm dying, Birch," I whispered with terrible certainty, the words no more than a breath on the air.

## Also by Azalea Ellis

**Seeds of Chaos Series**

Gods of Blood and Bone

Gods of Rust and Ruin-Coming Soon

Sign of for my newsletter to get news about new releases.

http://bit.ly/SeedsofChaosNewsletter

# About the Author

I am an author of science fiction and fantasy. I love to hear from my readers, so feel free to reach out to me.

*For more information:*

www.azaleaellis.com
author@azaleaelis.com